*H*eath slid his hand down her half-bare shoulder to her waist, urging her into him. "Julia," he murmured.

"Go ahead," she said in an undertone. "Do it. We're both dying of curiosity. Perhaps we shall feel better if we get it over with once and for all."

"Do what?" he asked in a deep, deliberate voice.

"This." She angled her head to bring her full red mouth to his. Her warm breath taunted his jaw. "Kiss me, and then we shall know."

He cradled the back of her head in his hand. Her lips parted.

She had the softest, most erotic mouth he had ever tasted. Forbidden fruit. He wanted to eat his fill of her, taste her from top to bottom. Incredible that this feeling could flare up between them, hotter, more dangerous than before.

God help him. He had not counted on this, that his talent for seduction would meet its match in the one woman he had wanted and lost.

The Wedding Night of an English Rogue

A Novel

Jillian Hunter

BALLANTINE BOOKS • NEW YORK

The Wedding Night of an English Rogue is a work of fiction. Names, characters, places, and incidents are the products of the author's imagination or are used fictitiously. Any resemblance to actual events, locales, or persons, living or dead, is entirely coincidental.

An Ivy Books Mass Market Original

Copyright © 2005 by Maria Hoag

Published in the United States by Ivy Books, an imprint of The Random House Publishing Group, a division of Random House, Inc., New York.

Ivy Books and colophon are trademarks of Random House, Inc.

ISBN 0-345-46123-1

Cover and stepback illustrations: Jon Paul

Printed in the United States of America

www.ballantinebooks.com

OPM 9 8 7 6

For my talented editor, Charlotte Herscher, who has worked so hard to bring out the best in the Boscastles and in me as a writer. Working with you is a pleasure.

Chapter 1

Until this evening Lieutenant Colonel Lord Heath Boscastle had been living under the pleasant illusion that he was the master of his own fate. It wasn't that he had escaped bad fortune. On the contrary. He had met and overcome more than his fair share of adversity. It seemed that he deserved peace. After all, he'd survived war, torture, espionage, two volatile mistresses, and a family that challenged the rules of Society on a regular basis.

It was, perhaps, a credit to his cumulative experiences that he managed to hide his astonishment at what his friend, Colonel Sir Russell Althorne, had just asked of him.

A man less adept than Heath at concealing his emotions might have given himself away. He displayed no reaction whatsoever. Most likely he was in a mild state of shock. He'd half expected Althorne to call him back into military service. As a soldier, that is, not a lady's companion. He had not anticipated a reminder of a past sexual escapade . . . as unforgettable as that escapade had been.

"Well," Russell asked him for the second time, "will you do it or not? I would prefer to leave London with an easy mind. Will you take care of Julia for me while I'm gone?"

"You might have given me a little more notice."

"You've been in Hampshire."

"You could have written."

"What? So that you had time to refuse?"

Heath shook his head. "You're all damned heart, aren't you?"

The two men stood at the top of the Mayfair mansion's magnificent stone staircase. To anyone observing them from the candlelit ballroom below, they appeared to be a pair of bored male guests who had retreated from the noisy crowd to puff their cigars in peace.

They had strengthened their friendship as raw light cavalry officers in Sahagun when ambushes and battles, intelligence gathering and patrols in the icy dark had beckoned to their thirst for adventure. Unfortunately Heath had gotten caught on one of those adventures, and it had been Colonel Sir Russell Althorne, his superior officer, who had rescued him, losing his left eye in the process, and earning a hero's acclaim.

"I can't do it." Heath gazed through a cloud of smoke at the figures that wove through the porphyry marble columns below. He wondered distractedly if the woman he and Russell had been discussing was down there in the crush. Would they recognize each other? What would they say? It would be damned uncomfortable, considering their short but memorable history. "I haven't seen Julia in years. I had no idea her husband was dead, or that she'd returned to England."

Or that Russell, predator and hero of the hour that he was, had already gotten himself engaged to her. Althorne had always been an ambitious, competitive sort, even as far back as their college days. He seemed determined to leave his mark on the world. "I had to talk her into accepting my proposal," Russell said, his voice more than a little baffled. He stood several inches shorter than Heath, with a heavier frame, rust-brown hair, hazel eyes, and rugged features. His was a rough appeal; what he lacked in refinement he made up for in resolve. "Can you believe it? Julia refusing me."

"What could she have been thinking?" Heath murmured.

"Obviously she wasn't." Russell smiled down at a young debutante who had caught his eye. Flustered, she bumped ungracefully into her dance partner.

Russell laughed.

Heath sighed. "Is she in danger?"

"I don't know," Russell replied. "Julia's aunt is convinced that their town house is being watched. I doubt it. Lady Dalrymple is a notorious corkbrain. Still, I do not think it is wise to underestimate Auclair. The man fights deadly duels for amusement. His quest for revenge seems personal."

"How do you know this?"

Russell's jaw tightened. "He's made it known in underworld circles that he wants to destroy me."

"The war is over."

"Apparently Auclair's taste for violence has not been sated. He was last seen haunting Tortoni's and other cafés in search of a good fight. His behavior is nothing a rational mind can understand."

Heath lapsed into silence. It was no secret to either man that Armand Auclair was their mutual nemesis, a former French spy who had tortured not only Heath but countless other English soldiers and had eluded capture in Portugal. Neither Heath nor Russell had ever seen Auclair's face. He had conducted his interrogations wearing an executioner's mask. Russell was well aware of the horror that Auclair had inflicted on the men he had taken prisoner. Most had died.

But did Russell have any idea what the woman he planned to marry had meant to Heath? What had happened that August long ago?

Of course not. Presumably Julia had not told him. This conversation would not be taking place if she had.

Heath's encounter with Julia Hepworth had been a passionate if too-brief private affair. There was not a soul in the world who knew that he had desired her ever since the day she had shot him in the shoulder several years ago. That she was the only woman he wished he had not lost. He'd hesitated to acknowledge it even to himself. It was only as he grew older that he realized he had never replaced her.

She hadn't permanently hurt him, but he'd never been quite the same. Damaged where it didn't show.

He'd been sneaking up on Russell from behind a carn to play a prank, and Julia had taken a shot at him from her horse.

The shot had grazed his shoulder.

The first look at her had pierced his heart. It still bled from time to time, although he'd learned to live with the pain. He smiled a little as he recalled their initial encounter.

"Are you all right?" she asked, throwing herself down on the ground to examine him. "Please tell me I haven't killed you."

He didn't move, awash in a sea of conflicting sensations. The searing pain in his upper body, the indignity of being shot by a female. The intrusive heat of her hands as she matter-of-factly tore open his riding jacket to examine his torso. Her dark red hair brushing against his belly, inflaming his senses. How he could desire a woman who'd almost killed him defied reason. But damnation, she had stirred him. He narrowed his eyes and considered the situation.

"Well, say something," she said in panic.

She was tall and lushly built, deep-bosomed and supple. She was imperious. She was the most compelling woman he had ever met, and he'd wanted to bed her on the spot. Right there between the rocks like a barbarian.

"All right," he said between his teeth, suppressing all his barbaric instincts. "You've killed me. I am dead. Does that make you happy?"

"There's no need to be rude."

"Isn't there? Forgive me if I find it difficult, lying flat on my back with a pistol wound, to dredge up my party manners."

"I don't know why you're being so horrible. It was an accident. I was frightened. I really thought I might have killed you."

He grunted. "Came close enough. You shot me. What in heaven's name possessed you? You *shot* me."

"Well, no wonder," she said, sounding a little indignant herself now. "What were you doing jumping out at me from behind that cairn?"

"I thought you were someone I knew."

"Well, I thought you were the rabid fox that had attacked the livestock last night."

"Do I look like a rabid fox?" he demanded crossly.

He was disconcerted by the wicked gleam in her gray eyes, and drawn to it, too. He didn't know which was

worse, that she'd injured him or that he desired her in spite
of it. Certainly it was not a normal response to being shot.
He sat up abruptly as she pulled his cambric shirt off his
shoulders to study the injury she had inflicted. "It doesn't
look as bad as I feared."

"That's easy for you to say."

"I am sorry."

He turned his head, her strong chin grazing his cheek.
"It's a nice shoulder," she said very quietly, "as far as
shoulders go."

"Is it?" he asked, grinning reluctantly.

"Of course, I'm not an expert."

He stared at her mouth—red, moist, inviting. He'd heard
one of the young men at the party comment that Julia Hepworth was something of a hellion. But it had been voiced
more as a compliment than a criticism. He'd wager that the
man who said it had never been shot by her and then suffered the delicious agony of her practically crawling on top
of him to tear off his shirt. Or perhaps he had. For all he
knew she'd left a slew of victims in her wake.

"Do we have to tell anyone?" she asked, her eyes meeting his appealingly.

"That depends." He decided he was going to kiss her.
Any young woman who could shoot and half undress him
the way she had deserved to be kissed. If not more. God,
she was fetching, he thought, enjoying the warm weight of
her belly against his side.

She let her hand slide down the front of his shirt, her
gloved fingertips skimming his chest. Heat flooded his
groin. "Depends on what?" she whispered, drawing her
head back to give him a suspicious look that told him he

wasn't the first man to find her attractive. He assumed he was the first man she'd shot though.

"On how sorry you are."

Her full lips lifted in a smile. "Everyone has warned me what a rogue you are, Heath Boscastle."

"Pity they didn't warn me about you," he murmured.

"That I'm reckless and impulsive?"

"No. That you're tempting and—"

A shadow dropped over this heated exchange like a shroud, dampening the air, dousing the invisible flames that leaped between them. The chance to kiss her red mouth was lost. All of a sudden Heath's shoulder hurt like hell. He made a face. Julia jumped up, stepping on his hand. He might have sworn. Bloody careless female.

"I think you're going to live," she announced in an impersonal voice as he pulled his shirt back over his bare shoulders.

"What in God's name happened?" demanded the shadow.

"I shot him," she said, not looking half as sorry as she should, in Heath's opinion.

"What?" The shadow sounded shocked. Heath realized that it was Russell, the last person on earth he wished to witness his humiliation. "You shot my best friend? Answer me right now, Boscastle, what did you do that Miss Hepworth had a reason to shoot you?"

Heath had ridden back to their host's home alone, not in the mood for Russell's snide remarks. He decided that he would find Julia during the party when she was by herself. He didn't have to.

* * *

She found him alone in the library several hours later. The rest of the party guests had gone off on a scavenger hunt and would not return until early evening. Only the infirm and the children had been left behind.

He put down his book when he saw who had interrupted him. His anger had died down. His attraction to her hadn't. "You haven't come to shoot me again, have you?" he demanded, sounding sterner than he felt. His shoulder was actually fine, and he knew it had been an accident.

She pivoted in surprise, her eyes widening with recognition. Her cheeks were flushed a deep rose against her pale skin. Her hair cascaded rather untidily down her shoulders, and her riding habit was a little rumpled. She looked as if she were trying to hide from someone. "I don't have a weapon." She held her hands up in surrender. "Search me if you like."

He grinned at her. He couldn't even pretend to be angry, not when she disconcerted him like that. "I think I will search you."

"Please yourself. Just don't—"

There were footsteps outside the door, young voices whispering, "Did she go in the library?"

"No. She ran upstairs. I heard her."

"She's hiding in the dressing closet. Come on, troops. After her!"

Julia spun around and locked the door. By the time she turned back, Heath's hands had encircled her waist, drawing her slowly toward him. This was an opportunity he wasn't about to pass up. She owed him. He lowered his head, skimmed his mouth over the curve of her cheek. Her skin was as soft as cream. He wanted a taste of her.

Her lips opened, inviting, soft, and lush. "Don't give me

away," she whispered, her soft breasts brushing his arm, "or I'll have to spend the afternoon reading to the cousins."

"Boscastle cousins?"

She was studying his face, resisting only slightly as he tugged her with him to the sofa. "Yes."

"My sympathies then," he murmured, drawing her down beside him. "You could read to me if you like."

"We shouldn't," she whispered, hiding her face in his neck. "I really shouldn't be alone with you like this."

"I know." The soft weight of her body, the scent of her hair, was driving him mad. "Let's elope."

"You scoundrel," she said, biting her lip, her gray eyes a little dreamy and wistful. "As if you would."

His heavy-lidded blue eyes drifted over her. "I'm wild for you."

"You're going away to war!" she said with a scandalized laugh.

"What if I die and never come back?" he asked, pulling her back toward him.

Her gray eyes danced with mischief, and a healthy dose of doubt. Even then she had her feet firmly planted on the ground. Sensible and sexual. He had never encountered such a combination. "What if?" she teased.

He slid his hand under her riding jacket, flirting with the underside of one firm breast. There was something about her he couldn't resist. Something that balanced his serious nature. He wasn't sure if he was seducing her or was being seduced. He couldn't remember ever falling into intimacy so easily with a woman. He'd known from the moment he'd seen her that she was different. "Your skin feels so warm and soft."

She caught her breath. "No one has *ever* touched me there."

He nuzzled the side of her neck. She'd never believe him that this was not his usual behavior, or that of all his brothers, he was the most restrained. "No one has ever tempted me like this."

"So you say."

"Do you think I would lie?"

"I think you're a dangerous rogue and—"

He kissed her ripe tempting mouth, pressing her back into the sofa. He would have killed anyone who'd interrupted them. He wanted her all to himself.

One thing had led to another. They had both been young, impulsive, and passionate. Even then he'd known how to arouse a woman, but there was nothing rote or planned about this encounter. He spent almost an hour kissing her, ravaging her mouth, learning little things that pleased her. They had talked between caresses. He had slowly led her, coaxed her, introduced her to the secrets of sensuality. He'd lowered her inhibitions without her even realizing it, and although she was sexually innocent, she was so sharp-witted that he couldn't predict how she would react to him. He couldn't predict his own responses. All he knew was that he'd never felt like this before.

He lost track of time. The rest of the world faded from his awareness, centered on this one woman. He remembered that they had rolled onto the floor, her riding jacket thrown over a card table, her breasts exposed above her unhooked bodice.

His own shirt hung open to the waist. He was practically panting with lust, already thinking of how to keep her away from his friends for the rest of the party. She had pressed her palms against him as he leaned into her, holding her captive between his thighs. He was aching for sex, hard and desperate for relief. He heard her moan softly as he rubbed his erection against her. He felt the heat of her body, her shiver of helpless excitement, the soft enticement of her skin. He shoved up her skirt, frantic for more of her. The future didn't exist. He had to have her even though he knew that it was too soon.

His fingers gently parted the damp curls of her sex. She went still at the invasion, at the penetration of his finger. "What are you doing to me?" she whispered, her voice breathless, unsure.

"Does it hurt?"

She shook her head, her inner muscles tightening, her breath coming in broken gasps of pleasure. He delighted in touching her, kissing her mouth, her breasts, as he played with her. His fingers were soaked with her essence. Never before or since that day had he known such desperate excitement. She responded to everything he did, her body ripe for his touch.

"What if someone notices we're missing?" she asked, her gaze on his face.

"You were doing a good deed," he said, his fingers sinking deeper, his mouth sliding down her throat. He feasted on her creamy skin, filled his senses.

She laughed. "A good deed?"

"Yes." He grinned at her. "You were reading to the man you wounded."

She lowered her gaze to study his shoulders, his bare chest and belly. "There isn't a thing wrong with you."

"Except the hole in my shoulder."

He hadn't given much thought on that sultry afternoon

to the rest of his life. He was going to war and knew he might not return. It was a miracle, considering how rashly they'd behaved, that he hadn't ruined her completely. If he'd acted on his animal instincts, he would have coaxed her to sleep with him. But sanity returned to them both in time. He didn't want to hurt her.

He'd helped her dress, conscious of how long they had been missing. "I'll look for you tonight at supper."

She let him kiss her one last time at the door. They lingered, bodies flushed, aroused to the point of aching awareness. "Don't."

"Why not?"

"Please, don't tell anyone."

He sighed into her neck, breathing deeply of her scent. He wanted her to stay with him, didn't want to unlock the door. "Never."

"Promise?"

He caught her strong chin in his hand. "I promise, but I want to see you again. I *have* to."

But he hadn't. She had not shown up at dinner that evening, claiming she caught a cold. He considered going to her father, making a confession, demanding her hand in marriage.

But she'd made him promise he wouldn't tell.

And he hadn't.

But sometimes he wondered what would have happened if he had.

Until this evening he'd assumed he would never see her again. Years had gone by since they had sworn to avoid each other. She had married another man and left Heath to nurse a wounded shoulder as well as bruised feelings. More than likely she had done her best to forget what had happened.

"The problem," Russell said in irritation, breaking the silence between them, "is that Julia believes she can take care of herself. She always has."

"Perhaps she can."

"Not against a cold-blooded assassin." Russell straightened the edge of his black silk eye patch. Heath was not sure whether this was a nervous gesture or a not-so-subtle reminder of what Russell had sacrificed to save a friend.

"She shot a man in India; did you know that?" Russell asked.

Heath hadn't known. He'd thought her lost to him forever. He had not wanted to hear the details of her married life in a foreign land. He was not a good loser at love. He had convinced himself he did not care.

"A sepoy?" he asked.

"No. A drunk English soldier who was assaulting one of her maids. She shot him right in the arse."

Heath laughed. "I hadn't heard." He wasn't surprised though.

"Thank God it isn't common knowledge," Russell said with feeling. "It's not the type of thing a decent young woman would brag about."

"You hold it against her?"

"Or course I don't," Russell retorted with a boyish smirk. "But there's no need for the civilized world to know I'm besotted with a damn Amazon, is there? Let that be our little secret."

Heath raised a brow. Besotted. She did that to a man. "I shan't tell a soul."

"I know that, too." Russell broke into an insulting grin.

"She shot you in the shoulder once, too, didn't she?" He started to laugh. "God, I'd almost forgotten. That was a time. You wallowing in the muck, white as a ghost, and Julia certain she had killed you. I thought at first there was something else going on between you. I was livid with jealousy. It looked as if she were lying on top of you."

Heath paused. The image remained vivid in his mind. Mud, pain, blood, Julia leaning over him with those clear gray eyes and her luscious, tempting body. "I remember you laughing your head off when you realized what had happened."

"I think that was the day I decided that I would marry her if I married anyone at all."

Heath glanced down at the ballroom, his expression unchanged. There was a woman attempting to hide behind one of the columns below the balcony. He couldn't see her face, but there was something about her that caught his interest. What the devil was she doing? Playing hide-and-seek? "You and half the men at the party."

"Except you." Russell leaned his elbow against the balustrade. Light from the multitiered crystal chandelier illuminated half his face; shadow blurred the rugged contours of the rest. Part hero, part cad. He was a human being with flaws, and Heath knew this, knew he was probably no better at heart. Russell had not had the easy Boscastle upbringing. He had practically pulled himself out of the gutter to achieve his success, and he was a damned fine soldier. "You and Julia took an active dislike to each other, didn't you? I suppose it's natural. The pair of you are complete opposites."

"I did not—do not—dislike Julia."

"You most certainly did. I have never seen a man and

woman go to such amusing lengths to avoid each other. Julia made me switch places with her at the dinner table that night so she wouldn't have to talk to you. And then she never showed up. She left the next day, and I lost her. At least until her husband had the consideration to get himself killed in an uprising."

Heath shook his head. Time had been good to Russell, carving masculine angles in his face to replace the pleasant boyish appeal of his youth. Of course the eye patch, added to his reputation for death-defying heroics, had enchanted England's female population. At heart though, Russell remained the same rough-around-the-edges, likable bastard he had always been.

But he had saved Heath's life once. And he would probably do it again without a second thought. He was a brave man for all his shortcomings.

Heath nodded distractedly at a friend who had just walked beneath the balcony. He should have known the day would come when Russell would take advantage of his rank, their friendship. But in his wildest dreams he hadn't expected it would involve Julia Hepworth.

He was astonished to discover that his feelings for her had remained this raw, this bittersweet . . . this ambivalent. He'd believed her memory to be buried beneath the many other issues of his past that were best left undisturbed. He didn't particularly care to be reminded of what he'd lost.

"If she and I are so ill suited, well, that's all the more reason why we should not spend time in each other's company."

Heath waited for a response, watching the graceful movements of the waltz below them. He could feel Russell appraising him, thinking, reshaping his strategy. Apparently he no longer harbored suspicions about what had happened between Heath and Julia years ago. Perhaps his sense of self would not allow him to imagine that the woman he planned to marry might have been involved with one of his friends.

"You owe me, Boscastle," he said in a quiet, deliberate voice. "I'm calling in the favor. I only want you to do this for a month."

Heath's blue eyes darkened. A month with Julia? He hadn't been able to trust himself with her for a few hours. "I had plans to go to Paris."

"Did Wellington's staff invite you to help play ambassador?"

Heath almost laughed. Russell was so predictably ambitious. "Worried you'll miss an opportunity?"

"*This* is an opportunity. Help me to catch Auclair and I guarantee you shall be rewarded."

"For playing nursemaid to your fiancée? Do they give medals for that? What am I to do, stop Julia from shooting someone? Are you serious?"

Russell smiled without warmth. "Are you a man of your word?"

A man of his word. He was, and always had been. It was his one infallible code in a world of war and chaos, the lodestar to follow when he began to lose his way. And the irony of it was that this one virtue, or flaw, prevented him from confessing why he had to refuse.

To explain the truth meant breaking his word to Julia. It would damage Russell's opinion of her. It would conceivably bring a dramatic end to their engagement. Heath would appear to be a cad, a scoundrel, a seductor of young ladies who kissed and told. He'd rather cut off his left foot. It would probably be less painful.

He shook his head in resignation. Hoisted with his own honor. That should humble him for thinking himself so bloody self-righteous.

Russell started to laugh. "For a moment I thought you would refuse. Why don't you go downstairs and talk to her? Make friends."

"You've told her?" he asked, amazed at Russell's arrogance.

"Yes. You try keeping a secret from Julia."

"How did she react?"

"I don't think she quite believed I—"

Aware of furtive movement on the stairs, both men turned at the same instant. A young footman in dark livery glanced up with an air of self-importance as he approached.

"This came for you, Sir Russell. The earl directed me to find you."

Russell unfolded the sealed letter and read it. "Auclair has just left for the country," he said with a soft curse. "I don't have time to convince you, Boscastle. You *have* to do this. It seems I'll be in Paris before you."

"Playing up to Wellington?"

Russell shot him a frown. "You do remember what she looks like, don't you?"

"I remember," he said in a clipped voice.

Not only did Heath remember what Julia looked like, he also remembered the spellbinding pitch of her voice, her easy laugh, the texture of her skin. He remembered the glint of gold in her red hair. And how her hair had fallen across his bare chest like a mermaid's net, alluring and sensual.

It seemed as if he had been attracted to her since, well, since forever. Since before his sexual tastes had grown jaded, leaving him empty, unfulfilled. She had not been the first or the last woman he'd seduced. But she was the one who had left the deepest mark on his memory. The one who had left him hungry, aching for more of her, curious to know what could have been.

No one else in the world knew that, of course, including Julia. He had not even told his brothers of his feelings. Heath kept his personal affairs and desires to himself. He'd take his secrets to the grave before getting potted at the club or bawling his eyes out on some whore's perfumed shoulder.

His thick black eyebrows met in a scowl. "When are you leaving?"

"In a few hours. He isn't going to get away."

Chapter 2

꧁ꕥ꧂

Julia stood concealed behind one of the columns in the ballroom, watching the two men on the balcony above her. It was impossible to decipher their conversation. She could hardly see their faces from this distance, but she would have recognized Heath Boscastle anywhere. The handsome devil still drew attention. Several debutantes, in fact, had made a show of walking back and forth directly beneath him.

Her fiancé was drawing attention, too. Julia frowned as two giggling young women stopped directly in front of her.

"Do you think they noticed us?" one of them whispered.

Her friend glanced up at the balcony. "Boscastle is looking *right* at me."

"What about Sir Russell?"

"I heard he'd gotten engaged, but he's looking, too."

"Let's look back. They're like gods."

Julia cleared her throat. The two younger women appeared startled, taking a step into each other. "Ladies," she said rather coolly, "haven't you been told that it is not only impolite but unforgivably forward to stare—even at the gods."

As they scurried away, duly shamed, Julia, hypocrite that she was, resumed staring at the two compelling figures on the balcony. They couldn't be discussing her all this time. They seemed perfectly calm, which meant that Heath could not have told Russell their secret.

Heath looked down to the exact spot where she stood. She slipped back behind the column. If Russell found out what had happened between her and Heath years ago, he would be understandably appalled. The mere fact that Julia had kept it a secret would seem to compound her guilt.

She had good cause to feel guilty. For heaven's sake, she had shot a man and practically invited him to ruin her all in one unforgettable day.

Her blood still went cold when she remembered Heath lying between the rocks, silent and unmoving. How relieved she'd felt when she had flung herself down on the ground and discovered him still alive. Very much alive, in fact. His blue eyes had seared her like a naked flame, disbelieving, furious . . . and disconcertingly male.

She'd had the distinct feeling he was undressing her with those eyes despite the fact that she could have blown him to kingdom come.

"You *shot* me."

"Well, no wonder." She was terrified. He had a magnificent body, and she'd probably scarred one of those muscular shoulders. Her father would hide her gun again. "What were you doing jumping out at me from behind that cairn?"

"I thought you were someone I knew."

"Well, I thought you were the rabid fox that had attacked the livestock last night."

"Do I look like a rabid fox?" he demanded.

No, she thought, biting the tip of her tongue. He looked

like a lean, angry wolf who would leap up at any moment and eat her. Even wounded he gave the impression of dangerous strength. And sensual appeal. She had been warned about him, of course. Every debutante wished to snare a Boscastle. Well, she had just shot one. Did that count?

Then, to make matters worse, she had proceeded to pull off his shirt. Her relief that the wound was only superficial gave way to a sting of pleased shock to discover that he was every bit as gorgeous as she'd suspected.

"It doesn't look as bad as I feared."

"That's easy for you to say."

She was beginning to feel better. She hadn't really hurt him. "I am sorry."

And that had been the start of it. A humiliating incident that had led to the most magical interlude she had ever experienced.

The eroticism of his kisses, the sinful thrill of being captured against that hard male body, still haunted her like a sensual dream. She'd never imagined, before or since, that she could respond to a man that way.

She certainly couldn't imagine what she would say when she came face-to-face with him tonight.

But she was about to find out.

Sometimes, examining how her life had turned out, she wished he had told. She might never have gone to India. Her father would probably have forced her to marry Heath and advised them to make the best of it. She would never have shot that soldier in the buttocks. Of all her sins, that was the one that had shocked Society the most.

She realized in alarm that he and Russell had left the balcony. That Heath was suddenly standing at the opposite end of the hall. Just that one glance at his profile, the hawk-like nose and strong, clefted chin, made her heart beat a little faster. She leaned against the wall, watching him in resentful fascination. Why couldn't he have grown fat, or lost his teeth? Perhaps he had. She could not properly see his mouth from where she stood. She remembered it, though. His firm, sensual lips with the small white scar, his beguiling smirk, the dizzying kisses they had shared.

She had never met a man who possessed the lethal elegance of Heath Boscastle, or who even came close. A man who had once seduced her down to her stockings at a hunting party when they both had been too young to know better. Or had it been the other way around? Had she clumsily attempted to seduce him? Wild Miss Hepworth her friends had called her in those days. They probably called her far worse now. The Wicked Lady Whitby.

She'd had plenty of time to reflect on what had happened between her and Heath. Years, in fact, for reflection and regrets. Naughty woman that she was, there were moments when her truest regret was that the two of them had not followed their heated encounter to the end. She hadn't always felt like that. It had taken a lonely marriage to make her face what she had wanted, what she could have had. That there wasn't only one path to contentment.

But on the day that she and Heath had parted, she had felt only an overriding panic and a guilty relief that they had stopped themselves before anyone discovered them.

And that he had kept his promise he'd never tell.

Heath was coming closer.

He walked toward the column with the same languid grace that had once set her nerves on fire, that took her breath away even now. He was tall, broader in the shoulder, than she recalled, a little leaner perhaps, but still dangerously attractive in a long-tailed black evening coat and pantaloons. Older, more experienced, more on edge, as elusive to the female heart as ever. Her throat closed as she stared at him. She'd believed she would never see him again. The ache of unresolved feelings inside her made her wish that she had not. It hurt to realize what might have been. And yet she could not deny the anticipation that rose inside her. Clever, handsome, an irresistible rogue. How silly to assume he would remain preserved as he was in her memory.

Six years, she thought, astonished that so much time had passed. She had been married and widowed in India. She had seen a side of life that the haut ton could only read about in the newspaper and gasp at in horror.

What had Heath heard about her?

She knew he could see her, that he was perfectly aware of who she was. His stride was unhurried, yet powerful.

Did he remember what they had done together that day in the library?

She steeled herself to look up into his heartbreakingly beautiful face, the chiseled features, the hard, sculpted chin. His dark blue eyes danced with restrained amusement, answering both her unspoken questions. He stopped as she stepped into his path.

He knew everything about her.

And he remembered perfectly well what they had done.

Furthermore, he hadn't lost even a single white tooth.

Even worse, she couldn't stop staring up at him, drinking in all the details of his appearance. One would think she had never seen a handsome man in her entire life. Of course there was a little more to it than that. They shared a secret.

"Julia," he said in the deep, cultured voice that brought another rush of forgotten memories to the surface, teased her starved senses. "Still hiding, are you? I trust you aren't armed tonight. Should I search you?"

She studied him in feigned puzzlement. "I'm sorry—do I know you? Have we been formally introduced?"

He took her by the hand, drawing her forward without a qualm. "Very funny, considering the fact that you almost shot me dead the first time I saw you."

"You shouldn't have been hiding behind that rock. I thought you were a fox." Now that she found her voice, she seemed to have turned into a chatterbox. The warmth in his eyes made it too easy to talk to him. "Oh, Heath, have you forgiven me? Did I leave you with a scar?"

"Yes. And yes. Actually I have gotten several scars since we met, but yours is the only one associated with a pleasant memory."

There was a pause. She was aware of how hard her heart was beating, of other guests glancing at them, that time had only intensified his personal magnetism. She'd been surprised when Russell told her that Heath had never married, but then he was young enough and could afford to wait, could take his pick from the entire female population of England. A man who looked like Heath Boscastle would hardly have to search for a companion.

She was staring at him again. And he was smiling, although not out of any sense of superiority or conceit that she could tell. A perfect gentleman, he didn't launch into gloating reminiscences of their sinful interlude.

It was more emotionally charged than she'd imagined it

would be, meeting him like this, and she had imagined it countless times. He was the same charming rogue she remembered. The war had changed so many of her male acquaintances, and Heath had been captured, had survived a great deal.

He cleared his throat.

She gave herself a stern mental shake and glanced away.

"Would you care for something to drink?" he asked, drawing her to the end of the corridor.

"A drink?" She wished she would not keep remembering how he'd looked half naked, how the hand that was guiding her in such a gentlemanly way had plundered the private recesses of her body. He was so poised. It must amuse him to remember what they had done.

"Yes," he said in a light voice. "A beverage. You know, that liquid stuff one swallows from time to time."

"A drink," she repeated.

"Do you need me to draw you a picture, Julia?" He waved his free hand in front of her face. "Julia?"

His voice was warm, teasing, as seductive as she remembered, had tried to forget. He'd always had a wicked, wry sense of humor, and it took all of her wits to pretend she was not affected, that every word he said, every gesture, did not take her back to the past. The lure proved too strong. She adverted her gaze, afraid she would give herself away, afraid that he was too intelligent to deceive. How humiliating that she could still recall every word.

I had one glass of claret, Heath.

Yes, well, it's all gone to your head.

No, it hasn't.

It most certainly has, or you wouldn't be kissing me like this.

Do you mind?

Of course I don't mind, but I daresay you will tomorrow.

I won't. I never do anything I regret. Well, until now . . .

He'd threaded his long fingers through her hair and pulled her back into the sofa, his sensuality overpowering, the heat of his chiseled lips on her throat drugging her senses. The other house guests had gone off on a hunt, and she and Heath had been locked together in the library for three hours, unable to open the door, or at least pretending that the lock was jammed. Three fateful hours. Her life had never been the same, the stolen pleasure of their interlude overshadowing her to this moment. The ache inside her became more persistent, bittersweet and unfulfilled. There was something about him that inspired confidence and penetrated her defenses. Yet he had kept his promise to her.

She forced her mind back to the present. He was no longer holding her hand, but she had felt the warmth of his strong fingers all the way down to her knees. A blush of pleasant awareness washed over her.

She met his curious, perceptive gaze and sighed inwardly. It was far too easy to lose herself in those eyes as she had once learned. Guests were milling around them, staring at them in recognition now. Clearly those in the know had heard that Julia was engaged to Sir Russell, and Heath was a Boscastle male—eligible if elusive, a conquest to be pursued by the marriage-minded at any price.

She started to laugh. "Yes. I'd like a drink—anything as long as it's not claret."

A flame kindled in the depths of his dark blue eyes. His mocking smile was irresistible. "Ah, yes. I've heard it goes to one's head."

Chapter 3

Heath walked beside her, deep in thought, trying to assess his position. He could not quite believe it. Perhaps this was the price he paid for being such a private man. For the most part he ignored Society, its whims and scandals, unless absolutely necessary. He'd accepted this invitation tonight to the Earl of Odham's ball only because Russell insisted, and he hadn't seen Russell in ages. He should have suspected an ulterior motive.

He'd been ready to be called back into service. London had begun to bore him silly. He was between mistresses, restless, seeking something he could not identify. Perhaps a distraction from his inner demons, his own thoughts. Nothing seemed to satisfy him lately. He didn't want to be alone, and yet he grew impatient with his small circle of friends.

The last woman in the world he'd expected to see tonight was Julia Hepworth--or Lady Whitby, as she was now known. He stole a speculative look at her. That pale mint-green gown of hers wrapped her delicious curves like gossamer. Green wasn't an appropriate color for mourning in London, was it, or had she adopted some foreign fashion? It *was* good to see her again. How long had her husband been dead? She hadn't lost her wits or her earthy appeal over the years.

Or her ability to provoke him. Why in God's name was she marrying Russell? What an unlikely match. The pair of them would drive each other mad. He decided that green wasn't worn in mourning, or half mourning, for that matter. He wondered whether she'd loved her late husband. And how he was supposed to "take care of her" while Russell played the hero. How was he supposed to pretend that he hadn't almost taken her virginity years back? No matter how detached either of them appeared, there was no point in pretending the past had never happened.

"Where did Russell go?"

The sound of her voice wrenched him back to his present dilemma. She had asked for Russell. The joker who had arranged this perplexing affair, the man for whom Heath would play reluctant placeholder. He frowned and noticed in surprise and some relief that they had almost reached the refreshment room. A reprieve from being alone with her might give him time to think of a solution.

He studied her covertly as she went through the door. She was Julia and yet quite different than the last time he'd seen her. More confident, all the discordant aspects of her character melded into a more intense, more interesting package. He could not read her thoughts, guess what she made of their situation. Of him.

She seemed sure of herself. Her eyes no longer gazed at him with that disconcerting innocence, but were knowing, with a steady stare that challenged. A handmaiden who had turned into Hera. He felt a shift in his perception of her, a disorientation. There was no other woman with whom to compare her. He could not think of a single one. His past relationships had been uncomplicated and open. What he and Julia had shared was shadowy and undefined, a desire left to dangle like an unanswered question.

He knew her, and yet he didn't. Well, he assumed, hoped, that he had changed for the better, too. They could hardly be the same two people who had gone at each other with thoughtless abandon in a library a lifetime ago. Years had passed. What had experience done to them? Had time fulfilled her expectations or erased them?

Her gaze lifted to his. She took a sip of lemonade, and he remembered suddenly the taste of her kisses, the ripe softness of her lips, the sensual hunger that she had stirred in him. She'd laughed the first time he kissed her. They had laughed themselves silly over nothing. The echo of that memory, that sweet blinding innocence that they had both lost, stabbed him with a sense of poignancy. He hadn't laughed like that since then. Still, they could never go back to that time.

"You're staring at my mouth," she whispered, catching him off guard.

"Oh." He removed a crisp white handkerchief from his vest pocket. "Lemonade. On your lips."

She took the handkerchief, her expression doubtful, although she went along with him. "Where did Russell go?" she asked, glancing around them.

"He was called off on an urgent matter."

She dabbed at her mouth. There wasn't any lemonade there, and they both knew it. She raised her brow. "Again?"

"Apparently." He took her elbow, to guide her away from the line of guests crowding the table. "Is he called away often?"

"Yes. And—"

"He's asked me to watch—"

"Over me." She made a face, her eyes darkening in disapproval. Apparently this whole thing hadn't been her idea. "It's ridiculous, Heath."

"I don't know. Auclair is a monster."

She set her glass down on the sideboard. "I can't believe it. Why would Auclair not have given up? Didn't you and Russell suffer enough at Sahagun?"

"Auclair is hardly a man of reason," he said quietly.

"Let someone else make a sacrifice for a change."

"We're still alive, Julia. Others have lost far more."

She faced him squarely, reminding him without words that she had made her own sacrifices.

"How is your family, Heath?"

He paused, admiring the adept change of direction. "Well enough, thank you. Grayson has recently married."

"I heard. Who would have thought it? The original scoundrel leg-shackled for life."

"It happens to the best of us." He laughed as he thought of his older brother's reckless past. "And to the worst, apparently."

"You're next in line, aren't you?"

"Not if I can help it."

She looked up at him. "I always thought you'd be married with at least five children by now."

She couldn't have been further from the truth. He'd never even come close to marriage. Not that he had anything against it. Did she love Russell? Of course she did. Half the ladies in London swooned when Sir Russell Althorne made one of his dramatic appearances at a party. How long had she been engaged to him? And when had their romance started? They seemed so incompatible, Julia, the free spirit, and Russell, who wanted so badly to impress the world. Well, opposites were supposed to complement each other.

It was arrogance on his part, really, to judge her so easily, sheer masculine conceit. Why did he presume to know her on the basis of one unforgettable interlude in the past? Just because her memory had haunted him over the years did not mean that she felt the same way about him. She may have come to regard him as the rogue who almost ruined her. What had been a significant moment in his life might have been no more than a humiliating experience for her.

"You don't have to do what he asks," she said over her shoulder as she led him back into the hall to the ballroom.

"No," he said mildly. "I could be a perfect cad and discard any sense of honor. Russell did risk his life to rescue me."

"Honor," she murmured offhandedly. "What is it anyway?"

"You don't believe in honor, Julia?"

"I believe men die for it."

She edged away from him, absorbed into a group of guests who greeted her with guarded smiles. Honor. He was incensed, at a loss as to how to respond, frozen to the spot. She seemed to hold the concept in disdain. Did it have anything to do with the fact that her husband had died a brutal death as an officer in India? The war had left more than one woman embittered, hurt, disillusioned.

Samuel Breckland, a family friend, and Heath's own brother, Brandon, had also lost their young lives upholding the notion of honor.

He felt like giving her a shake. She had touched a raw nerve, and the result was a rather irrationable sense of outrage. Wouldn't the world collapse without honor? Who was she to mock the one thing he valued above almost everything? Who was she to make him question what he had become? And, why, for God's sake, was he allowing her one careless question to unsettle him? Grayson, his brother, had repeated the same sentiment a dozen times. But from Julia, the words assumed a deeper meaning.

She turned unexpectedly, looking annoyed, perhaps embarrassed to find him hovering over her. She was presumably as uncomfortable with this arrangement as he was. Attempting to blend in with the other guests, she whispered in his direction, "Do go away, Heath. You're following me like a mother hen."

A mother hen. Heath Boscastle. No one had ever referred to him in such terms. He almost laughed. God, if his brothers could see him now. If she only knew how he really felt. If only *he* knew.

"Heath," a young woman behind him whispered. "Did she say Heath?"

"Heath Boscastle?"

"*He's* here?"

"Where is he?"

"I haven't seen him. He rarely attends these functions."

"I heard he attended his brother's wedding."

"Were you invited? Do you think—has he got marriage on his mind?"

He heard his name repeated, murmured, discussed by a small group of aggressive young women who'd just noticed his presence at the party. He could thank Julia for that. He disliked being the focus of attention. It went against his secretive nature, his ability to blend into the shadows and watch the rest of the world. They probably could not manage a single intelligent thought among them.

He tactfully brushed aside all the female bodies that began clustering around him like warm, perfumed moths. He was in serious danger of being smothered by a flock of fluttering fan-waving debutantes.

He made a covert escape to a chorus of disappointed sighs. By the time he managed to extricate himself from the siege Julia had set upon him, he glanced up to see her silk-clad form glide through a door at the opposite end of the ballroom.

Reaching her would bring all his skills as a cavalry officer into play. But their conversation was not over. He would not be dismissed like a raw youth, no matter what had happened in the past. Or what the future would bring.

Chapter 4

Julia took several deep breaths and proceeded down the candlelit hallway, her green silk gown rustling in the silence. She walked in long, precise strides. On a good day she could outpace most men her age.

Heath Boscastle was another matter entirely.

He always had been. She should have known his instincts would only sharpen over time. Well, so had hers. She wasn't a giddy nineteen-year-old virgin who drank a glass of claret and tumbled onto a library sofa with the most attractive man in the world and gave herself up to him with shameless abandon.

She pursed her lips in self-disdain. Heavens, no. She was a twenty-six-year-old widow who could calmly walk away from the most attractive man in the world because it was the right thing to do.

Wasn't it?

She had warned Russell that to order Heath to protect her was a horrible idea, an insult, an invitation to trouble. That she did not want a protector, at least not one who knew her a little better than she could ever admit.

The problem was that Russell, in his well-meaning male

arrogance, had assured her that *he* alone knew what was in her best interests. *He* knew whom he could trust, could depend on, could manipulate with Machiavellian skill. Well, to be fair, he hadn't said he could manipulate Heath, but the implication was resoundingly clear. He meant to leave her safe with the most competent man he knew, the one man he claimed to trust above all others.

And Julia could only sit on the sofa in silent misery while her celebrated fiancé lectured her in his paternal way until she'd finally managed to get a word in edgewise to protest.

"Not Heath Boscastle. Find another Hussar, a Horse Guard, a Bow Street runner, a . . . retired wrestler, or even a reformed convict."

"Julia, darling." He sat down beside her and gave her a hard, earnest look. "Trust me. I'm a man. I know what's best."

He was definitely a man. He might even have known what was best, but he did not know, and never would, what had happened between Julia and Heath years ago in Cornwall. On a sofa very much like the one they were sitting on, as a matter of fact.

And on the floor.

She stared down at the patterned Turkey carpet, transfixed by the memory of a half-naked Heath Boscastle on top of her, his clever hands, his sensual mouth, branding her with his unforgettable imprint. He'd had the body of a young god and the seductive powers to match. She felt a little breathless at this moment, thinking about him.

It had been the most earthshaking sexual experience she had ever known, even after five years of marriage. An extravagant invitation to pleasure, a stunning discovery, a raw awakening—

"And so you agree, it really is for the best. He's a heartless killer, Julia, a—"

"Heath Boscastle?" she said in disbelief, blinking guiltily.

Russell subjected her to an irate stare, his single eye managing to convey a wealth of displeasure. "No. Not Boscastle. Do pay attention. I am referring to the man I intend to bring to justice. The French spy who has promised to kill me, Julia, Armand Auclair."

"Oh, him," she said in embarrassment. "But why? I mean, why not allow someone else to be a hero for a change?"

She already knew the answer. Russell was about to receive a viscountcy for his bravery in the light cavalry, for the risks he had taken protecting his brigade, some of which had been, in Julia's private opinion, downright foolhardy. But he had caught the great Wellington's notice, and rumor had it that Sir Russell had a golden political future ahead of him. She knew it meant a great deal to him, and he deserved the acclaim.

She thought he was well-suited for a public career. She was a little less sure of her skills as a social hostess. Out of practice. She could probably survive a monsoon more calmly than London Society. She'd grown far too accustomed to behaving as she wished. Perhaps if she and her husband, a light dragoon officer, had lived in Calcutta instead of a bungalow in a remote country district, she would have been better prepared for her return to the social arena.

She had married Sir Adam Whitby only a month after meeting him at a horse race. Her father had encouraged the match, presumably because it was his duty and Julia's other suitors had gone off to war. Adam was sweet, attentive, and so infatuated with her she knew that he was a man who would never deliberately hurt her, and he hadn't until his death. Neglected her, perhaps, but not on purpose.

Like so many other young Englishmen he'd been caught up in a dream of serving in India and making a fortune there. He had assured Julia it happened all the time. She'd had enough adventure in her soul to agree to follow him, even though they'd needed special permission from the army to marry.

She had been unbearably lonely in India, soon realizing how much she missed rainy, green England and her father. She'd had a French cook and a great deal of freedom, but the only time she'd spent with Adam had been a stolen moment here and there. They'd been married for three years when he was killed. Now she was starting her life all over again and discovering how difficult it was.

She could not simply resume her former position in Society. Most of her friends had married and were raising children. If it hadn't been for Russell's support, she would still be struggling to find her bearings. He had helped her to take care of her father, Viscount Margate, while he was dying. Russell had been exceptionally kind and patient, handling the details of the funeral and legal matters, and he wanted a family of his own, having grown up as an orphan, an only child. He was quite a self-made man.

In fact, Julia was not sure how she would have gotten through her father's death without Russell. Her mind had been in a fog. It was only now beginning to clear. She had felt quite bewildered, losing her husband, then coming home to see her father die while she watched helplessly.

She had accepted Russell's proposal without really thinking it through. She was certain her heart would become more engaged when she settled back into her new situation. He was an enormously attractive personality.

She stopped in the middle of the hall to take stock of her present surroundings. It was one in the morning by the brass hands of the tall rosewood case clock behind her. She had an appointment. She was already late. She had to hurry before Boscastle realized she had left the ballroom, if he hadn't already. She would not be wise to underestimate him. Or to underestimate his effect on her. As wonderful as it had been to see him again, she wasn't convinced it had been good for either of them. It bothered her to discover that she had not quite gotten over their encounter. Or that time had not diminished his appeal. And yet . . .

She still did not trust herself alone with the man. What a horrid thing to discover at the age of twenty-six.

She pulled out her ivory fan, snapped it open, and peered at it in the dark. Tucked inside was an amateurish map, a layout of the house.

A large X marked the private study of the ball's host, the Earl of Odham. The room appeared to be located just around the corner, to her left, four doors down.

She found her destination without further difficulty; the door, however, was locked. She pressed her ear to the panel and heard the unmistakable rustling of papers inside the room. She frowned in disapproval before raising her knuckles to rap quietly at the door.

Once.

Twice.

A third time, then, in an impatient whisper, "For heaven's sake, Hermia, open this door before I am caught."

The door flew open. Her aunt's pale elongated face in its

coronet of silver-blond curls scowled at her in recognition. Julia squeezed in around her, praying no one had seen her.

"Why didn't you let me in?"

"You did not use the secret knock."

"My goodness," Julia said, glancing around at the letters and unfolded envelopes strewn around the room. "This room is a shambles. I hope you found what you are looking for."

Her aunt straightened the vase of peacock feathers she had knocked over. "I did not. The scoundrel has guarded his secret papers very well indeed."

"Well, clean up this mess."

"Why should I?"

"Do you really want the earl to know you are a housebreaker?"

"I do not give a fig for his opinion of me."

Julia knelt and efficiently began to gather the scattered letters into an orderly pile. "Help me, please."

"Oh, all right. No, those went in the lower-right-hand desk drawer. These with the red ribbon go over here in the box."

Julia crawled under the desk after her aunt. "Did you see these?" she asked, peering into a leather portfolio of old letters.

"No." Hermia frowned. "It must have fallen out of the drawer. Can you read any of the papers inside?"

Julia sighed. "I can hardly tell in the dark. They appear to be business letters. Let's look at them properly, shall we?"

"We're running out of time. I told Odham I would meet him at half-past one."

"How can you look the man in the face after you have

just ransacked his personal possessions?" Julia asked crossly as she crawled out backward onto the carpet.

"That's a very good question," a deep, cultured voice drawled above her. "Perhaps you'd like to practice your answer on me before I escort you to the earl."

Julia straightened quickly, her eyes dark with emotion. So he had followed her. She should have known. He'd never been like anyone else she'd met, a man always several moves ahead of others. He enjoyed analyzing human nature. His quiet façade hid a dangerous perception, which was, oddly, one of the things she'd liked best about him. One of the many things.

"Boscastle!" the older woman behind her exclaimed. "What in the name of Zeus are you doing here?"

"I should ask—"

"He's guarding me," Julia broke in impatiently.

"He's what?" Hermia asked in confusion.

"Protecting me while Russell goes off to find that Frenchman. Isn't it the most hideous idea you have ever heard?"

Lady Dalrymple eyed Heath with open admiration. "I think it's a stroke of genius. A Boscastle as your own personal bodyguard. Splendid. I had no idea he was up for hire, or I'd have snapped him up myself."

"He wasn't," Heath said, shaking his head in obvious chagrin. "Isn't. Well, at least not for money."

Hermia's brows rose toward her widow's peak. "Then why?"

"Because Russell is afraid that this man who means to kill him might decide to send someone after me while he is hunting the villain down," Julia said curtly. "He fears I shall be held for hostage, if you can imagine why anyone would bother."

"You can't blame him for wanting to protect you," Hermia said.

Heath pivoted. "There's someone coming. A man, by the sound of the footsteps. I suggest we finish this fascinating conversation later."

Hermia took hold of Julia's arm. "It must be Aldric. Hide me."

Julia looked at her aunt's large-boned figure in exasperation. The red silk gown with its taffeta bustle hardly underemphasized Hermia's substantial frame, or enabled her to blend into the furnishings. "Where do you suggest I put you?"

"Behind the desk . . . we should all hide to save us an explanation."

"I'm not hiding," Heath said, folding his arms across his chest. "I haven't done anything wrong, and I refuse—"

Hermia grasped him by the sleeve of his evening coat while simultaneously giving Julia a strong push toward the desk. "We shall explain everything later, Boscastle. It is crucial that Aldric not discover us." She looked Heath in the eye. "You are a man of the world, and Julia's chosen protector. I doubt any of Society's trivial scandals could shock you. You see, Aldric is blackmailing me."

"The earl, black—"

The three of them dove down behind the desk as a key turned in the lock and the door slowly opened. Heath found himself on his knees, sandwiched between Julia's bare shoulders and Hermia's ample bustle. There was hardly room to move a finger. If he had ever been trapped in a more preposterous situation, he could not remember when.

Julia lifted her head and looked up at him. Their eyes locked. The corners of her full red mouth lifted as if she were about to burst into laughter.

She had laughed a lot the day he'd spent with her, at little things, at the larger ones, too, such as shooting him by mistake. He felt suddenly, inexplicably, like having a good laugh, too, despite the fact that he could still be drawn to her after years of believing he would never see her again, that she was marrying his rival, that her knee was propped up against his backside. It was tempting to laugh at the sheer capriciousness of life.

Instead, he focused his attention on the pair of leather-shod feet that shuffled around the room. The Earl of Odham wasn't what one would call a young man, in his mid-sixties, but his mind had seemed agile and alert when he and Heath had met at their club.

Alert enough to notice the letter he had just stepped on.

"Hello," Odham said softly, bending at the waist to pick it up. "Someone's been rifling through my desk. That isn't a very nice thing to do. Quite unfriendly, in fact."

He got down on his knees, practically eye level with the trio of guests huddled behind his desk. By some miracle he did not appear to see them. Another inch closer and he surely would.

Heath frowned. He had no idea how he would explain being caught snooping around his host's private study when he really did not understand it himself. He had no excuse for his behavior. Hell, he didn't even know *why* he was hiding.

"Sloppy, sloppy, sloppy," the earl muttered. And then

clearing his throat, he added in a loud voice, "It's a very good thing I don't hide my *personal* papers in here."

A few moments later he was gone, humming to himself as he locked the door behind him.

Hermia crawled out from beneath the desk and straightened her gown and bustle. "Well, that was an invigorating experience."

Heath came to his feet, eyeing her darkly. "Invigorating is hardly the term I would use to describe a crime."

"It wasn't a crime," Julia said in her aunt's defense, smoothing out her gown. "Odham issued us a personal invitation."

Heath snorted in disbelief. "Surely not to rifle his study."

"Stay here a few minutes while I make sure the coast is clear," Hermia said, unruffled by his disdain. "You've done a bit of spying, Boscastle. I'm sure you understand what I mean."

"Actually, I don't. Nor, I suspect, do I wish to be involved."

"I don't either," Julia whispered over his shoulder. "Not exactly, anyway, but she is my aunt, and I will not see her wronged."

He turned, aware of her standing behind him, and examined her face in the darkness. He had always been attracted to the contrasts of her vivid coloring, her fire-red hair, wide-set expressive eyes, and smooth-textured skin. But there was more beneath her subtle beauty to draw a man. There was substance, intelligence, a warmth. He wondered if Russell really knew what he was getting into, or how fortunate he was. "I trust you don't do this sort of thing often."

"This is our first attempt at housebreaking, believe it or not."

He withdrew from his waistcoat pocket the map she had dropped in the hall, grinning at her. "Oh, I believe it. I hope it shall be your last."

Her full mouth curved into a faint smile. "Once is more than enough for certain experiences, isn't it? Especially those of the more sinful variety."

There was no mistaking what she meant. His pulse quickened in response. "I don't know, Julia. A few of us find a taste of temptation merely whets the appetite."

"Then what a good thing it is that I am not a hearty eater."

"Perhaps you've been sitting at the wrong table," he said smoothly.

She arched her eyebrow. "Perhaps I prefer to eat alone."

He smiled slowly. He couldn't remember the last time he'd matched wits with a woman and not known whether he would win. The challenge aroused him.

"Come on, you two," Hermia whispered back at them. "This is not the time for renewing old acquaintances."

He shook his head in bemusement as Hermia pushed open the door, peered outside again, then disappeared into the hall. He wasn't even sure what they had just done and how he'd ended up in the thick of their conspiracy.

"What," he said as he turned back to Julia, "was all that about? You don't really expect me to believe that harmless old Aldric is blackmailing your aunt?"

She gave an apologetic shrug. "It's true."

"Then it should be dealt with in a proper manner. That is to say, through the authorities as opposed to two females breaking into a man's desk."

"This is not a proper affair," Julia said matter-of-factly. "It is a personal one. Aldric is threatening to publish Hermia's past love letters if she does not comply with his demands."

"That is—" Heath broke off, curious despite himself. For a man who rarely attended parties, he seemed to be making up for lost time. "How did he come into possession of your aunt's letters, anyway?"

Julia shook her head. "The letters were written *to* Aldric."

He fought a grin. "Are you serious?"

"I'm afraid I am. You see, Aldric and Hermia had a torrid love affair many years ago, and she was foolish enough to describe certain details of their liaison in their correspondences."

She looked him straight in the eye, as if warning him not to bring up certain details of *their* past. He schooled his features into a bland mask.

"And Aldric has threatened to publish her letters unless she pays him some exorbitant price?" he asked, trying to sound appropriately disgusted.

"No." Julia brushed around him. "Not quite. He has threatened to expose their affair unless she agrees to marry him."

Heath could not suppress the smile that tugged at his mouth. This explanation was not what he expected, but it made more sense than an image of a malicious, blackmailing Aldric. An elderly earl obsessed to the point of blackmail, in love with a buxom widow who had apparently been quite the temptress in her youth. He rubbed the bridge of his nose to hide another grin. Perhaps youthful indiscretions ran in Julia's family. They certainly ran in his.

No wonder that the two of them, caught alone together, had created such a volatile combination. It was heredity's fault.

"Well, my goodness," he said. "Who would have thought it? Aldric and your aunt?"

"My aunt is mortified at the prospect of having this embarrassing part of her past revealed for public titillation."

"Yes, I can imagine. Hermia and Odham must have been quite a pair in their day."

Julia gave him another quick warning look as if to remind him that she, too, wished to have the past buried and private. She needn't have worried. Heath had absolutely no intention of bringing up their history, which made it all the more surprising when she said, out of the blue, "Just to clear the air, I have not forgotten what happened the last time we were together in the library."

He drew a breath and pretended to study the globe on a brass stand in the corner. Where was this leading? Clear the air, indeed. If anything her revelation only fanned whirls of smoke. Now that their past was out in the open, it begged for further discussion. "Neither have I."

"Perhaps we ought to check the door," she said with a meaningful look. "Just in case we find ourselves locked inside a room."

He glanced up, his smile dark. "Perhaps."

There was a pause. Heath allowed it to expand. He had long ago realized while intelligence gathering that one could learn far more about a person during a silence than a conversation. What would he learn about her? He studied her covertly. He'd never been sure exactly what she had felt for him. Perhaps he had made an irrevocable mistake that day, and she could not forgive him. He might have frightened her away.

She was as cool as a snowdrop in a February frost. The silence did not appear to unnerve her in the least. Well, she had lived quite a life, shooting a fellow Englishman to defend a native servant. The old rules did not apply, or she had never bothered to follow them in the first place. She swept past him to check the door for herself. Her confidence and purpose woke up all his dormant senses, attracting him to a danger he had never encountered before.

She was Julia Hepworth all right, but not the Julia he fondly remembered in his robust sexual fantasies. Perhaps she was more, temptation multiplied by ten. His heart gave a heavy, dangerous thump. How could this be? Part of him yearned for the reckless young girl of their youth, the girl who'd laughed at life and shared her innocence with him. At least with her he had been able to take the lead.

"I heard your father has died," he said, seeking balance in the safe, the expected. "I am sorry, Julia."

She sent him a half-grateful, half-searching look over her shoulder. "He would have loved it if you'd visited him. Most of his friends couldn't be bothered. His mind wandered at the end, but when it returned, it was as sharp as ever. You'd have done him a world of good."

"I wish I'd known." And he meant it. Her father had been a big, kind-hearted man whose passion for life had been infectious. Generous to a fault, a gentleman. He'd passed on much of his character to his only daughter.

"I lost my father, too," he said after a pause.

"Russell told me," she said, shaking her head in sympathy. "I suppose it helps, though, having all your brothers and sisters."

"They're a distraction. But . . . you were close to your father."

She smiled, taking him off guard. Maturity had created a flattering effect on her face, defining the strong bones, her rather wide mouth, and sharp chin, bringing her features into proportion. Arresting. A woman of character. "He liked you. I never knew how much until the month he died. . . ."

He had no time to ask her what she meant.

Voices in the hallway outside the study broke the unwelcome intimacy between them. They moved apart, toward the door, managing to appear as if they were two guests who had wandered off separately for a breather. Heath stood and watched her disappear into the cloakroom. He had no idea exactly what excuse he would use, but one thing was certain—he wasn't about to spend a month guarding Julia for another man.

Julia retreated into the cloakroom, completely chagrined with her behavior. All these years of deceiving herself. Of believing she had changed, grown stronger, learned from her mistakes. All the lectures and imaginary conversations she'd held in front of the looking glass. The clever comebacks, the cool distance she would put between them.

All gone the moment she had stared up into Heath Boscastle's unforgettable blue eyes. She might have been an empty-headed girl again, not a widow who was well past the first blush. Incredible, embarrassing that he could raze all her defenses to so completely unsettle her. The only difference between now and then was that she could hide her feelings. But she still felt them. She couldn't blame him for her reaction to his appeal.

She dabbed the pulse points of her wrists with a sponge

soaked in orange water, hoping the cool fragrance would settle the flurry of her thoughts. It hadn't helped that he was as charming as ever or so genuinely kind about her father. Or that her father's dying regret had been that she had not "married Boscastle."

"Damn it all anyway," she said, and threw the sponge into the ceramic washbasin. "Damn all men."

"Surely not *all* of them," an amused female voice remarked behind her.

Julia revolved slowly to see the petite figure of a woman in her early thirties reclining on the velvet settee. The woman rose with the languid self-indulgence of an empress. Her name was on the tip of Julia's tongue. She knew her.

"You're—"

"Audrey Watson," the woman said with a warm smile. "Do you remember me?"

"Of course. We met at Hyde Park ages ago." Julia forced a smile, reminding herself she was in London and the rules she'd almost forgotten now applied. At the time of their meeting Audrey had just become the mistress of a well-known portrait painter. Apparently, from what Julia had read in the papers, that affair was only the beginning of a successful career as a courtesan. London Society adored Audrey. She threw scandalous parties and sold sexual favors for outrageous sums.

A courtesan. Good heavens. What an auspicious start to Julia's entrée back into Society.

Audrey smiled as if she could read Julia's mind. "You've heard the gossip about me, naturally. Don't worry, darling— it's all true."

Julia blinked. She understood immediately why Society

liked this woman. She exuded a great sense of fun. "Well, in that case, congratulations. You've done better with the opposite sex than I have."

Audrey regarded her with concern. "You're Lady Whitby now, aren't you? Julia Hepworth, the girl who likes guns."

"Guilty as charged."

Audrey laughed in delight. "You're as notorious as I am, and we've both made our name using men."

"The similarity ends there, I'm afraid," Julia said with mock solemnity. "You see, I've become infamous for shooting them, and you . . . you . . ."

"Allow them to shoot," Audrey said with a sly grin. "I have left a few of my lovers with injuries, though, if it makes you feel any better."

Julia sighed, remembering why she had ducked into this room to hide. "I wish my affairs were that simple."

Audrey lowered her voice, nodding meaningfully toward the young maidservant who was arranging cloaks and shawls, while avidly listening to every word of this conversation.

"Did I see you sneaking off a few minutes ago for a rendezvous with Heath Boscastle?" she asked under her breath.

Julia's mouth fell open. She'd happily forgotten that Society had eyes and ears in every corner. "It wasn't a rendezvous."

Audrey smiled as if she knew better. "It is said in female circles that to be in the mere presence of a Boscastle is to have a rendezvous, Julia. A woman's senses are overwhelmed."

"That's certainly true," she said without thinking.

"They're the very best rogues in the world," Audrey added with enthusiasm. "I adore each and every one of them."

For some odd reason Audrey's announcement did not make Julia feel better. Knowing that other women found Heath irresistible did not give her an added advantage. In fact, it only seemed to enhance his unholy appeal, and to drive home how impossible this arrangement between them would prove. Heath Boscastle, her bodyguard. He did not appear to be any happier about the situation than she was, and she could hardly blame him. What an imposition on his life. She'd already involved him in her aunt's silly affair with the earl.

Audrey's eye widened in scandalous delight. "Don't tell me Boscastle has asked you to become his mistress."

Julia sighed. "Of course he hasn't."

Audrey gave a gasp. "Your wife? I shall swoon with envy."

"Obviously you have not heard the news," Julia said crisply, realizing how out of practice she'd become in social arts. "I am engaged to Sir Russell Althorne."

"Althorne?" Audrey had allowed her voice to rise again in unmistakable disappointment. "Oh."

The young maidservant glanced up at Julia in astonishment, subjecting her to a closer scrutiny. The door opened to admit three chattering debutantes. Audrey drew back gracefully to allow them room, jostling for space. She sent Julia an apologetic smile, recovering her composure, but her next comment only reinforced her true feelings.

"Well, in that case, I agree with your previous sentiment."

Julia wavered. It was the perfect moment to escape. She

did not want to be lured into revealing anything she regretted about her past association with Heath. Or her current one, either. But Audrey had cleverly piqued her curiosity, and Julia found she had to take that first bite of the apple, never mind what the serpent would do to her afterward. Clearly the woman disliked Russell.

"My previous sentiment?" she asked in a soft voice. "What do you mean?"

Audrey shook her head. " 'Damn all men.' That was what you said when you came in here, wasn't it?"

That was what she'd said, but by now two other women had squeezed into the small room. It was neither the time nor the place to continue the conversation, and it probably would not help her reputation to be seen openly seeking the advice of a known courtesan. Did Audrey have private knowledge of Russell? A reason to disapprove? Perhaps Russell had shunned her in public. Or was she merely so smitten with the Boscastle line that all other men paled in comparison?

Julia told herself that this must be the case.

The Boscastle men, as she knew from experience, were spellbinding devils who cast lesser beings into their shadows.

Chapter 5

Julia sat in a corner of the ballroom with her aunt for the next half hour, patiently answering questions about her life in India. How had she survived so long removed from civilization? Did she still have nightmares? Did her servants all smoke hookahs and consider her an infidel? The Earl of Odham tried repeatedly to draw Hermia onto the floor, but she refused and scolded him for behaving like a vain old fool. Julia suspected that her aunt enjoyed all the attention, and that she still had deep feelings for the earl, even if she could not forgive his infidelity. Julia did not judge her. She might have done the same in her place.

"Did you know," Hermia asked behind her fan, "that the notorious courtesan Audrey Watson is here tonight?"

"Yes." Julia stared across the room, not meeting her aunt's eyes. "I talked with her earlier."

Hermia lowered her fan, aghast. "You talked with her?"

"Yes. She's a lovely woman."

"What did she say?" her aunt asked eagerly.

"She—" Julia broke off in exasperation. It was impossible to concentrate on normal conversation. Heath had kept her under his scrutiny the entire evening, and didn't try to hide it. When she had emerged from the cloakroom, there he had stood, waiting patiently, his presence probably adding fuel to Audrey's speculation that there was *something* between them. He'd insisted on escorting her back to the ballroom and had watched her ever since. Twenty minutes ago she had attempted to sneak out into the garden to escape the stuffy, perfumed air. By some preternatural instinct, he had proceeded her and was lying in wait on the terrace, calmly smoking a cigar.

"Fancy meeting you here," she said, her heart lodging in her throat. "Again."

"Would you care to take a walk?" he asked, the practiced rogue concealed behind the perfect gentleman as he extended his arm.

Julia ignored the tempting gesture. She had to admit to herself that if one had to choose a bodyguard, he could not be bested.

"Yes, I would like to walk, thank you. But alone, if you don't mind. I grew accustomed to strolling by myself in India."

He glanced down into the garden's shadowed walkways. "I can't allow it," he said, shaking his head in apology.

"You can't *allow*—"

"Military discipline, and all that." He crossed the terrace to where she stood, depositing his cigar in a potted fern. "For the moment I am merely obeying orders."

She folded her arms across her midsection, feeling breathless, unbalanced. He really was taking his responsibility too far. "This will not work."

"I agree," he said, his smile rueful.

"You do?"

He moved into a circle of moonlight, meeting her surprised gaze. Silvery shadows deepened the angles of his attractive face. "When did your husband die?"

"Fourteen months ago."

He said nothing. She could almost see his clever mind calculating the passage of time. Four months to sail from India. Another month or so to visit relatives—Russell's support had seen her through when she had been too distressed to think clearly. He had been waiting for Julia at Dover, with a private suite prepared for her at the inn before he rushed her off to her father's side. He'd taken care of every detail. Swept off her feet, that was what she had been. She was beginning to feel more grounded now, more capable of thinking for herself. Sometimes she regretted accepting Russell's proposal without a little time to catch her breath. But she did not want to be alone again, and he had proved himself a true, reliable friend who would make a good father. They both wanted children. Julia's only fear was that perhaps they did not know each other as well as they might have.

"Do *you* want to walk?" she asked Heath suddenly, a little unsettled by his guarded silence, reminding herself that he was only acting in her best interests. It was hardly his fault that her heart pounded wildly in his presence.

He studied the garden. "On second thought, no. We're probably safer inside."

Safer? From what? She fell into step with him, the unspoken question hanging in the air. Was he acknowledging that he felt unsafe in her company? If he felt anything for her at all, he certainly hid it well. For which she ought to be relieved. "Do you really think that Russell is in danger?" she asked.

"Russell thinks so." He turned to her, his perceptive blue

eyes cutting straight to her heart. "Auclair is capable of anything. This I know from experience. What I did not know was that he had become active. I'd hoped we had heard the end of him."

She had to admit that it was a pleasant feeling, walking beside this solid, broad-shouldered man. He might undermine her composure, she might not trust herself alone with him, but no one could question his ability to protect her. Nor could she argue with Audrey Watson's assessment, that to be in the company of a Boscastle was overwhelming to the senses. And how could she ever forget that this particular male had an absolute talent for seduction? She guarded those wicked memories deep in her heart.

She glanced back into the garden, gasping softly. "Your cigar—it's still smoking in the pot."

He grinned down at her. "Let it smoke."

"But where there's smoke—"

"There's usually a Boscastle in the vicinity."

Let it smoke, indeed.

Julia was the one who felt as if she were doing a slow smolder as they reentered the crowded ballroom a minute later, engulfed in the airless, candlelit warmth. As expected, several guests stared at them, some merely curious, others openly surprised. Heath seemed not to notice, or care. In fact, he drew even more attention than Russell, who thrived on attracting public interest. She held her head high and allowed a half smile to linger on her lips. If not for Heath, she might have stayed outside for another hour. Russell did not believe her when she warned him she had lost her social graces. Or maybe she no longer had the tolerance for such nonsense. She had dealt with far larger issues of life.

Heath turned to talk to a middle-aged couple, placing his hand on Julia's arm to keep her from wandering off again. She heard a few snatches of gossip drifting from a small group of overdressed matrons who stood a few feet away.

"—and doesn't even have the decency to wear half mourning."

"Well, what would you expect from a widow who shot a man in the— I cannot even say the word."

Heath glanced around, interrupting his conversation to announce, "In the arse. She shot the bastard in the arse. I don't know if it was in the left or the right cheek, or even straight in the middle. You'd have to ask her yourself."

"Well, I never!" the matron exclaimed.

"Perhaps you should," he retorted with a devilish smirk. "It might do you a world of good. It might even keep you from repeating gossip at parties."

He nodded cordially to the couple, who smiled at him in approval. Then he took Julia's arm and whisked her into the center of the ballroom under the shimmering glow of the three-tiered crystal chandelier. Where everyone could see them. The sought-after rogue and the notorious widow who had shot an English soldier in the backside.

"Thank you," she said drily as the gay music of a country dance floated from the dais. "That should help my reputation immeasurably."

She could not hear his reply. His deep voice was drowned out by the sudden burst of fiddles, cellos, and violins from the orchestra, but it seemed to Julia that the impertinent rascal said, "Well, was it the left or right?"

To which she replied as their shoulders touched, "Nei-

ther. It was in the middle. I gave him a third dimple to remember me by."

She felt as stiff and ungainly as a wooden nutcracker.
The other couples on the dance floor were sneaking glances
at them, probably comparing Heath's natural grace to
Julia's hesitant movements. Expecting her to pull out a pistol and start shooting out the candles one by one. She hated
that she wondered what people thought. She hated the
thought that something she said or did would embarrass
Russell when he'd worked so hard to earn his reputation.
She was a liability and afraid it might be too late to change.

She turned the wrong way; Heath locked his arm in hers
and firmly guided her back in step, weaving through the
line as if he could do so in his sleep. Dancing with him was
not easy on her nerves. His masculinity was a little too distracting for her to concentrate on what she was doing, and
whether she wanted to admit it or not, she did feel awkward and inelegant, her talent for decorum rusty from
years of neglect.

But gradually her nerves begin to relax. She followed his
lead, his grace. His calmness calmed her. She sensed he was
determined to put her at ease in his subtle way.

He had always been observant. He noticed every mistake
she made, and yes, she should have worn half mourning;
Russell thought so, too, but she could not bring herself to
observe tradition. She had lost both her father and husband, and by not wearing black, she didn't mean to dis-
honor either of them. Her father had despised mourning
garments, claiming that widows looked for all the world
like black crows. She refused to follow etiquette out of respect for people she did not know. And the truth was that

she had barely known Sir Adam Whitby when she'd married him. She had not known him much better when he died, but she would have been a good wife if she'd been given the chance. She believed in commitment.

She and her young husband had seen each other only a few times a year in India. Adam was always traveling to one outpost or another, and she had read and sketched to fill her lonely hours. She felt guilty that she did not miss him more. She did not even have a child to console her. What she did have was her father's sizable fortune, and she had inherited his confidence, his belief in her, his passion for life. It would see her through.

"You're going the wrong way again," Heath whispered in amusement, swinging her around in the opposite direction.

"I was trying to escape."

He flashed her a wicked grin. "From me? Darling, how could you?"

"Unbelievable, isn't it?"

"Unprecedented. And here I thought I was behaving at my best."

They came together for an instant in the dance, bodies touching, heat flaring, their eyes locked. Julia lost her ability to think, to move, to breathe. Her breasts tingled against the confines of her bodice, a shiver of raw sensation slid down her spine. His gaze darkened in acknowledgment—he knew seduction inside and out—then the dance separated them again.

She took a breath.

And she'd thought that India was a dangerous place? She felt an unexpected urge to run from the ballroom and hide. Russell had convinced her that she could step back into Society and survive, but she suspected he was wrong. Anyway, he already showed ominous signs of becoming an absentee spouse. She was beginning to wonder if she was destined to spend the rest of her life alone while he set off proving his valor. He had always felt inferior in the haut ton, aware of his humble origins. Nothing Julia said seemed to bolster his belief in himself. He was insecure and arrogant at the same time. So flawed and human.

But he was also one of the few men in the civilized world who wanted to marry a scandalous widow. And they had known each other for ages.

Almost as long as she'd known the blue-eyed devil whirling her around the ballroom.

The dance ended.

She took another breath of relief and glimpsed Audrey Watson smiling at her from across the floor. Audrey's gaze drifted to Heath and lingered. She was not the only female guest present to gaze at him in wistful longing. Apparently, understandably, he had developed quite a following himself in the beau monde.

It was too easy to blame him for what had happened years ago. Even now she was not sure whether she had instigated that first kiss, or whether it had been him. She wondered how she would react if the opportunity arose to relive that memorable afternoon. Would she prove to him, to herself, that she was wiser? She would never know. The chance to recapture that time was gone.

He led her over to her aunt. She turned decisively. It could not continue. It had been wrong of Russell to ask this of Heath, wrong to place him in an uncomfortable position. The temptor's hand was at work here. The past could not be resurrected.

"I release you of your obligation," she said in an undertone.

He stared at her, his face impassive.

"Did you hear me?" she asked, her voice low with emotion. "We cannot do this. It . . . brings too much back, at least for me."

He nodded, his blue eyes glittering with dangerous flames. "I understand. And agree."

And although he watched her for the rest of the ball and escorted her home, he did not murmur more than a few words to her again.

Chapter 6

Heath took a hansom cab to Russell's leased lodgings after making sure that Julia and her aunt had safely arrived home. When no one answered his quiet knock, he hesitated, then took the liberty of letting himself into the town house.

He assumed that Russell had already retired in anticipation of tomorrow's early journey to Dover. Both of them observed an officer's discipline to this day. If this were not a matter of urgency, he would not intrude.

He stood at the bottom of the stairs, debating how to proceed. He disliked getting Russell out of bed, but on the other hand, he couldn't allow him to think that Julia had a protector in Heath when she did not. Russell would have to make another arrangement, whether he wanted to or not. Heath was willing to risk his life for his country. Risking his heart was a different matter. He saw no point in pretending to himself that he wasn't still drawn to her. Why place temptation in his path? He had been through enough torture in his life.

There was a light burning in a room upstairs. The rest of the house was absolutely dark, cloaked in silence.

He walked slowly toward the stairs, his senses alert, his brow furrowed in thought.

He found it odd that the front door had been carelessly left unlocked.

Odd that not a single servant stood duty when Russell was allegedly being hunted by an assassin. Had he already gone?

He heard muted laughter from a room upstairs, a woman's unfamiliar voice.

A prickle of foreboding slid down his spine.

He proceeded cautiously up the narrow staircase.

He heard Russell's rough voice responding to the woman's laughter. He could not make out the words, but it was definitely not a hostile exchange. He debated turning around. The thought of Julia unprotected was suddenly stronger than propriety.

A door stood open at the end of the hall. For a moment Heath did not move, not believing what he saw. A slender woman dancing on the carpet, her slippers held loosely in one hand while with the other she tucked a pin into the pale blond curls that spilled over her naked breasts.

"Lady Harrington," he said with a faint smile. "How nice to see you again. All of you." His cool gaze traveled from her incredulous face over her flushed, unclad form. The slippers dropped to the floor. She snatched her pastel tissue dress from the rumpled bed to cover her nudity. She needn't have bothered. He wasn't the least bit interested.

She gave a horrified gasp and darted past him, disappearing in a blur of pink flesh down the stairs.

He let her go. The bedroom door behind her was still open. He pushed it wide and saw Russell standing at his desk, bare-chested, a sheaf of papers in one hand, a pistol in the other.

"Damnit, Lucy," he said in annoyance. "I told you I had to sleep. What have you forgotten now?"

"Perhaps her virtue?" Heath replied, leaning one shoulder up against the wall. "Her marriage vows?"

Russell looked around, the papers falling in disarray on the desk. "What the devil, Boscastle?"

"Sorry," Heath said without inflection, staring at the disordered bedsheets on the floor. "I had no idea you were entertaining. I came to tell you I can't do what you asked of me. I won't take care of Julia."

"This isn't what it looks like," Russell said, sounding desperate, embarrassed.

Heath returned his appraising stare to Russell's face. He had no sympathy for this. "What does it look like?"

"I'm going away. A man has certain needs, and Julia is rather . . . reserved about the art of love. You won't tell her, will you?"

"Why should I?" And when had Julia become reserved? Reserved did not describe the Julia who had writhed under him on a library carpet, the woman who had left him panting with lust, with a longing that had never been fulfilled.

"This is the first time—"

"Shut up, Russell."

"I say, there's no need to be nasty. You aren't exactly a monk, are you?"

"Put your shirt on."

Russell reached casually for the white lawn shirt thrown over the chair behind him. "What are you doing here anyway? I told you to keep an eye on my fiancée."

"So that you could play on a clear field? That doesn't seem fair."

Russell began to button his shirt, his scowl black. "How the hell did you get into my house?"

"The door was unlocked. Rather careless for a man who is supposedly being hunted by an assassin."

Russell stared at him in disbelief. "My butler didn't try to stop you?"

Heath straightened, realizing his instincts had been right. Both he and Russell employed only servants who had been personally trained former soldiers and had proved their bravery on the battlefield. "No sign of him."

Russell strode toward the door, his face dark with alarm. "Then something has happened. He's never failed me before."

Three minutes later they found the butler and two footmen gagged, bound, and beaten in the pantry. Their assailant had been masked, and none of the men had heard his voice, or could describe him, having been taken off guard.

"Could it have been Auclair?" Heath asked as he and Russell searched the rest of the house.

"Of course not," Russell snapped. "He's obviously hired a thug to play hell with me."

"Why?"

"He's the enemy, and it is no secret that I intend to destroy him. I should not have to explain that to you." He fingered the edge of his eye patch, his voice thick with emotion. "This is exactly why you are needed. You know London. You know Julia, at least well enough to watch over her."

"Yes, but—"

"I witnessed what Auclair did to you in Portugal. I found you half dead, a raving lunatic tortured beyond human endurance. How could you have forgotten how many of our men he killed? Or that he enjoyed cruelty?"

"I didn't," Heath said curtly. "Are we going to look for the man who broke in here or not?"

Russell shoved his arms into his greatcoat. "I'll take care of that part. I want you to go to Julia's house. And stay. Please, Heath."

"Dear God."

"Don't question me. Do it."

Heath left St. James's Street in a dark, unsettled mood, wondering how the hell he would handle the situation. Of course what Russell had asked him to do was logical; there was justification, and Heath might have done it anyway had he been given time to make his own decision.

But it all came back to Julia, who had dismissed him hours earlier. Not out of any maliciousness but a common sense he had to admire. She had recognized the danger between them, the attraction. She had gained self-knowledge, a quality he found very beguiling.

He stood outside her town house for several minutes, allowing his feelings to cool, to settle, like ashes from a smoldering fire. He had enjoyed seeing her again tonight, but he was not sure he cared to repeat the experience. He disliked the challenge to his self-control, disliked not knowing how he would react to her.

She had always made him feel . . . well, she made him feel strongly. He had not yet decided if this was a state to be desired. Certainly his instinct to protect her warred with the unholy lust that she reawakened in him. An attractive, sexually appealing female who could become a trusted friend. Could there exist anything more dangerous in the world? How disconcerting to realize at his age that he could not always predict the next twist on the path. Well, wasn't that what made life interesting?

Lady Dalrymple was asleep in bed when he announced himself at the door of Julia's town house in Berkeley Square. The elderly butler who answered his sharp knock refused at first to let Heath in. He changed his mind when Heath explained the situation, that Lady Whitby needed to be on guard against the man who had broken into Sir Russell's home and beaten his domestics.

"I say them Frenchies are not to be trusted, my lord," he called down the hallway after Heath. "We should have taken their entire country prisoner."

"Splendid idea," Heath muttered. "I wonder why no one ever thought of it."

"I don't trust that Napoleon," the butler added, placing his mottled hand on the hall stand to steady himself. "I say we should have—"

Heath spun on his heels, walking backward. "Where *is* Lady Whitby?"

The butler blinked. "Upstairs in her bedroom, my lord, reading. She enjoys reading late at night. But you don't think that anything—that anyone—" He swallowed hard. "Sir Russell wanted a footman put outside her door, but Lady Whitby wouldn't have it. Said it would give her nightmares. Said—"

"Too much," Heath finished under his breath. "Lord help me, is this what I have trained for?"

He ran up the stairs, two at a time, and strode straight to the room where a glimmer of candlelight showed beneath the door. It was unlocked, an oversight for which he would take her to task. Julia was lying across the bed on her stomach, her face buried in what was clearly a very engrossing book.

The first thought that entered his mind was that she was alive, obviously unhurt, unaware that she had a visitor, unaware of the attack on Russell's servants.

The next thing that drew—and held—his attention was the potent sensuality of her body, the rise of her well-shaped backside under her nightrail, her sleek, muscular legs exposed to the thigh, her ankles crossed. In that unguarded pose, Julia could have brought most men to their knees. He stood frozen, fighting a surge of sexual desire in a silent if brutal battle. He could not understand his own response. His fascination with a woman who belonged to his friend. Where was the sense in this?

Her hair had lighter glints than he remembered; her arms and shoulders were becomingly burnished a pale gold, but then she had spent years in India. He wouldn't be a bit surprised to learn she had defied convention and not shunned the sun as a proper Englishwoman should. Julia being Julia, he wouldn't be shocked if she had swum half naked in a river with man-eating tigers every day. He could take a bite of her himself, could join her on that bed and let his male instincts take over. A tremor of unadulterated temptation rocked him.

His heart was beating hard. As much from the relief of finding her unharmed as from how her unstudied sexual appeal stirred his blood. He found it far too easy to imagine removing her simple nightrail. To picture himself running his hand over her curves, pinning her strong body beneath his and finishing what they had begun years ago. Reserved? Was that how Russell had described her? Not the woman who had gasped at Heath's illicit kisses, who had allowed him the intimacies they had shared. His groin tightened; he remembered too well how she had tempted him. She would never believe him if he admitted how he'd felt about her. He did not believe it himself, or know what to make of it.

The image of their past encounter dissolved as she rolled without warning onto her side. The temptation lingered, moved to the back of his mind to haunt him later. Her long red hair tumbled down her around her shoulders. Her gray eyes narrowed into bright, dangerous pinpoints of emotion. He blinked, his attention refocusing.

She was holding a gun in her hand. Pointed at his chest with unflinching accuracy. He drew a breath. Julia shooting him again was not the part of their history he wanted to repeat. Sex and laughter, yes. A pistol wound, no.

"It's me." He said the first thing that came to his mind; Julia did have a reputation for shooting men, and the third time was said to be a charm. "For God's sake, Julia, it's only me."

She lowered her hand, staring past him to the door. "What has happened?" she asked. "Is Russell with you? Why did you burst in here like this?"

"Your fiancé is fine. His butler and footmen were assaulted tonight while Russell was . . . packing his bags." Packing his baggage, he should have said. He wouldn't tell her. He would not be the messenger of bad news, or she *would* kill him on the spot. He had absolutely no intention of getting any more involved in this than was necessary. Or so he told himself.

She drew her nightrail down over her bare knees, a little

belatedly to do him much good. He'd already seen enough of her delectable body to keep him awake the rest of the night, to resurrect all his latent demons and desires. "Then why are you here?"

He frowned at her. God, she had given him a good scare with that gun. The woman deserved her reputation. "Russell sent me to make sure you were safe."

"Do you think I'm in any danger?"

He met her gaze. He wasn't about to insult her intelligence with a lie. Nor did he care to explain to her exactly how cruel, how insane a man Armand Auclair was. "I don't know."

"Perhaps I should leave London."

"Perhaps. There is not always safety in a crowd."

She slid to her feet. She looked younger with her hair down, defenseless, although with that pistol in her hand, she was not, and for that he was actually glad. As long as she didn't point it at him again.

"Thank you," she said, her eyes suddenly full of her familiar mischief, the color returning to her cheeks. "What a competent bodyguard you are, Boscastle."

He felt a tight sensation in his chest, a stirring of . . . what? Apprehension? Affection? Or sheer sexual attraction, the devilish sort that toppled kingdoms and destroyed careers, that made bloody fools of its victims? In a thousand years he would never have believed himself vulnerable to its snare. How blithely arrogant he had been. "Thank me for what?"

She grinned, and the sensation inside him deepened, heated, spread. He did not know how to fight it. He did not even know what it was. "For coming to my rescue.

"Ah, yes." She stared at him with an arch smile. "Rescued from reading. How shall I every repay you?"

"I'll think about it. Let me see that gun."

"Here." She held out her hand. "Be careful. It is loaded."

His eyes widened in surprise as she handed him the weapon. "Where did you get this? It's a Manton flintlock dueling pistol."

"My husband gave it to me."

He glanced up appraisingly. "Your husband?"

"He was gone a great deal."

"This is a beautiful piece, Julia."

"I know."

He stared down into her face. It came as a shock to realize how close to each other they were standing. Had she closed the distance, or had he? He could not tell. It was almost as if they were magnetized, drawn together against will and common sense. He could see the tiny mole on her throat, and lower, the rise of her full breasts. A woman in full bloom. A woman who belonged to someone else. His blood heated as if in rebellion at the reminder. Why did she have to be so damned alluring?

"Look, Julia, I—"

She leaned forward and stunned him by kissing his cheek. He did not move, not a muscle, but every sense, every blood vessel, every part of him reacted to the lush warmth of her lips. He did not show it. He did not show her how suddenly he ached to take her in his arms and teach her a thing or two about teasing. It astounded him, the raw-edged power of his desire for her. That years could pass, and she could break through his guard without even trying. She had gotten under his skin. He thought he'd recovered, God help him. He had hoped himself over her.

"Dear Heath," she murmured as she drew away. "You are too honorable for your own good, I fear."

Honor was the furthest thing from his mind. She had no idea of the things he had been forced to do since they had last met. He had killed men. He had walked away from women who wept and begged him to stay.

He could walk out of this house right now and tell Russell to go to Hades. His career would probably end, not that he'd seen any action lately. He would miss the danger, the excitement, the distraction from ordinary life. Still, he had more than enough money. He should probably look for a wife, beget an heir or two. He really did have a choice. He did not have to torture himself. He could hire another man to take his place. He stared at her, trying to read her thoughts. God help them both if she touched him again.

"What a frightening look you have on your face." She bit her underlip as she regarded him. "Stop thinking whatever it is you're thinking."

He took a sharp breath, his senses filling with her all over again. The scent of her hair, the inviting warmth of her body, the brush of her muslin nightrail against his knuckles. She had kissed him on the cheek. Of all the nerve. After all they had done, she thought a chaste peck would soothe him? It was practically an insult, an invitation, to what he did not know. He was angry and aroused at the same time, a dangerous combination.

He smiled unwillingly. "Do I frighten you?"

"Don't be silly. I hate to admit it, but I find your dark brooding looks rather attractive." She backed away from him, reaching for the brush on her dressing table. "But then you know me. I seem drawn to trouble, don't I?"

"Am I trouble, Julia?"

Her fingers tightened on the scrolled handle of the hairbrush, the only indication that his question had unsettled her. She glanced at him over her shoulder. She looked like a goddess with her hair unbound. "You certainly could be. You were once that I recall."

He smiled. "You survived."

"So did you."

He leaned his hip back against the bedpost, watching the slow glide of the brush through her hair. He ached to take over the task. "How do you know?"

Her hand stilled. She seemed startled, as if she'd never considered the possibility that she'd hurt *him*. "What do you mean?"

"How do you know what I felt for you?" he asked, his gaze piercing hers. "Whether I survived or not?"

Her eyes lifted to his. He saw his own confusion mirrored there. "You aren't serious, are you?" she asked softly.

He wished suddenly he had not spoken. It was unlike him to reveal his deepest thoughts. And what was there to gain by it? He stared at her sweetly sculpted body, noticed how her long hair curled beneath her full breasts. "Answer me," she said, lowering the brush.

"You never gave me a chance to—" He stopped himself. He wanted to tell her and yet did not. There was no point. Let past desires lay dormant.

"To finish seducing me?" she guessed, her gray eyes a little sad.

"I don't know." He paused, his gaze frank. "Perhaps."

She swiveled around on the stool. No coward, she met

his eyes with an unflinching stare. "Then we both escaped."

"Did we?"

Her lips parted. He dropped his gaze, noticed that her fingers had loosened on the brush, that her breathing had quickened. In that moment he knew how badly he wanted her, admitted it in his heart, accepted the truth in all its punishing honesty. She might belong to someone else, but she should have been his.

"You speak of seduction as if it were a goal in itself," he said. "But it can be more. I do not blame you for mistrusting my motives. Men seduce women every day and leave them. Still, if I had made you mine that afternoon, I doubt it would have been an ending for us."

Color mounted her cheeks. She took a breath.

He smiled with regret. "It might have been a beginning."

He went downstairs, satisfied that he had done his duty even at the cost of his dignity. He had never meant to make a confession. It hardly helped the situation. But at least she seemed safe enough for the night. He would remind the servants to be on the alert for intruders, to take special precautions, and then he would pace in front of her house for a few minutes. And try to think up a way out of this preposterous dilemma. It was clear that he and Julia could not be trusted in the same room together. He would seduce her. Or she would shoot him. Either way, they'd both end up on the floor.

Payton, Julia's silver-haired butler, met him at the bottom of the stairs. "Is all well, my lord?" he asked in an anxious voice.

Heath frowned. "Everything appears to be fine." If one

did not count his own mental state, which was too complicated and disgraceful to share with a butler.

"You were rather a long time upstairs in her ladyship's
room. I wondered—"

Heath cleared his throat. "There's nothing to wonder
about. Just don't go into her room unannounced. You're li-
able to get shot."

Payton allowed a knowing smile to show. "Oh, the staff
is perfectly aware of Lady Whitby's talent with firearms,
my lord. I assure you."

"Talent, eh?" Heath put on his gloves. "That's a polite
way to put it. Well, her talents aside, I will remind you of
what Sir Russell said before: you must be extra vigilant in
protecting this household. The garden and the street
should be watched day and night."

"I am vigilant, my lord." The butler followed him to the
door. "I carry my own weapon."

"Very good. Don't shoot me when I return in a few minutes after I take some air."

"Of course not, but—" The man stepped forward to
open the door onto the dark night for Heath. "Ah, your
companion appears to have gone."

Heath turned immediately to the deserted street. "My
companion?"

"The man in the black carriage who followed you here,
my lord. I was going to ask him in, but then I thought perhaps you had instructed him to watch the house." He gave
Heath a conspiratorial nod, pleased with himself. "For
safety's sake. I knew this was a secret operation."

"For safety's sake." Heath clenched his jaw, pivoted, re-
tracing his steps back to the door in resignation. So, a man
had been watching the house. Someone who worked for

Russell? Possibly, but then where had this mystery fellow gone, and why hadn't Russell forewarned him? "I don't suppose you could describe this man to me, Payton, or his carriage."

"Well, heavens, my lord. I did not wish to be impolite by staring at him. But I did get a good look at the carriage. It was small, and black, I believe. Or dark blue. Come to think of it, it could have been brown."

"Your powers of observation are remarkable."

"Thank you, my lord. Are we going back into the house?"

Heath pulled off his leather gloves, thinking of Julia upstairs in her room. "I'm very much afraid that we are."

Chapter 7

Julia and her aunt were listening to the conversation between Heath and Payton from behind the door of the
downstairs drawing room, decorated in tasteful shades of
cream and pale gold. Aunt Hermia had been awakened by
all the noise in the house and had come to Julia's room to
investigate. When Julia explained what had happened to
Russell's servants, Hermia had declared herself too agitated to return to bed. They had come downstairs together
for a cup of calming chamomile tea.

"What is Boscastle doing?" Hermia whispered.

"He's leaving."

"Leaving?"

"Yes." Julia peered through the crack in the door. "No.
He's coming back."

"Coming back where?"

"Here. Goodness, Aunt Hermia, he's headed straight for
this room. Move away from the door. Quickly."

They scurried back moments before the door flew open.

Julia could not believe her eyes. Heath strode straight
past them without so much as glancing their way. She was

certain he could see them, huddled together in their night-clothes in the middle of the room.

He shrugged out of his jacket, tossing it over the back of the carved damask sofa. He took off his shoes and socks and placed them neatly under the gaming table.

Julia and her aunt exchanged startled looks. Neither of them said a word.

Julia's lips parted. What in the world was he doing? Surely he realized they were in the room. He did not seem the least bit concerned that he had an audience.

He unknotted his white silk cravat and laid it neatly on the table beside one of Julia's books. Lying down on the sofa, he folded his muscular arms behind his neck and stretched out his legs. He did not look at the two ladies gaping at him only a few feet away. Fortunately, he seemed to have finished undressing. She was at a loss. She'd not even recovered from their most recent conversation. She dared not wonder what he had meant. Had it been the ploy of a clever man to lure her to his bed? No. Heath needed no tricks. Why had he spoken? It made it worse for her, reawakened the familiar ache.

She took a step toward him.

He appeared to be studying the fresco of frolicking gods and goddesses above the fireplace.

"Heath." She cleared her throat. The sight of him reclining on that sofa in all his lordly grace brought several disturbingly erotic images to her mind. He looked as if he were settling in for the night. In her drawing room. "I know this cannot—you *cannot* be doing what you appear to be doing."

He granted her a brooding look. His heavy-lidded blue eyes pierced her like a dagger tip that had been dipped in a heady aphrodisiac. He had the most sensual, unsettling stare of any man she had ever met. No wonder she had succumbed to him before. His gaze could melt a woman's heart at twenty paces. She felt an unwelcome stab of longing deep inside her. He was going to sleep on her sofa to make sure that no one hurt her. His gallantry touched her. Tempted her. He intended to stay the night.

And he had taken off his cravat and shoes in front of her and her aunt. What would come next?

"Do you require something of me, Julia?" He sounded resigned and a little resentful all at once.

She stood directly over him, gathering her wits. He took up the entire length of the sofa. He'd taken up the entire length of her once, too. Her face grew warm as she recalled how strong, how sinfully hard his elegant body had felt crushing her to the floor. She'd had years to analyze the sensation. Perhaps every woman never forgot her first encounter. She'd lost count of how many times she had secretly recalled the sensual pleasure of that afternoon. The thrust of his hips, the touch of his mouth. Her body had a memory of its own.

"What do you think you're doing?" she demanded in a low voice.

He closed his eyes as if to dismiss her. "Obviously I am going to spend the night here. Do you mind leaving the door open?"

"In this room?" She held her breath. "In my house?"

"I wish a clear view of the street."

"This is unnecessary, Heath," she burst out, exhaling. "I have footmen who can patrol the house."

"So did Russell."

Aunt Hermia edged over to the window, clutching her

dressing robe together. "I don't know about you, Julia, but it does make me feel better to have an able-bodied man about the house."

Julia examined Heath from the corner of her eye. He was a little too able-bodied to have around for her peace of mind. Talk about temptation. Was she supposed to behave in a normal fashion? As if a gorgeous rogue sleeping in her drawing room were a regular occurrence?

She backed into the tea table. "How will this look to our neighbors?"

"Far better than if either of us were found dead in the morning," Aunt Hermia said feelingly. "I shall sleep better tonight knowing Boscastle is at hand."

"Well, I shan't," Julia muttered. "He should be guarding Russell, not me."

Heath opened his eyes and glanced past her to the window, apparently unmoved by her distress. "A man was parked on the corner shortly before I arrived. Do you have any secret admirers, Julia?"

"She certainly does not," Aunt Hermia said. "It's a miracle Russell is marrying her considering how she has damaged her own reputation by shooting that soldier."

"Has Russell had anyone watching the house?" he asked Julia.

"No." She frowned, realizing he perceived the danger to her as real. He'd gotten her so addled that she had forgotten his true reason for being here. She felt ashamed of herself for wanting to shake him witless. "He suggested it once or twice, but I rarely go out alone. Having a guard did not seem necessary."

"Would you like a robe, Boscastle?" Hermia asked, as solicitous as a society hostess at a ball. "A little brandy—"

"He doesn't drink," Julia said, then almost bit her tongue for revealing she remembered that detail. "At least he never did before."

She caught the impudent glint in his eye as she backed toward the door. Little by little she was giving herself away, revealing how imporant he had been to her. A smile curved his sensual mouth. "I still don't," he said, sounding rather pleased. "What an excellent memory you have, Julia. I am quite flattered, really."

She did have an excellent memory, she thought a few minutes later as she returned to bed. That was a great deal of her problem. She remembered quite well what Heath Boscastle could do to her composure. Too much had happened between them to pretend theirs was a normal friendship. Every time they met it would be a test of temptation, a clash between who they had been and who they had become. And hoped to be. If they were both men, they would probably have engaged in a heated round of fisticuffs to settle their feelings. Being man and woman, however, they did not have such a simple option.

When she went downstairs the following morning, she fully expected to find he had gone. After all, no one had threatened her directly, and she should be safe enough at home during the day. She was not without common sense. She had no intention of leaving the house without a male escort. Her self-protective instincts were quite intact. Those instincts clamored like alarm bells a moment later.

Heath was sitting in the breakfast room, immaculately shaven, dressed in fresh clothes, reading the newspaper. He looked up briefly, one heavy black eyebrow lifting.

He scrutinized her for only a few seconds, but the heat in

his eyes raised her temperature as if she'd just walked into a furnace. For several heartbeats she did not move, mesmerized by his dark presence. Not for nothing did the mothers of debutantes warn their precious daughters to guard their virtue against the passionate Boscastle brood.

Still, Julia had managed to live without this particular Boscastle for six years now. He'd lived without her, too. She ought to be able to handle him for a month.

Handling her private feelings might pose another challenge. The moment he smiled at her, she felt a pleasant ache in the pit of her stomach. A lock of black hair had fallen across his forehead. She suppressed the impulse to brush it back for him. He looked tired, but in good spirits, despite spending what must have been an uncomfortable night on the sofa.

He was a good man, Heath Boscastle, no matter how she complained she did not need him. He was here only because he believed it was the right thing to do. She'd behaved impetuously with him all those years ago. What did he think of her now? She'd be afraid to ask, thinking her past conduct must seem quite undignified compared to the present-day sophisticated ladies who desired him. Presumably, he conducted his affairs with far more discretion than he and Julia had shown. She wondered suddenly who his current lover was, a woman who would surely resent lending him to Julia.

"Have you had breakfast?" she asked him, reining in her unruly thoughts.

"Yes, thank you."

She sat down at the table, smoothing out a wrinkle in the linen tablecloth. Of course, six years of marriage hadn't exactly left her without certain resources. She was no longer naïve. In her own way she'd had as much experience in love as Heath. Well, perhaps not as varied, but she certainly was capable of conducting herself in a proper manner.

Wasn't she?

Why was she even thinking of such a thing?

It was Russell she was marrying. London's brave, handsome hero of the hour. He had been loyal to her over the years, jokingly referring to himself as her last link to civilization. Perhaps he was. She had never been entirely civilized in the first place, even when she lived in England. Her mother had died when Julia was three. Her father had taken her hunting before she could walk, and she had spent most of her young life at his side in the company of gamekeepers and sportsmen.

Russell seemed to love her. Sometimes she wondered if she was truly suited for the social life he sought. He had always quietly pursued her, begged her to return home the few times they'd written to each other during her marriage. She was afraid sometimes that the challenge of the unattainable had attracted him to her, and he was not even aware of it. Would it wear off after she became his wife? Certain men enjoyed the chase more than the conquest.

"Is there any word from Russell?" she asked.

Heath put down his paper. "He's gone. He left word that two of his contacts managed to trace his attacker to a pub in St. Giles. A ruffian from the wharves was bragging quite openly about breaking into Russell's house. He claimed a foreigner put him up to it and paid quite well."

"A foreigner." Julia frowned. "And Russell still believes Auclair is in France?"

"He seemed more convinced than ever. He suspects the attack was a ploy to mislead him. In any event, he's gone."

She took the silver teapot in her hands. It was still hot, a momentary distraction from the intense blue eyes that watched her. "What about the man in the carriage last night?"

"Whoever it was never came back."

"Perhaps it was coincidence," she murmured, lowering her gaze. She could not concentrate when he stared at her.

He stood and came up behind her, his voice disturbingly low as he leaned over her chair. "Perhaps it was not. Or perhaps you really do have a secret admirer."

She raised her head, her nerve endings tingling in reaction to his nearness. The warmth of his square jaw against her chin momentarily arrested her powers of speech. She could not possibly affect him as he affected her. He'd had six years to subdue his impulses, to learn restraint, to hide his reactions. So had she. Why then was her heart racing? Why did she feel as if he were in control of the moment? It might have something to do with the trembling heat that swept over her.

"A secret admirer?" she said in amusement, her voice deceptively steady. "A widow in London who shot a man in the buttocks for assaulting her maid? I had no idea Society had developed a fashion for violent women."

"You possess beauty, wit, and some wealth, Julia," he replied calmly. "I'd say a secret admirer was a definite possibility."

Unbidden pleasure swept over her. She poured a bracing cup of tea from the silver teapot, surprised that her hand was not shaking. "I'd prefer my admirers to come to the door then, not lurk inside parked carriages."

"Except that you're going to marry Russell, and he

might not appreciate men coming to your door," he reminded her. "You attended a ball last night. Did you notice anyone staring at you?"

"Yes, you," she replied with a frown. "Every time I turned around."

"That was different," he said drily.

His chin brushed her cheek. Julia was afraid she would drop her teacup.

"People certainly stare at you," she murmured.

The sharp yapping of small dogs in the hall interrupted their conversation. Heath straightened dutifully from her chair, and Julia found herself suddenly able to breathe. "Ah," he said. "Your aunt and her ferocious pack of Lilliputian hounds are here."

"And shall protect me." She took a sip of tea. "You may go home now, Heath, and by that I do not mean to sound ungrateful. Hermia and I have plans for the day. Please get some rest."

He crossed his arms over his chest and smiled. "Where are we going?"

"What do you mean?" she asked slowly. "Odham is escorting us to a garden party."

He turned from her chair as the door opened, and Hermia appeared in a peacock-blue satin gown and feathered turban. "The earl may escort your aunt, but I shall accompany you, Julia, unless you find my company undesirable," he said in a deep voice that no woman could possibly resist.

She hesitated, ignoring every warning that raced across her mind. It wouldn't hurt, would it? Russell wanted her to make friends, to feel comfortable at social gatherings. She could use the practice. "The party might be a pleasant diversion," she admitted reluctantly.

His eyes glittered with devilish humor. "Perhaps I shall discover your secret admirer."

Julia gave a rueful laugh. "You shall discover that he does not exist."

Heath was ensconced in the drawing room, skimming a book on ancient Sanskrit, when the earl arrived to escort his beloved Hermia to the party. Heath lifted the curtain of the front window and studied the crowded street, as he had done throughout the night. Aside from the usual parade of cabs and carriages, vendors, and merchants making business calls, there was nothing in the noisy congestion to arouse suspicion. It was not difficult to move undetected in the bustle of London, to commit a crime and disappear into the underworld of alleys, warrens, and dens.

Still, Heath was suspicious by nature. His patience and perception were part of the reason he had been chosen by his superiors in Portugal to join the elite corps of guides, or secret British Intelligence officers, who could serve as dispatchers in battle, or even as double agents should the need arise. Unfortunately, he had been captured early in his career as a cavalry officer and put to torture by a French soldier named Armand Auclair. The experience had left him with both physical and emotional scars, but had also strengthened his character. He had survived hell. There wasn't much that frightened him now.

To this day he enjoyed solving puzzles, mysteries, putting things to right. He was a passionate cryptographer. Solving codes gave him a sense of stability that he seemed to require in what he perceived as a disordered world. Human affairs, of course, posed the ultimate challenge. Unpredictable in nature, typically without rhyme or reason. He'd yet to crack the mystery of emotion to his satisfaction.

Take the attack on Russell's servants last night. It bore the marks of a personal element that intrigued Heath. Apparently Auclair was playing a game. He wanted to instill fear and prolong his revenge. Why? He'd made a career as a duelist in Paris. Napoleon was in exile. Why would Auclair bother to hunt down Russell?

The door behind him opened.

The Earl of Odham bound into the room, his round face as dark as a thundercloud, his thick white hair untidy. "Damned London traffic will be the death of me yet," he announced. "Is that woman ready?"

Heath turned from the window, his reverie broken. Odham was as spry and alert as any dandy. He dressed like one, too, in a bright gold jacket, white embroidered vest, and buckskin breeches with gleaming Hessian boots that seemed to swallow up his short frame.

"If by 'that woman' you are referring to Lady Dalrymple, than I believe she is waiting in the garden with the dogs. If you are referring to Julia, then no. She is not ready."

Odham grunted, but appeared to calm down at the sound of Heath's voice. "Hello, Boscastle. I suppose they've both told you what a villain I am."

"Just tell me one thing, Odham, are you blackmailing Lady Dalrymple?"

Odham dropped like a stone onto the empty sofa. "I shan't deny it. Yes, I am."

Heath shook his head in disbelief. "You actually admit it?"

"Why shouldn't I?"

"Because it is unsavory, ungentlemanly, and illegal."

"Love ought to be illegal," Odham said, lacing his hands over his potbelly.

"Love?" Heath arched his brow. "Pray explain how love and blackmail go hand in hand. I must have missed that concept in my social education. It sounds a little primitive to me."

"If I didn't love the wretched woman, I wouldn't be blackmailing her into marriage, would I?"

"I fail to see the logic."

"Who said anything about logic? Good God, I am not a monster, Boscastle, merely a man, one who is utterly and miserably in love with the cruelest and most desirable female in the whole of England. If not the world."

Heath settled back in his chair. This proved his theory: that human affairs followed no predictable course whatsoever. "We *are* discussing Lady Dalrymple?"

"Who else?" Odham asked, thumping his head back on the sofa. "I don't suppose you've ever lost your senses over a woman? No, not you. You have a reputation for restraint. In fact, now that I think about it, your affairs are never in the newspapers. You're rather an anomaly in the Boscastle line, aren't you?"

"Just because my personal life is not public knowledge does not mean I do not have one."

"I did not mean to offend you. I wish I'd had your sense in my earlier years. I might have never lost Hermia if I'd been discreet. The woman is a goddess, and I worship at the altar of her charms."

Heath held back a grin. Hermia was twice the size of Odham, in height and in weight. "It's my understanding that Lady Dalrymple does not wish to marry you."

"Of course she does. The woman is wild for me."

"She certainly hides it well," Heath retorted.

"She's as stubborn as a goat."

"A goat or a goddess? Do make up your mind."

Odham rubbed his face in distress. "I shall do anything to win her. Anything. Do you understand?"

Heath grimaced. "I'm afraid I do."

"Then it's agreed—you shall take my cause?"

Familiar female voices drifted from the hallway. Heath leaned forward in his chair. "I've agreed to nothing of the sort. I do not think I should become involved in this business at all."

"Men have to stick together."

Heath shook his head. "Not when blackmailing older women into marriage they don't. I should feel ridiculous, and cruel."

Odham leaped up from the sofa. "I am lost without her—I shall pursue her with my dying breath."

"Pull yourself together, Odham. The ladies are right outside the door. If you wish to win Hermia, I suggest you find a more suitable way to do so."

Chapter 8

❧❧❧

The breakfast party did not begin until two o'clock that afternoon, in a small village on the outskirts of town. Heath had hoped for a quiet affair, the easier to keep an eye on Julia and perhaps to agree on a strategy for their arrangement. But the party turned out to be a crush, with at least three hundred guests in attendance. The master of ceremonies lost his voice before he ended his list of announcements.

Julia, Hermia, and Odham watched a match of cricket and played bowls on the lawn. Heath made an effort to participate, but he was more interested in observing Julia, and not in the line of duty either. She looked exceptionally striking in a pale yellow gown that set off her lustrous red hair and creamy sun-gilded skin. As they finished their final game, their hostess, Lady Beacom, who happened to be Odham's niece, brought out her five pet monkeys, who cleverly escaped their wicker cages to play gleeful havoc on the long tables. It was an unplanned entertainment, and the highlight of the party.

Several ladies shrieked in mock terror. Heath and Julia rescued three of the monkeys between them, but one female became particularly attached to Heath, refusing to release him when her mistress held out her plump white arms.

"You discriminating creature," Lady Beacom said in delight. "You would choose the most attractive man in London."

Julia laughed as the monkey buried its face inside his jacket. "I think you're the one with the secret admirer."

He flashed her a grin and gently attempted to coax out the animal. "This is rather embarrassing."

"Don't tell me it's the first time you've had trouble detaching yourself from a female."

"They generally smell a great deal better," he said, wrinkling his nose. "And I don't recall one with this much hair on her body."

She reached inside his jacket to help him. "Come on, you naughty girl, you're ruining his lordship's shirt."

All of a sudden the monkey tired of the game and crawled back onto Heath's shoulder to launch herself into a crowd of unsuspecting gentlemen. Guffaws of startled laughter filled the air. Heath straightened his dove-gray morning coat while Julia watched in amusement.

"Fickle female," she said. "She's already found another man to replace you."

"Was it something I said?"

"I don't think so. Her new friend appears to have a bag of sugared almonds in his pocket."

"If only the women I knew were so easily pleased."

"You mean your charm isn't enough?"

"Hardly."

They began to walk toward the garden, winding their way past the guests dancing on the lawn. The day was warm, the music a pleasant accompaniment to conversation.

"Who are they anyway?" Julia asked after a slight pause, darting a curious look up at him.

He glanced behind them, his gaze searching the grounds before returning to her face. "Who . . ."

"Your women." She bumped against him as the path became uneven. "Woman. For heaven's sake, you know what I am trying to ask."

His mouth quirked into a wry grin. "Yes, I know." But it was fun to make her explain anyway.

"Then you aren't going to tell me?"

"Tell you what?" he asked, taking her arm to steady her before she took another misstep.

"The name of the lady who has captured your elusive heart."

He stopped in his tracks and stared at her. Her golden-cream skin shimmered in the sunlight. The band had begun to play a waltz in the background. He studied her in astonishment. Trust Julia to cut straight to the bone. But then hadn't unexpected intimacy characterized their connection from the start? How easily they were falling back into their former association. He didn't know how to thwart it.

"Who said I was in love?"

"Aren't you in love?" she asked.

"Am I?"

She sighed in surrender. "Why don't you fetch me a glass of champagne? It's obvious I'm not going to get a straight answer from you."

"Good idea," he said, enjoying the chance to make her wonder. He wondered himself why he'd never fallen in love. "If I'm gone too long, I've probably run off with the monkey."

He found a footman attending the large group of guests standing in line at the bottom of the breakfast tables. He snagged a glass from the tray in the hope of escaping before anyone cornered him. Unfortunately, he turned to discover Lady Harrington lying in wait for him behind a boxwood hedge.

He didn't know what to say. So nice to see you with your clothes on? How are you enjoying the party? I'll bet it doesn't compare with your adulterous evening with Althorne? She had gall, to stop him in public after what he'd seen of her. Or what he hadn't seen.

"Good afternoon, Lucy," he said with a breezy smile, holding the champagne flute aloft. "I'd love to stay and chat with you, but I'm on a mission. By the way, it was charming to see you last night. All of you."

She stepped in front of him, her voice deep and urgent. "Don't you dare try to escape, Boscastle."

"Lucy," he said, "in all fairness I do not wish to become involved in your private affairs. One of Russell's women appears to be all I can handle at the moment." And that was the truth. He hadn't decided if Julia had him coming or going. Or which way he even preferred.

"Did you tell her?" she demanded, sounding more afraid than threatening.

His eyes narrowed in speculation. They stood in full view of the other guests, and although he didn't give a damn what anyone thought of him, he realized Julia was watching. The last thing he wanted was to arouse her suspicions or hurt her, or even Lucy's old sod of a husband. God forbid the man might think that *Heath* was having an affair with his faithless wife. Heath rather liked the old sod, and he did not conduct affairs with married women on principle.

"Never fear," he said in a bored voice. "Your sordid little secret is safe with me. I won't tell a soul you were giving Russell a proper send-off last night."

She released her breath. "It wasn't the first time, you know."

He glanced past her, his attraction diverted. He had just noticed a dark-haired, rather intense young man who seemed vaguely familiar standing behind Julia. She was edging away from him as if she were unconsciously uncomfortable. He kept creeping a little closer, working his way through a group of people toward her.

"Did you hear what I said, Boscastle?" Lucy asked, her voice shrill.

He looked around in irritation. "Yes. You said it wasn't the first—what are you trying to tell me?" he said impatiently. "I am not a priest, you know, and this is a garden party, not a confessional."

"Russell and I have been seeing each other off and on for years. I told him it would stop once he's married. I think . . . well, I've heard he's got a proper mistress."

"A *proper* mistress? Isn't that a contradiction in terms?"

"I'm going to break off with him," she said with a sniff of emotion.

"Well, good for you," Heath said, raising the champagne flute to toast her.

He wondered how all of a sudden he had become involved in this complication of human misconduct. He avoided emotional entanglements as a rule. In some ways he felt safer facing a bayonet on a battlefield or searching the Portuguese countryside for spies. He was a private person, and he preferred keeping his life to himself. Other people's messy affairs really did not interest him.

Julia interested him, though, far more than he cared to admit. He felt insulted on her behalf by Russell's secret dalliance with this woman. Why would any man tryst with a vapid twit like Lucy with a wife like Julia in his future?

"How do you know he's got a proper mistress anyway?" he asked, suddenly curious.

"I know what pleases him," she said a little sourly. "Russell wants a wife for one reason, and a mistress for another."

Which didn't explain where she fit into his plans. He gave her a dark smile. "Julia's been married, too. I suspect she might know a few things herself about pleasing a man."

Lady Harrington's smile faded. Heath nodded cordially and headed back toward Julia, bearing the champagne flute like a trophy. Obviously his parting remark had left Lucy with something to think about. Unfortunately, it set his thoughts running down a rather dangerous pathway, too. He had no idea what had come over him, except that he'd felt a compulsion to defend her. He had just made her sound like some sort of legendary concubine. Was that how he secretly thought of her?

"Why were you talking to that woman?" she asked with an uneasy smile when he reached her side.

His guard went up. He had to be careful what he revealed. Women had sharp instincts about these things. "I know her husband."

"Russell knows him, too. I always thought Lucy had a wandering eye, if you know what I mean."

He handed her the champagne flute. She took a deep sip. He hoped to God she didn't ask him any more questions.

He wouldn't get away with lying, and he didn't particularly want to deceive her, which didn't mean he had to tell her *everything*. "How well do they know each other?" he asked casually, following her farther down the secluded walkway to a stone bench that sat hidden in a leafy bower.

She sank down on the bench and examined her shoes. They were fashioned of Indian gold brocade and curled up at the toes, like the slippers a genie in a fairy tale would wear. They looked rather peculiar, but they suited Julia's adventurous spirit and sense of fun, and they matched her butter-yellow muslin party gown.

"I think Lucy was attracted to Russell before she was married," she said in a thoughtful voice. "I'm not certain if he noticed."

He raised his brow and tried to ignore the languid stretch of her spine as she leaned down to pluck a leaf from her shoe. He couldn't think of another woman who moved with such grace and determination, and it should not have aroused him, but it did. Made him imagine challenging her to a tussle in bed. A legendary concubine?

"I should think," he said, although he didn't really believe it, "that all that sort of nonsense will be over once you two are married."

"Yes." She sighed, and suddenly did not seem confident at all. She seemed like a vulnerable, charmingly headstrong woman who made his heart race for all the wrong reasons. "I'm not sure, actually. I'm not sure that Russell's acclaim will make for an easy life."

He frowned, aware that they were treading hazardous territory. A sparrow had swooped down from an overhanging branch in search of a beetle in the foliage. "Why would you say that?"

"Russell is concerned with his public image. I'm sure that part of him must enjoy having women admire him. Most men do."

"Not all of them." He had grown tired of being chased himself, honestly. He had enjoyed it when he was younger, but now he wanted so much more.

"For heaven's sake, Heath, none of you Boscastles are working toward sainthood."

He couldn't deny that. "With the possible exception of my sister Emma."

She laughed. "Perhaps she hasn't met the right man."

"You mean the wrong one."

Her amusement faded. "Do you know what I overheard one of my servants say? She said that Russell was a rascal, that he was only marrying me because I've inherited a fortune."

He frowned. "That's ridiculous, Julia."

"It isn't, actually. I'm quite well off."

"Well, Russell wanted you before you became an heiress." And so had he.

"Yes."

"How did your father die?" he asked quietly.

"He had a stroke." She looked him in the eye. "I'll tell you a secret. He hoped you might ask to marry me."

She gave another laugh, kicking up a few leaves with her silly pointed shoes, and something inside him turned dark and fierce. The desire to protect her, to spare her pain. A fortune she had said. Could it be true? The old viscount had not flaunted his wealth. Yet Heath still believed that Russell loved Julia for herself, even if he was betraying her behind her back, the stupid bastard.

Heath didn't know how to respond. After their past encounter, he never would have imagined that Julia would discuss him with her father. "I had no idea. I didn't know that he even thought of us in those terms."

"Neither did I until recently." She grinned wickedly. "He only told me right before he died. He didn't dislike Russell, but he preferred you to all the young men I'd met."

Heath's face showed no reaction. "Really?"

"He didn't disapprove of my engagement," she said as an afterthought. "But he caught Russell cheating at cards once, and never felt the same about him again."

Heath smiled.

"Of course that would never happen to you," she said tartly. "You'd never cheat at cards, would you?"

"I wouldn't get caught."

"But would you cheat?" she asked again, teasing him, he suspected.

They turned to each other at the same moment. Without thinking he put his hand on her shoulder and drew her toward him. There was no one around them, no one to witness their behavior. It was only the second time in his memory that Heath had given in to basic impulse. The rest of his family happily submitted all the time.

But he had always prided himself on his restraint. He was admired for it. He was the one his siblings sought for advice, for intervention. The level-headed male member of the Boscastle line. The one Russell had chosen to be the protector.

A protector turned predator. He couldn't help it.

He slid his hand down her half-bare shoulder to her waist, urging her into him. She bent but not without initial resistance, or was it surprise? It didn't much matter. He placed his other hand on top of her knee. To balance himself or hold her in place? Both perhaps. That didn't matter either. Her body heat stole through his jacket and shirt, into his skin, into his bones, where his memories of her smoldered. The tempting fire of her blazed a direct pathway into the guarded regions of his heart. She'd found her way there once before, he remembered, but he had assumed a scar had formed around the spot.

She moistened her lips, meeting his gaze. The sensuality in her eyes stirred his deepest senses. "Julia," he murmured.

"Go ahead," she said in an undertone. "Do it. We're both dying of curiosity. Perhaps we shall feel better if we get it over with once and for all."

His heart quickened. He felt the burning warmth deep in his belly now. A heat, a hunger. A wanting that gnawed into his bones. He brought his hand to her face, traced her jaw, her cheekbone with his thumb. "Do what?" he asked in a deep, deliberate voice. Yes, he was a patient man. He understood what she was saying, but he wanted to hear it explained in her own words.

"This." She angled her head to bring her full red mouth to his. Her warm breath taunted his jaw. "Kiss me, and then we shall know."

"There's no excuse for us this time," he said in a thick voice. "You can get up and walk away." But he prayed she wouldn't. He wished for this so badly his heart hammered in desperate violence.

She leaned into him, lacing her left hand around his neck. Her fingers trembled, stroked his hair until he shivered. "So can you."

"We both know better." His body was already as hard as stone.

"Do we?" she whispered, her gray eyes wistful.

He knew what he wanted. He cradled the back of her head in his hand. Her lips parted.

She had the softest, most erotic mouth he had ever tasted. Forbidden fruit. He wanted to eat his fill of her, taste her from top to bottom. Incredible that this feeling could flare up between them, hotter, more dangerous for their years apart than before.

God help him. He wasn't kissing an innocent debutante. She was experienced now, a woman who had lived a life, who knew how to please a man, to take her own pleasure. He had not counted on this, that his talent for seduction would meet its match in the one woman he had wanted and lost.

It was not like him to underestimate what he must face. He'd assumed time would dampen his attraction to her. He who analyzed every aspect of human behavior, who followed a precise blueprint for his own life, had not taken into account that Julia matured would be more than his equal.

Everything he secretly desired in a woman wrapped in one package.

A package labeled: Forbidden. Do Not Open. Property of Another Man.

But he had not bargained for this. To desire her all over again. This time with his full awareness and knowledge of what they were, the risks so dangerously high. They both stood to lose more than they could afford. He would give up any aspirations to his career, the respect of the man who'd saved his life. Julia would surrender whatever respect and standing in Society she had left.

She broke the kiss, her breath warm on his lips, lingering

with the aftertaste of fine champagne to tease him. Forbidden sweetness. He felt her hand lift to his chest. Felt her fingertips fleetingly explore the ridge of muscle that sheltered his pounding heart. He didn't move, didn't encourage or discourage her. She had kissed him with the cool skill of a courtesan. He couldn't help wondering what else she could do, would allow if they were alone. What she could be in a man's bed. In his bed. If she kissed like that, what else had she learned?

He pressed his tongue between her parted lips. Her mouth was sweet and moist. He tasted the sigh she gave, felt the quiver that shook her supple frame. His fingers tightened possessively around her neck. He deepened the kiss, his other hand curling around her waist to draw her against him. Her tongue met and circled his with a sensuality that made his body clench.

She moaned, the creamy globes of her breasts crushed to his chest. He cupped her hip through her pale gown, tested the tempting softness of her flesh. His blood pounded through his veins in a powerful wave of desire. This wasn't enough. He needed more. He'd kill for the chance to sleep with her. Six years of lust coming to an uncontrollable boil.

"Julia," he whispered in a thick voice. "Oh, my God."

Her mouth trembled. He pulled her closer, tangling his fingers in the hair that had fallen down her shoulder. He pushed his knee between her thighs, desperate to feel more of her. He moved his hand from her waist to the swelling underside of her breast. He heard her breath catch. His thumb teased the taut nub of her nipple. A dark mist of desire swam in his head. He had to stop before someone saw them.

"Your cravat is a little crooked," she said, staring at his neck. "Shall I straighten it?"

"Please." *Just keep touching me.* He glanced down at her averted face to the creamy sun-kissed skin of her shoulders. A pulse fluttered at the hollow of her throat, the only telltale sign of his effect on her that he could discern. His heart was thundering like a bloody war drum.

"Are you and Russell—"

"No," she answered quickly, her eyes lifting to his. "We're not lovers."

He smiled slowly, wondering why her answer pleased him. "I meant, are you going to live in London after you're married?"

"I think so. At least for part of the year." She gave his cravat a final tug. "Are you going to tell him?" she asked carefully.

He forced a smile. "Tell him what?"

"That I kissed you."

Her cheeks were flushed, and her mouth looked delectably moist.

"I kissed you first."

"Yes, but . . ."

"But?" he prodded gently.

She released a sigh. "I didn't have to reciprocate."

He shook his head. "I didn't have to tempt you."

Julia patted the end of his cravat, her pensive frown giving way to her natural merriment. She had never struck him as the type to cry over spilled milk. Or stolen kisses. How could he have forgotten her delightful irreverence for dignity? "It was a kiss, Heath. Not the Treaty of Paris."

He pretended to scowl at her. His body was still aching

and hard. His heartbeat was only now slowing to a more normal pace. "Do you kiss other men often?"

"Every chance I get."

"Did I satisfy your curiosity?"

She took another sip of champagne from the glass she had set beside her on the bench. He noticed that her hand was not completely steady. Good. "Did I satisfy yours?"

"Satisfied is not quite how I would describe my present state, Julia."

"I'm not satisfied either," she confessed, drawing her hand back into her lap. She lowered her gaze. "I feel very unsettled inside and annoyed at myself, if you must know."

He turned his head, ending their lighthearted exchange with regret. Lady Dalrymple and the earl were coming toward them, their voices raised in a quibble. He straightened, his face deliberately impersonal as he murmured, "Well, I'm not complaining. And, Julia, it should go without saying that I'm not telling either."

Chapter 9

Julia wandered over to her bedroom window, slowly pulling the pins from her hair. Evening had fallen, and she wasn't at all tired. She'd had the loveliest day she could remember in a long time. She'd had three glasses of champagne at the party and had fallen asleep on the ride home with Heath sitting opposite her. Now from where she stood she could hear the patter of light rain on the rhododendrons in the garden. She could hear the muted *clip-clop* of carriages in the street.

She'd retired to her room at ten o'clock that evening. She had not bothered to light a candle. Heath had refused to go home again. She'd left him downstairs with a book, his cravat loosened, his arm stretched across the back of the sofa. It had been a struggle not to stay with him.

She was going to have to find a way to release him from his promise.

Today only proved that they could not be trusted alone together.

She had seen other women stare at him throughout the party. Stolen, yearnful looks. Bold flirtatious smiles that invited seduction. She knew he'd noticed. But he'd only smiled politely and refused to linger. Russell would have stopped to talk to half of them, always the political creature. At the theater two weeks ago, he had made friends with everyone except the footmen. Julia had thought she would collapse from pretending to be so polite. Heath didn't seem bothered.

Would one of those women at the party today capture his heart? It was bound to happen soon. What would it take? She sighed at the thought of Heath setting out to seduce a debutante, a beautiful heiress. She wondered suddenly if he would be a faithful husband. And what he thought of her after their kiss today. Had it settled anything or left more questions unanswered? She was still weak from the wonderful power of it. Weak and wistful. She felt a little ashamed of herself too, but . . . she couldn't stop thinking about him. The dizzying pleasure of his hand on her breast, his hard mouth claiming hers. She had wanted him to touch her all over. She was ashamed, but she had wanted it just the same.

A creak from the misty darkness of the garden below arrested her attention. It was the cat banging against the shed door as it did every night when the gardeners forgot to lock their tools away, or when Hermia's little spaniels bedeviled it.

She tossed her brush down on the bed. She tugged the bellpull to summon a servant, but no one answered. It was late anyway, and she would be faster solving the problem herself.

She encountered a far more intimidating problem on her way down the stairs. Her heart accelerated at the tall lean figure who appeared without warning to intercept her. He had unbuttoned his jacket and stood below her in his white linen shirt and gray pantaloons. The shadows accentuated his deep blue eyes and the chiseled power of his face, the lines that bracketed his lean cheeks. Unwelcome heat suffused her as she met his gaze; her breasts felt heavy and sensitive. She couldn't remember when a man had aroused her with a mere look.

A dangerous man, she warned herself, recalling the rumors that he had efficiently, ruthlessly hunted down foreign agents after recovering from his experience in Portugal. Russell had often bragged of how he had rescued Heath, of how he had carried his abused body across the countryside in a wine cart, how they had begged refuge at a convent, disguised as peasants. She'd heard stories about Heath, too. How many lives had he saved? He did not brag of his deeds.

"Is something wrong?" he demanded, bringing her unruly thoughts back in line.

"Yes. It's a Crown crisis, Heath. My cat is banging against the shed door. At least I assume it was the cat. Call the Horse Guards while I fetch the prime minister."

His firm mouth curled into a sardonic smile. "And the light infantry?"

She attempted to slip around him. "Let's not lose our heads."

She did not see him move, but suddenly his hand captured her bare arm. The subtle pressure of his fingers encircled her wrist in an inescapable yet protectively gentle hold. She felt her breath hitch in her throat. "Wait," he said. "It's raining, and your dress is thin. I shall close the door."

She glanced up. "One of the footmen—"

"I sent them all to bed."

"Honestly, Heath, you cannot keep spending the night at my house. It really makes me feel terribly guilty."

He drew her down onto the step beside him. She felt a spark of shock, allowed herself to be swept into warm confusion. In the blink of an eye it engulfed her—shimmering heat, temptation. The very air that brushed her skin seemed to burn.

"Only until I make a more suitable arrangement," he said. "Do you really object?"

Breathing became difficult. The virile allure of his body drew her forward, magnetic and irresistible. She couldn't bring herself to pull her hand from his, enjoying his possessive touch far too much. "I object only because I feel it is an unfair imposition on your time."

"Is my company unpleasant?" he asked, his gaze playful, dangerously enticing.

"What do you think?"

"I say we will do what we are told."

She laughed softly. "As if either of us has ever done so. What must your family think of this? And my servants?"

The latter was a poor excuse, and no doubt he knew it. Julia had never lived an orthodox life. She had barely managed to cling to the fringes of convention, even during her marriage, and her household had been in her employ since her first days in India.

His roguish grin caught her off guard. "Your servants are loyal to you and understand the danger of your fiancé's mission. Furthermore, your butler and I are becoming fast friends. We played cards with the housekeeper last night."

"You didn't," she said in chagrin. What was going on in her household?

"I did. I won a silver carving knife and an Irish linen apron."

"With the servants," she exclaimed, not as disapproving as she pretended. "Gambling. My aunt would be scandalized."

"She wasn't, actually." His deep chuckle sent a shiver down her back. "She kept score for us."

"How could you? A carving knife. An apron."

"I won them fair and square." He leaned toward her, his voice wickedly conspiratorial. "And it's keeping your aunt out of trouble. She planned to break into Odham's bedroom tonight. She's convinced that he sleeps with her love letters under his pillow."

She swallowed. She wanted for once to unsettle him, as he did her, to see him lose his poise. She wanted . . . to melt into his arms again, to savor his hard strength, to resurrect the beautiful passion they had known. How could she have guessed that he would haunt her heart for the rest of her life? In self-defense she changed the subject. She could not think of him in such terms. "Speaking of my aunt, you're in for a surprise if you're still here in the morning, Boscastle."

"Am I? That sounds promising."

She lowered her gaze, staring inadvertently at his firmly molded mouth. She'd wager he wouldn't be smiling like that in the morning when he found the house taken over by a flock of amateur female artists.

"Aunt Hermia's painting club meets here every Tuesday after breakfast. The ladies are ever in search of a suitable model for their Greek deity collection."

And what a model he would make. The man radiated raw masculinity. What woman with artistic aspirations would not be tempted to immortalize that classically handsome face and perfectly sculpted torso? He would cause a sensation tomorrow if Hermia's friends got hold of him. She grinned a little slyly at the thought. It served him right for being so unfairly gorgeous.

"A painting club." He shifted his weight, smiled down into her eyes. "That sounds innocent enough."

"Doesn't it?" she murmured, remembering the risqué conversations, the wicked fun of her aunt's female friends. Innocent they weren't.

"Have you posed as Aphrodite for this worthy endeavor?" he asked, clearly unaware what fate held for him.

"No, I haven't. I did stand in for a Trojan once."

His gaze traveled over her in expert appraisal. Her unbound hair draped in wild disarray down her back. He'd mentioned moments ago that her muslin dress was thin. Now, by the way he stared right through it, by the sensual glint in his eyes, she might well have been naked, laid bare by his scrutiny. He really was a shameless man. She wondered if he could sense the emotional turmoil that flooded her whenever he looked at her like that, the deep craving that could never be fulfilled. Of course he could. He was a clever rogue.

She brought her arm back to her side. The pressure of his grasp had sent a tingling warmth through her wrist to her fingertips. "Are you going to close the shed door or am I?"

He squared his shoulders. "Boscastle to the rescue."

"Be careful out there."

"Is the cat dangerous? Good Lord, Julia, you didn't bring a tiger back with you from India?"

"Of course not. That would be cruel, to take a wild creature out of its native home."

He pulled his collar up high on his neck. "I'm only asking. After all, I was attacked by a monkey today."

She pursed her lips. "I meant be careful in the rain. Don't trip over a wheelbarrow or one of my boots. And don't hurt the cat. He's old and defenseless, as misplaced in England as I appear to be."

"You're sure it was the cat that disturbed you?"

She wavered. "Well, no. Not absolutely. Do you want my gun?"

"No, thank you. I think you should keep it. Just don't shoot at me from the window."

Heath stood for several moments in the light rainfall, orienting himself to the unfamiliar green-gray shadows. A large brown object curled around his ankles. He glanced down to see Julia's cat rubbing itself dry on his trouser cuffs.

"All right, Puss. Let's put a stop to your nonsense."

He pulled his collar up again over his nape, hoisted the tomcat into his arms, and took off at a sprint down the flagstone path. The shed stood at the very end of the garden, dark and enclosed behind a tangled wall of chestnut trees.

"Here's your home, my boy, and what a nice kitty castle it—"

The captive tomcat apparently did not appreciate being held. Without warning, it raked a razor-sharp claw across Heath's exposed throat, bunched its muscles, and sprang free into the heavy pattering rain.

"And she called you old and defenseless," Heath muttered, pressing his hand to the stinging cut before he scooped the escaping cat back into his arms and kicked open the shed door.

The shed was predictably dank and redolent of humus and mildewed bulbs. Heath froze in his tracks. The darkness, the angle of shadows, the scent of wet dirt assaulted his senses. Took him back to a time he could barely remember and yet was unable to forget. The brutal days of his torture, the pain that had seemed to have no end.

From out of nowhere a sense of suffocating panic consumed him. His mind struggled against darkness; deep, unwelcome memories unleashed. A harsh black-gloved hand gripping his hair and forcing his head into a vat of stagnant water, the taste of mildew. Holding him under until his lungs screamed and black terror blanketed his brain.

Then blessed air, and the soft lethal voice of the enemy. A hooded Frenchman expertly applying a red-hot poker to the most tender parts of his body. Armand Auclair's father had been an executioner during the Reign of Terror, a man infamous for how many aristocrats he had murdered at the guillotine. He had passed down his passion for cruelty to his son.

The cat in Heath's arms fell still, its muscles taut. He had not remembered the details of his torture so vividly in years, hoping that the wounds to his mind would heal. Scars, perhaps, but he had believed he would lay his demons to rest one day. He'd never told anyone what had happened. He never would. The mere memory made him feel insane, violated, more animal than man. He would never allow himself to be that weak again.

He heard rather loud footsteps behind him and swung around to see a robust silvery-haired figure raise an object over his head.

"Dear God, Lady Dalrymple," he exclaimed. "Put down that flowerpot before you do me or those geraniums a fatal injury."

Hermia peered around the uplifted pot. The cat squeezed out of Heath's arms and disappeared inside the shed.

"For heaven's sake, Boscastle," she said as she lowered the flowerpot. "I nearly brained you. What are you doing out here in the rain?"

"I should ask . . . did you see someone sneaking around the garden, too?"

"Yes, you." She nodded past him to the door. "I'd heard the shed door banging shut and came down to investigate. One cannot trust the servants with the job. They are fiercely loyal to Julia, but afraid of their own shadows. Between you and me, I think the lot of them have spent too much time out in the Indian sun."

"The sun?"

"Bakes the brain, you know."

"I don't think standing in the English rain does much for it, either. Would you mind waiting here a moment while I inspect the shed again?"

She stared past him in alarm. "You did not think that someone was watching the house from the shed?"

He brushed a bruised geranium leaf from his rain-spangled sleeve. "That remains to be seen."

He ducked inside the shed, his gaze lowering to the gleaming eyes of the cat in the corner. The pungent scent of mildew that he had detected earlier was fainter now, over-powered by the more pleasant aroma of moss and damp aged wood. After a thorough search he could not find a trace of a recent intruder. The rain would have blurred away any footprints outside the shed by now. His gaze lifted to a small window above the crowded shelf of bulbs and gardening tools. His skin began to crawl as he realized he could see into Julia's bedchamber from where he stood.

His eyes dropped to a dark object on the shelf. He reached up. It was a man's black glove, placed beneath a gardener's spade. The glove looked worn, more of a gauntlet style than part of a fashionable gentleman's wardrobe. It seemed vaguely familiar.

"Well? What is it?"

He turned to see Hermia's worried face, outlined in a halo of frizzy silver-gold curls, peeking into the shed.

He stepped outside. "I don't know." He handed her the glove. "Have you ever seen this before?"

She shook her head. "I can't say that I have. Did the intruder drop it?"

"No. It was sitting on the shelf."

"Well, an elderly gentleman did lease the house until a few months ago."

He glanced into the garden. The rain had eased, and through the misty gray veil of drizzle he could see Julia standing at the window watching them.

If anyone had hidden in the shed, he would have had a perfect view into her room.

He stood still. Was someone watching her or trying to discern whether Russell was in her room? Auclair, or an agent who worked for him, would surely know by now that Russell was on his way to Paris.

His every instinct awakened, warned him not to let down his guard. Never underestimate the enemy.

Hermia followed the direction of his gaze, shuddering in reaction. "Do you really think my niece is in danger? I admit that I'd hoped Russell was exaggerating."

"I had hoped the same, Lady Dalrymple." He studied the glove, his mouth thinning. He was suddenly glad he was here. "For now perhaps it is wise to believe him."

Julia had returned to her room, convinced she had sent Heath on a fool's mission. Of course it had been the cat she'd heard, not an intruder lurking in the garden. What on earth was he doing with her aunt? Both of them appeared to be getting soaked, from what Julia could make out from her vantage point. She pressed her forehead to the window-pane. What had Russell gotten Heath into? She felt so very self-indulgent, claiming him as her bodyguard. Under other circumstances . . . She blocked the thought before it could bedevil her.

The true danger was to Russell in Paris, a city not predis-posed to welcoming English heroes, despite the fact that Wellington had been set up there as an ambassador.

She felt dreadful, sending Heath out in the rain after he had been so generous with his time. She would apologize to him. Then she would insist he resign as her personal pro-tector. For both their sakes.

The door behind her opened. She turned, startled from her thoughts. He stood before her, his silky black hair plas-tered to his finely shaped skull. The front of his white linen shirt was molded to the superb musculature of his chest. He looked anything but happy, and no wonder. She shook her head in apology.

"You're soaked to the skin." She came forward, her hands lifting to his shirtfront. The damp brought out the masculine scent of his shaving soap and starch, the pleasing musk of his skin. "I should—"

"Not touch me like that," he said in a rough voice. "Julia, please, I am only a man."

"As if anyone could forget that," she retorted unthinkingly. "I'm sorry to have sent you out in this weather."

Their gazes met. The blue fire in his eyes took her breath away. "Try to think," he said, his face giving nothing away. "What exactly did you see or hear in the garden?"

"I heard a banging, and . . ." She noticed the thin trickle of blood on his throat. She raised her hand again, aghast. "What happened to you? There *was* an intruder."

"Julia, please do not distract me." Dark humor glittered in the depths of his eyes. "I think I'll survive. Compared to my past wounds—"

"Let me cleanse it."

"It's nothing."

"It isn't nothing," she said in concern. "You're bleeding. How did it happen?"

" 'Old and defenseless.' I believe those were your exact words," he said with a droll smile.

"My cat scratched you?"

"Apparently it didn't like me as much as that monkey earlier today."

"Take off your jacket and shirt this instant."

He unbuttoned, then shrugged the garments off his broad shoulders, grinning at her. "Anything else while I'm at it? Socks? Trousers? Boots?"

"How can you joke when your throat has been cut?"

He lowered his voice. "Because your cat did it, that's why, and it is only a scratch."

She frowned at him. "Do you want that scratch to become infected?"

"Sorry." He reached into his pocket and removed the worn black glove. "Does this look familiar?"

She shook her head. "No. I've never seen Russell wearing it. It certainly isn't mine." She glanced up at him again. "Where did you find it?"

"On the shelf in the shed. Hermia thought it might have belonged to the previous owner."

"Possibly. Or one of his ancestors. Please let me clean off that scratch."

He leaned back in resignation against her dressing table while she located a clean towel from under the washstand. He did not move as she dabbed astringent on the cut. He didn't feel the scratch at all. He couldn't say the same for Julia. He felt every movement of her body, a sweet agony that built by the moment. God help him, he would disgrace himself if he didn't find relief soon. His attraction to her had become unbearable, a physical as well as emotional ache.

He tried to ignore the soft brush of her breasts on his upper arm. He succeeded at first, but soon his body began to rebel. She was standing too close to him for comfort. His trousers still felt damp from the rain, and Julia's skin radiated a warm invitation. His cock stiffened, and he was certain she must be aware of his arousal, pressed against him as she was. He ground his teeth, studying her through half-closed eyes. He could just make out the rosy circles of her nipples through her nightdress. A dangerous fire ignited in his belly, spread through every part of his male body. He didn't give a damn about the scratch. He *wanted* this woman.

"Hold still," she murmured.

"I am holding still."

She leaned into him, and his throbbing groin was suddenly molded to the rounded softness of her stomach. He sucked in his breath, feeling her slight hesitation. By now she had to realize he was one hard, aroused man. Yet here they stood, a heartbeat away from each other, and he couldn't have her. And he needed her. God, he needed her.

He stared down at her as she drew a deep breath. He kept his hands braced behind him on the dressing table, but in his mind he was removing her nightdress, kissing her beautiful breasts, sucking on the dusky tips until she could not stand up. He exhaled slowly, tantalized by the yielding softness of her body, the scent of her hair, her sweet breath on his cheek.

The bed was only a few steps away. He could have her undressed and gasping for mercy in seconds. He could put himself out of his aching misery, impale her, ride her for the rest of the night to slake the longing that he had suppressed for so long. He wanted to grasp her firm bottom and drive into her until she could barely walk. He'd never needed to take advantage of his appeal to the opposite sex before. He was sorely tempted to test his skill now.

"What in the world are you thinking about?" she asked unexpectedly.

His smile gave him away, revealed every dark thought that he had entertained.

"Never mind," she said quickly. "That is a smile I recognize only too well. I don't think you need to explain it."

"How perceptive of you."

"You're right," she murmured, ignoring his remark. "That scratch is not deep enough to kill you."

"Thank goodness. I hadn't made out a proper will yet."

She looked up into his darkly mocking face and felt her

heart miss a beat. She struggled for equilibrium. "What are we doing alone in my bedroom?" she asked in a hesitant voice. "There wasn't anyone in the garden, was there?"

"Only your aunt," he replied, taking the cloth from her hand. "At least by the time I arrived, there was no one in sight."

"What did she think she was doing?"

"She almost bashed my brains out with a flowerpot."

"A flower—" She shook her head in dismay, not quite managing to smother a laugh. "How traumatic for you. First my cat, and then my aunt. I do apologize. Being my protector certainly comes at a high price."

She had no idea. It was killing him to control himself. He leaned forward, his bare chest brushing against her breasts. "That grin on your face doesn't look at all sorry to me."

"Do you need sympathy?" she asked, eyeing him in amusement.

Cruel woman, he thought. "It never hurts in these situations."

"Odd," Julia said. "I always thought of you as the stoic, long-suffering type."

"With everyone else."

She lowered her hand, gazing up at him in curiosity. "Am I different then?"

He hesitated. "I think we both know you are."

Her eyes darkened. "I'm not sure whether you should have told me that."

"Neither am I," he retorted. "Nonetheless, it happens to be true."

She swallowed, but he noticed that she did not draw away from him. He wished she would. He was going to take her into his arms in a moment and do something shocking to her. Something indecent and inventively sexual. She sensed that, too. She might not acknowledge it, but she must realize that he desired her. His treacherous male body gave him away all too well, and Julia was certainly experienced enough to recognize the signs of sexual arousal.

Her voice broke the tension building between them. "I suppose it's Russell we should be worried about. It has always seemed odd to me that Auclair would lure him so openly to France. What if this is a trap?"

He narrowed his eyes. What a tactic. There was nothing like the mention of another man to dampen one's libido. "Russell is prepared for that. I think he's ready to end the game once and for all."

"But not his life."

"Are you afraid, Julia?"

"Of course I am. I know you men believe yourself invincible, as did my husband."

He brushed a strand of hair off her shoulder, the gesture instinctual. She looked vulnerable again with her emotions unmasked; he reminded himself he was meant to defend her. And yet the drugging need spreading through his veins like molten wine made him feel more like an aggressor than protector. His body tightened like a fist. Her kiss today had intoxicated him, left him aching for more. His desire seemed to intensify every time he saw her. At this rate he would be raging mad by the end of the week.

Resolutely, he placed his hands on her shoulders. "Go to bed."

"What about you?"

"If I stay another moment—"

"Don't," she said, pressing her forefinger swiftly to his

mouth. "Don't say it. If you say it, then I shall want it, too, and heaven help us then."

His hands moved slowly down her back, slid around her hips to draw her into the hot core of his body. He thought she would resist. But her spine arched as if she were magnetized to him. He groaned with longing into the luxuriant coil of hair at her nape. There was no other woman like her. He'd always known that.

"God help me," he whispered.

"Go home, Heath," she said softly. "Nothing is going to happen to me tonight."

Chapter 10

He did not go home. Not to defy Julia, or to prove a point. He stayed because he had begun to wonder whether Russell's fears for her might be justified. No matter what he had to do, he could never let her fall into the hands of Armand Auclair, the man who had broken his body and had hoped to break his soul. Although he returned to the garden several times that night, he could not find any evidence of an intruder. The shed remained undisturbed. The rain had washed away even his own footprints.

He spent the remainder of the night in the library where he'd decided to set up headquarters until he could decide upon a more suitable solution. Would the ton talk? Unquestionably. This was something to talk about. Naturally, it would be assumed that he and Julia were in the throes of a passionate affair, and for his own part he did not particularly care. Russell could hardly complain. He had set the stage for this drama.

Heath would not be a Boscastle if he had not managed to stir up his share of scandal. Although to his credit, he had never deliberately provoked gossip. In fact, he had studiously tried to avoid it. Julia, in her day, had set tongues wagging. People were bound to talk. It was the least of his worries.

His primary concern was not the shallow-minded rumors that circulated in Society. It was protecting her while not seducing her insensible, a dilemma that weighed heavily on his mind and which might have explained why, when he strolled into the drawing room after breakfast the next day, he realized he had forgotten her sly prediction that the morning would bring a shock.

Lady Dalrymple's painting club. He knew the instant he looked around that he had made a grave error in underestimating Julia's warning. When would he learn? The woman surprised him at every turn.

The room had been transformed into an amateur artists' gallery. The damask sofa and delicate gilt tea tables had been pushed aside beneath white sheets to allow room for a semicircle of sketching tables, easels, and chattering women in muslin smocks who perched on Chippendale chairs.

Heath froze in the doorway as a dozen or so female heads turned in his direction. Julia glanced up from the corner where she sat with a sketchbook before her. She waved her pencil at him and declared loudly, "Oh, look, it's Lord Boscastle. He must have come to pose as our Apollo. Let's give him a warm welcome."

He turned on his heels to flee. Lady Dalrymple sprang up from her chair and caught him by the long tails of his morning coat. He found himself being unceremoniously reeled back into the room like a fish.

"Don't by shy, Boscastle."

"Shy? I'm not shy. I am merely not given to self-exposure."

Julia cleared her throat. "There's no shame in the human body being used for artistic purposes."

"Not to mention the orphans it will clothe," said a thin-voiced matron from behind her enormous easel. "Do you mind removing your shirt? For artistic purposes."

Heath blinked. "Do I—"

"It's not as if you haven't done it dozens of times before," said one of the Misses Darlington seated at his right.

"Hopefully not in front of this large an audience," murmured a low familiar voice beside Julia's spot in the circle.

He groaned inwardly. That ascerbic voice belonged to none other than Jane, his sharp-witted sister-in-law, the Marchioness of Sedgecroft, who was married to Heath's older brother, Grayson. All he needed was for a member of the family to witness this humiliating moment. He would never hear the end of it.

He directed an indignant scowl at Jane. "The first—and last—time I posed for anyone was at your house. I do not recall it as a pleasant experience."

Jane smiled wickedly. "Only because the housekeeper found you and the artist—Miss Summers, wasn't she—in a rather unartistic pose."

"That is untrue," he said, aware of Julia staring at him. "My toga merely unraveled, and Miss Summers was offering to straighten it."

"My dear brother-in-law," Jane said in a patently sweet voice. "Think of all the charities you will fund by posing for us. I should have considered you myself."

He gave her a sardonic look. "I would be more than happy to make a donation, Jane. In fact, I shall instruct my secretary to draft—"

"If you can pose for Eloise Summers," Julia said, looking

up over her sketchbook, "you can certainly pose for us. Do be a good sport, Heath."

"And make a donation afterward," Lady Dalrymple added.

A storm of excited chatter swept around the circle.

"I cannot believe we have a Boscastle in our midst."

"Have you seen his eyes? I shall have to mix a dozen colors before I start to paint."

"Is he really going to pose for us? How shall I do justice to that manly form, that face? Ladies, my pencils are starting to blush."

Heath retreated several steps toward the door. "I'm sorry. I completely forgot that your club was meeting this morning. Do forgive the intrusion. Please continue. Without me."

"Intrusion?" one of the amateur artists squealed, waving her hog-bristle brush in the air. "You mean he isn't going to stay?"

"Of course he's staying," Lady Dalrymple said, moving quickly to block his path. "He promised Julia last night that he would."

Heath frowned; was it possible to tackle a woman of Hermia's age without hurting her? "I did nothing of the sort. Julia, did you misrepresent me?"

She was fidgeting with her charcoals. "I am representing you as a Greek god. I should think you'd be flattered."

He managed to slip around Hermia before she could catch him again. "Use the butler."

"We've already used the butler," one elderly lady with rouged cheeks remarked. "We voted to fashion our Hermes after him."

Julia was staring down at her sketchbook with an evasive smile. "Because he's so fast on his feet."

He backed into the doorway. Payton, the silver-haired butler, stood behind him, bearing a tray of refreshments and shaking his head in sympathy.

"You may as well give in, my lord," he said in an undertone. "They shall hound you unmercifully until you do. Take my word. A graceful surrender is easier in the long run."

"Please, Heath," Julia said in a dulcet voice.

He didn't trust that voice. Julia's sugary façade hid Satan's heart.

"I'm not posing," he said, squaring his shoulders. "Do not ask me again. I did not come to this house to be . . . exploited. And that is the end of it."

"Do you mind lifting up the leg of your trousers, dear?" Mrs. Hemswell asked the tall figure standing in the center of the room, his handsome face frozen in a disdainful scowl.

"Yes, I mind," Heath snapped. "I feel bloody ridiculous as it is. As if I were a Christmas goose being examined at the market."

"You don't look at all like any Christmas goose I've ever been served," Julia murmured, nibbling on the end of her pencil.

Heath's sister-in-law, Jane, grinned in agreement. "Nor I."

One of the Misses Darlington raised her head. "He reminds me ever so much of the prize stallion my uncle brought at a private auction."

Heath threw down the white silk sheet that had been draped over his shoulder. "Apollo is fed up. In fact, he's about to ask Zeus for a few lightning bolts to hurl."

Lady Dalrymple frowned at him. "For charity, Boscastle."

"Somebody ought to show me a little charity," he muttered.

"I say, Boscastle," Julia said, squinting her right eye, "could you flex your shoulder again? My lines are a little off."

"Give us a rear view, dear," Lady Dalrymple murmured.

"Give you a what?" Heath asked, his brow shooting up.

"I should like to see some fluidity. Some movement," Jane said, studying her drawing with a critical frown.

"So would I," Heath snapped. "As in movement out of this room."

Julia's eyes twinkled in delight. "Ladies, I think we should let our deity stretch a bit. He's becoming a little stiff."

"I'm mummified," Heath muttered, pulling his shirt back over his one exposed shoulder; he had refused to remove the garment, despite their pleas. "Are we finished?"

Lady Dalrymple lowered her pencil. "Not by any means. It's a good thing we have you in our midst. The portrait of Apollo is one of the most important pieces in the collection."

Heath stepped down from the makeshift dais. "I'm feeling more like Hades at the moment, if you take my meaning. Let me have a look at these masterpieces."

Julia hugged her sketchbook to her chest. "You mustn't look at mine until it's done."

He pivoted, leaning across the back of her chair to gaze over her shoulder. "Fair is fair. I ought to be allowed a look. Give us a gander."

"Just a peek then," she said, holding up her sketchbook with a flourish.

His eyes widened. He stared in shock at the artless drawing. "God in heaven. I'm—"

"Apollo au naturel," Julia said gleefully. "Have I got your proportions right? I had to use my imagination for the covered parts."

He studied the sketch in horror. He'd no idea he was being reduced to such basic terms. "I'd say the fig leaves need to be larger. As in large enough to cover the entire drawing."

"What do you think, Jane?" Julia asked the marchioness, who had just risen to examine the sketch. "Are Heath's parts all in proportion?"

"I'm married to Grayson, Julia," Jane replied in amusement. "I am hardly an expert on Heath's attributes."

"But they are brothers," Julia said, meeting his dark stare. "They must share certain . . . characteristics."

Heath held her gaze. "I keep my characteristics private, thank you."

Julia smirked back at him. "Perhaps Miss Summers could enlighten us."

"Jealous, Julia?" he asked under his breath.

She hesitated. "Of course not. Eloise has no artistic talent at all."

He stretched his arms over his head. "I shall have to see that sketch in more detail before I give it my approval."

She bit her lip, crossing her arms over the sketching table. "It's not ready. I still need to draw in some more details. This is merely the framework."

"Oh, good," he said, staring at her. "Then it can be fixed if I have a few suggestions. Such as adding clothes."

"I intend to sketch a chariot in the background," she said thoughtfully, tapping her pencil against her chin. "I haven't decided whether Apollo should carry his bow or a lyre."

"He should wear clothes," Heath said firmly. "And possibly a mask to hide his identity."

"Look at mine, Lord Boscastle," one of the Darlington sisters called, waving her fingers in his face. "What do you think?"

He glanced down politely, managing to hide his smirk at her amateur scribbles. "I don't recall that Apollo went about Olympus pointing his arrow at people. Especially from that angle."

The young lady peered down at her sketch. "Oh, that isn't an arrow. It's his—"

"I trust that none of this shall be on public display?" Heath said quickly, casting a rather menacing smile upon the group.

Julia gave him a chastising look. "Any works of art the club creates are auctioned off for charity."

"Do you mean that my disrobed likeness shall be hanging in someone's drawing room?"

Lady Dalrymple beamed at him. "Just imagine, Boscastle—the Duke of Wellington could be staring up at you from his dinner table every evening."

"What a chilling thought," he said.

"You could become the talk of London," Julia said slyly.

He turned to glare at her. "The joke of it, you mean."

Julia merely shook her head as if she had no idea what he was upset about. And suddenly it didn't matter. He could not imagine why he was allowing this to happen to him. But one thing he knew for certain. She was the only person in the world who could place him in this position with impunity. No one else would have dared, or would have gotten away with it.

There was a quiet knock on her door. Julia rose from the fireplace, where she had been burning old letters, a hot poker still in her hand. Her heart began to race, although not with fear. It was well past midnight, and the house had settled into its usual nocturnal silence.

A servant would never knock at this hour. A certain rogue would. What could he possibly want? She refused to let her mind wander. She was far too fascinated by the possibilities.

She pressed her cheek to the door, whispering in a stern tone, "Who is it?"

"Who do you think it is?" a deep male voice asked.

She closed her eyes. Her pulse was already thrumming in anticipation. "If I knew, I wouldn't be asking, would I?"

She could almost imagine his smile. "I don't know."

"What do you want this late at night?" she whispered, her hand already at the lock.

"Open the door, Julia."

"You sound . . . intense. I'm not sure I should let you in."

"Open the door."

She pressed her left shoulder against the doorframe. Her smile deepened. "Why should I?"

"I can unlock it from here if you prefer."

"Then why didn't you?"

"Because I'm damned polite, that's why, and I didn't want to give you a fright." He hesitated. His voice dropped an octave. "Are you dressed?"

She glanced down at the thin nightrail of ivory silk she

had brought back with her from India. "Barely. I mean, not for a ball, I—"

There was a click, the sound of the tumbler turning, and she was staring into his sinfully blue eyes, unable to breathe, to say a single word. She should have known better than to call his bluff.

"There," he said. "That was easy, wasn't it?"

"What are you doing here?" she demanded.

"I'm on a mission."

He edged around her, his eyes narrowed. Julia felt a chill of foreboding slide down her spine as she followed at his heels. He looked dangerous, intent, determined. Heath Boscastle, the spymaster, the trained officer, the professional assassin. In her room. On a mission. A sense of lightheadedness swept over her. What was going on? She had expected something else entirely. How embarrassing to be thinking he meant to seduce her when he was only doing his duty. She straightened, struck by a disturbing possibility.

Could it mean he had spotted a genuine intruder and suspected he was hiding in her room? She hoisted the poker a little higher as he knelt to look under the bed.

"What are you doing?" she said in an alarmed voice.

"Trying to find a hiding place."

"A hiding place? In here?"

She held her breath. The thought of someone breaking into her house, into her own room, turned her blood cold. If an intruder had gained entry, he might have been lying in wait the entire time she was undressing for bed. Perhaps there *had* been someone in the garden watching her. Perhaps she should have taken Russell's warnings more seriously.

She watched, her heart pounding in her throat, as Heath

sprang to his feet, his face grim but not frightened at all. In fact, he almost seemed to be enjoying himself. "Not under there."

"Do you need my gun?" she whispered, her mouth dry. "You really should have one."

He frowned at her. "A pair of scissors should do. Otherwise I'll use my bare hands."

"Your bare hands?" she said with a gasp. "That's a little brutal." She backed away from him, reaching behind her for the door. "Let me fetch help."

He sprang to his feet. His voice was matter-of-fact. "No. I do not want any witnesses."

Her jaw dropped as he strode resolutely toward her wardrobe. "In my armoire? In my dresses?"

He glanced almost casually over his shoulder. "Put down that poker before you burn yourself."

She obeyed and lowered it carefully to the hearth. "I really wish you would take my gun," she said in an undertone.

"Is your wardrobe locked?"

"No—*no*, but don't open it. . . ."

He smiled in satisfaction. "It's in here?"

"It?" Her pistol was under her pillow. "Wouldn't a gun be a quicker way to handle this?"

"A bit overdoing it, don't you think?"

"What are you going to do if he's in there?" she asked unsteadily.

"Cut the damned thing into a thousand pieces."

"The thing?" She flinched as he wrenched open the wardrobe door with an utter disregard for his safety that seemed more foolhardy than courageous. "You mean him, don't you?"

"Him?"

He stuck his head into the row of morning dresses, cloaks, and evening gowns that were arranged in no particular order. Julia reached behind her for the pistol she had hidden.

"The spy. Russell's nemesis. He isn't in there, is he?"

He turned to her in annoyance. "I have no idea what you're talking about. I'm looking for the sketch of me you did today. I will not have that seen in public. Where did you hide it?"

She straightened, looking appalled. No wonder he'd been so calm. "Are you telling me that you broke into my bedroom—that you came here this late at night—to find my sketch of you?"

He advanced on her, one dark eyebrow arched. "What did you think I was looking for? I want that sketch, Julia."

She turned, lunging for the pillow. "I want my gun."

"Oh, no, you don't." He dove around her and flattened himself out on the bed, crossing his arms under his head. "Where's the sketch?"

"Hermia has it."

He stared up at her, looking more perfectly at ease, more appealing in her bed than was decent. "Hermia?"

"Yes. Why don't you break into her bedroom?"

He gave her an engaging grin. Her breath caught in reaction. "I don't think she'd be nearly as much fun as you."

"Fun?" she said in indignation, as angry with herself as she was at him. "I thought you were trying to protect me. I thought you were about to kill a man."

"I'd hardly do so with a pair of scissors." His grin faded, replaced by a dangerous intensity. His smoldering gaze traveled down her silk-clad form, then slowly returned to her face. Her body temperature rose. "Do you always look this desirable when you're going to bed?"

"Only when I'm expecting a rogue to come to my room and drape himself over that bed." She laced her arm around the bed's wooden poster as if to anchor herself against temptation. He'd done it again. Seduced her with a single look. "Up with you."

"I was just making myself comfortable."

"Too comfortable by the look of it." Too attractive for her comfort.

She turned to the right as he rolled his muscular frame from the bed, uncrossing his arms with agile grace. She glanced up and glimpsed his face in the mirror. She could not miss the unguarded look of raw longing that darkened his features.

A shock of surprise, of fierce pleasure, shot through her, electrified every nerve ending. She turned back slowly toward him, her gaze questioning. His face was so devoid of expression that she wondered if she were imagining things. Seeing only a reflection of her own hidden desire.

"I aim to examine that sketch of me before you unleash it on the world," he said in a disgruntled voice.

She laughed as he walked past her to the window. "Your body and my art shall belong to posterity, I'm afraid."

He pushed aside the curtains. "Now that's a frightening thought."

Her laughter died away as she came up beside him and gazed down into the dark shadows of the garden. He seemed too serious. He had something else on his mind beside the sketch. "You still haven't found anything out there, have you?"

"No. The pathways were awash in mud this morning."

"Perhaps there really wasn't anyone there last night."

"I don't know." He let the curtain fall back into place. "There's no point in taking any chances." He turned, started to move past her, then stopped. Julia felt her heart race at his scrutiny. Clearly there was something troubling him. "What is it?" she asked, her gaze holding his.

He gave her a rueful smile. "Do you know," he said, "I thought for years that if I ever kissed you again, I would be cured?"

"Cured?"

"Of my desire for you. I believe that I shall always regret we were not lovers. Well, call it a young man's folly, wanting what he could not have."

She glanced away, an unwilling smile settling on her lips. "Lovers?" She pretended to look surprised, as if she had not considered this countless times herself. But hearing him admit that he felt the same way—she did not know what to think. It was a dangerous door to reopen; she stood on the threshold of temptation. "You sound ever so tragic," she said gently.

"Don't I though?"

"I don't believe it for a moment. It sounds exactly what a rogue would say to lure a woman to his bed."

"It was worth a try."

"You are shameless," she exclaimed. "I think you're worse than when I met you."

"It's quite possible. I've had several years of practice."

"Well, so have I," she retorted. Not that it appeared to have done her much good. She wanted him now with a woman's desire, not a young girl's impulse. If they'd been lovers, would they still be together now? The thought taunted her. He had gone off to war.

He smiled at her, then walked back to the door. She watched him go, aware of an ache deep inside her. Regret, he'd said. Was that what this bittersweet pain was called? "Don't let any other rogues into your room tonight, Julia," he said over his shoulder.

"I don't think there's any chance of that."

His eyes met hers, sternly reprimanding, and the ache settled deeper inside her. What had she lost? "Lock the door anyway."

Chapter 11

Three uneventful days passed. There were no intruders in Julia's garden. No more reasons to suspect she was in any immediate danger. Little opportunity for Heath to act as hero unless one counted a small drama at the end of that week when she and Lady Dalrymple became involved in a minor street riot. It had started innocently enough.

Heath had agreed with reluctance to escort the two women early in the evening to a lecture in the East End on the plight of homeless soldiers. He knew he should have refused.

His coachman had instructions to return in three hours to collect them. Heath should have obeyed his instincts and insisted they stay home.

A scuffle broke out at the back of the lecture hall as the talk came to a premature and an emotional end, a veritable shouting match over soldiers being denied pensions that quickly escalated into a pushing war. A disgruntled youth set off a firecracker and tossed it into the air. The audience gave way to panic, dispersing in all directions.

"Head right for the carriage," Hermia shouted above the confusion of shoving bodies and shrill voices. "Heath, do not let Julia out of your sight. These crowds can turn vicious."

Julia's voice floated out of the chaos. "I'm fine. Each man to himself."

Heath caught a glimpse of her face, looking calm if understandably aggravated by the jostling of elbows and shoulders around her. As long as he could keep her in his view he would not be overly concerned. How had they gotten into this situation? He supported social reform but through Parliament, not public debate.

Suddenly the double doors at the back of the hall banged open, and a horde of ragged street ruffians appeared. Heath recognized danger when he saw it. A rush of cool evening air reached the wall sconces, extinguishing the candles that cast wavering light upon the scene of panic. He gazed across the swarm of fleeing attendees, searching for Julia's face in the chaos.

He could not find her. His heart began to hammer.

"Julia," he shouted, vaguely aware of how silly he sounded, how the elderly couple beside him started in alarm.

"Over here!" Her white-gloved hand waved valiantly above the sea of bobbing heads. "We seem to be moving as one to the back door. . . . Take care of Hermia—"

He shook his head in frustration. "Hermia is right—" He glanced around, realizing that the older woman had also vanished from his sight. An unfamiliar bespectacled man stood in the space she had occupied only moments earlier. "Where did she go? Hermia, where the blazes are you?"

"Down here."

He followed the muffled reply to his feet. "Good God.

What happened?" he demanded, reaching down to help her. "Were you pushed?"

"I dropped my hat, Boscastle. No need to panic."

"Panic?" he muttered, pulling her to her feet. "Tell that to the hundred or so people charging like a herd of elephants. Why did I let myself be talked into this?"

She straightened, her cheeks brightly flushed, her hat clutched in her hand. "Where is Julia?"

"Gone out the back way, if she had any sense." He took firm hold of her arm. "Let's join her, shall we?"

"Excuse me," Julia said as a Hessian boot trod down hard on her big toe. She had been swept into a dusty, stygian back passage with a small group of frightened lecture attendees. "Would you mind not stepping on my feet?"

"Sorry, madam," the disembodied voice replied. "I cannot see where I'm going."

"There's a door leading out into the alley," a woman called back from the front of the crowd. "Three steps going up."

"I can't seem to breathe," an unseen man said in a frantic voice. "I've always hated the dark."

"There's another way out," a refined male voice whispered in Julia's ear. "Take my hand, and I'll help you."

She hesitated. She'd completely lost sight of Hermia, but she knew that her aunt was with Heath, and that she could trust him to take care of her. The owner of the polite voice sounded young and gentlemanly, and Julia could not discern any ulterior motives for rescuing her other than simple kindness.

"I can't see a thing," she whispered back.

He grasped her wrist in his leather-gloved hand. "Don't worry. I can find the way."

She glanced into the void of utter darkness. "How? It's as black as a grave."

"I used to explore caves as a child. I was never afraid of the dark. My name is Raphael, by the way. Baron Brentford."

Heath had one arm hooked around Hermia's thickset waist, the other raised to protect them against the barrage of rotten eggs and stones that the rioters in the street hurled in abandon. These weren't sincere protesters, merely thugs who reveled in wanton violence and the chance to steal a purse or two.

"Soldiers' pensions?" a man jeered, launching a moldy cabbage at Heath's head. "I'll give you a pension!"

He ducked, shielding Hermia from the missile with his body. "Where the devil is the carriage?" he muttered as he herded her away from the agitated crowd. "And where the hell is Julia?"

Hermia straightened her russet velvet pelisse and peered over his shoulder. "Do you think she might have found the carriage before us?"

He glanced down the gaslit street, his mouth tightening. Where could she have gone? Why hadn't he asked his coachman to stay? Genuine social protestors had begun to intermingle with pickpockets and ruffians from the rookeries. No one had been seriously hurt so far, but he was uneasy not knowing where she was. The mood of the crowd was turning uglier by the moment. Armed with rotten food and clubs, a mob of male troublemakers had banded together to overturn an empty carriage.

The coachman of the abused vehicle cringed behind a lamppost, emerging moments later as a Bow Street van veered around the corner. The ruffians broke formation to scatter into lanes and alleyways as several patrolmen wielding staffs came running down the street.

"Get in quickly!" a familiar voice shouted above the chaos.

Heath turned in time to see a trim black carriage draw to a stop alongside them.

"It's Odham," Hermia said. She gave Heath a tug in the direction of the street. "My ancient enemy is finally making himself of use. Do you think he might have rescued Julia?"

"I doubt it," he said, glancing behind them in concern. "She could have escaped through the back of the hall. Or perhaps my driver returned early and found her."

"I hope so." Hermia shuddered and glanced back at the unruly crowd.

An egg sailed over their heads and splattered on the pavement. "Heavens!" Odham exclaimed from his carriage. "This place has become a battlefield. Do get inside."

The carriage door swung open. Odham's liveried footman hurried forward to help Hermia ascend the folding steps. Heath stared into the carriage's interior, his face darkening with worry. He was going back to find her, and if anything had happened to her, he could blame only himself.

"You haven't seen Julia anywhere, have you, Odham?"

The earl sat forward with a frown. "Not a sign of her. Don't tell me you've left her alone in that brawl."

Heath drew back outside, his voice brusque. "Take Hermia home."

"We are not going anywhere," Hermia said stoutly. "Not until Julia is found."

"Move along here." A craggy-faced constable in a woolen overcoat strode up behind them. "What the blazes—that isn't you, Lord Boscastle?"

Heath gave the Bow Street patrolman a grim smile. The man was one of Heath's informants and a good soul. "Yes, it is, and don't ask me why I am here. Just help me find—" He pushed around the constable in relief. "There she is." Thank God. He exhaled slowly. He felt his entire body relax. Only to tense again with an altogether different concern.

His eyes narrowed in speculation as he noticed a slender young man in black beside her, his arm placed protectively around her shoulders, his body both a shield and a weapon against the boisterous mob. Julia looked neither frightened nor overly distressed by the experience.

"Is she all right?" Hermia demanded impatiently from the carriage.

Heath shook off the disturbing sensation that seemed to squeeze his heart. What was it? Fear for her? Some arrogant sense of damaged pride that he'd failed as her protector? Was it jealousy? Sheer jealousy to see another man holding her? That would be ridiculous considering that she would marry his friend a few weeks from now. The emotion raged inside him nonetheless.

"Julia appears to be fine," he heard himself saying. "There is a man with her."

"A man? A stranger? Well, for the love of heaven," Hermia said, "stop scowling like that and rescue her."

He forced a smile. "I'm not all that sure she wants to be rescued." But she would be, whether she appreciated it

or not. She had not just put him through hell while
another man stepped forward to do his duty.

Julia wriggled away from her rescuer, discreetly shrug-
ging off his arm. He was a sweet young man, if rather over-
bearing and full of himself, but he seemed to believe she
was as fragile as a glass figurine. Which was a precious if
erroneous sentiment. Julia had realized long ago that there
wasn't a trace of crystalline delicacy in her character. She
was composed of more durable stuff, basic English chalk-
stone with a sturdy vein of granite. Not that she could not
break, but it took a strong blow. She suspected she'd suffered quite a few good cracks deep inside where they didn't
show. She could not take many more, however. Even chalk-
stone crumbled over time.

She sighed in relief as she spotted Heath standing on the
pavement. Amazing that the man could threaten and make
her feel safe at the same time. How awful to realize that she
had already come to anticipate his presence. That the lack
of it affected her.

She disengaged herself once again from her rescuer's
arm, which had somehow slipped back around her shoulder while she was searching for Heath and Hermia.

"I have to go now." She turned briefly to look up into the
man's brown eyes. He had the tousled black curls and
spoiled, sensual mouth of a romantic, this gallant baron
who had come to her aide and attached himself to her like
a limpet. "Thank you ever so much for acting as my
guardian angel."

He glanced past her to the street. Heath had just dodged
a carriage, his stride purposeful and swift. "Your hus-

band?" he asked with the deep sigh of a man accustomed
to losing at love.

Heath. Her husband. Her gaze drifted back to the broad-
shouldered figure hurrying across the street. The mere suggestion of belonging to him swamped her with a wave of
guilty pleasure. What a pair they would make. Was it possible they might have married if the war had not taken him
away? What was she thinking? He'd said he regretted that
they had never been lovers. Not anything more.

"Heavens, no. Not my husband."

"Your fiancé?"

She laughed a little uneasily, edging away. People were
rushing about them in all directions. Another police van
had pulled up at the pavement.

"No. He's not my fiancé. Look, we're going to get arrested in a minute. You really have to escape."

His heavily lashed brown eyes widened in understanding. "Your protector? Ah."

Julia's lips tightened, and she found herself quite at a loss
for words. How was she supposed to explain her complicated association with Heath to a virtual stranger? She did
not quite understand it herself, and Heath probably didn't,
either. "Well, you might call him my protector."

He nodded, studying her with renewed, mildly insulting
interest. "It's all right. You needn't be embarrassed. I am a
man of the world."

Julia choked back an indignant denial. Now he thought
her a ladybird, a woman of loose morals. That was exactly
what she needed. "I'm quite sure you are, my lord, but that
does not make me your equivalent."

"Please call me Raphael."

"Fine." She was growing nervous, more concerned with

their present situation than anything. Two policemen were heading toward them with heavy clubs. Even more menacing was the disapproval that darkened Heath's face as he advanced on the baron. It gave her pause. He was famous for hiding his feelings.

His anger was certainly evident now, bare and elemental.

Her rescuer must have noticed it, too. The baron dropped her arm and attempted to melt back into the dwindling crowd. Suddenly she felt him freeze, and his gaze met hers in dread. "Boscastle," he said, sounding none too pleased at the realization. "You're under *Boscastle's* protection?"

"In a manner of . . ." She glanced around, dimly aware that Brentford had made good his escape. A moment later she felt herself jostled up against a taller, harder male body, familiar and yet not. Heath's arm encircled her waist. A sultry warmth flooded her as their eyes met. In the back of her mind she wondered why she responded to him like this. Did Russell have the same effect on her? Of course not. The Boscastle charm was legendary.

"I've been looking for you everywhere," he said in a steel-edged voice.

The concern in his piercing blue eyes warred with the anger of his tone. She had not meant to worry him. Heaven above, she had not planned the riot. "I came out the back door with a man."

"So I noticed," he said coldly. "Did he introduce himself?"

"Baron Something or Other." She was fully aware he had not removed his hand from her waist. The closeness felt possessive, personal, a little sinful, and far too pleasant. Heath's eyes narrowed in realization. "Baron Brentford," he said in contempt. "I knew I'd seen him before. He was staring at you at the breakfast party. He's a known rake, Julia."

"I gathered that. I take it you don't like him?"

"Like him?" He stared over her shoulder into the street. "The rotten little bastard kissed my sister Chloe behind a carriage in the park. In front of witnesses."

"My goodness. How criminal of them."

"Chloe was exiled for her part. Brentford narrowly escaped with his life. My brother Grayson wanted his head."

"It's still there. His head, I mean."

"Move along please, my lord." One of the policeman, apparently recognizing Heath, gave him a friendly warning. "It's about to turn nasty, I'm afraid. We don't want the young lady to witness any acts of violence."

"Thank you," Heath said, drawing Julia past the police van. "I'll deal with Brentford later."

"He didn't do anything except to help me outside."

"His arm was around your shoulder."

Some devilish impulse got the better of her as they made a dash for the earl's carriage. "Your arm is around my waist."

He glanced down at her, his blue eyes both reproachful and a little wicked. Julia's heart gave an unexpected, painful flutter. "So it is." He shook his head. His usual good humor seemed to be returning. "You're rather like her, you know."

She paused as he handed her up the carriage steps. Was a confession in the offing? "Like her?"

"My sister. You have a way of finding trouble."

"I've never found trouble in my entire life, Boscastle," she said with a rueful smile, then added, "I've never needed to, unfortunately. Somehow it has always managed to find me."

Heath laid his head back against the squabs, staring out the carriage window to the cobbled street. He hoped his coachman did not encounter any troublemakers. Now that he knew Julia was safe, he had the luxury of analyzing the situation a little more logically. Brentford, the sneaky bastard, had made a furtive getaway when he'd spotted Heath coming toward him. He knew that the baron had recognized him, even though they had never actually met. The man appeared to be a bloody coward as well as a rake. He shouldn't be surprised.

Baron Brentford, the handsome buck who had all but led Heath's younger sister down the road of social ruin. Not that Chloe had needed a helping hand. She had practically paved the original path with her own missteps. She had all but sent out engraved invitations to every eligible bachelor in London. If she hadn't ended up happily married to Viscount Stratfield, the Boscastle brothers would have made Brentford pay.

The Earl of Odham rapped his cane on the roof, and the carriage lurched forward. Hermia settled back breathlessly on the seat that faced him.

"What are you doing here anyway, Odham?" she asked with a sniff of grudging gratitude.

"I thought you might require help," the earl said, shaking his head. "This lecture was bound to end in a rumble. I did tell you that."

"I wish someone had told me," Heath said, crossing his arms over his chest. He'd never been involved in anything like this. He'd probably read about it in the paper tomorrow.

"There was no need to come, Odham," Hermia said, but not with great conviction. "Boscastle is our bodyguard. He protected me as a knight would a queen."

"Look at the egg on his sleeve," Odham pointed out. "He didn't protect himself from that."

Heath caught the fleeting grin that crossed Julia's face. The irritating thing was that he found himself tempted to grin back at her. She probably thought it was quite amusing that he'd been frantic to locate her. He cleared his throat. "Odham, kindly have your driver drop me off at my home after we see the ladies safely inside."

"You cannot go home tonight," Hermia exclaimed. "We have plans to go to the theater. Isn't that right, Odham?"

"Indeed," the earl replied with a frown. "And a far better choice of entertainment for two tender-hearted damsels such as these. Don't you agree, Boscastle?"

Heath drew a breath at the unexpected pressure of warm, gloved fingertips on his knee. He looked down in fascination and saw Julia's hand sliding back to her lap. Heat suffused his body, as disconcerting as a flame against bare flesh. Without even knowing how it had happened, he had an erection that throbbed inside his trousers. He raised his eyes to hers and hoped his stark hunger did not show. Hoped he could hide it from her if not from himself.

She hesitated, her lips parting as his gaze fastened on hers. He ought to teach her to touch him at her own peril. Did she not realize her own appeal? "I thought, well, I was thinking of a—"

"Yes?" Obviously she'd guessed what was on his mind. He had admitted his desire for her the other night, after all, and she had more than a rough notion of how she'd affected him in the past. She shouldn't touch him, not knowing how he would react. The frightening part was that he did not know himself. She frowned, looking suddenly confused, on guard. Well, good. Wasn't that what he wanted?

"You don't have to go with us tonight, you know," she said in a quiet voice. "I will be perfectly fine with Hermia and Odham."

Chapter 12

Heath had no intention of allowing Julia to attend the theater without him, although in his heart of hearts he wondered whether it had less to do with protecting her for Russell's sake than it did with his own personal feelings. He enjoyed her company far too much for comfort. But having begun this game, he would play it to the end. He owed her that, no matter if he did not know the rules they were to follow. Neither of them were innocent, but perhaps knowledge was not an advantage. He liked a challenge, yes, but a challenge to his wits, perhaps even to his life. Gambling at love posed a different liability, more powerful than sexual need, more dangerous. Lust he could control, pay the cost, and even raise the stakes.

He stood alone for several moments in the welcome darkness of his own private study. If he were a drinking man, he would get foxed, let his demons out on a long leash, and revel in hell for the duration.

As it was, he would have to wrestle those demons, balance his secret desire for Julia, in bleak sobriety. At least here at home he had the peace to prepare for battle, to brace himself against temptation.

Peace, that was, for approximately ten seconds. The pounding at the front door, the boisterous male voices that followed it, alerted him to the arrival of his brothers, Grayson and Drake.

Peace, alas, would have to be postponed. Family came first.

His brothers took over the drawing room, filling the house with male energy and lighthearted, bawdy banter. Grayson Boscastle, the eldest, the Marquess of Sedgecroft, lounged across the white brocade sofa in all his arrogant grace. Blond, muscular, gregarious, he had recently married and vowed to reform his wicked ways.

Their younger brother, Lieutenant Lord Drake Boscastle, more closely resembled Heath in both looks and temperament. Tall, lean, with short black hair and angular features, he shared Heath's talent for espionage, his intensely private nature. He'd also developed a taste for adventure and dangerous women. He was like Heath and unlike him, an unknown element in the family line.

All three brothers claimed the compelling blue eyes and passionate character that made them irresistible to the opposite sex. Devon, their younger brother, who was not present, was a rogue in his own right.

"To what," Heath demanded, leaning back against the sideboard, "do I owe the dubious honor of this visit?"

Drake's firm mouth curved into a smile. "Rumors abound about you, dear brother. The women of the family have sent us to investigate."

The women being Jane Boscastle, Grayson's lovely and lively wife, and their sisters Emma and Chloe, the last of whose wings had hopefully been clipped by her recent wedding to Viscount Stratfield.

Grayson's handsome face brightened with friendly deviltry. "Word on the street is that you, our discreet, most secretive sibling, almost got himself involved in a riot."

Heath did not say a word.

"And," Drake continued, "there was a woman involved."

Grayson grinned. "Isn't there always?"

Drake sighed. "In the best situations."

Heath pushed away from the sideboard. "You hopeless fools have not investigated well enough, or you'd realize that there were *two* women involved." He paused, allowing himself a strained smile. "And one of them is our old friend Julia Hepworth."

Drake's eyes met his in brief acknowledgment, indicating that he'd known all along and had not betrayed him. They shared the same passion for secrecy in their personal affairs. "Dear Julia, gorgeous and redheaded, if I remember correctly."

Grayson lowered his arms. "The woman who shot you from a horse? She's got you rioting in the streets now?"

"I'm afraid it's rather more involved than that." Heath glanced again at Drake. "In fact, I think you ought to visit her yourself, Drake. Keep her company for an hour or two until I see her later tonight."

Drake pulled down the cuffs of his tailored sleeves. "Done. I never refuse the opportunity to visit a beautiful woman, even if I am a replacement."

"As I am," Heath said drily.

"Done?" Grayson said in confusion. "Just like that, and—" His face cleared. "There's something more going on. And Drake knows. When will I ever learn? The pair of you have always dabbled in intrigues. Dear God, don't tell me this woman who shot you is a spy?"

Heath threw back his head and laughed. "Not exactly. I am acting as Julia's escort for Althorne, who *is* a spy. We might have lost the war if we'd had women like Julia and your wife working against us."

"Which reminds me," Grayson said, not questioning him further even if he might suspect there was more to this story. "Are you coming to Jane's dinner party tonight, Heath?"

"Could we arrange another night? I'm escorting Julia and her aunt to the theater, I'm afraid. With the Earl of Odham."

"Odd old Odham?" Grayson asked in disbelief. "That aging roué is still kicking about?"

Heath nodded in amusement. "We could all learn a thing or two from him, I suspect."

Drake rose from his chair. "What or whom are you investigating anyway?"

"What do we know about Baron Brentford?"

Drake frowned. "Probably not enough, if it's the same man who disgraced Chloe. It's past time we looked into his background."

Two minutes later Drake Boscastle had taken a cab from the fashionable bachelor's town house to fulfill his promise, leaving Heath and Grayson alone. "What has Brentford done now?" Grayson asked, his voice deep with displeasure.

"He was a bit too friendly with Julia at the lecture hall earlier this evening."

Grayson stretched out his legs. "He had his eye on Jane once, before his botched attempt to seduce Chloe. Jane, fortunately, was too involved with me to respond to him, and the rest is history."

Heath smiled. "Naturally."

"So tell your older, wiser brother," Grayson continued, folding his hands over his flat stomach, "what is this sudden devotion to a woman who shot you in the shoulder? Spill the soup."

"Are you referring to Julia?"

"Unless another female has shot you. Confess. What is she to you?"

An obsession. A need, a desire so deeply entwined in the past and present that he could not seem to remove her without cutting to the core of who he was.

"I suppose she is duty."

Grayson looked skeptical. "Odd way to put it."

"No, she really is. I have been commissioned to protect her."

"Do explain."

Which he did, grateful that Grayson listened without bursting into laughter or inserting a snide comment here and there. Grateful that he was part of the passionate Boscastle clan and could depend on its collective loyalty even if he had spent half his life getting his siblings out of trouble, defending the whole sorry lot of them.

Yet now *he* was in trouble, of the very worst sort. An affair of the heart, the sort of hazardous entanglement he had managed to elude until now.

"Am I asking you for advice, Grayson?"

"If you are, it's a first. In fact, it has always been the

other way around. You, Heath, are the one we all seek for direction and cool logic."

"I believe I am in this too thick to advise myself."

"Heath Boscastle, spymaster and unwitting heart-breaker, seeking the advice of one of London's premier, re-formed rakes," Grayson mused. "Well, who better to ask?" He sat up, frowning in realization. "And you say that Julia is engaged to that male whore?"

"Sir Russell Althorne?" Heath was taken aback. He'd assumed that Russell's sexual indiscretion had been a well-kept secret. He'd certainly never told. "Grayson, are we talking about the same man?"

Grayson snorted in contempt. "I've never told you, and I doubt Althorne has any idea, but I happen to be his land-lord. I don't want it to become common knowledge, mind you. Collecting rent makes me sound rather mercenary, al-though the money never touches my hands."

"And how does this make *him* a male whore?"

"He was looking for a convenient place to keep his mis-tress near the club."

"Near the club?"

"Well, it makes sense. Pop into the club for a brandy, then pop down the street for a different sort of stimula-tion."

Heath's chest tightened with an unpleasant sensation that he vaguely identified as resentment. He should have known that Russell's promise of future fidelity to Julia was a lie. He felt betrayed on his own behalf, but even more so on Julia's. If Grayson knew, then it was only a matter of time before she discovered the deception.

"I'm glad to be done with that sort of life," Grayson added as an afterthought. "You've never been that type, though. I've always admired your discretion. A little more trouble, but worth it in the end."

"I suppose," Heath said drily, "that Lady Harrington has ordered every kind of refurbishment under the sun for their love nest."

"Lady Harrington?" Grayson looked blank. "What does she have to do with anything?"

"She's Russell's mistress."

"No, she isn't."

Heath's forehead creased in a frown. "Yes, she is. I caught them red—well, red all over, actually."

"You could have caught them tupping upside down on the staircase, but Lucy is not the woman Russell has set up on my property. This female was a voluptuous opera singer who is quite obviously breeding. She also has incredibly large breasts, not that I notice such things."

"A pregnant opera singer?" Heath said in a cynical voice. He was tired of making excuses for Russell. "And there is no chance that this is his payoff to her, his way of thanking her for her *past* services?"

"There was nothing 'past' about their affair as it was reported to me," Grayson said, raising his brow. "The expanding chanteuse let my factor know that she and Russell intend to put their nest to good use after he returns from Paris."

Another mistress. Another infidelity. Another lie. And now a child would be involved. It was a mess of the most distasteful nature. Heath was sure Julia did not have any idea. She would have shot Russell right through his disloyal heart if she'd known. He felt like shooting him himself.

"Why did you not tell me this before?" he asked, more incensed by the moment.

"I thought you were above gossip."

"I am, but . . ."

Grayson's blue eyes danced with unholy perception. "You're not above Julia? Good Lord, this is rather sudden."

Heath ground his jaw. He wouldn't call six years sudden, but Grayson had no way of knowing that. "I have cared about her for some time," he admitted after a long hesitation.

"Give me a few moments to recover from my shock. There. Now. What are we to do?"

Heath came out of his chair, restless, aware that he had only an hour or two to make inquiries about Brentford. "What do you think I should do?"

Grayson grinned like a satyr. "I know exactly what you should do. This happens to be my area of expertise."

"And?"

"Seduce her. It's quite simple."

"There's nothing simple about my relationship with Julia."

"There would be if you reduced it to basic terms." Grayson gave a deep pleasurable sigh. "It worked well enough for Jane and me. I seduced that woman senseless before I married her." He paused. "She seduced me in a far more subtle way. I am more convinced every day that I could not live without her."

Grayson's reference to his wife and to the tantalizing game of seduction they had played in the period before their marriage gave Heath pause. Grayson and Jane belonged together. Everyone knew it. And yet the course of their true love had been a crooked road indeed.

"You desire her," Grayson said, the words a statement of fact.

Heath picked up an unopened letter on his desk. A half smile played at the corners of his mouth.

"She desires you," Grayson continued. "You care for her, and she cares for you. This is mutual misery."

"I—"

"Then what the deuce are you waiting for? Take her to bed. Make her your own. It is your turn."

"There is the matter of her fiancé. My superior and friend. He did save my life."

"The male whore?" Grayson snapped his long elegant fingers. "He's sent you into danger as repayment several times since then, and reaped the acclaim. Besides, a Boscastle recognizes no competition. Don't be so damn decent that she slips away from you."

Heath turned the letter over. "I have no wish to hurt her."

"Hurt her? My God. Devise an infallible strategy. Seduction is a pleasurable game, not a mortal battle."

"A pleasurable game. A strategy." He had never thought of plotting out a love affair. He rather liked the idea. Why not apply intellect to winning the woman he wanted?

Grayson shrugged expansively. "Always glad to be of help, Heath. Having been taken out of the game of love as a free spirit, so to speak, I can at least share my secrets. And wish you as much happiness as I've been given."

The game of love. The game of seduction. Heath wondered why he'd never thought of romance or courtship in such a provocative manner before. Perhaps because he had not cared enough. And yet was it not the most tantalizing challenge of all? To lose oneself in a woman only to emerge as a victor? Russell obviously intended to continue betraying her. To have his cake and eat it, too. The rules had changed before Heath had even grasped them. How far would he take his role as protector? Did it include defending her against Russell's infidelity?

He was not certain where his loyalty should lie. With Russell? With Julia? Or with himself? Or was this soul-searching an exercise in self-deception? Was he merely looking for an excuse to take what he wanted?

He'd been so blindly arrogant in his previous romantic affairs, taking the ladies who loved him for granted, secretly believing himself above the web of deceit and aimless desire that ruined lives. In sympathetic amusement he had watched his brothers pursue their conquests like a pack of animals, wild, unrestrained, merciless seducers of the opposite sex. How many times had he laughed at friends trapped in the throes of love, complaining at the club of their misery?

He had been the lone wolf, preferring to remain unattached unless he could have the woman he wanted. Julia's marriage had been an obstacle, and the timing had been off. War had come between them, as had the impetuous mistake they'd made in their youth. Then Russell had barred the way, erecting the thorns of friendship and duty. Heath could only blame himself for missing his chance with her. But he was not about to make the same mistake again. He wouldn't learn to live with losing her again.

Russell had broken the most basic of rules. He had betrayed both his friend and his fiancée. He'd lied too easily to Heath as well as to Julia, and apparently would continue to do so. He would be unfaithful to his wife as he climbed the ladder to the top of the castle and made the betrayed princess his queen. Such behavior might be common in Society, but not in the Boscastle breed. Seductions were a family trait. Betrayals, no.

"The hero of London." Heath tossed the unopened letter on his desk in disdain. "The king of the castle—no, cad of the castle is more like it."

There was a faint clumping of footsteps in the hall, a movement at the door. A behemoth shadow fell upon the thick Oriental carpet, obscuring its masses of bloodred peonies. "Are you in for the evening, my lord?" a deep voice like a funeral bell intoned.

Heath turned toward the imposing personage who blocked the entire doorway. Hamm had been a trooper in his brigade, a capable swordsman and loyal friend who had charged in the cavalry alongside him. Together they had cut down their fair share of French dragoons in ice and mist. Hamm presented a ferocious enough appearance that he still frightened the housemaids, whom he teased and protected in his lumbering way.

"Actually, Hamm, I am going to the theater."

The gigantic footman stepped into the room, giving his master a covert once-over. His gaze lingered on the egg that had dried in a crusty mess on Heath's sleeve. "You will require a fresh change of clothes, my lord?"

"Yes, and a shave. I don't suppose Sir Russell has sent word from Dover?"

"No, my lord. The War Office has promised to alert you should the need arise."

Heath met the middle-aged Yorkshireman's gaze. It was

Hamm, along with Russell, who had rescued Heath from the tiny Portuguese convent where he had hidden after his escape, after suffering tortures he'd mercifully forgotten. His body bore the scars, but his mind had found a welcome oblivion. Hamm had lost both his brothers and his father in the war. He never spoke of them, but Heath knew he grieved in his quiet way.

"It's too soon yet," Heath said. "I expect he has more important things to accomplish than sending letters home."

Hamm nodded, his gaze oddly guarded. "Sir Russell can fend for himself, my lord," he said after a pause. "He always has."

Chapter 13

Hermia entered Julia's bedroom unannounced, her long-sleeved dark-gold crepe dress reflecting the soft glints of candlelight. "Good heavens, Julia, put down that sketch pad. You're not dressed, and we shall be leaving in a few minutes."

"Hmm?" Julia did not look up. Her frown of displeasure deepened as she regarded the sketch propped against her upraised knees.

"It's criminal," Hermia said without preamble, plunking her sizable posterior onto the bed.

Julia sighed. "That I'm not properly dressed or that you barged in without knocking?"

Hermia attempted to peer over the hillock of Julia's knees. "Neither. I was referring to Odham's shameless pursuit of a woman my age."

Julia covered her sketch with her hands. "I think it's rather sweet."

"Sweet. The old scoundrel. What is it you are drawing in such secrecy, Julia? Do show me. Is it a naked man?"

"A naked man? Oh, really."

"A naked Heath Boscastle?"

"Honestly, Hermia. All I can say is thank goodness he has gone home for an hour. I can finally catch my breath."

Hermia compressed her lips as Julia carefully leaned forward to bury the sketchbook in the brass-hinged chest at the foot of the bed. "I could put several meanings on that statement."

Julia decided she would have to find a new hiding place for her sketch later tonight. She didn't trust Hermia's sneaky nature for a second. Or her curiosity.

She slid off the bed and carefully smoothed out the folds of her shimmering eggshell-white silk evening gown. "Have you seen my sapphire bracelet?"

"Don't try to change the subject, my dear. I feel safer with Heath here, Julia. Protected."

"Well, I don't." She tugged a fringed paisley shawl out from beneath Hermia's posterior. "I feel rather endangered, if you must know."

"Endangered?" Hermia's brows lifted in disbelief. "By Boscastle? He'd kill anyone who came near you. Unless you are referring to a different kind of danger."

"Damnation," Julia muttered, "where *is* that bracelet?"

"On the table in front of you. How does Heath endanger you, Julia?"

Julia fastened the clasp of her bracelet. Hesitating, she picked up a pair of elbow-length kidskin gloves from the bed. "It is not a comfortable situation, not for either of us."

Hermia's light green eyes glittered with understanding. "I'd say he looks more than comfortable with you."

Julia stared at her other glove as if she couldn't remember how to put it on. "I'm afraid Russell blackmailed Heath into guarding me."

"Blackmailed? Do you mean that Heath has a criminal past to be held over his head?"

"I mean nothing of the sort. It's just that Heath is too honorable for his own good." And Russell did not realize what he had done, putting the two of them back together.

"How can a man be too honorable?"

Julia struggled to fit her fingers into the glove. "I wish you'd convince him he doesn't need to stay here any longer."

"I shall do nothing of the sort," Hermia retorted. "I enjoy him, Julia, and so do you. I have come to view him as our personal Apollo. A bit on the devilish side, perhaps, but what woman could complain?"

Hermia rose and went to the door to wait.

Julia shook her head in chagrin. "Our personal Apollo."

"You do not find him unbearably handsome?"

She allowed her aunt to exit into the hall before her. "That is hardly the question." It was, however, a great part of her dilemma. Handsome, sexually irresistible, gentle at all the right times. It distressed Julia to discover that, at her age, after all her experience, she could be tempted.

Hermia paused at the top of the staircase, her breasts quivering below her Baroque pearl necklace. "A god in the hand is worth two on Olympus. I shall be quite crushed if you dismiss him as our protector."

Julia had just come down the stairs and stepped into the hall when she noticed a dark, arresting man standing alone in the dim, tapestried recess. He swiveled on his heel at her approach. Her gloved hand clutched the smooth mahogany handrail, and she paused, meeting his gaze in silence.

A shock of pleased surprise ran through her, followed almost immediately by a sting of disappointment. At first glance he could have been easily mistaken for Heath. He had been blessed with the same thick black hair and devilish elegance, that air of breathtaking virility that commanded attention. Strong shoulders, the deceptively lean frame that wore evening clothes so well.

And his eyes. Those deep Boscastle blue eyes, that assessed and consumed a woman with a polite hunger that left her breathless. She felt herself scrutinized by an expert stare that was flattering and not at all insulting.

"Hello, Julia," Drake said, striking her as warm, manly, and altogether disconcerting, in the best of ways. "I'm Heath's brother, Drake. Do you remember me?"

"Of course, I do." Heavens, one wouldn't forget him. "How good to see you after all this time. You're looking, well . . ." She could hardly say he looked almost as indecently attractive as his brother. "Well. Yes, *very* well."

His gaze took another appreciative journey over her silk-draped form. "So are you. Very, *very* well."

She laughed. There was a wealth of playful sensuality in his eyes that must drive women wild. He resembled his older brother, although his face seemed a trifle harder, the angles broader, the appeal more raw than refined. Drake definitely fell into the category of dangerous but oh-so-desirable rogues. She could hardly imagine growing up in that household of untamed males. One Boscastle man was more than enough to keep her on her toes.

"Are you my gaolkeeper for the night?" she asked.

"That obvious, is it?" He smiled into her eyes. "Ah, and I was hoping to pass myself off as your companion."

She released a sigh. Her instincts told her she could trust him. "Your brother is breathing down my neck like a dragon. I swear the man never lets down his guard. He has eyes in the back of his head, and he can see through doors."

Drake gave a deep appreciative laugh. "That would be Heath. The Sphinx, we call him. There's no one in the whole of England quite like the clever fiend."

"Yes," she said, glancing away guiltily. "I knew that."

He grinned at her as if they'd become instant allies. They had his enigmatic sibling in common. "You could always shoot him again if he really becomes unbearable."

"I shall never live that down."

He gave her a conspiratorial smile and took her arm, his strong hand curling over hers. "And why would you want to?" he asked with open approval. "I'd be proud of myself, were I you. We have all wanted to shoot him at one time or another."

Chapter 14

❧❧❧

Heath stood unseen at the back of the private theater box, his eyes adjusting to the dimness. The ripe odor of spilled ale, half-eaten oranges, and candle wax from the pit below thickened the air. Countless footmen hovered at every turn, and he'd had a struggle reaching the upper boxes. He seemed to have timed his arrival well; the green baize curtain would close at any moment.

The performance had just concluded, the new Irish actress Miss O'Neill had brought down the house, and the audience had burst into wild applause.

In the private boxes around him, however, various other, more interesting dramas were still being played out, low-voiced introductions, flirtations over fans, whispered invitations to seduction.

He frowned as he scanned the figures still seated before him, none as yet aware of his presence. The Earl of Odham appeared deep in discussion with Hermia. The top of Julia's head, that lushly coiled auburn hair, shone in the candlelight, but the rest of her curvaceous form was blocked by a man leaning a little too intimately across her seat.

Who, he wondered, straightening, was this nuisance?

Not his brother Drake, who was sitting with a pair of binoculars trained on an opposite box. On some comely female, Heath would guess. At least Drake had not left her side. He moved closer, unable to identify the face of Julia's admirer. The man turned his head. Heath's eyes darkened in recognition.

Julia's companion was the same intense young man who had come to her rescue earlier in the day during the minor riot. Baron Brentford. The same man who had disgraced Chloe in public.

Coincidence or not?

Heath did not anger easily. Nor did he typically jump to conclusions. It was not remarkable to meet a member of the ton at the opera. In the brief rush of their encounter at the lecture hall, Julia had conceivably not mentioned that she was engaged to Russell.

Perhaps she *had* mentioned that she would be at the theater tonight.

Heath tensed at the sudden movement from the box. His rushed inquiries into Brentford's past on his way here had yielded no helpful information. Brentford was a self-indulgent buck, a gambler, a ne'er-do-well who was fast squandering his inheritance. His family line was authentic if not impressive.

Julia's ivory lace fan had risen in the air and come down on Brentford's wrist. Coincidental meeting or not, a fan brought down upon a man's hand held a universal meaning. Either Brentford's attention had strayed where not invited, or Julia was flirting with him. Either way, Heath intended to put a stop to it.

"Well, good evening everyone," he said with forced

friendliness, sweeping Brentford a hostile look before his gaze pierced Julia.

She glanced up, her eyes widening in surprise. And welcome. She did not bother to hide her pleasure at his arrival. A sense of satisfaction softened the edges of his anger. The hunger he felt for her temporarily swept all other thoughts from his mind. He drew a breath. This would not do. He could not afford to lose sight of his purpose just because she looked at him in a certain way.

He glanced at Drake. "Kindly escort everyone to the carriage. Julia's friend and I are going to have a few words alone."

Odham, grasping the situation, nodded in understanding and bent to assist Hermia from her seat. Drake extended his hand to Julia. She stared up at Heath in resigned appeal. "Words only," she said in an undertone. "He is quite harmless."

"Is he?" Heath said, his smile tight.

Brentford straightened as if he had just received a death sentence; his soulful brown eyes followed Julia from the box. "Will I see you again?" he called after her, clearly not realizing he had overstepped his bounds. "Will I—"

Heath cleared his throat. "I appreciate your gallantry at the lecture hall earlier, Brentford, but I shall take over from here. You see, the lady is engaged."

"Well, yes, but I meant I might see her at another time."

"Engaged to be married," Heath said between his teeth.

Brentford's horrified gaze returned to Heath. "Married? To *you*?"

"To my friend."

"Oh, thank God," Brentford said, closing his eyes in such relief that Heath almost felt sorry for him.

"You're pathetic, Brentford. I really should have thrashed you to kingdom come for kissing my sister in the park that day. In fact, if I didn't suspect Chloe was as much to blame for the incident, you would not be standing here tonight."

Brentford held up his hands in self-defense. "I would have married your sister had Sedgecroft allowed me anywhere near the house to ask. I dared not even show my face at his door."

Heath gave him a cold, unforgiving look. He disliked Brentford, but there was some truth to what he said. Still, the baron was the sort of moonstruck fool who fell in love with every pretty lady he met. He needed to be taken down a peg or two. And he needed to stay away from Julia. Heath intended to make that point perfectly clear.

"You're too late to propose anyway," he said. "Chloe is happily married to a man who would murder anyone who looked at her twice."

Brentford nodded in defeat. "Dominic Breckland. Yes, I know. Lucky devil."

"*Dangerous* devil. As is Julia's betrothed, Sir Russell Althorne. I assume you know of him?"

The baron flinched for all the world like a frightened schoolboy. "Of course I do. You're all dangerous, aren't you?"

Heath glanced around, assessing his surroundings. Drake and Julia had probably not battled their way through the crush in the lobby yet. He was suddenly impatient to be with her alone. His earlier conversation with Grayson had helped crystallize what he felt for her. Observing her with Brentford had brought all his deeper instincts into play. He meant to make a move.

Having confronted the dark truth of his desire, there was no turning back. If he did not act to win her, she would marry Russell, and he would lose her forever. For years he had denied what she meant to him. He would not deny his need for her now. Nor would he be denied. Nothing mattered now but keeping her safe. And keeping her for himself.

"I think," the baron said, casting a doleful look around the empty box, "that when I take my private fencing lesson in the morning, I shall ask my instructor to strike me straight through the heart."

Heath shook his head. He'd had enough of Brentford's self-pitying disposition. "If you do not control your amorous impulses with Lady Whitby, you will not need to seek death. It will be waiting on your doorstep, I promise you."

He did not know why he had been so lenient with Brentford. The bloody fool deserved a good scare once and for all. Brentford had no idea how fortunate he was to have escaped the wrath of the Boscastle clan not once, but twice. Heath did not consider himself to be hotheaded. If he had to confront the baron, it would be on a field at dawn and not in a public place. But for now seduction beckoned more than battle.

He fought his way through the swarm of attendees crowding the candlelit lobby, politely brushing off the friends who called to him, the ladies who looked at him in hopeful recognition. He had no time for them. No interest in their invitations, the talk of politics or parties.

One single goal burned in his mind, one desire, a single destination.

He caught sight of her near the door, Drake guarding her

on one side, Odham and Hermia standing sentinel on the other. Julia glanced up unexpectedly and grinned in recognition. Her semibare shoulders gleamed in the candlelight. She looked so beautiful tonight he could not stop staring at her.

A wave of fire consumed him. A white-hot awareness of her that electrified, galvanized him into action. She beckoned him over to her, her gray eyes warm and unguarded, a woman who had no reason to play games. A woman he wanted so badly he could feel the heat of it igniting in his bones. The more he saw of her, the more he desired her. Or perhaps he was of an age when he no longer cared to wait for what he wanted. He felt his blood stir in anticipation, his senses thrum with arousal. He savored the feeling, allowed it to spread.

He smiled back at her, took an instinctive step around a cluster of people. Then stopped, his senses frozen by a primordial chill of apprehension, a warning, a very different awareness from his incendiary attraction to Julia.

A sense of being watched. An unease that gnawed at his nerves. He glanced around, his gaze studying the sea of innocuous faces that swam before him. He strove to discern the source of the sensation. It was impossible in the crush of overperfumed humanity to trace the stare that had singled him out.

He felt a hesitant touch on his arm.

He spun around, his voice sharp. "Who—"

"What is it, Heath?" Julia asked with a concerned smile. "You look as if a ghost had just walked over your grave."

He looked back over her shoulder, his hand closing protectively around hers. Nothing appeared the least bit out of

the ordinary; there were no menacing shadows, no reason
for his reaction.

Still, his primary instinct was to get her safely home. Was
she in danger? From what? From whom? He did not waste
time considering that his urge to protect her from an invisible threat might be irrational. The impulse was too strong
to ignore, and while not infallible, his instincts rarely
proved wrong. He was not willing to take risks where she
was concerned. A friendly voice called his name from behind him. He did not acknowledge it.

Gripping Julia's arm, he guided her swiftly outside the
theater where Odham and Hermia had gone to await them
on the pavement. Julia complied without questioning him,
but her voice dropped to a puzzled tone when the carriage
pulled up alongside them.

"Where," she whispered over her shoulder, "are we
going in such a hurry? I assume there's a reason why we are
in such a rush."

He slid his hand up her arm to her elbow, let it drift to
the small of her back. The threat he felt had dissipated, allowing him to focus on more pleasant matters. He settled
his palm on the firm swell of her backside. She drew a
breath. He drew her nearer. For a moment he simply delighted in the feel of her, the sensual distraction of her
earthy appeal. Julia had opulent curves, well toned but
generous, a woman to arouse, to answer every fantasy.
Imagining her moving underneath, or on top of him, be-
guiled him. He'd learned a lot about pleasing a woman in
the last few years, and what pleased him.

She would please him in bed. He would please her, too.
He took a breath to slow his heartbeat. The fragrance of
her hair teased his senses.

She turned without warning, her eyes slowly lifting to his. Her gaze acknowledged the licentious wandering of his hand. The fleeting smile she gave him did not chastise as much as question his intentions.

"You're touching me," she said under her breath.

He pressed his palm down harder on the rise of her rump. "Yes."

She looked a little mystified, perhaps uncertain why he had stepped outside his role as the stalwart protector in public. His fingers flirted with the warm hollow of her spine. He'd noticed that she did not move. His mouth curled in a smile.

Naturally, he could not tell her that Russell's betrayal had altered his strategy. Not this early in the game. It was unnecessary. Let her assume that his rogue Boscastle blood was finally showing through, coming to a slow boil. He intended to win her fair and square, but with a liberal revision of the old rules. Protecting her would still be his primary concern. Beyond that he would allow himself carte blanche on the playing field. His guidelines for seducing her were fluid, subject to change at a moment's notice.

It was going to be the most pleasurable conquest he had ever made, worth whatever wiles he would have to use.

Hermia gave a loud cough behind them. Heath suppressed a laugh and reluctantly lifted his hand away. Touching Julia tantalized all his senses. He could caress her lovely body for hours on end.

"Are you all right?" she asked, her voice low with curiosity. "Did you quarrel with Brentford?"

"He should not bother you again. I think I made that clear to him." He waited for her to enter the carriage before he climbed up and took the seat across from her, next to Odham. His body felt heavy as he watched her in the dark. Just looking at her, hearing her voice, stirred him.

Julia fussed with a loose button on her glove. "There is no need to hover over me like a nervous nursemaid. The next thing I know you shall be turning me over your knee."

He stroked the scar on his upper lip. "Do not tempt me."

She leaned forward, away from Hermia's watchful guard. "As if you could," she said softly.

"As if you don't deserve it."

"I probably do," she admitted, her eyes glittering.

"Did your husband spank you?" he asked with a challenging smile.

"He wouldn't have dared."

"Not after he gave you that gun."

"I'll have you know that I *never* took a shot at him."

"Did he know how lucky he was?" And he meant in more ways than one.

"I think he was happy enough," she said after a long hesitation.

Which meant that Julia had probably held the upper hand in her marriage. How deeply had she loved her husband? What kind of man had won her heart? Was Russell like him in any way? Before Heath could probe deeper, Drake made an untimely appearance, whistling as he swung his lean, muscular frame into the carriage.

"Good evening, all," he said, his charm undeniable, his black hair spangled with the light rain that had begun to fall. "I hope you haven't been waiting long. I met up with a friend. We're going to a ball after I leave your enjoyable company. That is unless my escort services are required again."

Julia sat forward, her voice firm. "No, they aren't, but

thank you for offering. I won't require your services—I mean, your company—as pleasant as it is. This is beyond absurd. The only person who has approached me in weeks is Brentford, and he is a harmless fool. I can handle the likes of him."

Heath gave Drake a pointed look. "I asked you to take care of her."

Drake's smile was cool but meaningful. "Brentford would not have gone any further, believe me. I had one eye trained on him."

"He certainly is no French spy," Odham remarked.

Hermia shook her head. "One never knows. I daresay, Drake, this means we won't expect to see you again later tonight for cards and conversation."

He gave her an apologetic smile. "Probably not, ma'am. But I did enjoy the play."

"You're going to get soaked," Heath said with a glance at the window. "Borrow my coat."

Rain had begun falling in earnest by the time he removed his black woolen greatcoat to hand to his brother. Hermia lifted the curtain to watch the young man charge off into the rainy night with a friendly wave back at the carriage.

"Enjoyed the play, my foot," she said in amusement. "He did not follow a single scene for flirting across the box at his lady friend."

Julia shivered under her shawl. The night had taken a chill turn. "I believe the tendency to flirt runs in the family."

"He has a marvelous physique," Hermia murmured, returning her shrewd gaze to Heath. "I don't suppose you could talk him into posing for the painting club next month? We still have not found our Hades."

Julia was intensely aware of Heath throughout the short ride home. The way he'd touched her in the street, *where* he had touched her, had stirred her senses into a sweet confusion. She was almost afraid to meet his regard. Or to question what she felt.

The rain had not eased up by the time the four passengers in the carriage made a collective dash into the town house. Hermia insisted that the two men wait out the storm before leaving for the night. Which in Heath's case appeared to be a moot point.

He stated that he had no intention of returning home until he was ready, and nothing Julia could say seemed to shake his resolve. He was as calm and unreadable as usual.

Still, there was a palpable tension about him tonight that intrigued her, a brooding sensuality that she could not overlook. Even the way he studied her had changed. This was a darker Heath than she had encountered, a man whose sharp edges enticed when they should have warned her away. She was drawn to this enigmatic facet of his character. She was drawn to the heated desire he allowed to smolder in his eyes.

She poured brandy for Odham and Hermia as the four of them gathered in the drawing room to talk. Heath settled into an armchair by the window with his gaze searching the rainy street. The servants had lit a robust coal fire.

The room still felt rather cool and damp.

Until Heath turned to scrutinize her, his chin in hand, his gaze heavily lidded and frankly sensual. Unmistakable, the meaning, the fire that flared in those guarded blue eyes.

The power of his look penetrated her entire body, excited her so that she could not think of anything else. She felt his gaze raze through the barrier of her clothes, her promise to another man, their past relationship.

Her knees suddenly weak, she poured herself a generous glass of brandy and sat down on the sofa to sip it. Odham and Hermia were discussing the sensational actress Miss O'Neill, but Julia could not follow the conversation. It was all she could do to appear composed, to hold the glass steady in her hands.

The dark smoke of Heath's stare lingered in her awareness. If she hadn't known better, she would have sworn that for the past hour or so, her protector had been priming her for seduction, and doing a dashed good job of it, too. With only a few looks, a touch, he had, well, reduced her to a state of . . . She didn't want to admit what she felt for him, not even to herself. If she admitted it, then all hell would break loose. She would not be able to go on acting as though he meant nothing to her. She stared down at her hands.

She had finished her brandy without tasting a drop of it. Heath's questioning gaze traveled from her face to the empty glass, then back to her eyes.

"I'm going to bed," she announced suddenly, and feigned an enormous yawn. "Sweet dreams to all of you." She lingered beside her chair, collecting her evening gloves. She wasn't truly tired at all. She would probably read in bed, undress, and— "My bracelet is gone," she said with a soft gasp. "I just realized it's missing."

Heath rose from his chair and came up beside her. "I didn't notice it on you in the carriage. Perhaps you lost it somewhere in the theater."

She frowned. "It's very possible. There was such a crowd. Do you remember seeing it in the theater, Hermia?"

Hermia shook her head. "Come to think, I didn't. You had it on when we left the house."

"I'll check in the morning," Heath said, following her to the door. "Let me walk you up the stairs."

She smiled, her back to him, her nerve endings sizzling at his nearness. "Do you think mortal danger awaits me somewhere between here and my bedchamber?"

His eyes narrowed as he gazed down at her profile. "One never knows. Something more welcome might. Perhaps we'll even find your bracelet."

She felt her heart quicken as he moved up against her. She went still, conscious of the hard length of his body against hers, the muscular support of his thighs through her evening gown. If she turned, she would be flush against him. He hadn't given her room to draw a breath. "You rogue, Heath Boscastle," she said, closing her eyes for a moment. "To think the world believes you are the honorable one."

His jaw brushed the coil of hair at her nape in a blatant caress. Her voice caught at the unexpected pleasure that assailed her. "Did Hermia see you do that?" she asked in an undertone.

"I doubt it," he murmured without a hint of apology. "Let's remove ourselves to the hall just in case."

She broke off. She had been so engrossed in her provocative exchange with Heath that she had not been paying attention to the two other people in the room. All at once she realized that Odham had risen from the sofa and was approaching them, leaving Hermia chattering midsentence. "I shall see Julia safely delivered to her room, Boscastle," he said.

Heath turned in surprise, too much a gentleman to

argue. Julia could have laughed aloud that whatever dev-
ilry he'd had in mind was foiled. Her gaze lifted to his; his
eyes hinted that Odham's interruption was only a reprieve.
But from what?

A moment later she and Odham stood alone together in
the hall.

She had no idea what had brought on the earl's sudden
act of chivalry. It was not characteristic of their relationship. In fact, he looked subdued, uncomfortable, almost
sad. The harsh lines of his face softened as unexpectedly he
took her hand. What had come over him? She realized that
he seemed quite serious, that something must be wrong.

She stared down in trepidation at the gnarled knot of fingers clasping hers. "If Hermia has ordered you from her
life again, I shall remain impartial," she said. "You two are
worse than children. Unless, of course, you resort to
bribery. I—"

He cleared his throat. "I know how unforgiving women
are, Julia. How you never forget an insult."

"What is this about, Odham?" she asked quietly. "You
know Hermia does not take my advice. Hand over those
letters she wrote you, and let us be done with threats."

"Poor Julia." He squeezed the life out of her fingers.
"This does not concern Hermia. It's the rumors about Russell that I heard today at the club."

Her smile felt stiff and artificial. She listened to the
rhythmic patter of rain hammering the streets, the unsteady beat of her heart. "Rumors? What rumors? Has he
been hurt?"

"Nothing of that nature." His gruff face looked almost
pitying. "Infidelities are common enough, and I am certainly not one to cast stones. Yet it becomes altogether dif-

ferent when children are involved. He's having a child with another woman. Well, that is what is being said. Forgive me for being so blunt."

She should have been more shocked, more distraught, more . . . something. Instead, she felt a welcome numbness seep into her bones as she listened to the strangely soothing violence of the rainstorm, the even more soothing sound of Hermia and Heath's voices from behind the drawing room door. She heard Heath's low-pitched laughter, the notes beguiling. He had a lovely, deep voice. How could she have ever forgotten it? How could Russell have been so kind and then betray her? How could he commit his heart when another woman was carrying his child?

"Does Hermia know? Does Heath?"

"Good heavens, no. I have not breathed a word. But perhaps the gossips have got it all wrong," Odham said. "If you wish me to investigate, I shall."

"I don't think that will be necessary." She gently pried her hand from his. "I do appreciate your honesty."

"We don't *know* yet that there's any truth to it."

She swallowed. He must have believed it, or he would never have told her. "You're right. There's no need to rush to judgment."

He heaved a sigh of relief. "I'm glad that's off my chest. At least you will be prepared if it is true. You are all right, Julia?"

Her gaze drifted to the closed door, her thoughts to the darkly alluring man who stood behind it. Her protector. She wanted suddenly to be with him. "I'm perfectly fine, Odham. Thank you. It takes courage to do what you have done."

* * *

She laid her brush down on the dressing table, swiveling around on the stool. The knock at her bedchamber door had been quiet but rather too insistent to ignore. Too tempting, if she were honest with herself. Not Hermia's perfunctory knock when she even remembered to knock. It could only be Heath. Was she ready to face him again? She felt very vulnerable at the moment.

The seed that Odham had planted in her mind had already begun to grow roots. Ghastly, subterranean roots that choked trust and spread insidiously to her heart. That Russell had been unfaithful was painful enough. But Odham had used the word *infidelities*. And a child. There was to be a child.

The knock sounded again. She waited a moment, debating. "Who is it?"

"It's Heath. Are you all right?"

She rose to open the door. Having to defend herself against his dark elegance and sardonic smile pushed her other concerns to the back of her mind. He had removed his evening jacket, and looked all too virile in his black silk vest, white linen shirt, and tight broadcloth trousers. A vulnerable woman, and a virile rogue. A fatal mix, indeed.

"Why would I *not* be all right?" she asked as he invited himself inside.

He brushed around her. "I thought I should make a thorough inspection of your room before you retire. After all, we were gone all night."

"I checked my room," she said, watching him.

"Well, I wanted to make sure your windows are closed. It is raining."

"As if it does not do so every other day in England."

"Ah, yes, but this is the *evening*." He prowled around

the perimeter of the room, making a show of checking behind chairs and furniture. "Did you forget what happened
the other evening when it rained?"

He had come to the window, gazing down in apparent
concentration into the stygian wilderness of the garden.
Julia's arms lowered to her sides. With a worried frown,
she walked toward him. "There isn't anyone in the shed
again, is there?"

He shook his head, glancing at her briefly as their shoulders bumped. Despite the drop in temperature, or perhaps
because of it, Julia found herself drawn to the familiar
warmth of his body. It was tempting to burrow against his
hard-muscled form and not think.

"Julia," he said, staring at her.

"If you're here again in search of the sketch, I've hidden
it elsewhere in the house."

"I don't want the sketch. Well, I do, but that isn't why I
came here."

She brushed her knuckles across the damp windowpane.
His confession intrigued her, but she could not bring herself to ask him to explain, as badly as she wanted to. The
safe thing was to shift the subject. "I wish you had seen the
play tonight. It was quite entertaining."

"Look at me."

Her heart raced at the arresting command in his voice.
She didn't trust herself to look at him. She would probably
melt at his feet like a raindrop on a hot stone. Or go up in
a wisp of steam.

"Miss O'Neill caused a sensation," she murmured.

"Do you think I am the least bit interested?" he asked
mildly, turning to pull her against his chest.

She laid her face on his shoulder, felt the beating of his

heart against her cheek. She could smell the deliciously spicy scent of his shaving soap. He wrapped his arms around her. She allowed herself to relax. His hand moved down her arm, tracing the curve of her elbow. His body hardened. Hers softened in aching surrender. His quiet strength was irresistible, she thought with grudging admiration. So was his timing.

Heath Boscastle. Cool, restrained, detached, the demon of her lost dreams. No one could unnerve him. Still waters that ran too deep to fathom or a woman might drown in them. The perfect Englishman. The consummate gentleman.

The gentleman who was calmly untying her nightrail, shoving it down to her waist, and suddenly kissing her breathless as he walked her bare-breasted to the bed. It had all happened in seconds. Her head swam. Her breasts pressed against his hard chest.

"I don't think I need to ask what does interest you," she whispered against his mouth, unbalanced, fighting for breath, for sanity. "I— Do you realize what you're doing?"

He grinned and caught her swiftly in one arm before she collapsed across the blue silk coverlet. "Of course I realize." He lowered her deftly to the bed, his hand fondling one breast in sensual possession. She arched her back, shivered in reaction. "I realize a lot of things now."

"Perhaps," she replied, with another deep shudder, "I shouldn't ask what those things are." No, she wanted him to show her. She wanted to feel him without restrictions, to experience the sexual hunger she had seen in his eyes. She did not want to think of Russell's betrayal. If she were honest, what Odham had told her tonight had not hurt her as deeply as it should have. She knew why . . . her mind had already been lured away to another man.

Heath sensed his advantage. He captured her mouth in a deep, sensual kiss before she could question him. He wasn't sure that anything she could say would have changed his course. Her hot-blooded response to his behavior granted him all the license he needed. Her half-naked body was trapped beneath his. Her slim white hands had already lifted to his chest.

Not to push him away. But to explore. To tease. To learn what he liked. He was only too delighted to show her, to give her a hint of how fully they could enjoy each other. Perhaps not tonight. He'd learned restraint over the years. He wanted her to want him so desperately that there was no doubt at all in her mind that she would be his. But the rogue in him wanted to taunt her with a taste of what she was missing.

She raised up on her elbows to take a gentle bite of his shoulder. A moment later her tongue caressed the small injury. "On second thought," she murmured, "perhaps I should ask."

He buried his face between the valley of her beautiful breasts. "Ask what?" he said, his attention more focused on continuing what they'd begun than conversation.

"What are we doing in my bed?" she whispered, her hand positioned directly upon his heart.

He snared her wrists in his hand and held them above her head. "Whatever you suggest," he murmured with a devilish smile.

"I'm not suggesting anything." But her eager response told him otherwise.

He eased her left knee up over his hip, opening her lower

body to his exploration. His gaze drifted over her, taking in every detail. "In that case, I'll have to take the initiative."

She strained her wrists. He tightened his hold.

"Now wait just a minute—"

"I think I've waited long enough."

"No, you haven't," she exclaimed, giving a helpless laugh. "Heath, you aren't supposed to be here."

"I've been ordered to be your bodyguard." He pressed his groin to hers. She was half undressed. He was still clothed. "Agreed?"

She narrowed her eyes, a faint smile on her lips.

"Yes, but—"

"Well, I'm protecting you."

She laughed softly. "No, you aren't."

"I guarantee no one will get to your body with me on top of you."

She started to speak, lost the thought as emotion and sensation inundated her. She felt exposed, damp with desire, caught up in only him. He demanded—and got—her full attention.

He'd left his mark years ago. Her heart, her body remembered all too well, responded, yearning for completion. To be part of him, to take him inside her. Unfinished pleasure. A shadow ache. He shifted position, pressed himself into the moist hollow between her legs. His stiff arousal branded her, and she moaned. She could feel how hard he was for her, how he needed her, and her instincts urged her to give him fulfillment.

She ached, arched, twisted into him. His mouth closed around one nipple and suckled hard until blackness swam behind her eyes. His hand stole up her nightrail, his fingers stroking her flesh before sinking into the moist cleft that welcomed the invasion.

Her body clenched. She heard him draw a deep breath. His fingers penetrated her in tantalizing degrees, withdrew, repeated the play until she shivered with raw sensation, her breathing suspended. He teased her without mercy, pinned her writhing form down with his powerful thigh.

"I can't believe . . ." The words caught in her throat, a gasp of surprised pleasure. "I can't believe that we're making the same mistake."

"The only mistake," he whispered, pressing his fingers deeper inside her, "is that I let you run away from me six years ago."

"I didn't know—"

"I've waited forever to touch you like this," he said quietly.

She felt tears well under her eyelids as he kissed her again, a kiss that tasted of desire too long denied, of loyalties questioned, of male conquest. How many times had she ached for this moment? How had she existed without him?

She was supposed to marry Russell. His face floated like an elusive cloud in the back of her thoughts. She fought to remember what it had felt like to kiss him, to remember how good he had been to her when her father was ill. Had Russell betrayed her? She knew it must be so. But no one on earth could kiss like Heath Boscastle. His mouth was like a medieval torch that could raze an entire castle, a village, a woman's heart. Deep, soulful kisses that made her head reel, made her ache for hot, uninhibited sex.

She uttered a soft cry, the pleasure he gave her cresting like a wave. She had tried to hold back. She wanted to cling to one last thread of control. He took her further than she'd ever dreamed she could go, deeper. She throbbed against his hand, drenched him, inhibition washed away in a rush of rapture, flooded.

His hand gripped her hip as the contractions subsided. He smiled at her, a knowing smile, as if she did not realize what he had just proved.

How effortlessly he could seduce her. And how many times had this fantasy, or a variation of it, dominated her awareness when her late husband visited her bed before hurrying off to his beloved army. So now she and Heath both knew. She heaved a deep breath, felt her heartbeat begin to slow.

"I knew there was something different about you in the theater tonight," she whispered, twining her arm around his neck. Her fingers threaded through his thick hair. He closed his eyes. "And then when you touched me in the street, the way you stared at me. What has come over you?"

"Perhaps I've come to my senses."

He shifted, drawing her into him. His eyes flickered open. For a dangerous moment she began to move with him, against him, not knowing what she was doing, except that her feelings for him were overwhelming, complicated, too potent to deny. Her nightrail had twisted around her hips, completely exposing her to him. Even through his evening trousers she felt the hard power of him, his erection arousing a deeper ache inside her, pushing against the slick folds of her sex. The fact that he was fully dressed made their position even more erotic.

"Poor rogue," she said slowly, her eyes locked with his. "You did not find your release."

"You'd be surprised how much self-control I have learned to exercise in six years."

"Nothing about you would surprise me," she said very softly.

And if he hadn't shown the willpower to stop right then, Julia had no idea what might have happened. More than likely she would have dredged up some control before they went any further. But it was as if they both realized at the same moment that they must stop.

For Heath it was more a matter of what was best for her than gratifying his physical lust. His body craved her with a gnawing need that would keep him awake for hours, but he decided he'd gone far enough for one night. Too fast and he risked losing her. He wasn't merely playing a game of seduction. He was playing to win her heart, her devotion.

He eased away from her, casting one last rueful look at her lying on the bed, her breasts and dark rose nipples flushed from his kisses, her mouth moist and inviting. In the end she would be his, but he would make certain before he played his hand that the odds were in his favor. Heath would make her admit what she wanted.

She wanted him. He saw the naked desire in her soft gray eyes before confusion and concern set in. She sat up, making a belated attempt to cover herself as she did. She gave a reluctant laugh. "I *am* worried about you—"

They glanced around at the same instant as a door slammed downstairs. Raised voices reached them from the hall below. Julia had already slipped into a dressing robe, straightened the bedcover, and Heath was on his feet by the time the knock came at the door.

She made a face. "It's probably Odham and Hermia in another battle."

He shook his head. "I don't think so."

He was right.

Hermia stood in the doorway, her face an unnatural shade of white. She didn't question the fact that Heath and her niece were alone together in Julia's bedroom. In fact, Heath was not sure that the woman really noticed.

"Come downstairs, both of you," she said, motioning in distress. "Drake has been stabbed in the street. Odham has already gone for my physician."

Julia took stock of the attractive man who was half reclining on the sofa, his expression one of tolerant resignation. Her face paled as he repositioned himself, and she noticed the blood-soaked cloth he was holding almost casually over his left hand. She thought again how easily he could be mistaken for Heath.

The same compelling hawk-nosed profile, the crisp black hair. And in that black greatcoat—he was wearing Heath's coat.

"He looks like you," she said to Heath, who clearly wasn't listening, reaching Drake moments before she managed to move.

"Who?" she heard Heath ask his brother, his voice controlled but clearly shaken. "Where? And why?"

Drake shrugged, accepting the glass of brandy that Odham had passed him. "A ruffian—a foreigner by the looks of him. Devon chased him into the rookeries."

Heath's face hardened as he examined the wound on his brother's wrist. It wasn't fatal, but who knew what had been his assailant's intention? "How did you and Devon end up together?"

Drake hesitated. "We were apparently on our way to the same young lady's lodgings. A private dinner party."

Heath's mouth thinned in amusement. "Not very discriminating as to whom she invites, is she?"

Drake lifted his brow. "I resent that. And stop making such a fuss. It's a pinprick. He cut my hand. I came back here only because I felt guilty for leaving you the way I did. It was rude of me."

Heath straightened. "I suppose you'll live, and yes, you were rude, but I'll forgive you. Did your attacker take your cash?"

"No, he didn't. I think I surprised him. At least he looked surprised when I turned to plant him a facer." Drake examined his hand. "He'll be more surprised, I wager, when he realizes he's lost two front teeth."

The physician arrived, a trim-bearded Scotsman who announced he had just been about to attend a dinner two houses down, and wasn't it fortunate he was available? In the flurry of activity that followed, Julia could pick out only snatches of Heath and Drake's private conversation.

"Did he follow you from the theater?" Heath asked.

"I'm not sure," Drake said. "I wasn't paying much attention. We stopped by Grosvenor Square for Devon to change. We could have been followed from there."

"Was he French?"

"No. Hired from the gutter. German or Dutch, I'd guess."

"Why did you let him get away?" Heath gave a deep sigh. "Don't tell me. It was the woman again. I hope she was worth it."

"She wasn't," Drake said emphatically, wincing as the

physician began to poke and prod. "She had another man there and wouldn't let us in. A very rich one, she claimed."

Heath stood to allow the physician more room to examine the wound. He turned to look at Julia. She caught his hand.

"Look at him, Heath."

"I did. I believe he will live but probably not learn."

She lowered her voice. "That isn't what I meant. *Look* at Drake."

"Yes?"

She met his gaze, and found herself frustrated that his face revealed so little of what he thought. "He looks exactly like *you* in that coat. You don't suppose his attacker had the wrong brother?"

He smiled fleetingly before he turned to the door. "Probably not. Keep him company a moment, would you, but don't get too friendly. He's like me in more ways than one. I won't be long. I want to look around the house a little bit."

"Why?" she asked.

"Just to be safe, Julia."

Heath walked through the servants' quarters, searched the wine cellar and scullery, then exited into the garden by the kitchen door. The rain was lighter than before but still falling steadily, turning the small rectangular garden into puddles of muck. Julia's cat streaked past him for the warm haven of the house. He headed for the shed.

As he turned onto the rhododendron-lined pathway, he heard a door creak open at the back of the house. He hoped to God that Hermia had not followed him again. Not that he anticipated finding anything in the shed, but it never hurt to be cautious.

He pulled open the door and stared into the dank gloom. Pots, a wheelbarrow, the odor of humus and damp wood. No ghosts from the past. What had he expected? He should have felt more relief instead of this vague unrest.

He did not realize until that moment how he wanted to face his fears, to dispel the shadows that still haunted him. He wanted to be in Russell's place, hunting down Auclair. It might have brought Heath a measure of peace to confront his former captor himself.

There was a hesitant footstep on the leaf-strewn path that led to the shed. He backed out of the door in resignation, hoping he did not encounter Hermia and her flowerpot again. As he turned his head, he caught sight of Julia's elderly butler Payton sneaking behind the trees. The old servant was probably trying to be helpful, and Heath was grinning as he reached back around to close the shed door. He didn't call out. No point in giving Payton a fright—

"Stop right there!"

He swung around, expecting Payton to recognize him, to stammer an apology—expecting almost anything except the sharp blow to his head and the black oblivion that followed.

Chapter 15

The murmur of voices brought Heath back to consciousness. He forced his eyes open and examined the woman leaning over him. Her lovely oval face was pale with concern. Her gray eyes reminded him of English mist. And his head hurt like bloody hell.

He sat up, embarrassed to find himself smothered under layers of perfumed silk sheets and a pink silk coverlet, which had been tucked around his shoulders. His brother Drake, his left hand bandaged, grinned at him like a gargoyle from the bottom of the bed.

Julia's hair spilled across his chest as she leaned lower to plump up his pillows. "Did you shoot me again?" he asked her. "What am I doing in bed anyway?"

"Do not jest, Heath. I almost died when I saw you. But no one shot you."

He grunted, glanced down, and realized that his shirt had been removed. "Someone undressed me. I hope it was you."

Julia caught her breath and glanced back at Drake. He shrugged helplessly, his eyes gleaming, and slid off his stool. "I'll leave you two alone for a moment. Let me tell Grayson the patient will live."

Heath cursed softly, testing his shoulder, his arms. "What happened, Julia? I was in the garden, and I saw Payton—"

"My butler hit you with a shovel," she said, chewing the edge of her lip. "He thought you were another intruder. Apparently, you had warned him to be on guard."

"Bloody hell."

"He thought he was being helpful, doing his duty. Oh, Heath, if only you'd told the servants you were sneaking out into the garden . . . Payton feels dreadful."

"He feels dreadful?" He rubbed his neck. "Why am I in bed?"

"You fell against the shed quite hard and hit your head. There's a sizable knot on the back of your skull."

He lifted his hand behind him, glancing past her with a disgruntled look. "This isn't your room. Where am I?"

She brought a cool cloth to his head. "In Hermia's bed."

"Hermia's bed? Was that necessary?"

Julia's eyes sparkled with warmth in the candlelight. "It was Drake's idea, to be honest. Her room was closer. Heaven knows I expect the disapproval of the whole Boscastle brood to come down upon my head. Both of you injured in the same evening."

"You do not think Drake's assault was a coincidence?"

"No," she said slowly, shaking her head. "He looked too much like you in that coat."

"I'm not sure I share your suspicion."

"Well, at any rate," she said, giving his pillow a final plump, "I shall have to protect my bodyguard, won't I?"

"Only against your aunt and butler."

He leaned back thoughtfully against the headboard.

Julia turned the cloth over in her hands, then stretched forward to straighten the bedclothes. The bedclothes that had covered him had slid down off his shoulder, revealing his bare chest. For a moment Heath did not realize what had happened. Then he heard Julia's sharp intake of breath, looked up and saw the compassion in her eyes.

"Your chest," she whispered. "Oh, Heath. I saw it when Drake and I removed your shirt."

"I should have warned you."

She shook her head, holding back tears. "I'm not thinking of me. Only of what you must have suffered."

"It's past, Julia."

She nodded slowly, knowing he was too proud a man to desire her pity. There were faded, vicious scars on his chest. Deep and puckered purple craters of flesh that resembled healed burns. Julia pressed her fingertips gently upon each one. Deliberately inflicted by another. She felt sickened. How fortunate he had survived. Burns.

He was tortured in Portugal, Russell had told her when he was explaining that he wanted Heath to watch over her. *Nothing a lady needs to hear about. He's healed. We all went through hell, and there's no reason to discuss it. He survived.* No other details. All very matter-of-fact, a soldier's duty. The pain must have been unendurable.

He frowned, clearly aware where her gaze had fallen. "Julia," he said in faint irritation, "I do not wish to be coddled like an invalid. Please leave the room so that I may dress."

"Of course," she murmured.

He caught her hand as she twisted around in her chair. "Do I sound ungrateful?"

Her heart clenched at the warmth of his hand on hers,

the sight of his half-bare, muscular body sprawled out on the bed. He was a man to dream about. But the scars on his chest reminded her of how vulnerable even the strongest man could become. Her husband, Adam, had died before he was thirty, certain he was invincible. She fought down a surge of anxiety, of fear for Heath, and Russell. They both were trying to protect her, but who would protect them?

"At least you didn't shoot me this time," he said with a weak attempt at a smile.

"Thank heavens."

His voice lowered an octave. "I'd be shot by you all over again if I had another chance to change what happened afterward."

A current of heat went through her as his hand tightened over hers.

"I wish . . . well, we can't change it now," she said after a long silence.

"I remember everything, Julia."

"This—"

"You remember, too. Why did you leave me?" His eyes searched her face, unguarded and dark with emotion. "Why did you run off to get married after we'd found each other?"

She stared at him in astonishment. She could not believe what he had said. "Leave you?" She shook her head in confusion. "I didn't leave you. *You* left *me*."

"You told me never to talk to you again. I thought you were ashamed—"

"I was."

"I thought you needed time to realize what we meant to each other."

She kept shaking her head. Never once in all these years

had she considered what had happened from his viewpoint. He was a known rogue. "I assumed you would think I was fast, too forward. I—"

"I thought you were wonderful. I couldn't believe my luck or my subsequent bad fortune. I couldn't believe that I had met someone like you right as I was going off to war."

"You thought *I* was wonderful?"

"Yes." He gave her a black look. "And you told me to go away or I would ruin your life. You called me a demon with blue eyes."

"All this time," she said in wonder, "and you remember my exact words." She remembered, too. She'd revisited those hours often enough. Shed more than a few tears.

"I remember that you told me you never wanted to see me again."

"Yes, but . . ." She lifted her free hand to her heart. "I didn't mean it."

"The blue-eyed demon didn't know that."

"I wasn't about to become one of Heath Boscastle's women," she said defensively.

That seemed to catch him by surprise. "What on earth are you talking about? What women?"

"All the young women at that house party wanted you to notice them."

His frown deepened. "That doesn't mean I wanted any of them."

Julia searched his handsome face, completely unbalanced by what he'd confessed. It was the first time she had allowed him to speak in his own defense. She knew he was telling the truth, had no reason to lie to her now. She had thought him heartless. "But Russell told me that in all those years, you never once mentioned me, never asked how I was or where I had gone."

A flush of anger crept across his proud, chiseled cheekbones. "For God's sake, Julia. Of course I never discussed you with him. I promised you that what happened between us would remain a secret. I knew that if I started to talk about you, he would guess how I felt."

"How you felt," she repeated numbly. "How could anyone guess? I can forgive you, Heath, because I do not believe you would lie. And after all this time, there is no need. But . . . you're as difficult to understand as those Egyptian hieroglyphics you like to study."

He gave her a warning look as the door behind her opened. Drake and Hermia's physician suddenly entered the room to bring a standstill to Julia's revealing conversation with the man. She needed to think. So much time had passed. Wasn't his admission too late to matter?

"Is everything all right?" Drake asked, glancing from his brother to Julia as if he sensed the strange tension between them. "Heath? Do you want something for the pain?"

"What pain?" Heath muttered as Julia came to her feet.

And Julia smiled. She couldn't help herself. Yes, she was rather bewildered by their conversation, but deep down inside she felt a fragile stirring of happiness. Perhaps even hope.

I didn't leave you. You left me. Had she said that? Had their misguided sense of virtue come between any chance of happiness together they might have had?

She glanced back at his stark, masculine face, at his hard powerful body posed so incongruously in her aunt's bed.

"I'll come back to check on you when you're feeling

yourself again," she said as he gave Drake and the physician a forbidding scowl. "Do what you're told, Heath."

Naturally Heath did not remain in bed. He ordered Drake and the physician from the room. He had work to do. And it was degrading, really, beneath one's dignity for a former cavalry officer to be felled by an overanxious butler. Never mind that the butler's mistress had felled the officer once herself.

In fact, Heath reflected, as he threw off the feminine bed coverings, he had never completely recovered from his first encounter with Julia. In a sense, she hadn't just shot him in the shoulder all those years ago. She might as well have taken aim at his heart.

He stared around the room, looking for his shirt. Well, now Julia had seen the scars on his chest, which tended to fascinate or frighten women. She hadn't fallen into either category that he could tell. He assumed she understood that the scars were Auclair's handiwork. He wasn't about to enlighten her if she didn't.

He pulled on his shirt, noticed the mud stains on it, then pulled it off again. Someone had draped his vest and jacket over a chair. He dressed, scowling at his reflection in the beveled pier glass. There was something about a shirtless man in a vest and evening jacket that looked quite off.

"I'm not Beau Brummel," he told the reflection. "And as I'm talking to myself, I think I may have sustained a brain injury."

At least the reflection didn't talk back. He assumed that was a sign he'd retained a modicum of sanity.

It was probably shock.

Julia thought he had left her. All those years of hiding his wounded pride, of yearning, of searching for a woman to replace her. He hadn't done it consciously, of course. But every woman he had courted, every one he had taken to his bed, had been held to the light of Julia's joyous spirit and been found lacking. Ironic that they had not been reunited to realize their true feelings until she was engaged to one of his oldest friends.

"Hell," he said loudly. "Hell and damn."

He'd done more than initiate a seduction that afternoon long ago. He had lost a valuable piece of himself to her. In those days he hadn't been quite as self-contained as he was now, but he'd been wildly attracted to Julia from the moment they met. He would have pursued her after their sexual encounter. Except that she had never spoken to him again, and she probably would have murdered him if he'd approached her father.

Marriage had been the last thing on his mind, of course. Still, he resented not even having been allowed a say in what had happened. She'd underestimated him, or perhaps underestimated what he thought of her. She'd assumed he was another rogue in a long line of them. That wasn't untrue, but it didn't mean he could never change.

Then before he'd figured out the proper way to win her, or how badly he wanted to, she had sailed off to India to marry another man, not knowing how much she had meant to Heath because he hadn't really known it until it was too late himself.

Understanding this changed everything, and it changed nothing. He was still honor-bound to protect her. She was still officially engaged to Russell, a temporary situation he would remedy, but the fact was that the spark between Julia and him had never died. It had smoldered dangerously for years. Heath was of a mind to fan it; they'd both go up in flames before she got away from him again.

Now that he had finally seen their past from Julia's perspective, what had happened afterward made sense. Julia assumed that her "sin" had rendered her rather vulgar in his eyes. She'd been ashamed of her passionate response to his seduction, assuming it had been the kind of thing he did every day.

It hadn't been. Not then. Not now. He had been swept up in passion, in their encounter, had savored every sensual moment in his memory. But he'd hardly made a regular habit of ravishing young girls at house parties.

His mistake had been in believing that Julia had been liberal-minded enough to ignore the strictures of Society. But even a freethinker could not escape certain social conventions.

Until now.

She had assumed that Heath, having seduced her once, being a Boscastle male, was an irredeemable rogue. Well, it might be time to start acting like one. If it took a rogue to win her, he could play the part.

All he really had to do was follow his instincts.

And perhaps put on a shirt.

Heath appeared recovered enough the next day to go for a drive with Julia in Hyde Park. He assured her his head did not hurt. She relented but did not believe him. She frowned in concern as he put on his coat in the hallway.

She even insisted on holding the reins of the curricle. To her surprise he did not protest. She suspected he might be in greater discomfort than he let on, or perhaps he wanted to be on guard. Whatever his motive, he did not seem to be in a talkative mood.

Of course, after last night, they would be wise to think carefully before revealing any more secrets. By telling Heath the truth, Julia had placed herself in the most vulnerable position imaginable. Not to mention her uninhibited response to him in her bedroom. Six years of unsatisfied passion stored up. She had been quite shameless, almost insensible with need, although he hadn't appeared to disapprove.

She knew she could trust him to keep his silence the way he had for the last six years. But wouldn't she rather that he fight for her? For the first time she realized that a passionate commitment was what she had always secretly wanted, waited for, hoped he would offer. The truth dawned on her as they circled around the park in the warm afternoon air. His deep voice only reaffirmed her regret.

"I don't blame you for hating me for what happened years ago," he said, as if he, too, had been giving the matter a great deal of thought. "You were young. We both were, and I couldn't resist you. That's no excuse. I took advantage of you." He ran his hand through his gleaming black hair, then shrugged in helpless apology.

Julia drew back lightly on the reins. She didn't look at him. Those sensual Boscastle eyes always put her at a disadvantage. "I never hated you."

"Thank God. I deserved it."

She was tempted to laugh. "What a wicked pair we are." They were both equally guilty, or equally innocent, depending on how one looked at the situation. "There's only one reason, actually, why I can never forgive you."

She felt him turn slightly toward her. His body brushed hers like a warm iron, solid and strong, but capable of leaving a painful brand. A true warrior beneath that deceptively languid frame. A fluttering heat swirled in the pit of her stomach. She dared not look at him.

"What?" he demanded. "What is it?"

She stared at the young couple who rode past them. "What is what?"

"Answer me, Julia."

She slowed the curricle, afraid of where this conversation would lead. Yes, it was good to clear the air, but what would be left of them afterward?

He reached across her lap to grab the reins from her hands. His eyes searched her face, and in that moment she felt a shiver of empathy for the enemies he had confronted during war. There was a ruthless streak beneath all that refined beauty. His stare felt as though he had taken a scalpel to her soul. "Last night each of us confessed things that were unsettling and should have been said before," he began. "There is no point in continuing that course of stupidity. We are both old enough to accept the truth."

She bit her lower lip. "I was rather hoping we were going to do the civilized thing and forget that conversation. It was quite painful as I recall."

He would not back down. Merciless, these Boscastle men were when it came to having their way. "What have you not forgiven me?" he demanded.

Had she really hoped he would relent, be polite, and pretend she hadn't laid her heart open to him? No. She wanted him to know. The truth had been festering inside her like a thorn for too many years. Let him pluck it out, even if she bled to death. He was probably used to it. The Boscastles in ancient battle had been a bloodthirsty lot.

The curricle had come to a complete stop in the center of

the ring. They were interrupting the flow of fashionable traffic. Several riders cast them curious looks in passing. She wasn't accustomed to all the attention. Heath was. There wasn't a male in his family who hadn't attracted notice from his first nursery days.

"All right, Your Royal Arrogance," she said. "I'll tell you. And afterward you will never wish to talk to me again."

He raised his brow. "I doubt it."

She pulled off one of her gloves. "Do you *really* want to know?"

He leaned into her. "Julia, we are not budging an inch *until* I know."

He meant it. She could picture both of them sitting in this curricle through a complete change of seasons, having their meals brought to them by the Boscastle servants, coal braziers and blankets provided for the cold, plum pudding for Christmas.

"Oh, fine." Her throat felt tight and achy. "I don't forgive you for not fighting for me. For not asking me to marry you after what we'd done."

"For not fighting for you?" His blue eyes glittered with anger. "Who was there to fight?" His voice deepened in disbelief. "You?"

"Yes!"

His mouth flattened. "You told me you never wanted to see me again. You told me I was a devil, a libertine, a rake, a— You made me swear upside down that I would leave you alone." He shook his head incredulously. "You made me swear on my mother's grave that I would pretend nothing had ever happened between us, that, should we ever meet again, I was to act as if we were polite strangers, that—"

"I didn't *mean* it," she said in a quiet voice. "I wanted you to pursue me, but I thought you'd think I was fast. I thought—"

He started to laugh. "You're not serious."

"I'm afraid I am."

"You couldn't have told me this a little earlier? Say five or so years ago? When it could have made a difference?"

She reared back. Was he telling her that it didn't make a difference now? And if it didn't, why had they been together in her bedroom last night? "I shouldn't have told you."

"And you would have married me—if I'd gone to your father and asked for your hand?"

"I don't know," she said, giving a heartfelt sigh. "Yes, I would have. Of course I would. I'd have run off to China with you if you'd asked."

He shook his head again, looking utterly bemused. "Even though I *had* already asked to see you again, and you had refused?"

"Which I did only because I was afraid you were only asking me because you're such a gentleman."

He exhaled and readjusted the reins he'd wrested from her hands. At his expert touch the horses redirected themselves into the ring. Julia studied him from the corner of her eye. Obviously it wasn't easy for either of them to discuss the past.

"Julia," he said in a low voice. "I've had enough experience with women since then that I actually do understand your logic. Or *illogic*."

She took a breath. "Now you must think I am not only

fast but also a fool. A fool with no morals and a loose tongue. A—"

"Why did you marry?" he demanded, his temper rising again as he remembered how furious he had been, how he'd practically set sail for India when he had heard about her intended marriage. He'd ridden halfway to the wharves like a wild man before realizing that Julia would have been wedded and bedded before he could reach India. That she had forbidden him to talk to her again.

"I married him because he asked me, and you didn't."

"I asked you to elope," he said darkly.

"I didn't think you meant it," she said quietly. "Did you?"

"Probably."

She lifted her brow. "Probably? That doesn't sound very definite, does it?"

"I thought you were coming back in a year," he said, frowning at her.

"That was our original plan," she said, frowning right back at him. "I thought *you* were planning to fight in India with your brother Brandon."

"That was *my* original plan, but . . ." His face darkened as if he were on the verge of a violent outburst. "But Russell persuaded me to go to Portugal instead."

"Russell?"

Heath's eyes blazed. "He convinced us we'd be heroes, he and I."

"You were heroes," she said weakly. "He was right."

"He plotted out our brilliant military careers," he ground out.

"He's very good at plotting."

He narrowed his eyes. "An absolute master. That's why he's got all those medals."

Julia glanced around. The horses were skittish, as if they sensed the dark plunge of the driver's mood. No wonder Heath kept his emotions under such tight control. It was a frightening thing, just to watch that temper building. A sensible person would not want to be in the vicinity when it exploded.

What should she do? Calm him down?

"Actually, you both are," she said, smiling brightly.

He scowled at her. "Both of us are what? Masters of plotting? That may or may not be true, and I don't seem to have plotted out my personal life very well. Anyway, what does that have to do with the price of eggs?"

"I mean, you both have. You both have, or had, or *will* have brilliant military careers."

He snorted. "Perhaps he guessed how I felt about you all along."

Her mouth dropped open. "Do you really think so?"

He urged the horses into a smart trot, his voice low and savage. "Of course I don't. It just makes me feel better to blame someone." And then he swore.

It occurred to Julia to ask him how *he* felt about her now, as well as then, but it wasn't the sort of question an engaged woman could ask her betrothed's friend. Not in the middle of Hyde Park. Besides, he was still swearing under his breath, and he looked so angry, so discomposed, so . . . beautiful. She had not seen Heath so on edge since the first time they'd met. It was a temptation to provoke him.

She cleared her throat. "Well, what do you think?"

He flicked her an inscrutable look. He'd stopped swearing. He wasn't going to lose his temper, after all. "I'm not sure what to think. What do *you* think?"

She thought he hid his feelings far too well. "I think . . ." Her horrified gaze moved past him to the sandy track. "I think that we're about to crash into that phaeton."

They didn't crash. At the last moment Heath drew the curricle to the rail, skillfully avoiding a collision with an expensive black phaeton. The young male driver, also dressed in black, jumped down from the box to apologize profusely.

"Correction," Heath said, his voice sharp. "He was about to crash into us."

"It's Brentford," Julia said.

Heath lifted his brow. "You sound surprised."

Brentford strode up before them, his black cape fluttering in the breeze. His face looked drawn, unnaturally so, accentuating the liquid dark of his eyes. "I say, I didn't mean to give you a scare."

"Then why did you?" Heath demanded in an impatient voice. "This is the park, Brentford, not a race course. What were you trying to prove?"

"Well, actually, I was . . ." He glanced behind him, looking puzzled. "I was showing off to my friend, my fencing instructor, actually. He wanted to time my progress, but he's gone. He's gone."

Heath blew out a sigh. "Why don't you join him then?"

Brentford flushed as he stole a downhearted look at Julia. "Good idea. I will. If I can find him, that is." He pivoted on his boot heels, then began to stride off in the opposite direction.

"In your phaeton, Brentford," Heath called after him. "Don't tell me you're going to leave the blasted thing parked in the middle of the ring."

Julia shook her head in chagrin. "Poor Brentford. You've got him so flustered he doesn't know if he's coming or going."

"He's definitely going." He glanced at her, laughing with reluctance. "You mustn't feel sorry for him, Julia. It could hardly have been an accident that he almost ran into us."

Brentford, hearing their voices, turned and backed into his horse.

Heath sighed again. "Or perhaps it was. The fool, driving like that. Someone could have been killed."

"A bit of an exaggeration, don't you think?" Julia asked in a droll voice.

"Not at all. I could have killed him on the spot."

"For his driving?"

He hesitated. "No. For looking at you."

His gaze held hers, a smile of bewitchment lurking in his eyes. Julia felt a wave of liquid warmth wash over her. "For looking at me?"

"It's my job, isn't it?"

"Well—"

"Do you want me to fight over you or not? This seems as good a time as any to start, seeing that we've lost six years."

Julia could not help herself; she started to laugh with abandon. It felt awfully good to be honest with this man. Then as Heath, grinning, drove through the gates, she noticed the bank of swollen gray clouds gathered overhead into an ominous mass. She glanced back again, thinking of

Brentford caught in a shower. But as she resettled herself, her laughter died away.

A little chill chased down her backbone. She had just noticed a man behind the rail doff his black hat to her, the gesture almost impertinent, mocking, as if he'd been secretly watching the exchange with Brentford. The man stood alone, a walking cane tucked under his arm. Before she could see his face, he had turned to blend into the flock of gaily dressed pedestrians hurrying across the park to escape the impending rain.

"What is it?" Heath asked. "Did Brentford drive into the Serpentine?"

"No, it's . . ." His elbow brushed hers, and she forgot the man who'd been watching them.

"Brentford is going to get caught in the rain," she murmured.

"Good," Heath said, driving smartly around a slow-moving barouche. "I hope he does."

Chapter 16

Heath invited Julia to dinner that same night at his brother Grayson's Park Lane mansion. Her natural inclination was to accept, although after their straightforward conversation in the park, she did not know how they would act toward each other. Clearly neither one of them had meant to speak so frankly. For the most part she had welcomed the chance to bring her feelings to light. But being candid was not always helpful. Often honesty stirred up more problems than it settled.

Had she shocked him? No. Not Heath, although she had gotten an unexpected reaction from him.

She couldn't help wondering how different everything might have been if she'd had the courage years ago that she had today. She would never have run away from him.

She accepted his dinner invitation. Hermia had grudgingly agreed to attend the opera with Odham, and Julia was not quite sure that she trusted herself to be alone with Heath in the town house for an entire evening. At least not this soon after their emotional afternoon of revelations. She thought that Grayson and his wife might provide a buffer between her and Heath.

She was woefully misguided. Devils at heart, the Boscastle brothers apparently supported one another in sickness, and in sin. As it turned out, Grayson was only too happy to rekindle the sparks between her and Heath. With a pitchfork.

The Marquess of Sedgecroft's mansion reminded Julia of a small-scale palace. Elegant Greek frescoes edged in gilt adorned the walls, and large mirrors enhanced the sense of light and spacious luxury. The servants appeared as if by magic to take her green silk stole and to draw her chair. Those same domestics disappeared like smoke the moment they were not needed. The atmosphere was one of understated wealth and ease.

Her slippered feet sank into the plush Persian carpets that covered the polished black oak floor as she was led to the dining room and seated at an enormous mahogany table between Heath and his brother the marquess, a gregarious golden lion of a man. There was a definite air of conspiracy in the house. She felt a little like a pawn on a chessboard. But it was not wholly an unpleasant feeling. Not when Heath's brooding blue eyes met hers more than once, and held. To be in the presence of two dominant Boscastle men was to feel protected . . . and possessed. A mortal woman really could not fight it. A wise one would not attempt to try.

The dinner proceeded without a flaw. Then Heath and Grayson excused themselves during the dessert course for some private male conversation in the marquess's study.

Jane, the honey-haired marchioness, smiled warmly across the table at Julia. She had been notably silent during the meal, observing her guests. "I have only one word for you, my dear. Beware."

Julia stared down in feigned alarm at the wedge of cheesecake on her plate. "Poison?"

"Even more dangerous." Jane lowered her voice, her green eyes glittering in the light of the silver candelabra. "Seduction."

Julia put down her fork. "Seduction?"

"In classic Boscastle style." Jane leaned back with a sigh of regret. "That is all I am permitted to say, having married into the family of devils." She laced her fingers protectively over her abdomen. "And having conceived one."

"But . . . beware?"

"Or enjoy. Whatever you desire. Heath is an enormously attractive man, and you've been married before. I daresay you know how to handle this."

"Seduction?" Julia said again, as if she were surprised, although all the signs were there. But for his family to see? What could it mean? "Are you sure?"

"Trust me as one who has been seduced, Julia."

"Well, then, what am I to do?"

Jane took a small forkful of cheesecake to her mouth. "Savor. Enjoy. It's delicious."

Julia laughed. "What am I to do if he tries to seduce me?"

"I just told you." Jane's delicate face glowed with mischief. "Savor. Enjoy."

Grayson poured himself a generous glass of brandy and stretched his long legs comfortably across the tufted sofa. "I'll give you another piece of advice, as this appears to be very serious. Don't move too quickly with her. Take your time."

Heath smiled drily. "Six years is hardly what I call running a race."

"Well, you've waited this long for her." Grayson swirled the amber liquid at the bottom of his snifter. "Make her want you. Make her burn."

Heath sat down on the edge of the armchair. "I'm burning at the same time, you realize."

Grayson gave a low, wicked laugh. "Of course you are. That's why you're doing this with such care. You want to build the passion moment by moment, kiss by kiss, caress by caress. Let her smolder. Any fool can go up in flames." Grayson sobered. "I do believe you already know all this."

Heath shook his head. "It's never mattered so much before."

"Dear God," Grayson said. "It's fatal, isn't it?"

"I beg your pardon?"

"You're showing several of the symptoms. Trust me, I am a victim myself."

Heath removed a cigar from his waistcoat pocket. "You are making no sense whatsoever."

Grayson snorted. "Love does not make sense."

"Love?" Heath said, lowering the cigar to look at his grinning brother. "Symptoms?"

"The Six Deadly Symptoms of a Man in Love. Inability to think straight?"

"Well, I do have quite a bit on my mind." Heath smiled reluctantly. "Julia does challenge a man, yes."

"You're smiling."

"Yes?"

"You usually frown. And the second symptom is an alarming propensity to smile at the oddest moments."

"Is this an odd moment?" Heath countered.

Grayson narrowed his eyes. "Symptom three: Constant thoughts of the object of one's desire."

"For God's sake, Grayson."

"Is she or is she not the object of your desire? And do you or do you not think of her constantly?"

Heath leaned his head back. His refusal to answer was all too revealing.

"Four: Absolutely no interest in other members of the opposite sex."

Heath sat in total silence.

"Five," Grayson continued heartlessly, "a startling sense of goodwill toward the world in general."

Heath lifted his head. "That lets me out right there. I hate the world in general."

"And six," Grayson concluded, his voice soft, "a perpetual state of sexual arousal."

"Are you quite finished?"

"No. I'm just warming to one of my favorite subjects."

"You're enjoying this, aren't you?"

"Bring her to her knees." Grayson's smile was devious. "In a figurative sense, I mean, or a physical one, if it pleases you. Has she found out about her faithless Russell?"

"No."

"Are you sure you don't want a little help in that direction?"

"No. Absolutely not. I do not want her hurt, and I do not wish to win her by default."

"You don't have forever. When is Russell coming home?"

"I haven't heard. Not a word. It's too early anyway."

Grayson hesitated. "Any chance he might be dead?"

Heath rose from the chair. "Not likely. He's probably worming his way into Wellington's graces, and I imagine there's a pretty Parisienne or two on the side."

"Then to the devil with him." Grayson raised his glass in a mocking toast. "Remember my advice. Make her burn."

Julia knew the moment Heath returned to the dining room. A delicious tingle of foreboding shivered over her skin. She and Jane were discussing their mutual desire to visit the Louvre and admire its plundered art treasures when he and Grayson strolled up to the table. Heath's gaze went immediately to Julia, and lingered. She looked down, pretending not to notice as her heart leaped into her throat and pounded in response.

Seduction. That was what Jane asserted, and she did have experience. Was it possible? She glanced up to meet his steady look and felt a current of emotion electrify her. He lowered his lean frame into his chair with such unstudied elegance that she actually sighed aloud. And prompted him to smile, a small, private quirk of his sensual mouth that set her pulse racing all over again.

Grayson took his place at the table. "We must invite Heath and Julia to Kent next week, Jane, for our small family gathering."

Jane lowered the napkin she had raised to her lips. "Our what? Oh, yes, our family gathering. It must have slipped my mind."

"Don't apologize for being forgetful, my love," Grayson said with a tender smile. "It frequently happens to prospective mamas."

"Oh, does it?" Jane asked, widening her eyes. "I'd no idea you were so well versed on the subject. Do enlighten us further."

Heath glanced at Julia and grinned. She grinned back,

relaxing, despite her conviction that the two brothers were plotting something that involved her.

Grayson lounged back in his chair, unruffled. "Well, my mother did have six of us."

"And a handful we were," Heath said, giving his brother a droll look. "Julia and I would love to come. You enjoy the country, don't you, Julia?"

She glanced at Jane, who gave a small helpless shrug and shook her head, suggesting this was beyond her influence. "Yes, but Hermia—"

"Hermia suggested it, actually," Heath said in a silken voice, looking very solicitous. "She thought you were under a strain after the incident in the garden."

"And the street riot," Grayson added. "What a horrifying experience that must have been. Ghastly, to be caught in the midst of a mob."

Julia smiled tightly, feeling herself drawn deeper and deeper into their conspiracy. "Yes, it was entirely terrifying. Heath got hit by an egg. I still have nightmares about it, actually. The yolk everywhere, on his sleeve, his hand."

Grayson blinked. "Really? Well, flying eggs can be dangerous. Especially if they're rotten."

"Oh, yes. It was almost as terrifying as the time a tiger cornered me in my garden in India at twilight." Julia paused. "Almost but not quite."

"Hermia *is* worried about you," Heath said, dark humor in his gaze.

"How good of everyone to be so concerned about me," Julia said. "I'm feeling so delicate I'm not quite sure I shall make it to the door without assistance."

There was a long silence. Heath sat, in all his Sphinx-like serenity, while Grayson refolded his napkin into the shape of a boat, then asked, "Heath, did you show Julia the new Italian gallery yet?" He glanced at Julia with a smile. "Jane had it designed to duplicate the one at her house."

Heath stirred. "No, I haven't."

"What a splendid idea, knowing how interested she is in art." Grayson rubbed his large hands together in glee, as if he had not been the one to pose the suggestion. "You do know the way, don't you?"

Chapter 17

It was indeed, Julia thought wryly, a scene set with masterful skill for a classic seduction. She studied the private candlelit gallery with a wistful smile. There was an inviting deep-cushioned chaise lounge in the corner, and masses of hothouse lilies arranged in a crystal bowl on a low Chinese table that sat on lion-clawed legs.

The plaster ceiling fresco depicted helmeted cherubim. In the recessed alcoves stood life-sized marble statues to replicate ancient Roman gods. Julia made a show of admiring a vestal virgin pouring out an urn.

She was apprehensive, on edge, but certainly not afraid, or even offended. She was perhaps confused by what Jane had revealed. More curious than anything. Temptation thickened the air. Alone with Heath Boscastle in a room designed to encourage intimacy. Where was her willpower when she needed it? And what exactly were his intentions?

Yet she found herself too fascinated to stop him before he made his move. She had inherited a little of her father's gambling streak, his hunger for life. He had taught her by example that one should take a risk now and then.

Alarming, how intense her secret attraction to Heath

had remained over the years. Had it grown even stronger, unattended and allowed to deepen? Her heart gave a painful twist at the thought of what she might have missed. Would miss. He was a unique man, but she had lost him. Who could she blame but herself, the choices she had made? Was there a chance that they could build upon their past to make a future?

He moved up behind her, and her anxiety dissolved into a warmer, deeper whirlpool of emotion. The solid heat of his body sent a shiver down her shoulders into her very fingertips. His hard chin brushed her nape. Her dark, irresistible Boscastle. She ached to fall into his arms and simply surrender to his allure.

"What do you think of my brother?" he asked in a voice low with amusement. "Subtle, isn't he?"

"He's charming."

"A charming rogue."

She turned then without warning; she wondered if she could take him off guard. But he stood his ground, allowed her to reposition herself without moving an inch to accommodate her. She faced him now; she could feel the latent strength of his body against hers. His firm mouth tightened at the corners in a slight smile. She knew she was standing too close to him, but she could bask in his virile presence for hours. He was so disarmingly male, mesmerizing her.

"You're both rogues, I'd say," she murmured after a moment.

"Me?" He lifted a hand to his chest. "Gentleman that I am?"

"A gentleman rogue then. You're more subtle, therefore far more dangerous to the female heart."

He laughed. "You judge me unfairly."

"I'm in no position to judge you at all."

"Perhaps you should," he said, his brow arching.

Julia hesitated, aware that she was being led, but into what, she could not guess. Something undeniably inviting. "What do you mean?"

"I mean that I should rather be judged unfairly than be ignored."

It was her turn to laugh. "As if anyone could ever ignore a Boscastle."

He took her gently by the elbow, acknowledging the comment with a wry smile. "Sit down. Jane is playing in the salon below. She does so every night in the hope she will produce a pleasant-natured child. Listen."

"Do you think it will work?" she asked, allowing him to draw her deeper into the room. Into temptation.

He led her to the bisque-satin chaise lounge that sat in a shadowed corner. Julia could hear the poignant strains of an old English melody on the pianoforte, and the music had a magical, soothing effect on her, lulling her senses.

Heath traced his forefinger down the curve of Julia's cheekbone. She held her breath, transfixed, as he continued the seductive caress down to the swelling tops of her breasts. Her nipples tingled in anticipation. Warmth pooled in the hidden places of her body.

"I believe you just asked me a question," he said, bringing his mouth to hers. "For the life of me I do not remember what it was."

"It was . . ." She faltered, aware of his firm lips teasing the edge of her mouth. His tongue played with hers, enticed her into breathless submission. His kisses could have seduced one of the statues behind them.

"It was?" he asked, amused.

"I don't remember." And she didn't, heaven help her. All she could think of was him.

"Perhaps there are other things on your mind."

She decided she would die if he did not stop playing and kiss her. And yet her every instinct warned her that the precarious balance between them had shifted. But in whose favor? That depended on how she hoped her relationship with Heath would end. Or not end.

She leaned into him, her body softening, magnetized to his masculine power. The radiance of the wrought-iron wall sconces imparted a rosy warmth to the gallery. The dreamlike glow of candlelight and Jane's haunting music in the background conspired to wear down Julia's defenses.

"There's another thing we both seem to have forgotten," she said after a long hesitation.

His perfectly chiseled mouth touched hers again, aroused, invited. "What would that be?"

"I'm engaged. To Russell."

"Hmm." He met her gaze, his eyes heated, flagrantly sensual. "That shouldn't pose a problem."

Her heart missed several beats. "Shouldn't?"

"Well, he's not here, is he?"

"He won't be away forever."

"I'll take care of him."

"Take . . . care of him?" She heard her voice catch. This was another side of Heath she had never experienced. He guided her back in subtle degrees toward the chaise. "Take care of him?" she asked again. "You don't mean you and he would fight or anything so uncivilized?"

The shadow of a possessive smile crossed his face. His dark gaze drifted over her. "If it comes to that. Don't you consider yourself a woman worth fighting for?"

She felt the tufted arm of the chaise against the backs of her legs. Her knees felt unsteady. Her stomach clenched in a knot of sensation. "This isn't like you, Heath."

"Yes, it is." He caressed the curve of her hip with his palm. A shudder of longing slid down her spine. "It's more like me than anyone knows."

His hand slid around her hip to capture her more firmly. His gaze lowered to her mouth, lingered there for so long that she felt her lips part in invitation. He accepted, his eyes darkening, and bent his head to hers. He kissed her before she could draw another breath. He slanted his sensual mouth over hers and kissed her deeply until she could not stand. Her body melted back against his forearm as he lowered her to the chaise. A rush of excitement swept her senses.

He groaned, eating at her mouth. "Oh, Julia." He wasn't playful now, heat radiating from his hard masculine body. This was a lover's kiss, fraught with sexual fire, with hunger. A declaration of his intent to possess her. She leaned back into the crook of his arm, her eyes fastened to his. The smile that crossed his face promised seduction, offered trust and intimacy.

His voice sent a fresh shiver of delight down her back. "Here we are."

"At last," she whispered, her breathing suspended. It felt right to be with him, no matter how long it had taken her to find her way back to where they'd begun. It felt right in a way it never had with her late husband, or with Russell.

His smile deepened. His gaze devoured her. "I'm not letting you escape me this time."

"I hope not," she said faintly.

His knee pressed her down deeper into the chaise. She

sank in a rustle of silk, willing, her body receptive to whatever he demanded. Her bones had turned to water. She was aching for him to touch her.

"Do we understand each other?" he asked, his voice deep-pitched. "I will not let you go again, no matter what Russell says or does."

"I understand. I'm not sure whether he will."

"That doesn't matter. Just trust me to take care of him."

"Are we destined to relive our past mistakes?"

His devilish eyes darkened. "It is my intention to remedy them."

"This remedy sounds very interesting," she whispered.

"Doesn't it?" he replied.

She drew a breath. She felt as though she were dreaming. She had never expected to have this chance with him again. It was almost too much to take. Her sensuality overwhelmed her. He leaned over her, his blue eyes burning, and trailed his kisses across her collarbone, the aching peaks of her breasts. His tongue circled her nipples, licked through the fragile silk that covered them. Fire raced over her skin. His free hand drifted up the side of her knee as he sculpted her body through her thin dress.

Every curve. Every crevice. Every indentation knew his arousing touch, and she allowed it, made no secret of her enjoyment. He explored her, inflamed her with the merciless eroticism of a master. And he hadn't even undressed her. It intrigued her to imagine what he could do to her in bed. What they could do to each other. She wanted to show him pleasure, too.

"You are here now with me, Julia," he whispered. "If Russell did not wish to risk losing you, he should never have sent me in his place."

* * *

Make her burn.

Make her burn.

Heath pushed the tantalizing words to the back of his mind, but not the strategy. Grayson's advice seemed to have worked in reverse. Heath was the one who burned to the core of his being. And yet he was a patient man. One who got what he wanted.

What he wanted was temptingly positioned beneath him, her eyes misted over with desire. He smiled and brought his hand to her low neckline and lightly tugged. She shivered a little as the cool air of the gallery brushed her exposed breasts. She looked deliciously wanton, her milky white skin spilling out of her gown, the rims of her nipples rosy and enticing. His cock swelled inside his pantaloons.

"Heath," she whispered, catching her breath. "It's a little cold in here."

He lowered his head to draw an engorged nipple deep into the moist heat of his mouth. A fierce need filled him, pounded through his blood. He murmured, "Is that better?"

He suckled on the distended tip of her breast until she closed her eyes in helpless pleasure. With aching refinement he drew her other nipple between his sharp white teeth and soothed the deep pink crest with his tongue.

Julia moaned and buried her face in his arm. He moved his hand slowly beneath her silk dress, caressing the soft interior of her thigh. "You're not cold here, are you?" he asked. "Let me see what I can do to help the problem."

"You *are* the problem, devil," she whispered. "I'm shivering all over because of you."

"Well, you feel very warm here, darling. And so wet."

"You deceived us all," she whispered, biting her lip. "You *are* wicked."

He laughed, his hand parting her legs, his fingers probing the moist hollow of her sex. "Would I be less wicked if I asked politely?"

"Most definitely not."

"Please, Julia, please . . . may I do what I have wanted to do for years?"

"Asking like that makes it seem even more wicked, as you're well aware."

"You know what we Boscastles always say?" He shifted, his knee nudging her thighs even farther apart, forcing her into an indecent pose. Her dress was pushed up around her hips.

"No, and perhaps you shouldn't tell me," she whispered, her heart in her throat.

" 'There is a time to be wise and a time to be wicked.' " His clean-shaven jaw rubbed against the blushing undersides of her breasts. "Unfortunately my family usually chooses to be the latter."

"And everyone thought you were different."

"What do you think?" he asked, taunting her.

"I'm *not* thinking. That's the trouble." She gave a low, shivery moan, flexing into him. "What are you doing to me?"

He began to stroke the wet folds of her flesh, whispering in a soothing, seductive voice against her breasts as he did, "I'll do anything you let me. Everything." And he would. He couldn't imagine a man living with Julia and not taking full pleasure of her passionate nature. He wondered suddenly whether her passion was something he alone could summon. The thought gave him a primal satisfaction even as his body begged for release. *He* wanted to be the only one who made her wild. She did the same to him. His experience gave him a slight edge. Unless . . . how experienced was she?

He pressed her deeper into the chaise. How he craved her, needed her, delighted in stealing her control. A strong woman she might be, but in this arena he would dominate her. He held her soft body in place with his own harder frame. His mouth captured the deep-throated whimpers that she could not hold back. He eased another finger inside her dewy channel, his jaw firm with fierce restraint.

He would seduce her one step at a time, even if he could barely walk a straight line. God knew he felt dangerously close to falling into an abyss. Had he ever known such consuming desire? His head swam with the blinding red blaze of it.

"Heath," she murmured, her hand gripping his forearm. "We're in your brother's house. Shouldn't we stop?"

"Not yet."

She felt herself spiraling. She was caught in a force that demanded a surrender of her whole self. She sensed the need in him, saw the raw and unapologetic lust on his taut face as he brought her to a climax that almost stopped her heart. She did not think she would ever recover, shaken to her very core. Her spine arched as spasms overcame her. She buried her fingers in the folds of his black evening jacket, gripping the fabric until her knuckles turned white. For several moments it was all she could do to breath.

Awareness returned in degrees, and with it, embarrassment, regret that they'd lost so much time . . . a deeper longing, an awakening of emotions denied. She was hesitant to look at him again. Once a dutiful wife, she realized that his own needs had not been slaked. Slowly she regained her self-control and reason. Even then she wanted more of him, to show him a similar pleasure, to learn what brought him gratification. She almost cried at the sting of loss she felt when the hard warmth of his body lifted from hers. It hadn't been enough. Not for him. Not for her.

He had destroyed all her defenses. She met his dark gaze and felt a stab of illicit pleasure. There was no mockery on his face. Only a naked sensuality that made her shiver, a promise that this was not the end.

"What will happen next?" she wondered aloud, feeling his fingers closing over hers.

"It's all right, Julia. I will handle whatever comes our way."

"I have a feeling that it will be harder than you make it sound." Russell would not take her rejection lightly, even though he had betrayed her. But she could not marry him now. She wanted Heath. Was he offering her a future? A temporary arrangement? A position as a wife or as a mistress? She wanted to be both. She should have been his from the beginning.

She submitted as he deftly lifted her pale silk bodice back into place. Clever devil. Wicked and wonderful man, so full of secrets and sexual power. She stole another look at him, felt her heart beat wildly at the dark passion in his eyes.

How could he appear so collected, so elegant and devastatingly attractive when she had just splintered into a thousand fragments . . . well, it was unfair.

"The music has stopped," she exclaimed. "Where have Jane and Grayson gone?"

His sensually molded mouth curled into another smile.

The hard angles of his face, the muscular planes of his body mirrored the classical beauty of the male statues in the gallery. She loved his quiet strength, his humor. It felt beautiful and pure to be with him like this. Did Russell regard his love affairs in such a light? Would he have ever told her he was having a child with another woman?

"I wouldn't worry about Jane and my brother," he said. "This is their home, and while it is monstrously large, they're not likely to get lost."

"They can certainly find their way here."

"They won't," he said reassuringly.

"I shan't be able to look your brother in the eye again."

"Do you think Grayson is a stranger to seduction?" He drew her back onto her feet. "I am your protector, Julia. I wouldn't be touching you if I weren't prepared to stand beside you afterward."

Whatever that might mean, Julia thought feverishly as she followed him to the stairs. She was half afraid to speculate. He was not a man to make false promises. Or false threats. His family appeared to support him. Grayson and Jane had embraced her with unmistakable warmth tonight. She felt comfortable with his brother Drake.

She glanced back into the candlelit gallery. In the ethereal rose-gold glow it appeared that the eyes of the vestal virgin's eyes had widened. Julia grinned ruefully. If she had spent another minute alone with Heath on that couch, the poor statue would have had a good reason to drop her urn.

Chapter 18

Julia sat at her desk an hour later, trying to ignore the light tapping at her door. She'd been working again on her secret sketch of Heath. Well, she had been admiring it anyway. The last thing she needed was for Hermia to find her mooning over a drawing of a naked man.

Not just any naked man, either, and Julia doubted she'd done him artistic justice with her amateur effort. She had seen his beautiful scarred chest and strong powerful back, had touched the sculpted muscle and sinew with her own hands. The other undeniably male parts of his body remained more of a delicious mystery.

One she wanted to solve. After tonight, Julia's curiosity had been irrevocably aroused. She could still feel the imprint of where he had lain on her, the possessive strength of his body against hers. Her lips were lightly bruised from his kisses, her breasts still swollen from his love bites.

She took out a fresh piece of paper, grinning, and started to draw her personal Apollo in caricature. Absolutely no one would be allowed to see this rendition. It would be wicked and unspeakably naughty. One day, if all went well, she might show it to Heath. . . .

She threw her shawl over the sketch and stood as the door opened. Hermia, in a purple gauze wrapper and a frown on her face, regarded her in concern.

"I just wanted to make certain everything is all right. You were quiet coming in. Dinner with Sedgecroft went smoothly?"

A little *too* smoothly, Julia thought, but only said, "Lovely. The best. The meal was divine. The marchioness is beautiful and great fun."

"Great fun," Hermia murmured, her eyes reflective. "Well, that is fine then."

"Fine, yes."

Hermia hesitated, taking another step into the room. Julia reached behind her and smoothed out the shawl to keep the sketch from slipping. Hermia would be shocked if she saw what Julia had just drawn "Did you entertain Odham?"

"That old rascal. I am never speaking to him again. He kept trying to kiss me in front of the servants. Can you imagine? By the way, Madame Tournier has asked if you would be available at the end of the week."

Julia studied the carpet, remembering Heath's mouth as he had kissed her, the small scar on his upper lip, the hard weight of his manhood. She knew what she would dream of tonight. Would she dream of being kissed by him? She could dream of a lot more.

"Will you?" Hermia asked a trifle impatiently.

"Will I what?" she said, startled.

"Be available for the modiste? The fitting for your wedding gown, Julia. You do recall you are engaged to be married when Russell returns?"

Julia glanced up guiltily. How to gracefully end her

engagement had been the last thing on her mind, although of course she would have to do it. Heath's decadent kisses had taken precedence. It occurred to her the two of them had crossed a dangerous line tonight, and she ought to feel far more repentful. "Of course I recall, but I'm . . ."

Hermia gave a deep sigh. "Having second thoughts? I'd guessed as much. You were grieving both your husband and your father when you accepted Russell's proposal."

"Oh," Julia said, leaning back against the desk as the shawl began to slip. "I don't know what you mean—let's change the subject, shall we? Odham wasn't here tonight, which must mean he's been pestering *you* again with a proposal."

"It means nothing of the sort," Hermia said in annoyance. "It means—"

The sketch slid off the desk.

Hermia bent at the waist to retrieve it, her arm arrested in midair at the horrified shriek Julia gave. "No. It's all right! Don't touch it. You'll strain your back."

"There's nothing wrong with my back."

"Well, no point in taking chances, is there?" Julia asked, swooping down before Hermia could get a good look at the charcoal sketch.

It was all there, in shades of black, white, and gray. The details of Heath's body in its glorious, exaggerated beauty. Or at least the details that Julia half remembered and half imagined. Blown completely out of proportion. Sinful. A sight to rob a woman of all her wits.

For a heartbeat she thought that Hermia would faint. This was her aunt, for heaven's sake, and Julia had practically admitted to her that she was in love with Heath. Which didn't excuse her sketching naughty pictures of him. The older woman's face reflected a myriad of emotions, fortunately none of which she seemed able to voice. Finally she cleared her throat.

"I believe you should guard that sketch more carefully, Julia," she said, compressing her lips. "It shall fetch a fortune at our auction."

Heath lingered on the stone steps of Julia's town house for several minutes after he had seen her inside. It was a wonder he did not go up in smoke in the drizzling rain that pattered down on him. He hated to end the evening. He'd been reluctant to break the spell that the past several hours had cast over them, to let anything threaten their bond of sexual attraction.

Standing at the bottom of her staircase, he had invented a thousand excuses to follow her. Was her window secured? Did her door lock properly? It had been easy for him to gain entry to her room, he scolded. Would she like him to search inside her wardrobe for intruders?

"I do not think there is any need," she'd replied. Her clear gray eyes had sparkled with amusement at his warnings. He had felt like a parent guarding a child. But there was nothing paternal in the chained passion between them. Like a mythical beast, it roared to be unleashed.

Make her burn.

He was practically breathing fire himself, searing to charcoal everything in his sight.

Restraint was his forte. Wasn't it? Or had he never understood the true meaning of temptation before?

He stared in resentment at the small carriage that awaited him in the empty street. He intended to go home for a fresh change of clothes and to bring back a few books for the night ahead. He would not be gone long enough for anything to happen to her.

Unfortunately, he would not be gone long enough to bank his passion for her, either. His mind returned over and over to their encounter on the couch. He tortured himself with the memory of her response to him, how warm and inviting her body had been. She had been liquid fire in his hands, hotter than any woman he had ever known. He had known her for years, and he wanted to know her better, inside and out, in every way he could imagine.

He hurried out into the street, then half turned and looked back in longing at the town house. What would he do in the event that Russell returned before he had won Julia over completely? Ruefully he reflected that he and Grayson had neglected to include that crucial detail in their plot.

Of course, Grayson would have no compunctions about doing whatever was necessary to attain his goal. And when it came down to Julia, Heath suspected that the darker side of his own soul might indeed come into play. She was his. Russell had betrayed her. Too bad, but one did not gamble with affairs of the heart. After tonight there was no doubt at all that Heath would have her.

He turned to his carriage and saw the curtain shift slightly. His gaze shot in question to the well-trained coachman sitting on the box with his face hooded against the rain. The coachman gave him a faint nod to indicate that all was well.

Heath climbed inside.

"Good evening, Boscastle," a gruff voice greeted him. "Nice weather if one is a water fowl, isn't it?"

Heath relaxed his guard. He had not seen Colonel

Hartwell in ages. Not since Heath had been a raw intelligence scout who had patrolled incognito in the light cavalry and wracked his brains solving enemy codes. Hartwell had been a frequent guest at Wellington's war table. Word had it he was still attached to the War Office, although in what official capacity Heath did not know.

Hartwell appeared considerably older, his hair silver, his dark hazel eyes still sharp and insightful. "You look far better than when I last saw you," he said after a long pause.

He was referring to the battered, half-dead state in which Heath had been found when Russell and his men had staged their heroic siege on Auclair's headquarters.

He sat down opposite Hartwell. "I *feel* better, thank you. Are we going anywhere tonight?"

"Just to your house. I thought we could have a chat to catch up with each other."

A chat. Heath's chest tightened in warning. Normal conversation could have been held at the club over cards or brandy. He rubbed his upper lip, his face reflective. "Is Russell dead?"

"No. But the bloody idiot is halfway to Brittany following a false lead."

Heath glanced out the window as the town house receded behind a shroud of rain. Was Julia in bed yet? Had she locked her door and wedged the chair against it as he'd insisted? Was she undressing, remembering what they had done?

"Auclair is not in France," Hartwell continued. "He never was."

Heath turned his head. A sense of panic rose inside him. He'd left her alone. "He's here. Auclair is *here*?"

"Yes."

"It was a trick, all along." Julia's feminine intuition had been chillingly accurate. Russell had been so eager to act the hero again that he'd played right into Auclair's hand. Heath fought the urge to stop the carriage. To run back to her house. His heart was beating hard, a counterpoint to the clattering of the carriage wheels over the wet cobbles.

"What does he want?"

"We aren't sure." Hartwell regarded him in concern. "We do know Fouché has been in contact with Napoleon on Elba. There does not appear to be a connection. Auclair seems to be acting alone these days."

"But Auclair—in London. I'd heard he had turned to dueling for a living."

"He likes to kill people, apparently. We have several men looking for him."

Heath nodded. "And are my services needed?"

"Right now you can be of service to us by staying alive. Napoleon's staff have had plenty of time to devise a new cipher, and we may require your cryptology skills should problems arise in the future."

"A cipher? What about Auclair?"

"You are advised to do whatever you must to protect yourself against him should you meet him before he is captured. But for God's sake, be careful."

The carriage stopped in front of Heath's bachelor lodgings on St. James's Street. "Are you coming inside?"

"No. My wife becomes agitated when I am out late at night. Your coachman can drop me off, if you don't mind."

He sent Hamm to fetch fresh clothing, then went straight to his darkened study to gather a few books. The nerve endings on his nape prickled in awareness as he entered the room.

He stood for several seconds in front of the unlit fireplace and listened to the steady ticking of the enameled clock. The portrait on the wall of a hunting scene was off center by a nailbreadth. His collection of books on Egyptology were not aligned on the bookshelf as he had left them. Call it an idiosyncrasy of his nature, but Heath noticed such details and knew the room had been violated. Not by his small staff of well-trained servants, who knew what they might and might not disturb without permission.

Someone else, an intruder, had visited. He probably would not have even sensed the subtle difference if Hartwell hadn't warned him.

He turned his head and scrutinized the moonlit outlines of his furnishings, the desk, the armchairs. Whoever had been there was gone. What had been the objective?

He removed a small brass key from the heel of his boot and opened the private compartment in his desk. His files did not appear to have been taken. Not that secret Crown business had been committed to paper—he never put in writing the names of past operatives, or contacts even now maintained in foreign countries.

Such information, along with his deciphering skills, had been locked away in his mind.

He looked up slowly as a glitter of dark gemstones on the floor caught his attention.

Julia's sapphire bracelet. The one she had lost at the theater. He leaned down to retrieve it. The gold links lay nestled in the palm of a black gauntlet glove. The match to the one he had found in her shed, to be precise. He clasped the bracelet in his hand, fighting the wave of sick fury that coursed through him, the dark possibility that entered his mind. Did he know the identity of his intruder?

He remembered that Armand Auclair had tortured his captives wearing a hood and the same gloves his father had used to execute French aristocrats who went to the guillotine. Could Auclair have left the gloves here and in Julia's shed as a calling card? Did the bracelet mean that she was in imminent danger? But why? Why would Auclair go to such lengths?

Hartwell was right. Russell had been lured away to leave the field clear for Auclair.

A gigantic shadow filled the doorway. Heath released his indrawn breath through his teeth. "I have your things ready, my lord," Hamm said.

"A change in plans, Hamm."

The rough-featured face moved into the moonlight. "You are not returning to Lady Whitby's house?"

"Oh, I'm going all right." Heath straightened, the bracelet clasped in his hand. "We're both going, in fact. I have a job for you."

Hamm's huge shoulders lifted as if in anticipation. "A real job, my lord? A job that involves action and not standing on the back of a carriage like a trained monkey?"

Heath managed a smile, but there was no lightness inside him, only an urgent need to return to Julia's side, to protect her from a man who had made killing an art. No one would threaten her while he had breath in his body.

"Come with me to the carriage, Hamm. I shall explain on our way. You may send for your belongings and inform the staff later of what has happened."

Chapter 19

Julia was not in her bedchamber when he returned to the town house. Heath pushed past the sleepy footman who'd let him in, now accustomed to the odd behavior of Julia's friend. God knew he was providing the ton with enough fodder for a major scandal. Well, let them gossip. He had more important things on his mind.

She was not in the drawing room either.

His instincts led him to the narrow kitchen at the back of the house, where a coal fire burned low in the dark. He saw Julia standing at the kitchen door, letting the cat out for the night. For a moment he was so relieved to see her, he did not say a word. He simply stared. She had brushed out her hair for bed. It shone wine-red in the subtle glow of firelight.

She turned, her hand lifting to her throat. "Dear heaven, Heath. What is it?"

He strode toward her. He wasn't about to terrify her with the truth. That could wait until morning, and she would have to be told, to realize she could not let down her guard again. For now it was enough to know she was safe, and that he could hold her again, keep her beside him.

She glanced down at the glittering stones in his hand. "Oh, you found my bracelet, you clever man. Where was it lost?"

"On the carpet." He didn't elaborate. He would tell her that tomorrow, too.

"Did you come all the way back just to bring it to me?"

She looked irresistible in the hazy moonlight of the garden, her smile warm and inviting, her lush red hair lightly scented. Her robe had parted so that the tops of her breasts showed blush-pink against the cream silk lacing. His mouth went dry. The feel of her, his craving for sex, still dominated his senses.

"Has the cat got your tongue, Heath?" she teased. "You've gone awfully quiet."

He drew her into his arms. She didn't resist, huddling into his warmth. He kicked the door shut and bolted it. "Don't stand here in the dark again by yourself."

"What is it?"

"If it were in my power, I would lock you away from the rest of the world and keep you safe forever."

She pulled back a little to look up at him. "A dark desire, somewhat impractical, but not entirely unappealing."

"No?" He felt his body harden.

"No."

He leaned into her, pressing her against the heavy oak door. Julia's arms lifted to lock around his neck. "I'm sorry, Julia," he said.

She gave a dreamy sigh. "For what?"

He swallowed. "For not fighting for you."

"Oh." She lowered her gaze. "I shouldn't have said that."

"I'm glad I know."

"I think you know a little bit too much about me now."

"I want to know more."

"That sounds very wicked," she whispered. "Tell me something. Did you plan what happened tonight at your brother's house?"

"Why would you think that?" he asked innocently, moving against her.

She laughed. "You did."

"What if I did?"

He felt her hesitate, felt her body tremble. "I'd say I shall have to be careful of you in the future—careful to resist you, that is."

"You're not being very careful now." He gazed down into her face. "I think, with a little effort, I could make you completely careless, in fact."

She moistened her lower lip. "Confident, aren't we?"

"In certain things, yes."

He caught her face in his free hand. His tongue traced her plump bottom lip. She tasted of mint tea. She was wearing a cotton nightrail under a lavender lightweight woolen robe. He molded his body to her uncorseted curves. Black desire raged through his blood as she arched her back in response. He had to remind himself that they were standing at the kitchen door in the dark. He wanted to bury himself deep inside her silky dampness and take her up against the door until there was no doubt that she belonged to him. His. She should always have been his. He was still on fire from being with her earlier. He could only imagine, after the way she'd responded to him, how incredible it would be to ride her, to spend days and nights in bed together.

He ran his hand down her shoulder, her side, shaping the

rise of her heart-shaped bottom. He was discovering that even for him the Boscastle blood ran true. Had he ever hoped to escape his heritage?

He meant to seduce her to the point of delicious surrender. There was one advantage to winning her after all these years. He was experienced enough to appreciate her.

Her breathing quickened. She was becoming more sensitive to him day by day. She traced her fingernail down his nape. "Does this mean that you came back tonight because I am desirable and not some horrible duty you must fulfill?"

"You are the most desirable—" He straightened, turning his back on her at the smart tapping of slippers on the flagstone floor.

"Who's there?" Hermia whispered from behind the oak table that stood between them. "Show yourselves, whoever you are."

Julia released a rueful sigh. "It's only us, Aunt Hermia. We were just, um, letting the cat out."

"I see." Hermia stared directly at Heath. "And are you letting Boscastle out, too? Or is he staying the night?"

Julia grinned at Heath. "Are you staying, Boscastle?"

"Yes. He's staying," he said, grinning back. "I'm staying, Hermia, and, with your permission, ladies, I have brought along reinforcements. One of my servants." He shook his head as he remembered Hamm waiting diligently out in the carriage, on the lookout for unwanted visitors.

"A guest?" Hermia said, raising her brow. "Well, we have the painting club here again the day after tomorrow. You both might want to get some rest."

"The painting club?" Heath said in chagrin.

Julia began to laugh. "Perhaps your companion can pose for us, too."

Heath drew away from her with regret. It was clear that he had a dreary night ahead of him with Hamm for company. But at least he knew she would be safe. For now that was what mattered.

Julia had just begun eating breakfast alone when Heath entered the small morning room the next day. She looked up from the table and smiled. She had known last night that something weighed on his mind, and he confirmed her suspicion as they took coffee and toast together.

"So Auclair is in London," she said in a subdued voice after he finished explaining what he'd discovered the previous evening. "How frightening to think he has been in England without anyone realizing it."

He ran his forefinger across his lip. "Your intuition was right all along."

"And Russell does not know?" she asked in concern. Despite the fact that she no longer wished to marry him, she did not want him to lose his life.

"By now he might."

"So he will return," she said slowly.

He regarded her in the pale morning light, and Julia felt the heat of his scrutiny to her bones. Heath was one of those men who could chase down villains, sleep in his clothes, and wake up the next morning appearing as crisp and composed as ever.

"He will not take you from me," he said.

"How is your head?" she asked.

He lowered his hand. "My head is fine. Do you understand the import of what I have just told you?"

She nodded slowly. "I think so." To look into his eyes now, deeply concerned but unfathomable, she might have dreamed what they had done last night. "I certainly understand that the danger cannot be underestimated."

"Good," he said, his voice rough.

She knew that there were different kinds of danger. The danger that Auclair posed. The danger of an affair between Heath and her, the emotional repercussions.

The truth was, Heath was the only man who'd made a genuine effort to seduce her, and he was good at it. Far too good. Her husband had not needed or understood the art of seduction. She had been an inexperienced, headstrong young woman who'd married on impulse and learned to live with the choice she had made. Adam had been neglectful, but certainly not cruel. He had been passionate about his career, had given his life to it in the end.

Russell had not bothered with seduction. Pursuit, yes. The thrill of the chase. But Julia had not felt especially desired for herself. Her father's inheritance was a definite lure. Her experience with passion, perhaps. Russell had been kind to her; she knew he felt at least affection for her, but it was clear he shared a different passion with his mistress. He had never made Julia feel as attractive as she did now. Perhaps he did not even realize they did not belong together. She wanted more from a marriage than what he offered.

"Danger," she said, rising to fill his cup. "I should be used to it after living in India." She leaned over his shoulder. His lean cheek smelled of shaving soap. She ached all of a sudden to touch him again, to feel the intimate pressure of his body against hers.

The vehemence in his voice startled her. "You have never

known the sort of danger that Auclair poses; I guarantee it."

"I worry for you, Heath. Until I saw the scars on your body, I did not realize what a monster he is."

He studied her as she returned to her chair. "I've asked Drake and Devon to help me. I have another man waiting outside to take over those times I must be gone from you."

Julia made a face. "Another man?"

"My footman. He spent the night here with me."

She went to the window, gasping as she drew the heavy brocade curtains open and spied the massively built figure standing outside. "I do not see a footman, Heath. I see a giant with ham hocks for hands, scowling at me from the front steps."

He took a sip of coffee. "That would be Hamm."

"Where did you find him? In a Russian circus?"

"Not a bad guess. It was Prussia, at the academy. He comes from Yorkshire, actually. He served with me in Portugal." He put down his cup, smiling wryly. "I took him on originally as a butler."

"He was demoted?"

"Well, it was a mutual decision. The housekeeper said she would strangle him with her bare hands if he broke another dish."

Julia drew the curtains back into place. "I daresay he shall curtail my social life."

He draped his arm over the back of his chair. "I daresay he will. That is the point."

She backed away from the window. "I don't know what to say. He looks menacing."

"Wait until you meet him."

Before Julia could object, he rose from his chair to summon the footman into the house. Hamm nodded stiffly as Heath brought him to Julia for an introduction.

"He's quite helpful," Heath whispered over her shoulder.

"Quite huge," she whispered back.

Hamm stood at perfect attention, then said, "Shall I tend the fire, my lady? I notice the flames are low."

"Yes . . ." Julia glanced around his massive form to the woman who had just pushed open the door.

Hermia stood frozen to the spot, her ample bosom quivering. "Dear heavens! Who is this?"

"Hamm," Julia murmured, her lips pursing in amusement. Well, she would certainly be well protected now.

"Not the food," Hermia said, edging around the carpet. "*Him.*"

"This is Hamm," Heath said from the window. "*He's* Hamm."

"Whom?" Hermia said, her eye on the impressive footman at the fireplace.

"Hamm." Julia frowned. "His name is Hamm. He is a soldier turned footman, and Heath is stationing him here in the house. To protect us."

Hermia examined Hamm in thoughtful silence.

Julia cleared her throat. "Isn't he impressive?" she prompted.

Hermia started. "What did you say, dear?"

Heath leaned back against the window and smiled at the look of exasperation Julia shot him. "Isn't it a horrid idea to take Hamm away from his other duties, Aunt Hermia?"

"Hamm." Hermia shook her head. "I mean, *ahem.* A well-trained footman *is* a treasure, and he certainly cuts an intimidating figure. How kind of Boscastle. I shall feel quite well guarded between the two of them."

Julia sat down at the table in resignation. She did not object to Hamm's presence; it never hurt to have a capable man at one's call. But she was concerned that Heath had decided to go on a personal hunt for Auclair. The evil that Russell had intended to confront had come home. And Heath would be the one in the most danger. He would be the one to face the man who had almost destroyed him. Only now was she beginning to realize how much was at stake.

He stirred. "Ladies, I will be gone for only a few hours on some business matters. Hamm will not leave your side until then. Isn't that right, Hamm?"

Hamm dropped the brass poker on the hearth with a loud clatter. "Not for a second, my lord."

Julia's heart lodged in her throat as she watched Heath make a quiet exit. In a bittersweet flash of honesty she realized that she had not felt anywhere near this much anxiety when Russell had left her for France. It was all she could do not to run into the street after Heath. Where was he going? Did he have friends to help him? She held her emotions in check. She ought to be worrying about what would happen when Russell returned.

Her fiancé. Her betrayer. The hero of the hour. She could not picture herself standing before him, taking her wedding vows. The image was murky, dissolving all too swiftly. It felt wrong. Yet lying half naked in Heath's arms had not. She could not bring herself to ask him if he knew about Russell's infidelity. It did not matter. Heath was the only man she had ever wanted like this. Russell's deception merely gave her reason to face the truth.

She reached across the table, shaking herself inwardly. "Coffee, Hermia?"

Her aunt nodded as she took her chair, whispering, "Perhaps we should have our footman pour. Except he does look a trifle heavy-handed."

"Heavy-handed?" Julia stifled a giggle, whispering back, "He looks as if he could uproot an entire forest with his little finger. I suppose we could try to hide him. Do you have any Ionic columns close by?"

She and Hermia turned to study the massive footman. Julia whispered behind her cup, "I don't think there is a chest, or even closet, large enough to conceal him."

"Could we put him in another room?"

Julia gave a helpless shrug. "Heath has ordered him to follow me everywhere."

"My goodness."

"Shall we put him to the test?"

Julia waited until Hamm turned back to the fire, then made a beeline for the door. Before she could twist the knob, Hamm lurched around from the hearth and moved forward to open the door for her.

"Are we going out?" he inquired in his soft grumbly voice. "Shall I have the carriage brought around?"

Julia glanced back at Hermia in resignation. "Are we going out today?"

Hermia nodded. "You received an invitation to Audrey Watson's house—she would like to have tea with you. I would like a new turban to wear to the club tomorrow."

Shopping. With Hermia and Hamm. An invitation to have tea with a courtesan. Julia did not want to think how

Russell would react if he saw them, not that she much cared. He deserved to be engaged to a scandalous widow. Perhaps he deserved even worse. "Bring the carriage around in twenty minutes," she said decisively. She was suddenly curious to find out why Audrey Watson would issue her an invitation. "I have a call to pay before we shop."

Chapter 20

Julia instructed her coachman to drive her to Audrey Watson's two-story residence on Bruton Street in Berkeley Square. Hamm and Hermia accompanied her into an anteroom, where she asked them to wait while she spoke in private to the celebrated courtesan. She had never been inside Audrey's house, but she'd heard a few stories about the scandalous parties its owner gave. Despite the fact that she did not know the woman well, she had instinctively liked her. But why had she invited Julia here today?

Audrey, clad in a pale mauve gauze gown, was entertaining a young Cossack when Julia was announced. She gave her disgruntled lover a gentle shove toward the door and ordered him to go for a lengthy walk while she greeted her arrival.

Julia stood in the doorway, staring at the clutter of trunks and traveling bags that covered the floor. A plump white poodle barked at her from the sofa. The Cossack swept past her, his hat in his hand.

"Julia, it really is you," Audrey said, extending her arms out in greeting. "I wasn't sure you would come."

Julia waited until Audrey's handsome footman closed

the door, leaving the two of them alone. Rumor had it that more than one widow admired Audrey and had accepted her invitation to become a lady of pleasure. Becoming a wealthy man's mistress was a desirable position for many young women who found themselves without resources. Audrey was an infamous hostess, a well-liked former actress, and a sponsoress of the arts. Or of the artists.

Audrey was also privy to more of London's secrets than anyone else Julia knew. She entertained poets and politicians. She trained the mistresses of powerful men.

"I've heard the most delicious rumor," Audrey said, pressing a finger to her cherry-red mouth. "It involves an absolutely sinful sketch of Heath Boscastle, au naturel, to be auctioned for charity. I shall outbid anyone for the chance to display it in my receiving room."

Julia sat down beside Audrey, hoping her cheeks weren't as fiery-red as they felt. How quickly word spread. "I have a feeling this mystery sketch will *not* ever be on public display."

"I am crushed," Audrey said, her hand dropping to her heart.

"If this rumored sketch even exists," Julia added for good measure.

Audrey subjected her to a sly look. "Have *you* seen it, by any chance?"

"Audrey, really."

"I collect nude men, you see."

"Do you?" Julia glanced around in amusement. "Where do you keep them? And don't they get cold?"

Audrey laughed. "*Paintings* of nude men. Oh, Julia, my naughty heiress, you must come with me to Paris."

"To Paris?" Julia's gaze strayed to the assortment of

trunks on the floor. Paris was where many of London's ton had gone to celebrate peace . . . and the other pleasures of the city they had been denied during the war. Fashion, haute cuisine, beautiful women. She sighed. No doubt Russell had availed himself of all the delights and decadence that Paris had to offer while Heath protected her. "Are you traveling alone?" she asked Audrey.

"No. I'm taking my Cossack for company. My current lover is in the House of Lords. He's older, well, practically an antique, and does not travel well." Audrey lifted the poodle into her lap. "Julia, I know you must be wondering why I invited you here today. . . ."

"I am, actually."

Audrey gave her a frank look. "There are very few women who talk to me in public, Julia. Men do, but the ladies of the ton, although curious about my profession, are more cautious about my company."

"I am past the age of worrying about what the ton thinks of me." Especially when most of what the ton thought was true.

Audrey stroked the poodle, her gaze direct. "Your fiancé is unfaithful, Julia. The woman involved has been set up in private lodgings. She is expecting a child in the spring. Russell buys her jewelry and confesses at parties that he adores her."

Julia shook her head. So that was it. Audrey meant well. She was suddenly grateful that Odham had prepared her for this. "I appreciate your candor, Audrey, but I already know."

"And you will forgive him?" Audrey asked curiously.

"Of course not." Because she also knew in her heart that he would never love her as she wished to be loved. Russell had his good qualities. To most women he was considered a catch, and he probably thought that having a mistress was perfectly acceptable for a man in his position. But Julia had agreed to marry him for all the wrong reasons, and she was old enough not only to know her own mind, but to change it.

"Russell set her up in lodgings on Half Moon Street with his brother for safety," Audrey added after a moment's silence.

"Isn't he thoughtful?"

"That man thinks mostly of himself," Audrey said, indignant on Julia's behalf. "Shall I have my Cossack take care of him for you?"

Julia hesitated. "It is tempting, but I need to think about it first."

"You wouldn't consider working for me, would you?" Audrey asked half jokingly.

"That is not quite as tempting."

"Especially not with Heath Boscastle as your protector."

"It is a temporary position, Audrey."

"Perhaps."

"What do you mean?"

"I saw him chasing after you in the ballroom that night, Julia. In my professional opinion, his instincts were not entirely protective."

Julia smiled at the thought. Russell's deception had made it easy to follow her heart, to force her to face what she really wanted. She would never be happy being the wife of a man with political aspirations. She would, on the other hand, be perfectly content marrying a rogue.

"Take him," Audrey said in such an impassioned voice that both Julia and the poodle jumped.

Julia stared at her. "Take him where?"

"If you have to ask me that, then perhaps you do need my professional expertise."

"No, thank you, Audrey. I shall manage this 'journey' on my own." She rose, clutching her reticule in her hands. "You have been most kind."

"The sketch of yours would be lovely repayment." Audrey stood in a flutter of mauve gauze to kiss Julia on the cheek. "The Boscastle men are beautiful, every one of them, but Heath is probably the most intriguing. I suspect that he would be difficult to resist in the bedroom."

"I suspect he would," Julia replied. Which of course she already knew.

"Are you absolutely sure you won't take a few secrets with you? You could use them on Russell to teach him a lesson if nothing else. Leave the bastard breathless for you. What a wonderful revenge."

Julia wavered, more tempted than she wanted to show. Not to apply any such teachings on Russell, but on Boscastle. He was a highly sexual man. "It isn't really the sort of thing that can be taught, is it?"

"Oh, Julia, for a wicked widow, you do need your education broadened. Sit down."

Julia would never quite look at sexual relations in the same way again. Audrey's instructions had been simple and yet shockingly explicit. Julia did have a broad base of knowledge to build upon. But . . . she had never thought of pleasing a man as a skill to be acquired, much as sewing a sampler or speaking French.

"It would seem," Julia had said after a very graphic description of a certain act, "that a woman might be better off just doing what comes to her naturally."

Audrey's throaty laugh of delight had filled the room. "But nature always can use a little help. After all, one does not plant cucumber seeds in a strawberry patch."

Julia examined the book that Audrey had shown her. "Interesting positions. I'm suddenly feeling a little warm."

"We cannot cover every pleasurable act in a single day," Audrey said.

"I do not think my heart could take it."

"You have a crude understanding of what pleases a man," Audrey said thoughtfully. "Your instincts are your best assets in bed."

"I'm not sure that anybody outside this room would agree with you."

Audrey smiled slowly. "Boscastle would."

Julia felt a blush mount her cheeks. "That remains to be seen."

"It remains to be proven. Just think of me as passing on the torch of passion, Julia."

After she left Bruton Street, her mind brimming with sexual images, Julia kept her promise to go shopping with Hermia. They visited a perfumier on South Audley Street, then a bookshop and milliner's on Stafford Street.

Hermia tried on every hat in the shop. "What do you think of this one?" she asked from the mirror for what seemed to Julia to be the hundredth time.

"It's a lovely hat," Julia said absently.

"I'm not *wearing* a hat," Hermia snapped. "I knew you were not paying attention. What did you and Mrs. Watson discuss that has made you so distracted?"

Julia pretended to examine a pair of green gloves on the counter. "Cucumber seeds."

"Seeds?"

"Yes." As in planting them in places where they did not belong. Which was apparently what her faithless former fiancé Russell had done.

A child. A child changed everything. It meant family, obligation, a long-term association, and not just a sexual one either. Part of Russell's cucumber, well, his seed, anyway, belonged forever to another woman. Julia wished all three of them happiness. Without her.

Audrey had known, and Russell was comfortable discussing his love affair at parties. What about Heath? What did the inscrutable, seductive Sphinx know? Shouldn't he have warned her? Or had he been waiting for her to find out for herself?

She tossed down the gloves and followed Hermia out of the shop.

The woman, Russell's mistress, was staying here in London, which meant that he'd probably visited her after he saw Julia. If Odham had heard about the arrangement at his club, it would stand to reason that Heath would be aware of it, too. No wonder the sly devil had no compunctions about seducing her.

"You great, big, corrupt cad, Russell," she said aloud, startling Hamm, who nearly walked into a pedestrian at the sound of her irate voice. "Not you, Hamm," she added with an apologetic smile. "I have grown fond of you." And even more so of his master.

A gust of wind blew down the street. Julia's hair tangled in her face, and as she reached to straighten it, the book she had brought for Heath slipped from under her arm.

"Oh, blast it all."

"Please, allow me."

She nodded in gratitude as a tall, darkly cloaked man in a high black beaver hat, gold-knobbed cane under his arm, reached down to retrieve her book. Before she could properly thank him, he had disappeared in the crowd of pedestrians on the pavement.

"Is everything all right?" Hamm asked from behind his tower of Hermia's purchases.

"Yes." She gazed out at the procession of carriages that clogged the street. "I dropped a book. A polite man rescued it."

She turned and found herself blocked by a hard, muscular chest. A strong arm encircled her waist, holding her steady. A familiar thrill shimmered down her spine at his protective embrace. Heath. She had just spent an hour studying the rudiments of giving pleasure to a man. She was certain she looked guilty. She wondered suddenly what he would think if he knew.

"Don't you know better than to talk to strangers?" he asked with a strained smile. "Come with me. My carriage is closer than yours."

"What about my aunt?"

"Hamm will take care of her."

"Yes, but—"

He grasped her elbow, and she felt the length of his body, his strength, through her cloak. His eyes looked more charcoal than blue today—a reflection of the sky, or of his mood? He smiled at her, a reminder of how close they had come to making love last night. He had played her like an instrument, awakened all her senses. One day she would do the same to him.

The mere idea made her heart accelerate in anticipation. She felt her lips quirk into a smile. His grip on her arm tightened as if he could read her thoughts. Without another word he ushered her toward his waiting carriage. The entire ride home, seated opposite him, she sensed the controlled tension in him. Had he found out anything more about Auclair? As always he looked impeccable, his blue frock coat perfectly tailored, his white linen shirt pristine, his Hessian boots polished to a high gleam.

"Did you have a pleasant afternoon?" he asked as they finally reached the town house.

She watched as he studied the street before allowing her out of the carriage. "Well," she said, a little breathless, "it was a distraction."

"And how was Audrey Watson?" he asked as they approached the front entrance.

The butler left them alone in the hall. The book she had brought for him slipped out of her hand. "You followed me?"

"Only to Bruton Street."

"But why?"

"I wanted to see if anyone was following you."

"And?" she asked quietly.

"No one followed you to the house." His gaze held hers in an unwavering stare. "I admit to being a little astonished myself."

She bit the end of her tongue. She was flustered that he knew where she had been, flattered that he had taken the effort to guard her, but heavens, if he guessed what she and Audrey had discussed . . . The secrets to arousing and pleasuring a man. Specifically *this* man, in illicit and candidly graphic detail. Audrey's advice echoed in her brain.

The male organ must be revered, Julia.

Revered? Really?

Look at these pictures.

My goodness. I certainly hope they were not drawn to scale. That looks more like a canon than a—

Julia, you were married for years. Surely you examined your husband's body.

Well, yes, but I might have paid more attention if it had been this size.

"Julia?" Heath gave her a puzzled look. "Your mind has drifted away. What are you thinking?"

"What am I thinking?"

He folded his arms across his chest. "I confess *I* don't know what to think."

"It's a relief, isn't it?"

"What is a relief?"

"That no one followed me. Except you. Was that the important duty that you mentioned?"

"Audrey Watson is an accomplished courtesan as well as a family friend. On a professional basis, she has become known for dispensing sexual expertise to women eager to improve their bedroom skills."

Julia backed up against the hall stand. A shower of calling cards fell off the silver salver onto the floor. "Is she? Well, fancy that. I mean, who would have guessed?"

"The entire English population, I'd say."

"Don't forget I've been away."

He narrowed his eyes. "Some knowledge is universal."

"Is it?"

"The knowledge that Audrey imparts certainly is."

"You seem to know a bit about her yourself," she retorted.

"You're the one who went to her house. And stayed quite some time."

"And you've never visited her?"

The muted sound of voices, Hermia's and Hamm's, on the front steps, came to Julia's salvation. She would probably have blurted out everything if he'd continued to question her.

"A reprieve," he said in amusement.

She glanced at the door, rubbing her hands together. "It's getting late. Let's all have tea."

He caught both ends of her shawl and slowly drew her back toward him. "Just remember that I am always here if you need advice in the future, Julia."

"Advice?" she said faintly.

"From the male point of view."

"On . . ." She saw the devil issue a direct challenge in his eyes, and the hellion she was at heart ached to accept.

"Lovemaking," he said, as if she didn't know.

Hermia burst into the hall, dragging Hamm with his armload of boxes after her. "We're home, everyone."

Heath released the ends of Julia's shawl. Suddenly she could not seem to draw enough air into her lungs. All she could think of was doing the things to him that she had studied today. He stared into her eyes, and she felt his incendiary look scorch through her guard, felt an answering spark kindle deep in her belly.

"Julia?" he questioned softly, his wicked voice low with curiosity. "What were you up to this afternoon?"

"I—" She glanced down at the floor and brightened. "Oh, I bought you a book."

Chapter 21

꧁༺✦༻꧂

Heath sat in the corner of Julia's drawing room several hours later, the book of Egyptian hieroglyphs she'd purchased for him in hand. Hermia and Odham were playing cards by the fire, and Julia was serving as peacemaker to their squabbles.

The twin demons of desire and a growing premonition of danger put him on edge. There were too many uncertainties in the air to lower his guard. He stared out the window onto the dark London street to keep from staring at Julia. To keep from undressing her with his eyes. His mouth went dry every time he looked at her.

The warmth of her last night, the sensual openness she had shown, had tied him into knots. He gripped the unopened book in his hands. He was so hungry for her, so desperate for sexual relief that he could have run outside into the night and howled. His strategy for seduction could well end up killing him. Never had he been forced to exert this much discipline on his desires. Everything about her excited him, challenged the conqueror in him.

"Don't you want to play, Boscastle?" Odham asked him. "Hermia is cheating again."

"No," he murmured.

He wanted to play with Julia. Wanted to spread her naked beneath him and empty himself in her wet sheath. Wanted to make love to her until she was too weak even to walk.

His need for her, sexual and intensely emotional, had complicated his course. If he lost her again, he would never find anyone like her. There was no one else. They complemented each other, Julia with her joie de vivre that lightened his darker outlook on life. She was the only woman he knew who could set him on fire with a smile, a glance. Her lush body had always beckoned him, her laughter soothed him.

The thought of her consorting with a practiced courtesan intrigued him. He had to know exactly what she'd been doing. She had been uncharacteristically flustered when he'd questioned her. Did it have anything to do with what had happened between them in the gallery last night? Julia, soliciting advice in the sexual arts? He'd teach her anything she wanted to know, fulfill her every desire. He would be the most wicked mentor in the world.

"Heath?"

His entire body tightened at the brush of her hand on his arm. Last night she had touched him with a sensual promise that had ravished what control he'd maintained. By the time he'd carried out his plan, she would be begging for him to take her. If he didn't beg her first. He could go down on his knees this very moment.

"Do you like the book I brought you?"

He glanced up and allowed his gaze to travel slowly over her with a sensuality that left her breathless. "I haven't looked at it. My mind is on other things."

"I don't think I should ask you what those things are," she said under her breath.

He smiled lazily. "I think you already know."

The unmasked desire in his eyes mesmerized her. She'd felt him watching her all night as if she were naked before him. As if he were biding his time before making another move. She was drawn to him, her bond to Heath growing more powerful by the hour. She could hardly wait for Russell to come home so that she could officially break off their engagement. She would be honest with him even if he refused her the same respect.

He hadn't known about her past encounter with Heath. Or had he? She began to wonder. He had been at the same house party in Cornwall all those years ago. It was only afterward that he had started to pursue her. Had he guessed what had gone on between Heath and her? Or had he desired her simply because he was jealous of Heath and wanted to win?

The thought of Russell faded, replaced by the sinfully compelling man who sat before her. Heath looked dangerous tonight, more tense than she had ever seen him. Although he sat casually in the corner, Julia knew he was aware of every noise that disturbed the night. The rumble of a carriage in the street. The housekeeper's keys jangling in the back of the house.

Of every movement that Julia made.

He drummed his fingers on the spine of the book. "Thank you for the gift. I'll be able to look at it when we're in the country. I've decided we should accept Grayson's offer."

"The country?" She felt Hermia and Odham glance up

at her in curiosity. The country. On Boscastle turf. No where to run but into Heath's arms. Private evenings that invited intimacy. Long afternoons alone in the library behind locked doors. It would be an opportunity to learn more about him, to let down their guard a little. Perhaps Heath would have a chance to relax. It was a meaningful step for both of them.

"Taking me into custody, are you?"

He gave a low laugh. "For your own protection."

"I thought we would at least discuss it."

He shrugged. "We just did."

"Do I get any choice at all in the matter?" she asked with a teasing smile.

"Apparently not."

"Arrogant devil," she muttered. "I know what you can do with your book."

His eyes burned with amusement, and something that made her heart accelerate. "We'll have plenty of time in Kent for reading." His gaze indicated he had far less intellectual activities in mind. "Perhaps you should pack."

"But . . . I'm supposed to be fitted for some new clothes this week." One of which had been a wedding dress. Not that there would be a wedding.

He angled his head to smile at her. In the candlelight she wanted suddenly to sketch him. To undress him and run her hands over his marvelous body. "The wardrobe will have to wait."

"Fine. You can explain it to your family when I appear at the table in rags."

He laid his head back against the chair, the picture of sensual elegance. "I shall be happy to. In the meantime, you might want to pack those rags for our stay in Kent."

"I suppose I'll have to let a few friends know—"

"No. Absolutely not."

"Is this an abduction, Heath?"

"It might be if you're not ready in the morning."

She suppressed a smile. She liked the way he took control, and he was undoubtedly right. They would be safer on Grayson's private estate, and she was far more worried for Heath than for herself. Further arguing with him would not matter anyway even if she had not agreed. He had already made up his mind, and she might as well attempt to move the Sphinx with a wheelbarrow before she could change it.

The worst part was that she wasn't sure she wanted to. Audrey had said today that there was a little courtesan in every woman. Julia suspected she was about to prove that theory true.

As soon as the ladies retired for the night, Heath left Hamm on guard duty and went straight to Audrey's house on Bruton Street. She was entertaining friends: several politicians, a painter, and a pair of young pretty actresses who were apparently courtesans in training. Audrey had once been an actress herself, and she frequently said that playacting took a prominent role in pleasure.

The two young women examined Heath as if he were a full-course meal to be devoured during a famine. Audrey quickly came to his rescue and ushered him into her private room. Diamond-headed pins glittered in her hair, and she wore a choker of gemstones around her throat. Her copper taffeta gown rustled as she took her place on her chaise.

Heath went to the balcony window and casually studied the street below. He had not been followed.

"Boscastle, this *is* a nice surprise. Is it business or pleasure?"

He sat next to her and smiled. "Neither."

"But there isn't anything else, is there?"

"I want to know why Julia came to you today."

She widened her eyes. "I never tell."

He settled comfortably on the couch. "I shall sit here and stare at you until you do."

She fingered her choker, her gaze slowly drifting over his broad shoulders to his lower torso. "That's hardly a threat. Are you going to torture me?"

"I don't have the time."

She sighed. "What a shame."

"Audrey," he said softly, "I have to know."

She looked intrigued. "Why?"

"Why did Julia come to you?"

"Ask her."

"I'm asking you."

She began to fidget under his steady regard. "My lips are sealed."

He took her hand and kissed her fingers, one at a time. "Audrey, my beautiful temptress, how long have you been friends with my family?"

She quivered in pleasure, closing her eyes. "Too long, you devil. Oh, damnation. If I tell you, will you promise not to let Julia know?"

"My word as a gentleman."

"And as a rogue?"

He laughed. "That, too."

Two days later Julia had packed her bags for an indefinite stay in the country. She knew it was an irrevocable step, to agree to go with Heath to Grayson's estate. Hermia assured her it was the sensible thing to do, and Julia was grateful that she had her aunt's support, for all she teased her. Still, common sense had less to do with Julia's decision than the unreasoning power of emotion. She was only listening to her own heart. She wished she'd done so a long time ago.

She closed her bedchamber door and hurried down to the music room where she had hidden her sketches of Heath. She meant to take them with her. Heaven forbid that any of the servants should come across them. She'd have the devil's time defending that artwork.

"What are you doing, Julia?" her aunt demanded from the door. "Boscastle's carriage will be here at any minute."

Julia stared at the empty space behind the Irish harp that she had inherited from her grandfather. The sketches were gone. It couldn't be. No one used this room. It was the best hiding place in the house.

"Oh, no," she whispered. She turned to her aunt. "You haven't been in here recently, have you?"

"Not until today," Hermia replied. "This room is such a mess, one can barely move. I did, however, take the liberty of having two young chimney sweeps clean it out for you yesterday morning."

Julia gasped. "You didn't!"

"I just told you I did. Goodness, Julia. There was so much clutter in here, so many old papers. You would not have wanted to start a fire, would you?"

"What did they do with my papers?"

Hermia shook her head. "Disposed of them, I imagine. There wasn't anything of value, was there?"

"That depends," Julia said, not allowing herself to panic. "I wish you had asked me first, Hermia."

Chapter 22

The Marquess of Sedgecroft's country estate sat below a horizon of wooded hills on the outskirts of a half-timbered village in Kent. Built in the sixteenth century, the handsome house had changed over the centuries to accommodate the social needs of its owners. House parties and hunting pleased the current residents. The gregarious marquess and his wife enjoyed entertaining close friends in the tranquil surroundings of the grand manor.

But Grayson and Jane had yet to arrive. The two sent word that they had decided to detour to the coast to visit Jane's cousins. Heath and Julia had the estate practically to themselves. If one discounted Hermia, Hamm, and Sedgecroft's efficient servants. Even then the manor's wide-ranging rooms afforded plenty of opportunity for privacy.

On the first night of their arrival, they did little more than take a light supper and go to their assigned rooms to unpack. A servant led Julia up a spiral stone staircase and through an endless torchlit hallway to an arched oaken door at its end.

"A tower room!" she exclaimed, looking back at the tall

figure who had followed them. "What is the meaning of this?"

Heath grinned. "It is for your own protection."

"Protection? I feel as if I've been taken prisoner."

"That is utter nonsense." He gave the footman a slight nod. "Thank you, Collins. You may leave the traditional bread and water outside the door in the morning."

"Very funny," Julia muttered as he opened the creaking door onto a surprisingly intimate candlelit chamber furnished with a gilt dressing table, a writing desk, and a mahogany four-poster hung with burgundy velvet curtains. An inviting fire burned in the pink-veined marble fireplace. "I— Oh, it's lovely. The loveliest *prison* I have ever seen."

He smiled drily. "This is where the male members of the family brought their princesses."

She admired a watercolor above the fireplace of a shepherd and shepherdess in a meadow until she realized just what the bucolic couple were doing under the hay. One could hardly stare at it without thinking of uninhibited sex, of abandonment, of earthly pleasures. "I don't think I need to ask why they brought women here," she said, turning slowly . . .

To find him standing directly behind her, his gaze drifting over her with unmistakable sensuality. She put her hand to the fastening of her gray wool mantle. All of a sudden the room felt rather too warm. When would she learn that the Boscastle family never did anything in half measures? This must have been what Jane meant when she had warned her to beware.

"Why so uneasy, Julia?" he asked, his voice teasing. He circled her, laying his hands on her shoulders, his voice exuding magnetic male confidence. His body pressed into hers, the hard wall of his chest inviting her to lean back against him.

"Uneasy? Do I seem uneasy?" Faint. Light-headed, definitely.

She turned and saw the alluring image of the fire's flames in his eyes. If she dared to look closer, she would probably see the devil, too, or at the very least the reflection of her own desires. Her breasts felt flushed, and her breath seemed to catch in her throat. Warmth swept through her in swirling waves.

"Julia," he said, lifting one dark eyebrow in reproach.

There. For a fleeting moment she glimpsed Satan in his gaze as he added, "It's only me." His hands moved to the front of her mantle.

"Precisely."

With a flick of his fingers he unfastened the garment. "It's warm in here, isn't it?" he asked, looking deeply into her eyes.

"Roasting."

"Perhaps you're overdressed."

"I'm perfectly capable of undressing myself. I've been doing it for years, actually, ever since I was three."

"One can always use a helping hand."

"I think I'll manage."

He brushed his fingers down her back in a subtle caress that stopped her breath. "I happen to be good with my hands."

"Was that ever in question?"

She watched the mantle slither to the thick, patterned carpet. She wasn't sure, but she suspected the design woven into the heavy wool depicted another voluptuous scene to stir the senses. Not that the typical Boscastle male needed help in that field.

Neither did she. She was drowning in need, so desperately in love with him that she could not contain it. Having waited so long for happiness, she wanted to savor every moment of it. Moments that would lengthen into months, then years, if she had her way.

"Where is Hermia going to sleep?" she asked, a small gasp escaping her as his hands slowly crossed around her shoulders.

His eyes gleamed playfully. The scar on his upper lip thinned as he gave her a disarming smile. "Safe in the other wing."

"The other wing!"

"Hamm is in the room beside her. After all, I can't be expected to guard you both at the same time."

She stared down at the carpet, anything to take her mind off the desire that pounded through her blood. The pattern appeared to be an erotic tableau from a Dionysian orgy. "Interesting rug. Decadent, but interesting."

He lifted her chin with his knuckles. A wave of anticipation washed over her at his sultry look, his eyes heavily lidded. "Our rooms are connected."

She glanced at the door behind him. "You mean by the outer hallway?"

He brushed his thumb back and forth across her lower lip. The sensual friction almost brought her to her knees. She swallowed a gasp, her legs trembling. He spoke in the quiet voice of a hunter calming his quarry. "The dressing closet links our rooms. I'm only a call away."

"I don't see a lock. It must be on your door."

He shook his dark head. His smile held hers without

mercy, the message clear and beguiling. "No lock. Only the door to the hallway."

She stood immobilized on the carpet as he turned toward the closet. "Don't you feel safer knowing that I'm in the next room?"

"I might if there were iron bars between us," she said with a frown.

Another smile carved creases beneath his broad cheek-bones. She saw his compelling reflection in the cheval glass as he murmured, "Is that because you don't trust me, or yourself, Julia?"

Julia had undressed for bed but could not sleep. She felt like the princess in the fairy tale who fretted the entire night because there was a pea beneath the mattress. The chamber had been designed for comfort, to close out the rest of the world, to allow a woman to concentrate on only one thing.

"Seduction," she said, sitting bolt upright in the warm shadows of the bed. The book she had been attempting to read slid to the carpet. She pushed off the mound of lavender-scented bedclothes and leaned down to retrieve it.

When she straightened there was a man half reclining beside her on the bed. A very dangerous-looking one in a loose-fitting white linen shirt and black trousers that molded his sculpted musculature.

She opened her mouth to scream.

He silenced her with a kiss.

"Merciful lord," she murmured when she could speak, falling back onto the scented bedclothes, captive beneath the sensual weight of his body.

He leaned over her. "There's no need to thank me," he said in a husky voice. "I am here to protect you."

She stared over his shoulder into the indistinct shadows of the room. "From what?"

"I heard a noise."

"You must have the ears of a wolf, Heath Boscastle. And the instincts of one. I dropped my book only a moment ago."

"I thought there might be an intruder. I came to investigate."

"There *is* an intruder," she retorted.

His eyes narrowed in feigned concern. "Can you describe him?"

"Perfectly. He is sinfully handsome, sinfully devious and . . . and altogether sinful. Most intruders are."

His gaze flickered over her like a touch of flame. "I think I ought to stay in case he comes back," he said, his hand stealing up her arm, drawing her nearer. "Unless, of course, you want me to leave."

She closed her eyes with a shiver, whispering, "No."

"I didn't think so."

"What do you think?"

"I've waited so long for you," he whispered. "I'm warning you that after tonight, you won't get away from me again."

Her heart fluttered. "I wouldn't want to." She would stay with him now no matter what, even if Russell caused a scandal over their broken engagement. She would be Heath's until the end.

She had risen to her knees to unbutton his shirt, to pull it roughly from his shoulders to his lean waist. Between deep hungry kisses he untied her nightrail and tore it from her body. She rubbed her swollen breasts against his hard, scarred chest. She would devote herself to healing him with her love. She would help him forget everything he had suffered. He thrust his lower torso against hers, opening his thighs to balance her as her body softened, yielded to him. She wanted to give herself to him in every way that she could. Her heart had always belonged to him. At last her body would, too. How beautiful to love so freely.

"Oh, my God, Julia." Heath could feel the depth of her emotion in her response to him. She was a little wild, sweetly willing. He dragged his mouth down her throat to her breasts, drawing a dusky nipple between his lips. She arched, shivered, pushed against him. She craved this as badly as he did, but it wasn't enough. He wanted her to know fully that marrying another man was a mistake. That it was him she needed, had been meant for all along. He had resisted telling her about Russell's disloyalty, but he was tempted. He knew he would never betray Julia. He could not imagine why any man would want to, but Russell's loss was his gain.

He ran his hands possessively over her naked body, gripped her bottom so that she could feel how hard for her he was, how desperate she made him. She shook, burying her face in his shoulder. "I want . . ." Her voice was muffled.

He traced his thumb across the rise of her rump. No woman had ever excited him as she did. "I know what you want."

"Then don't you think it's time to make me stop wanting?" she whispered against the hard line of his jaw.

"You aren't going to leave me afterward." His hand

drifted down her hip into the warm hollow between her legs.

"I'm—"

"It wasn't a question." He lowered her to the bed, pinned her down with the muscled weight of his thighs. "It was a statement. And I won't leave you, either. There is nothing that can take me from you this time."

She strained against him, her spine arching. He stared down at her with a smile. He meant to show her imprisonment of the most erotic variety. When he was done, she would gladly be his slave in bed, as he was enslaved to her. "I crave you," he said.

She gazed up into his eyes. "I've wanted you since the very moment we met."

"We should have been together, Julia. How did we go so wrong?"

She lifted her hands to his chest, her touch both soothing and seductive. "We're together now."

His eyes met hers as she caressed him, her fingers exploring the mysteries of his male body, stroking the striated muscle of his flat abdomen. He leaned back to shed his trousers, so hard he could not hide it. His need for her raged through his blood, settled into his bones. It took all his willpower to remind himself that he wanted to prove his love, his desire, to make every movement with her something she would remember. To make up for the years they'd been apart. He had been too eager and impatient the first time they'd been together. He knew so much more now, about pleasure, about what truly mattered in life.

"I'm going to give you what you want, Julia."

"I want you," she said without hesitation.

"And—"

"*You—*"

She lowered her hands, taking his manhood between her fingers. His groin tightened at her arousing touch, and fire streaked through his body. He moaned in approval as she stroked him, showed him that in the game of desire she was not an opponent to underestimate. He mourned the years they had lost, shook at the pleasure of the moment, at the love he allowed himself at last to feel.

She was what he had wanted, had needed, had missed in his life. She raised up on her elbows to take him into her mouth, and he stared down at her in fierce longing, reveling in the seductive warmth of her lips, the unbearably sweet suction. The pressure in his loins built. He battled for sanity, for control. If she sucked him any harder, he would climax helplessly like a schoolboy, and he wanted so much to impress her.

He ground his teeth and caught her by the shoulders, forcing his knee between her legs. She fell back on the bed, open and enticing. He bent his head to kiss her; he felt her arms clutch his shoulders, and his muscles contracted, responded to her touch. He settled between her thighs and thrust. Wet heat welcomed him, closed around his throbbing shaft in blissful sensation. Years of waiting, of wanting, and she was his. He closed his eyes and let instinct take over, let himself join her in bliss.

Chapter 23

"There is something I have to confess," she said as they lay together; neither of them seemed ready to sleep, to relinquish a single moment of what time remained in the night.

He hesitated, his thoughts still distracted. He'd never had sex like that before; his body was practically shaking from the strength of his orgasm. And he wanted her again. Oh, God, she intoxicated him. What had she said? She wanted to confess? He sensed that she was going to tell him that she'd gone to Audrey for advice on how to seduce him. Well, it wasn't his duty to deflate her illusions of secrecy, especially not when her goal had been to lure him to her bed. He wasn't about to ruin the most enjoyable night of his life by admitting he had investigated her. And discovered her naughty secret.

He chuckled and folded one arm casually behind his head. His other arm pulled her closer to his nude body. "Confess away, sweetheart. I'm in a forgiving mood."

Not that there was anything to forgive. Julia's sensuality tonight was every man's private fantasy. But most women enjoyed a sense of mystique. He smiled indulgently as he felt her pull away from him. She looked a trifle shamefaced in the shadows that enclosed them, although she had done nothing to be ashamed of. Frankly, he couldn't wait to be the recipient of whatever sexual knowledge she had gained. He was primed for lovemaking.

She leaned forward, staring at the curtains. He walked his fingers down her spine to the cleft of her white bottom. "Spill it. It can't be that shocking."

"Oh, it could," she said quickly.

He sat up slowly. The sheet fell to his waist. The low pitch of her voice warned him she had more to confess than studying the sexual arts. What could it be? Something more serious. Hell's bells, could she have found out about Russell's infidelity?

His heart went out to her, even if he hated to see her upset over another man. He burned with jealousy at the mere thought that they had just made love and she could still even *think* of Russell. "What is it, Julia?" he asked, more coolly than he intended. He had never experienced such deep passion before.

She gave a little shiver. "Perhaps I should tell you in the morning."

"You'll tell me now."

"Why spoil a perfect night?"

He scowled at her shadowy, alluring form. "Do you think that I cannot be trusted?"

"No. That isn't it."

He laid his hand on her shoulder, turning her toward him. Her dark expressive eyes roused a fresh surge of fierce desire inside him. He had never been so satisfied and left hungry for more in his entire life.

"Then what is 'it'?" he demanded. "Russell?"

"Russell?"

"Russell. My former friend. *Your* former fiancé."

She frowned back at him. "What on earth does Russell have to do with anything?"

"That is what I'm trying to find out," he said impatiently.

She sank back against the pillows. "Will you promise to be merciful? Will you remember that I did not do this deliberately to hurt you?"

He leaned over her, suddenly alarmed. "What have you done?"

"I didn't do it on purpose."

He stared down at her, waiting, reassuring himself that she was incapable of an unforgivable act.

"Do you remember the sketch I did of you?" She pulled the sheet up to her shoulders. "The one I did for charity?"

He straightened. "Don't tell me you *sold* it?"

She shot him a reproachful look. "Of course I didn't sell it. This was my private sketch, not the one intended for the club. Do you think I'd share my vision of you with the world? At least *that* vision."

"No." He released a deep sigh of relief. "I don't. But for an awful moments there, you gave me a—"

"I lost it," she said, drawing the sheet up over her face.

"Lost it? You mean in the town house? Misplaced it, you mean? You don't remember where you hid it?" He tugged the sheet down from her face. Her eyes peered up at him beseechingly. "Tell me that it's lost somewhere in your house."

She swallowed. "I wish I could. But it isn't. It's gone. Aunt Hermia had the music room cleaned out by a couple of chimney sweeps she took off the street. We probably don't have to worry though. What would anyone want, besides me and a thousand other Englishwomen, with your naked likeness?"

"Naked?" he asked faintly. He was hoping he'd misunderstood her. "You never finished drawing my clothes? Not a sheet? A few more fig leaves?"

"Well, I was debating whether I should have you hidden by your chariot when the sketch disappeared. It's probably been thrown away by now, don't you think?"

"I am afraid to think, Julia. I am positively frozen at the possibilities of my naked likeness circulating around the streets of London." It was, in fact, a damnably embarrassing situation, but hardly worth spoiling the intimate mood between them. He would deal with the missing sketch in the morning, but the hours until then belonged to Julia.

She woke him in the middle of the night, her hands exploring his lower body. He stirred, and felt himself hardening at her touch. "Have you forgiven me yet?" she whispered, her body soft and warm from sleep.

He rolled over and trapped her between his heavily muscled thighs. "I think you should earn my forgiveness, don't you?"

She smiled. "I'll try."

He held his breath as she nudged him onto his back. It was almost dawn, and the estate lay in utter silence. His belly muscles tightened as he felt her arousing mouth brush his groin. She rolled the crest of his shaft between her lips with a light, tantalizing friction. He tunneled his fingers in her hair, his heartbeat escalating, the tension unbearable, sweet agony.

"Forgive me?" she asked in a temptress's voice.

He felt as if he would explode. Her agile tongue circled his engorged penis in skillful torture, teasing licks that set his nerve endings on fire. "Anything," he said, the word a hoarse cry wrung from him.

She brought him to the edge, testing the limits of his restraint. He allowed her to prolong his pleasure until the moment came when he knew that he had to return the favor or lose control. He stretched forward and rolled her beneath him in one fluid move, holding her wrists above her head with one hand.

She lay in breathless anticipation as he kissed a path down her breasts to her belly. Her legs parted at his urging. She moaned when he buried his face between her thighs to taste her. He felt her shift restlessly, and he wondered if she had ever known this delight before.

"Relax, Julia."

"But I haven't—"

He licked her slowly with his tongue, lapped the folds of her crevice in long, velvety strokes. She fell silent, her thigh muscles quivering, her lower body twisting. He threw his left arm over her belly to hold her still. She arched, whimpering low in her throat. She might have been married once. She might have been engaged to another man. But before the night ended, she would belong to him alone. Her body would remember no other master.

She gasped for breath. "That feels so wicked."

"God, it's heaven. Do you want me to stop?"

"I'll die if you do."

He penetrated her deeply with his tongue, the scent of her making him wild. He drew her nub between his teeth and took teasing nibbles of her until her entire body shook and she turned her face breathlessly into the pillow. He tormented her. He drew out every sensation, awakened her every hidden sense until she writhed beneath him. His heart pounded, but he refused to release her, bringing her to a climax with his mouth.

He did not give her time to recover before he splayed her thighs apart. Her eyes were closed, her body steamy wet, aroused, and ready as he sank inside her sheath. She quivered in pleasure at the invasion. She wrapped her legs around his hips and squeezed him; her sensuality challenged his control, inflamed his senses.

"Heath." She was begging, whether to stop or love her harder, he did not know. He was beyond stopping. He wanted only the release she could give him. He lifted her legs over his shoulders and rotated his hips with sensual abandon. Harder. Faster. Hotter. Deeper and deeper into the damp heat of her until her muscles contracted around his cock, his mind spiraled and pure feeling took over.

He arched his back and felt his body flood with pleasure, soul-deep shudders of satisfaction. When the last spasm subsided, he could only stare down at her in wonder, touch her cheek.

Her eyes met his. "My God."

She sighed.

He eased down beside her and took her in his arms. "I don't think I'll ever have my fill of you."

"I can feel your heart pounding, Heath," she whispered.

"That's what you do to me." His arms tightened protectively around her. "Were you this passionate with your husband?"

She sighed again. "No. Never."

"And with Russell?" he asked; the question had been

burning at the back of his mind. He would erase all her memories of every man she'd ever met if given the chance.

"No. Russell and I were definitely not this passionate."

"Don't tell me he never tried," Heath said, unable to believe that any man could resist her natural sensuality.

"I didn't say that."

"Bastard," he said darkly.

She laughed at that, angling her head back to study his profile. He did not look at her. He was afraid he would not be able to hide how he resented Russell, how wildly possessive and protective she made him feel. His pleasure at their physical union. He'd had long enough to learn to appreciate her, to realize what she meant to him.

"Heath?" she prompted gently.

He glanced down at her, his emotions softening. There was a note of anxiety in her voice. He wished he had not ruined the moment by letting his jealousy get the better of him.

"What is it?" he asked, meeting her troubled gaze.

"I know how the male mind works, Heath."

"You certainly know your way around the male body."

She smiled. "Mrs. Watson made it sound very academic. I daresay she will open a school one day and make a grand success."

He grinned. "Just don't volunteer to act as a schoolmistress."

Her eyes lifted teasingly to his. "I suppose that every man wishes to be a woman's first lover," she said softly. "I wish it had been you."

"Dear Julia." He bent his head to kiss her soft, tempting mouth. "You are so very wrong."

She nestled into his embrace, draping her leg over his muscular calf to draw him closer. "Am I?"

"Yes." He melded his hardening body to her appealing curves. "Every man wishes to be a woman's *last*. Which, in your case, I shall be."

He stirred an hour later, in the silence right before daylight broke. With a smile he drew the coverlet over her bare shoulders and stoked the fire so that in the morning she would awaken to warmth. For a blissful interval he did not move. He felt a contentment he had never known. To lie in bed beside Julia, listening to her breathe.

Here in the country, in his brother's house, the threat of Auclair, of explaining the situation to Russell, seemed distant and dangerously easy to push out of his mind. Julia, on the other hand, was impossible to ignore. Talk about making up for lost time. She would be aching all over after what he'd done to her during the night.

He would have loved to linger in her bed and keep her warm himself. But even a Boscastle rogue had to maintain a minimum of propriety in a social setting. It wouldn't do to have Aunt Hermia discover her niece being ravished while she was supposed to be under his protection.

He let himself into his own room, washed, shaved, and dressed in fresh attire. As he heard the servants moving about the house, he sat down at his desk and began to draft a letter to London. He had not forgotten about Julia's missing sketch. Best to find the blasted thing before it could cause him trouble.

Julia heard him stir and quietly slip from her bed. His lovemaking had left her too deliciously exhausted to call after him. She felt safe in this house, in his arms, and, if it had been within her power, she would have held the rest of the world at bay forever. She could pretend to be his princess in the tower indefinitely.

But she had an unpleasant feeling that Russell would not take her rejection gracefully, even if he'd been disloyal to her. Had she said that she wanted Heath to fight for her? Well, she had not meant so in a literal sense. Neither he nor Russell needed to fight over her to prove their bravery or manhood. How *would* she handle Russell? How would Heath? He had not told her. He was a man who thought carefully and was not prone to rash actions.

For now she could only wait and hope to break off with Russell with as much grace as he would allow. She and Heath, together, were certainly strong enough to withstand whatever came their way. Such, she supposed, was the benefit of experience. At least she had the wholehearted approval of her aunt; fortunately, Heath's family appeared to have accepted her with their famous warmth. The backing of the people she loved would see her through. Was loyalty in the face of life's trials what gave the Boscastles their resilience? It was a quality she admired, one she hoped that whatever children Heath gave her would inherit.

Chapter 24

The letter from his brother, Heath, reached Lord Drake Boscastle at a most inopportune time. He was just settling in Audrey's suite for an afternoon of artful seduction. He had been invited on the pretext of a poetry reading. He doubted he would leave the premises with literature on his mind.

The young actress in his arms probably could not recite "Jack and Jill" at the moment. He had agreed, at Audrey's persuasion, to let her budding new student practice her professional skills on him.

"I think," he murmured against her warm red mouth, "that you have a definite calling for this."

She twined her arms around his neck and began to loosen his cravat, cooing, "Do you really think so?"

"Well, I suppose we ought to—"

He glanced up in annoyance as the door behind her opened, and Audrey ushered in a young footman. Drake was of a mind to brain the fellow for interrupting until he recognized the family livery. He gently deposited the woman draped across him onto the sofa.

"Sorry, Boscastle," Audrey said with a sly grin that suggested she was anything but. "He insisted it was important." And obviously she intended to find out why.

The footman handed the letter to Drake, all the while examining the flustered actress on the sofa, who was covertly trying to readjust her gown and hair at the same time. Drake tore open the seal and scanned the message, his face darkening.

> *I need to see you on a mission of utmost urgency. The family name is at stake.*
> *Heath*

"Bloody hell," he muttered, slipping the paper into his vest pocket. "He certainly knows how to pick his times."

Audrey studied him in concern. She had always harbored a fondness for his family. "Trouble, Drake?" she asked, arching her brow.

"What would a Boscastle be without it?" he replied with a rueful smile.

She followed him to the door, her eyes regretful. The Boscastle footman had already fetched Drake's hat, gloves, and black cloak. "I suppose I can assume from Grayson's recent marriage and Heath's interest in Julia that you and your younger brother are the only Boscastles available to us for debauchery?" she called after his lean, retreating figure.

He pivoted, blowing her a kiss from the door. "At least in the immediate family."

Heath and Drake met in the oval drawing room of their elder brother's estate the following evening. Heath stood by the window as Drake paced the floor, restless after the rushed ride from London.

"I appreciate your fast response," he said, pouring his brother a glass of brandy from the sideboard.

"I practically broke my neck getting here," Drake replied. "Is it Auclair? Brentford again?" His eyes narrowed. "I knew I should have beaten him senseless."

"Auclair has not made another move."

"I suppose it's too much to hope he's disappeared for good."

"Probably." Heath handed Drake the glass, his smile strained. "This is awkward."

"Awkward? I left a nubile brunette half fainting on the sofa at Audrey's. I'd say it was agony, not awkward."

"I'm sure she'll wait."

Drake stifled a yawn and dropped into a brass-studded armchair. "If you really want me to dispose of a body, speak up. Hamm can help. Let's get it over with."

Heath paused at the sound of feminine laughter in the hallway. "It's not a body. Well, actually, it is. *My* body, or an unauthorized, naked rendition of it. A sketch Julia made of me has gone missing."

Drake choked down the sip of brandy he had just taken. An evil grin spread across his face. His features were similar to Heath's, but more hard-edged, the angles sharper. "*Your* . . . you, naked?"

"If you start to laugh," Heath said coolly, "there will indeed be a dead body that requires disposal."

"Where has it gone?"

"Hermia hired two chimney sweeps off the street to clear out the clutter of the music room. Julia had hidden the sketch of me there. For safety."

"Sink me," Drake said, flicking back his coattails. "A pair of sweeps could have dragged the damn thing anywhere."

"Precisely."

"Perhaps it found its way into the Louvre," Drake said. "We'll have to send Wellington to reclaim it."

"I have slightly lower aspirations of my artistic worth," Heath said. "I am personally appalled imagining my bare image being paraded through the alleyways of St. Giles. I know it wasn't exactly Julia's fault, but it *is* embarrassing."

"It ought to fetch a fortune on the black market," Drake said. "Think of all the women who would kill to possess it. What does it look like?"

"Like me in the nude, I assume."

"What in the blazes would possess Julia to do such a thing?"

"You'd have to ask her, wouldn't you?"

Drake paused. "Never mind. I already know. The question is: Does Russell?"

Heath glanced up, distracted by the door opening behind them to admit Hermia, and Julia, his wanton artist herself, in a lilac muslin dinner dress. He straightened, his gaze traveling over her in dark appreciation.

"Oh, dear," she said, hiding behind Hermia. "A family conference, and I think I know the reason why."

Hermia looked directly at Drake. "Have you found it yet?"

He rose politely to address her. "I haven't, but I am about to embark on my quest. Could either of you describe the sketch to me?"

Julia twisted the fringe of her shawl in her fingers. "Really, I'd rather not."

"It is me, rendered as the God Apollo," Heath said in exasperation. "It shouldn't be that hard to recognize."

"Well," Julia murmured, "except for the tiny fact that I rendered you a cartoon."

"A cartoon?" he said blankly.

She turned to the fire. Never in a thousand years had she imagined that her sketch would fall into public hands. No wonder the ton called her the Wicked Lady Whitby. What a horrid impression to make upon Heath's family, and to think she had only meant it in fun. "I distorted certain parts of your anatomy. You know, made one of those caricatures that are so popular in the press."

Hermia gasped. "Not *that* sketch?"

"Find the cursed thing," Heath said darkly. What an appalling thought, to be immortalized as a nude cartoon. "Find it, or there'll be the devil to pay."

Drake took a light dinner with Heath and Julia and retired immediately afterward so that he could have an early start on his rather amusing quest the next day. It was Julia who remarked on the situation to Heath as they sat before the fire in her room. "That sketch has begun to cause you embarrassment, and it has not yet been viewed. I *am* sorry."

"So you've said." He smiled reluctantly, unable to stay angry at her. Having realized how much he needed her in his life, he was not about to quarrel over this. Not when there were other more serious problems they must face. "I'm sure I will survive this, Julia. Do not lose sleep over it."

Although he might. Lord above, what an unprecedented embarrassment. He could just see himself walking into his club and finding that sketch on the wall. His friends would laugh themselves into a stupor. He would be known as the Naked Apollo until his dying day. He would *never* live this down.

"You haven't seen it yet," Julia murmured. Her voice indicated that he wouldn't be so forgiving if he had. "Perhaps the sweeps burned it."

"Go to bed, Julia." He stood and reached down for her hands. As she rose, he drew her into his arms.

He kissed her until he felt her hands slide around his neck, until she was relaxed, responsive, her breathing warm on his neck. He was hard as steel in an instant, the familiar molten heat flooding his body.

"How did I live without you all these years?" he asked, closing his eyes, rubbing against her.

"Don't live without me ever again," she whispered.

Already they had fallen into the secret world of their love affair. He undressed her slowly, going down on his knees to remove her garters and flesh-colored stockings. He placed his palms inside her thighs and pushed.

She gripped his shoulders, her hair gleaming like dark flames in the firelight. "Sinful man," she said in a broken voice.

"Sinful woman."

"Only with you."

"I shall have to be very good to make sure." His hands curled around the white globes of her bottom. He nuzzled her nest of fragrant darkened curls. "Or very bad. Which do you prefer?"

"I think—" She groaned and would have collapsed, but his strong hands braced her buckling knees.

"I think you prefer it when I'm bad," he murmured as he held her trembling body in helpless submission.

He rose swiftly to take her into his arms. Julia began to undress him, kissing each part of his body that she uncovered until he stood nude and fully aroused. She walked him backward to the bed and took his sleek rod between her hands. Now that she had allowed expression of her feelings for him, she could not seem to stop herself, to stop touching him. She could never deny what he meant to her again. He seemed to understand her so well, and anticipate her moods, her needs. "How bad can you be?" she asked, bending her head to kiss the knob of his erection.

He flexed his hips and anchored his legs around her lower body to imprison her. "I'm a Boscastle. There are no limits."

As if to prove this, he clamped his hands around her waist and lifted her onto his rampant shaft, only to impale her as he lowered her back down. He groaned with pleasure as he sank deeply into her wet channel. "That feels nice, doesn't it?"

She threw her head back and stretched her spine, the movement pure sexual reaction. He caught his breath and moved his hands up her belly to her full, flushed breasts, pinching and stroking the dark tips between his fingers. She moaned, her lips parted in pleasure.

He rode her harder, inflamed by her passion, his muscular thighs gripping her in a vise. He was in total control, loving how her soft bottom sat against his belly, how open and silky wet she was inside.

"You feel incredibly good," he muttered, pushing upward.

"You feel . . . incredibly big."

He lifted his lean hips and thrust. "Poor darling."

"It wasn't a complaint."

He rolled her onto her back, their bodies still connected. She hooked her legs up around him, absorbing every stroke of his thick shaft. He had never loved a woman like this before, with his heart, his soul, his physical being. He had never experienced this heady surge of emotional intensity and sexual need. There had been other women in his life, but no one like her, no one who had stolen his heart. Somewhere deep inside he had been waiting for her. He'd been afraid to admit it, afraid he would never have another chance with her.

"I claim you."

"I'm yours," she whispered, her hands braced on his forearms.

"I won't lose you again." He rotated his hips in a slow undulating rhythm. "I should have taken you like this years ago."

She strained upward. "Don't think I didn't dream of it." Her inner muscles tightened on his shaft. He groaned and felt her body trembling, on the verge. He loved to make her lose control. He drove deeper, to the hilt, in a black haze of desire. His heart hammered with the elemental fury of their mating, his emotions.

She was beautiful in her arousal, in her vulnerability, her trust, as she came apart beneath him. He held back another few moments to watch her take her pleasure. His own climax devastated him, swept him into a world of sensation, emptying him and filling him at the same time.

His chest was damp, his heartbeat had slowed, but its frantic pulse throbbed throughout his body as he held her tightly. His woman. He breathed in her scent, savored the warmth of her. "I love you, Heath Boscastle," she whispered against his neck.

His throat tightened. For her he had waited. For her he would fight and sacrifice his honor if need be. Their time together was precious but not illicit; Russell would be mad to surrender her without a struggle.

"Rogue," she said, shaking his shoulder. "I have just told you that I love you, and you answer me with silence?"

He gave a low devilish laugh. "Just remember you said that, Julia, and this time I am not a young man you can run away from. I won't give up for anything. I love you with all my being, even if I do end up disgracing us both."

"I wouldn't expect less of a Boscastle rogue," she said gently.

Chapter 25

On the following morning Emma Boscastle, the widowed Viscountess Lyons, was giving etiquette lessons in the drawing room of her younger brother Devon's London town house. It offended her sensibilities to be dispensing advice on proper conduct from a known rogue's headquarters. But at least the rogue was situated in the fashionable part of town on Curzon Street, and she did happen to adore him, faults notwithstanding. If only she could persuade him and Drake to settle down and behave themselves. Thank heavens Grayson and Chloe were married and that Heath conducted his private affairs with discretion. Emma had always been grateful that she could count on Heath to use common sense in his personal dealings.

She clapped her hands to bring her unruly female students back to order. In all her days she had never seen such a wild bunch, unless she counted the members of her own family. In fact, two of her most challenging pupils were Boscastle cousins, thereby explaining their misguided energy.

"That will be quite enough talking, girls. And giggling. We are not a gaggle of geese." She stood on tiptoe to see what had caused such a stir amid her pupils, who only minutes ago had been on the verge of falling asleep. "What is it you are all examining with such interest?"

"Just some artwork, Lady Lyons."

"Of a Greek deity."

"Ah." Emma sighed. "Dare I hope this signifies an appreciation for the Ancients?"

"He doesn't look ancient to me," one of the girls murmured.

"Goodness, look at the size of his arrow!"

Charlotte Boscastle giggled. "That's not an . . ."

The gleam in the girl's blue eyes set off alarm bells in Emma's brain. She marched into the middle of the circle. "Hand it over *this* moment."

Charlotte looked up innocently. "But it's only a drawing of Apollo."

Emma gasped in horror. "It's a pamphlet," she exclaimed. "One of those scurrilous caricatures that defile the streets and drawing rooms of our country! And, oh, my goodness, a *naked* man, of all things."

"It isn't just any man, Lady Lyons," a girl in spectacles said shyly. "It's your brother."

"My"— Emma stared down in disbelief at the cartoon in her hands —"heavens. Oh, my heavens. My vinaigrette, please. A chair. A fainting couch. It's Heath."

Charlotte pushed a stool under Emma's swaying figure. "Sit down. Take a deep breath."

The pamphlet fluttered to the floor. The bespectacled girl swooped down to retrieve it. "I always wondered what he looked like. Isn't he supposed to be one of the more respectable men in the family, Lady Lyons?"

Charlotte peered over her shoulder, shaking her head in wonder. "Not anymore, he isn't."

Two hours later Lord Devon Boscastle strolled into his club on St. James's Street. He headed straight for the group of young men gathered around the bow window. There was an air of wicked excitement around them that drew Devon like a magnet.

"What piece of frivolity are we betting on today?" he asked in a bored tone.

"Have you seen this?" one of his friends asked in an incredulous voice, hanging over the back of a chair.

"Have I seen what?"

"The pamphlet that's circulating all over town," someone in the center of the group replied.

Devon fought off a faint sense of foreboding. His family had a saying. Where there was smoke, there was usually a Boscastle in the vicinity. Where there was smoke *and* scandal, one could count on finding a member of his family in the thick of it. "It's a bit early in the afternoon for heavy reading, isn't it?"

"It's your brother, by God," a friend announced with glee.

Devon's first thought was of Drake. Grayson, the marquess, was married and practically dead in terms of scandal. Their youngest brother Brandon was gone forever. Devon had not gotten into trouble for, well, it must have been almost three weeks now. And Heath, sneaky devil that he was, played too discreetly to get caught.

"What's he done now?" he inquired, sauntering to the edge of the semicircle.

"I'd say it's what's been done to him. This is Heath, isn't it?"

Someone pushed the pamphlet under his nose. His eyes widened in amazement. It was Heath, all right, as very few members of the ton had seen him. Standing spread-eagle in front of a flaming chariot, in all his natal glory, with the biggest—

"Is that an arrow?" he asked aloud, choking back laughter. "Who the blazes would do this?"

"The Wicked Lady Whitby. Look, she's even signed her name to it, presumably never dreaming it would be seen. How the mighty have been brought low. By a woman, too. Won't Russell have an apoplectic fit when he sees Heath like this?"

Devon studied the caricature with a droll smile. "I expect Heath might be a little hysterical himself."

By the next day, the *Morning Chronicle* reported that Lord Heath Boscastle had eloped to Gretna Green with Lady Whitby, the infamous widow who had shot a British soldier in India. There was no mention of her having shot Heath. However, the article did claim that she was carrying his child.

Another column in the *Times* asserted that the scandalous couple had fled to France. The correspondent also stated that the most popular portrait painters of the ton had noted a sudden demand among their clients to be depicted as Greek deities.

Sir Russell Althorne read both articles in stark-faced silence in his mistress's bedchamber. He had been back in London for approximately one hour. Scarcely had he recovered his powers of speech than his mistress, who *was* carrying a child, produced the pamphlet of Heath, as Julia had sketched him.

Russell surged off the bed, practically choking with fury. He was fatigued from his frustrating mission in France, outraged at what he had returned to find. "How *could* they?" he demanded, shaking the pamphlet in the air. "My *honorable* friend. The friend for whom I sacrificed an eye. The woman I rescued from shame and scandal—"

"Does this mean you won't get her fortune?" His mistress lowered her plate of cake.

"How the hell do I know what it means?" he bellowed. "It means I have been played for a fool."

She brushed some crumbs off her bosom. "I thought it was a good sketch of him, actually."

"He was naked!"

"Yes, I did notice that." She peered up at the pamphlet. "It's very hard not to—"

" 'Do not cause a scandal,' I said. And what did they do?"

She hesitated. "Cause a scandal?"

"That clever mind of yours never stops, does it, darling?"

She smirked up at him and crossed her swollen ankles on the footstool. "I don't suppose this is a good time to tell you that Julia was seen visiting Audrey Watson."

"Audrey Watson?" he said in a weak voice. "Why?"

"I have no idea. I've considered working for Audrey a few times myself."

"Julia . . . visiting a courtesan?"

She leaned forward. "The Boscastle men tend to bring out the wickedness in women. Or so I've been told."

"Heath Boscastle is supposed to be a gentleman."

"Decadence runs in the family." She frowned up at his agitated figure. He was pulling on his pantaloons and shirt, stepping over her crossed feet to find his boots. "I thought you didn't care for her in that way."

He didn't answer.

She lowered her legs and covertly kicked one of his Hessians behind her chair.

"Why would she do this to me?" he muttered. "Does she have a total disregard for social opinion?"

She placed her plate on her abdomen and glowered at him like an ill-contented cat. "You're not going to see her, are you, not on your first day back?"

He slung his blue military coat over his shoulder, jamming his shirt into his waistband. "I am engaged to the bloody woman. Do you think I will suffer being the laughingstock of her scandalous behavior?"

"You cannot rush off after her . . . half dressed," she said, setting her plate on the floor.

"Why not? I have just returned from a wild-goose chase across France. An assassin is on the loose. My fiancée has published a sketch of my trusted friend, in the raw, with her name signed to it. Do you think I will tolerate this? Do you think I can?"

She picked up his missing boot and hurried out into the hall after him. "Heath Boscastle will kill you if you confront him."

He turned on her like a madman, the pamphlet clenched between his teeth as he snatched his boot. "Not if I kill myself first."

"Everything is perfect," Julia said late that same afternoon as she stood in the circle of Heath's muscular arms, her head on his shoulder. She hadn't felt so cherished and protected since she'd been a young girl with her father. She wished she could tell him how happy she was now.

She and Heath had been walking in the woods when it had started to rain. Heath had drawn his black woolen cloak around her, and they had kissed in the watery shadows of a sessile oak grove. Lightning flashed across the dark lavender sky. London seemed to be part of another life, the congestion and the petty scandals forgotten.

Heath kissed a hot trail down her throat through her clothes to the tops of her breasts. She closed her eyes, trapped between a rough-barked tree and his hard, warm body. "It will be perfect," he murmured, his hand slowly stealing down her spine, "when I get you back to the house."

"Are you unhooking my cloak and gown?" she whispered, laughing.

"Are you objecting?" he asked, cupping her bottom through her dress.

"I'm—"

She swallowed a shiver at the onslaught of wet air on her exposed breasts, followed by the welcome heat of his mouth. She gripped his forearms, her cloak sliding off one shoulder as fire engulfed her from head to toe. Why did it feel so natural to behave like this with him? It always had. Was there anything more beautiful than passion and love combined? Perhaps only when a child came as a result.

"You look very wanton," he whispered. "I don't think I want anyone else to see you like this."

She grasped his waistband, her fingers working at the fastening. "Shall we even the playing field?"

His teeth grazed the dusky peak of her breast. "I have a better idea."

Without warning he scooped her up in his arms, rain droplets running down the creases of his angular face, into his thick blue-black hair. Julia clung to his powerful frame. "This isn't the direction of the house, you rogue," she said, inhaling the virile musk of his skin.

"Isn't it? Fancy that."

"You can't carry a woman off into the woods, even if you are a Boscastle."

"That's exactly why I can do it. It's bred into me."

"Where are you taking me?"

"Here." He deposited her before a veil of ivy, virgin's bower, and thorn that concealed the mouth of a shallow sandstone cave. He swept aside the creepers and pulled his cloak off to cover the leaf-strewn ground inside. Julia surveyed the dark, mysterious interior while he made a quick inspection, presumably to be sure they were alone. There was an old brass-hinged chest in the shadowy void behind him, overflowing with broken wooden swords, tarnished silver goblets, a paste-gemstone tiara, and an assortment of childhood treasures. A skull sat in the dirt, leering at her.

He held his hand before her. "Welcome to the Boscastle lair, captive. On your knees. Now."

She walked him back a few paces. "And if I don't?"

"Well, in the old days I would have beheaded you."

She let her gray cloak drop to the ground, holding her bodice to her breasts. His eyes narrowed as he watched her, gleaming in the dimness. She circled him playfully like a proud pagan queen who had been captured by a peasant. "And now? What do you intend to do with me?"

He raised his chin as she brushed around him. "I thought I might make you plead."

"For my life?"

He caught her under the knees and drew her down with him to the ground, his mouth capturing hers. He tangled his fingers in her hair. His thighs lifted to trap her against him as he lowered her body to his. He kissed her with the rain pattering against the curtain of vines before gently rolling her onto her back. It could have been snowing outside, and Julia wouldn't have minded.

"I take it you've played this game before, Boscastle."

He smiled, his heavy-lidded gaze traveling over her supine form with an erotic message she couldn't miss. "Not as an adult."

"How do I gain my freedom?" she asked in a low voice.

"You don't."

They might have been the only two people who existed in the world. Julia glimpsed flashes of lightning outside the cave through the curtain of vines. She could hear thunder rumble in the distance, the lyrical splash of rain through the trees. The promises, both erotic and emotional, that Heath whispered in her ear.

If he had never revealed his gentleness to her, his vulnerability, she might have had a chance to resist him. She might have managed to fight her feelings and follow the course she had chosen. She would not have risked heartbreak again, not repeating the same painful mistake.

For years, she had built her case against him in her imagination. Based on the assumption that he had felt nothing for her, she had resented him. Even more she had resented the reckless aspect of her own nature that made her desire him all the same.

The true Heath Boscastle, in all his enigmatic darkness, was far more dangerous to her heart than her false image of him as a heartless rogue. The tenderness he had hidden was his secret strength. His unerring perception was a weapon against which Julia had no defense.

He was a lone wolf, intense and loyal. He had not left her, all those years ago, as she had believed. He had not married either.

Why not? She wanted to believe he had waited for her.

She looked up at him and gasped softly at the promise of wicked pleasure in his eyes. He slid his hands under her bottom and molded her to his hard, aroused body. He hadn't bothered to remove their clothing. She shivered beneath him, enjoying his touch, so absorbed in him that several blissful moments passed before she realized that her dress was bunched up wantonly to her waist; she could feel the jack buttons of his waistcoat brush her breasts as his thick shaft slowly penetrated her. Cool brass against her burning flesh. The breathtaking sensation of him pressing into her sheath.

"You're very wet," he said in a deep husky voice. "I like it."

He trailed kisses across her temple, down her cheekbone, onto her shoulder. He sank deeper inside her with every thrust until she gave a soft cry. She struggled to breathe at the friction of stretching fullness, the sinful feeling of sexual invasion.

"Do I hear a plea for mercy, Julia?"

She ran her fingers down the ridges of his muscular back.

She loved every inch of this man, his passion, and perceptive nature. "You're indecent."

He withdrew, then slammed into her, grasping her hips to hold her still. "So I've been told."

She trembled; his hard mouth smothered the instinctive cry she gave. He groaned deep in his throat. His unapologetic sexuality completely disarmed Julia. Considering their past, it did not seem terribly shocking that he was ravishing her in a cave. Or that she had encouraged him. She delighted in his hard powerful body, the ripple of muscle and sinew as he drove inside her.

"How many other women have you brought here?" she demanded.

"I don't know."

Her eyes narrowed.

"None," he amended, laughing at her response. "You're my very first captive."

He brought his mouth to hers. His tongue mimicked the movement of his lower body, thrusting, conquering her, driving deep inside, withdrawing with sensual self-control. She closed her eyes. Her muscles had melted to warm liquid. A trembling began in the depths of her belly. She was losing control, surrendering, spiraling.

"Only you," he said again.

He clenched his jaw, surging upward. She clasped his back, murmuring as the storm overwhelmed her, "Just as long as I'm the last."

Chapter 26

Julia hadn't noticed the ivory-inlaid pistol Heath carried on him until she saw him return it to his waistband. It sent a chill up her back to think they had made love with a loaded gun lying on the ground beside them. That no matter what they felt for each other, he might have to confront a man who took pleasure in killing, inflicting pain. She watched the gun disappear from sight.

She met his gaze and shivered. "I'm glad I didn't see that before."

"So am I." He helped her with the hooks of her sage-green woolen dress. "I wouldn't have wanted it to distract you," he added, grinning. "However, until Auclair is found it would not be a bad idea for you to keep your pistol with you as protection."

She followed him outside into the rain, pinning her heavy hair into a knot at her nape. She was jolted back to reality by his calm acceptance, the fact that he deemed his life in enough danger that a simple walk in the woods might not be safe.

Or perhaps the pistol represented a part of his past, his profession, that he would always carry with him. She remembered the scars on his chest. He had been tortured and mercifully lived. But he had not forgotten his ordeal. The memories of cruelty that he had kept to himself surely haunted him. He would never lower his guard.

And the man who had tortured him was in England. Why? Why had he lured Russell to France? Why would he hunt down an officer who had escaped him? Did Heath know the true reason? Did Russell? Or was Armand Auclair simply mad, obsessed with killing? Was there rhyme or reason to his actions?

She pulled the hood of her cloak over her head. "Perhaps we should wait out the storm in the cave."

"No. I want you safely inside the house." He glanced back wistfully at the cave, concealed again by its covering of twisted vines. "This was only one of our favorite haunts as children."

"It would seem your family's reputation is well deserved."

He grasped her hand, his eyes glittering with devilish amusement. "For a captive you are rather impertinent. Shall we make a run for it?"

She nodded. She loved that he had begun to share parts of his life with her. She was fascinated by the place he occupied in his family, the respect with which his brothers regarded him. He was a man like no other. She appreciated him more every day.

They were soaked to the skin when they burst through the estate's ornamental gates and into the house a half hour later. Hermia met them in the entrance hall, her face white with distress. A small group of servants, dressed in cloaks and heavy boots, stood behind her.

"There you are!" she exclaimed, wringing her hands. "I

was just about to send Hamm and a search party after you."

Julia felt a guilty flush wash over her. She pushed off her hood, not daring to glance at Heath in case she gave herself away. She lost all sense of time when she was with him. "We only went for a walk."

Hermia stared meaningfully at the brass buttons of Heath's coat. The row was clearly misaligned, and Julia could blame only herself. She had rebuttoned it. "You were gone for almost three hours, Julia," the woman said with a deep frown.

"Well," Julia said, motioning covertly for Heath to fix his coat, "we waited out the worst of the storm."

"In a cave," Heath added. "Our Aladdin's cave."

Julia nodded. "It was like a treasure cave."

Hermia subjected them both to a cold stare. "I think the two of you are more than a little wicked, and inconsiderate. Furthermore, I suspect you are wrong."

Heath turned toward her, his face skeptical but respectful. By some sleight of hand he had managed to straighten out his buttons. "Wrong?" he asked, his brows lowering.

"Yes, wrong," Hermia said in a miffed voice. "The storm has only just started. I predict that the *worst* of it is yet to come."

It stopped raining early that evening. Julia, Heath, and Hermia enjoyed a quiet supper of cold chicken, cheese, and apple tarts before retiring to the family's private drawing room. Hermia excused herself to change, her manner still offended but civil.

Heath and Julia settled in front of the fire as if, he thought ruefully, they were the picture of domestic happiness. He was sitting with his profile to her in a ladder-backed chair, the book she had given him on his lap.

"She's still a little upset with us, you know," Julia murmured as Hermia's footsteps died away.

"I think we gave her a fright today," he said.

She sighed. "I couldn't very well explain to her what we were doing."

His even white teeth gleamed in a grin. "I should hope not. But her worries are not unjustified. I was a little careless."

She made a face. "Careless? You took me captive. In a cave."

"Well, I do have a certain obligation to family tradition. You're lucky you didn't lose your head."

"But I have lost my heart to you."

He turned slowly in his chair. "Have you?"

"How can you doubt it?" she asked, studying his face.

"No feelings for Russell?"

"I don't believe I ever felt more for him than gratitude and friendship. Perhaps, I was afraid to be alone." She glanced at the fire. "How long have you known about him anyway?"

"Known about what?" he asked evenly.

"That he was betraying me."

He leaned forward, his voice deep. "How long have *you* known?"

"Not as long as you, evidently." She resisted as he turned her face to his. Understanding Heath as she did now, she decided that he must have had a time wrestling with his conscience. He would never deliberately hurt anyone. Perhaps by keeping Russell's secret, Heath had hoped to protect her. But it would have been so much worse if she had not found out the truth. "Why didn't you tell me? How could you let me be such a fool?"

"You were never a fool, Julia," he said quickly. "He's the fool for deceiving you."

"But *you* knew."

"I did not want to be chosen by default."

Was that it then? Her proud, honorable protector wanted her on his terms, for his own merit.

"Were you ever going to tell me?" she asked softly.

"Not unless I had to. It wasn't a card I wanted to play. All I am sure of is that I would not let you go again. He saved my life. I will always owe him for that." He shook his head, his gaze holding hers. "But I wouldn't have tolerated his taking you from me. In fact, I look forward to letting him know that you are mine."

"I dread it—only because I do not think he will react well." She scowled. "He's having a child with another woman. I suppose you know that, too."

"You could be carrying my child right now," he said, with a smile to counteract her scowl.

The mere thought sent a shiver of longing through her. His child. She wished it were true. Hadn't she realized a little earlier that a child would be the perfect expression of their love? Let Russell have all the acclaim and mistresses he desired. She wanted only a quiet life with Heath. Well, perhaps not quiet. Her missing sketch was certainly starting their affair off on an awkward foot.

"I shall never escape scandal," she said with a soft laugh.

"Not marrying into this family, you won't. I'd say we have a gift for it."

"I don't seem to be helping," Julia said ruefully.

The door opened, and after a cool glance in their direction, Hermia returned to the sofa, a stack of letters clutched in her hand. Heath and Julia drew away from each other like children caught at mischief.

"Do continue," Hermia said after a meaningful pause. "Heaven forbid that I should come between you."

Julia gave her a fond smile. "Are you still upset with us about being out so long, Aunt Hermia?"

Hermia sighed, her face softening. "I am recovering, but I do believe . . . well, I never thought I would say this, but seeing the two of you together makes me face the painful fact that I am missing Odham."

"Missing Odham?" Heath and Julia said in unison.

"Well, only a little bit," she retorted. "He's never given me back my letters, and I won't forgive him until then."

"But you are going to forgive him?" Heath asked curiously.

"I might. I haven't decided." Hermia glanced away, clearly flustered by this revelation. "Stop staring at me, both of you. Especially you, Boscastle. Those blue eyes of yours have a horrid way of unsettling a woman."

"Isn't that the truth?" Julia said under her breath.

"Read your book, Boscastle," Hermia added. "Julia, tear yourself away from the rogue and decipher these letters for me. My eyesight is not what it used to be."

Julia rose obediently, whispering to Heath, "Be a good boy for once, and do what you're told."

He grinned and glanced down at the book, but he was too preoccupied to concentrate. These stolen moments of pleasure would not go on indefinitely. He would not be truly content until they had faced Russell with the truth. He hoped that he and Russell could agree to find Auclair and deal with their personal dilemma in mutually satisfying ways. If Russell did not offer his forgiveness, then at least Heath could look forward to the future with a clear conscience.

And to a future with Julia, with family around them to share the rest of their lives with.

His gaze lingered on her profile as she bent over Hermia's letters. A dark red curl had fallen across her breasts. Lush. That was how he would describe the woman Julia had become. Lush. Layer upon layer of complex, captivating woman. The perfect mate to stand by his side through the years. Passionate. He ached to have her again right then and there, and his own impatience amused him.

That afternoon in the cave . . . well, he had *never* had such wild uninhibited sex, but everything about it, about *her*, had felt so right. He'd been comfortable with her from the moment they'd met. Somehow he knew that when—and if—he could ever reveal his deepest thoughts to anyone, it would be to Julia. And she would understand.

She glanced up at him, her smile seductive and mischievous. His blood heated dangerously at that smile.

He hoped she would still be smiling after he had dealt with Russell. He had a feeling that the confrontation between the two men would end badly. And there would be the inevitable flurry of gossip when Heath married her, as she had pointed out earlier. Funny how he'd always believed himself above this sort of thing. Well, he was in the thick of it now. They had lived through worse.

In a way, the whole situation only emphasized how potent the Boscastle blood was. For an honorable man he was behaving quite shamelessly. Which showed that he had not escaped heredity. He had only proved it. But Julia had found his weakness. She had carved a place in his heart before war had hardened him, filled him with more questions than answers. She balanced out the darkness inside him that he had not been able to fight.

She had known about Russell's betrayal. Heath would never have told her. He would have carried that secret to his grave before causing her pain or humiliation. But on the other hand, he felt relieved that she finally knew. Had the discovery influenced her decision to sleep with him? To give him her heart? He did not think so.

It should not matter. In a strange way, Russell had brought them back together. They were indebted to him. Russell would not see the situation in these terms, of course. He was a man who lived to impress others, a man of the world, of appearances. He would be outraged that anyone would defy or deny him. He would be outraged and unwilling to accept the fact that he had taken Julia for granted. And Heath would not back down.

He lowered his gaze, smiling as he listened to Julia read her aunt's letters.

What was it Julia had said earlier, when they'd been walking in the woods?

He had been so engaged in her, so physically aroused and attuned to their surroundings, that he hadn't really listened.

But he remembered now. The evocative scent of her, the beckoning warmth of her body against his as the rain washed down upon them.

Everything is perfect.

His fingers curled around the spine of the book that sat unopened on his lap.

She glanced up at him over the letter and raised one brow.

He gave her a slow smile in return, noticing how she caught the edge of her lip in her teeth. If he could preserve this moment in time, if it were in his power, he would do so without hesitation.

Hermia cleared her throat. Julia returned her attention to the letter. She looked so flustered that Heath laughed. The two of them were clearly past trying to hide their feelings. At this point they could not even deceive themselves.

The scandal of their love would rock Society. And then Heath would pass the reins of his roguedom down to Drake or Devon. Julia was more than enough to keep him satisfied.

Everything is perfect.

A noise, the muffled clamor of someone banging at the gates, interrupted his enjoyable musings.

At first Julia did not notice. But then her startled gaze met his, questioning and concerned. She lowered the letter she had been reading aloud.

He stood and strode to the window. The dogs, Grayson's pack of wolfhounds, began to howl in warning. He could see Hamm and three other servants hurrying toward the gate. He pivoted and headed for the door.

"Take Hermia with you to the tower," he instructed Julia in a calm but firm voice.

Hermia rose in concern, her hand grasping Julia's. "What is it, Heath?"

"I shall send Hamm up to stay with you. Just as a precaution. Do not worry. Grayson frequently has guests who arrive at all hours."

He opened the door to usher them out into the hall. The book he had meant to read had fallen onto the floor.

"It is probably nothing," he said. "Perhaps it's only Drake or Devon, in their cups, demanding to be let in."

Julia placed her arm around Hermia's waist. "It's rather late to be on the road, isn't it?"

"It could not be Auclair, could it?" Hermia whispered.

Julia shook her head. "I doubt a French spy would bang on the gates demanding entry. Still, whoever it is sounds quite insistent."

Heath watched them disappear up the stone staircase. The muscles of his shoulders were stretched taut with tension. Even if it were only a guest, it meant his privacy, his precious time with Julia, would be threatened. Just as he turned to go outside, he heard Hermia's voice drifting down.

"You don't suppose it could be Russell, do you? I wonder if he's found out. Oh, Julia, I hope the two of them don't kill each other over you."

The unexpected late-night visitor turned out to be neither a spy nor an outraged Russell. It was instead the Earl of Odham, his cheeks red with exertion. His white tufts of hair were disheveled from travel. To calm himself, he sipped a brandy in the drawing room with Heath, Julia, and Hermia watching him with a mixture of relief and curiosity.

"What is the meaning of this, Odham?" Hermia asked in a displeased voice, clearly forgetting that she had confessed to missing him only a short time ago.

He blew out a sigh. Hermia was seated stiffly in the opposite chair. Heath and Julia had withdrawn to play the neutral party on the sofa.

"I have come to surrender, Hermia," he announced, collapsing back in his chair.

Hermia frowned, alarm darkening her eyes. "Surrender?"

"Yes. You have won."

Hermia paused. "Exactly *what* have I won?"

"Your freedom. Your old letters." He produced a packet from the folds of his dark gray fur-lined cloak. The letters had been carefully preserved in a red velvet pouch. Odham's hand trembled visibly as he held out his peace offering. "There. I shall leave now. Do not worry about my traveling this late at night. My coachman can bury my body in a ditch if I expire. There's nothing left to live for if I lose you."

Hermia's brow shot up. "Stop it, you blustering fool."

Heath coughed loudly. "I think perhaps it is Julia and I who should leave."

Hermia said nothing, turning the pouch over in her hands.

Odham sent Heath a grateful look, as one old rogue to a younger member of their private sect. His dark brown eyes twinkled in appreciation.

Julia began to laugh as Heath swept her from the sofa and out into the hall. "Where, may I ask, are we going?"

"You'll see."

His strong hand claimed hers. She felt her heart race as he drew her down a portrait-lined hallway that she had overlooked before. The vast house had numerous rooms. "Another Boscastle hideaway?" she asked in amusement.

"Clever woman, how did you guess?"

He whisked her into a dark, dusty room, shimmers of moonlight catching glints on the swords and ancient weapons arranged on the oaken wall. Julia bumped into a helmeted coat of armor with Gothic gauntlets and stifled a scream, backing into Heath.

"A weapons room?"

He locked the door, watching her with glittering eyes. "Another excellent guess. We were forbidden to play here as children."

"Why did we have to leave Hermia and Odham? The conversation had just gotten interesting."

"I thought they deserved their privacy. As we do ours."

She turned to examine a huge spiked ball attached to a morning star, a vicious medieval weapon. "Interesting collection of arms you have here. Are you going to challenge me to a duel?"

He smiled. "I wouldn't dare. You might win."

She glanced up at the display of crossbows and battle-axes above the massive stone fireplace. He had unbuttoned his jacket and stood with his hip against the door, watching her. "Somehow I doubt that."

"I would never underestimate you, Julia."

She gave him an arch look. "You're certainly the stronger player in this game."

He pushed away from the door. Lean-hipped, handsome, he was temptation incarnate, right down to the way he walked, that commanding cavalry officer's control of his body. "How many captives have you brought here?" she demanded, striving to maintain her equilibrium. And failing.

"None, actually."

She felt a shiver slide over her skin as his firm mouth found a vulnerable spot above her shoulder. He bit her tenderly. Her breathing deepened. Was there an inch of her body that could resist this man's seduction?

"You see," he continued in a quiet voice, running his hand slowly up her side to cup her full breast in his palm, "I've never had to subdue a woman before to seduce her."

"I don't doubt that."

"We could try the chains if you like."

"On me or you?" she whispered, her mouth suddenly dry.

"Ladies first."

He moved his other hand up under her skirt, finding his way across her bare thigh to the moist heat of her sex. Julia felt herself grow wet, aching, throbbing, her knees giving way beneath her. His fingers pushed, probed, took possession. The hidden pulse points of her body quickened in anticipation.

She gasped and turned her head to look down. "You devil, you've unfastened my dress again."

He pulled her down onto the carpet, locking his arms around her firm white bottom. "If we're going to duel, we might as well do it naked."

She glanced up at the array of clubs and swords above her head. "Don't tell me you brought me here to show me your cavalry saber?"

"My saber isn't on the wall."

"No?"

"But if you want to examine it, I'm sure it could be arranged."

She stared up into his face. A vein pulsed in the hollow of her throat. He caressed it with his index finger. "Isn't that dangerous?" she whispered. "I've heard that a saber is the most effective of all swords."

"That's very true. A saber can inflict great impact when wielded in the proper way."

She breathed out a sigh. A warm tremor spread upward from her knees into her lower body. "How do you wield your saber?" she asked softly.

"For thrusting mainly."

"For . . . thrusting?"

"Yes." He moved against her, brought his mouth to hers. "You see, my blade is curved."

"And the advantage of this?"

"It allows the swordsman to penetrate his opponent's body more deeply."

"Fascinating."

"Are you interested in weaponry, Lady Whitby?" he asked, his mouth drifting down her neck to her breasts.

She felt as if she would faint against his hard, powerful body. The virile heat of him melted her, fused her to him. She had been made to belong to this man.

"I have recently developed quite a passion for it," she whispered.

"How encouraging," he murmured, as his sinful lips encompassed one distended pink nipple and suckled hard. "Perhaps I should give you a demonstration of my skill."

"In here—"

"Of course." He tore off his jacket with his right hand. "It is, after all, a weapons room."

He knew they could not linger for much longer, or they would be missed again. But she felt so irresistibly vulnerable and deliciously enticing sprawled beneath his body. Could he help it if she touched his senses without even trying?

"You don't need a weapon to conquer me," he said in a subdued voice. "Against you I am completely disarmed."

Julia released a wistful sigh. "We'd better get up and put ourselves together. I should die if anyone found us like this."

"You'll have to get up first."

She rose gingerly and pulled up the sleeves of her dress. He reached up to brush a cobweb from her hair. As he was buttoning his jacket, the rumble of carriage wheels on the crushed shell drive echoed in the night.

"Oh," Julia said, her face dismayed. "Odham and my aunt must have quarreled again. He's leaving. I'd hoped they would reconcile."

"That isn't Odham's carriage," he said as he glanced at the door. "That sounds like Grayson and Jane have arrived. Prepare yourself for a grand performance."

Chapter 27

The quiet countryside estate changed the moment the Marquess of Sedgecroft arrived. A procession of carriages lined the drive, and servants burst forth from the steps to unload the expectant marchioness and the vast array of trunks she had carted from London; Sedgecroft's vitality charged the air as if stardust had fallen from the sky.

The family dogs set up a joyful keening; bright lantern lights flooded the endless rise of clipped lawn. Julia had escaped from the weapons room just in time to present a respectable façade. Not that Sedgecroft, with his history of seduction, would be for one instant deceived. He knew the look of a woman well loved.

Heath lingered behind for her to sneak out. In one way, Grayson's arrival was a disappointment. He was a forceful personality, who tended to dominate one's time. On the other hand, Heath realized that Julia's guard would be increased. Grayson might be a gregarious, playful devil, but he was no one's fool, and a good fighter into the bargain. He would be another watchful eye.

From the window Heath observed the entire ceremony of servants welcoming the master home with a great deal of mayhem and merriment. Grayson enjoyed putting on a show. In this he was better suited than any of his brothers to his role in life. The Boscastle patriarch. The scoundrel turned respectable.

Heath far preferred to remain in the wings and perform his own role in private. Well, privacy in the house now would be almost, but not entirely, impossible. There was a devious advantage in keeping Julia in the tower, however. He would merely have to visit her in secret, and secrecy only added a pinch of spice to the pot.

He turned from the window, shaking his head in resignation. If he had to leave Julia in order to hunt down Auclair, who better to guard her than Grayson? She would be protected as well as entertained and befriended by his lively sister-in-law, Jane. As he stepped toward the door, his gaze lifted to the handsome sword collection mounted on the wall. An ancient Roman gladius. A Spanish rapier. A basket-hilted broadsword of a Highland warrior.

He'd loved this room as a boy. Had admired the warlords who had wielded these magnificent weapons.

He had always imagined that one day he would grow up to fight duels, but war had dulled his appetite for bloodshed. Had he and his nemesis Auclair shared the same childhood dreams?

And then, in an instant, as if it were a code he was deciphering, he began to make connections in his mind that he had missed. He had explored the possibility that Baron Brentford was involved with Auclair, but Brentford was to all appearances an innocent if foolish man.

He lifted his hand to the hilt of the French cavalry saber on the wall, tracing his finger along the cold blade.

Why had he not considered the possibility that Brentford

was an unknowing pawn in Auclair's game? The melancholy young man had probably never guessed that he was being used as a method of revenge.

But, unwittingly to them both at the time, Brentford had revealed the clue in his conversation with Heath at the theater. Heath could hear the words echoing in his mind, Brentford's voice, rueful and absurdly tragic.

I think that when I take my private fencing lesson in the morning, I shall ask my instructor to strike me straight through the heart.

And again at the park. Brentford had mentioned the man he had been racing his phaeton to impress.

His instructor.

Auclair, a member of the elite French Corp de Gards, a swordsman who lived to provoke duels, who profited by the death of others.

How long had he been hiding in London? Posing as a fencing master?

Where was he now?

Heath stared at the saber, removed his hand.

Auclair had not been employed at Angelo's fencing studio. He had given private instruction to the wealthy young males of the ton, a notoriously loose-tongued group. He could have easily followed Heath and Russell's movements.

He had to be found and eliminated before he made his next move.

The question was: Would it be safe for Heath to leave Julia to do the job?

Heath had plenty on his mind to keep him awake all night. The most pressing issue was to remove Julia from any threat of danger, then find Auclair. He had to admit a vital piece of the code still eluded him. Auclair's motivation.

Why had Auclair not been content to remain in Paris? Had he gotten into trouble with the authorities there? Yes, Heath had escaped him, perhaps made Auclair look inept and careless to his French superiors. But if every soldier went after his enemy counterpart after the war, the world would never enjoy peace. According to the War Office, and Hartwell's information, Auclair had not been demoted after Sahagun. In earlier reports Heath had read, Auclair was reported to have climbed ever higher in Napoleon's favor before leaving the army. For the first time he wished to meet up with Russell to understand. The two of them could have put their heads together to find Auclair.

"Heath? Is that you hiding in the hall?"

The graceful figure of his sister-in-law Jane flitted across his line of vision. She stood alone at the bottom of the stairs in a lynx-trimmed traveling cloak, her hand on the balustrade.

He smiled at her. "How is our expectant marchioness?"

"Carrying the devil's seed if one may judge by the peculiar cravings for food that possess me." She studied his torch-lit face in concern. "Oh, dear. I can see by your expression that you've heard the news."

His smile vanished. "The news?"

She laid her hand on his forearm. "I don't need to tell you to be brave. Having been born into the Boscastle family has of necessity hardened you to scandal."

"What are you talking about, Jane?"

She swallowed. "I'm sure that Julia did not mean any harm by it. There has to be an explanation."

He narrowed his eyes. "For what?"

"The scandal will die down eventually," she said vaguely. "Take it from one who knows."

"What scandal?"

She turned and climbed several steps, her cloak brushing the stone stairs. "Think of it as art, Heath," she called down over her shoulder.

Was she grinning? Did he hear laughter in her voice? "Think of *what* as art, Jane?"

She vanished from his sight. He barely caught her parting comment. "Think of it as . . . a compliment."

He found out a few minutes later exactly what Jane's elusive remarks had meant. Grayson was waiting for him in the formal gold withdrawing room. The room reserved for company. For dramatic occurrences. For lectures from their father and announcements of engagements. And deaths. It was not called a formal room without good reason.

The marquess was standing in front of the fire in his muddied traveling boots, his hands clasped behind his back. Any other man would have been intimidated by his posture. But Heath knew Grayson a little too well.

He glanced around the room, assessing the situation. Hermia and Odham were sitting stiffly on the sofa with Julia wedged between them as if they were a pair of bookends.

Heath tried to catch Julia's eye. She was deliberately avoiding his gaze. A very bad sign. Had Hermia or Grayson guessed what he and Julia had been doing in the weapons room?

She glanced up unexpectedly. Her gray eyes caught his.

He grinned, but she dropped her gaze. She *was* embarrassed. His grin deepened. He'd never have guessed, not after the things they had done to each other.

His attention was diverted by the loud timbre of Grayson's voice—his brother was shouting. Not an unusual occurrence, but . . . Heath glanced around in bewildered amusement.

"Are you shouting at *me*, Gray?"

Grayson sent him a black scowl. "Do you see any other of my scandalous siblings in the room?"

Heath straightened, the grin on his face frozen.

Grayson produced a paper from behind his back and waved it in the air. Heath did not immediately realize what it was. He might have paid more attention if he weren't distracted by Julia, Hermia, and Odham quietly sneaking to the door. Escaping.

"Is there something wrong, Grayson?" he asked quietly.

Grayson strode across the room. "I thought you were the responsible one."

"I am," Heath said. Wasn't he?

"Oh?" Grayson snorted. "I thought you were the brother I did not have to worry about causing a scandal."

Heath shook his head. "What has been written about me now? I cannot defend myself until I see it."

"Defend yourself? What defense is there against this?"

Grayson thrust the pamphlet at him. For a moment Heath did not recognize it for what it was. A caricature. One of those lascivious, sometimes clever, often vicious cartoons. A satire of Society that circulated the streets of London.

It was a printed sketch of a naked man, the anatomy distorted. He moved it to the light. Heath stared at his own image, dumbstruck for the first time in his life.

"Isn't that you?" Grayson demanded. "It says it's you."

Heath arched his brow. "I never saw myself in this way, but it's me." Exaggerated. Quite flattering if one wanted to be turned into a caricature for public consumption. Was this how Julia viewed him?

"How did you allow this to happen?"

Heath looked up. No wonder Julia and Hermia had sneaked away. "I did it for charity."

"Charity?"

Heath turned the pamphlet this way and that. No matter how one looked at it, he was larger than life.

"It's for the Greek God Collection."

"You agreed to pose nude for a public print for charity?" Grayson asked with a rude sneer. "Wouldn't it have been easier to make a donation?"

"How many copies of this were printed?" Heath asked quietly.

"I don't have any idea," Grayson said. "Usually the damn things are littered over the streets of London. One can hardly count all the copies."

"I see."

"I wish I did." Grayson sat down heavily on the sofa. "What am I to do? You were the model of exemplary behavior for the family. You were the one whom I ordered Drake and Devon to emulate. Do not follow my example, I said. Do not sin in my image. Aspire to be like Heath. Sin in secret. Do you have a defense for this?"

Grayson glanced around, realizing that his brother had not been responding at all.

"Heath?"

The room was empty.

Grayson was lecturing to the four wolfhounds that sat around the fireplace, tails thumping in friendly anticipation. They loved the marquess.

"And my parents thought I was the worst of the litter," he mused.

Heath let himself into Julia's room unannounced. She was sitting in her chair, pretending to read a book. He cleared his throat. She turned a page. He walked up to her and dropped the pamphlet in her lap.

"Is this how you see me?"

She whitened, slowly lifting her gaze to glance at the pamphlet. "It was supposed to be a joke," she said in a whisper. "I never meant it for public scrutiny."

"Public?" He circled her chair. "That is rather an understatement. By now it has probably sprouted wings and flown across the Continent."

She angled her head to gaze up at him. "I am sorry, Heath."

"How will I look to the War Office?" he asked, his strong hands planted on her shoulders.

She swallowed, braving a smile. "Exposed?"

"Quite." He bent his head to her cheek, *tsk*ing. "My anatomical proportions are enormous. What *were* you thinking, Lady Whitby, you wicked creature?"

She drew a breath. His hands were stealing around her shoulders. "It could have been worse—Grayson did say that there's a fortune being offered for the original."

He removed the book from her hands. "I think we shall have to find another hobby for you besides sketching."

"I think you might be right."

"How," he asked, kissing the sensitive spot under her ear, "are we ever going to explain this to Russell?"

She closed her eyes. "I'm very much afraid it explains itself."

"Then it saves me the trouble, doesn't it?"

"I think I have brought you only trouble," she whispered with a shiver.

He buried his face in her neck. "I seem to have acquired a taste for it, Julia. There's no need to apologize."

Chapter 28

Heath met alone with Grayson the following morning after a leisurely breakfast. Old friends had already begun to call on the well-liked marquess, who followed the family tradition of entertaining in grand style. Invitations to his parties were sought after by the aristocracy. Heath had always preferred more exclusive entertainments.

Still, Grayson could be the staunchest ally at times. He was nobody's fool, a man of his word, and Heath intended to enlist his help in the matter of Auclair before country life distracted him. Not to mention his pregnant marchioness. Grayson had a full plate of life's pleasures set before him.

"I can only conclude that Auclair holds a personal grudge against you," Grayson said after a long pensive silence. "God knows why. Do you not have a guess?"

Heath shook his head. "Aside from the fact that I escaped him, no. But . . . anything is possible. Who knows what I have forgotten? I do not remember most of my ordeal."

"Thank God," Grayson said with great feeling. "Having seen the scars on your body, forgetfulness is no doubt a blessing."

"I wish I knew. I wish I understood." Heath's voice deepened with emotion. "Perhaps if I understood, I would find the key to stopping him."

"Do you have something he wants?" Grayson leaned forward. "Could he possibly want Julia? You said he left her bracelet in his glove to taunt you."

"Why?" Heath's face hardened at the very thought. Until now he had not wanted to admit the same suspicion had crossed his mind. "She has done nothing to him. I cannot believe that her husband did, either. Whitby spent his short military life in India. He was not a spy."

Grayson sat back in his chair, gazing at the wall. "Auclair wants to intimidate you—he must hate you very much to take such risks to do so. It does not make sense. If this were a political assassination, Althorne would seem a better target."

Heath stood. He found it increasingly frustrating to fight such a lethal enemy and not even be able to recognize his face except from the drawings that Colonel Hartwell had shown him after the war. "I want it over."

"In the meantime, Julia is welcome to stay with us indefinitely," Grayson said, and clearly meant it. His generosity and sense of justice were two of his endearing traits that more than atoned for his past reputation as a scoundrel.

"I hope I do not have to take you up on that offer. Russell and I may yet be forced to work together."

Grayson looked at him in concern. "I think we will all be relieved when you get rid of Auclair. I fear your demons will never be laid to rest until the man is dead."

Feminine laughter drifted from the depths of the garden. Julia and Jane were playing cricket with Odham while Hermia kept score. Grayson stood up and walked with Heath to the door. "Whatever happens, the family is with you."

"Yes."

"By the way"— Grayson laid his hand on Heath's shoulder, lowering his voice—"I can see that my advice worked."

"Can you?"

"Yes, but that sketch of you, Heath. My, my. Julia has been burning all by herself, it would seem."

"I really can't comment. I never tell."

"You don't need to," Grayson retorted. "Julia's drawing speaks volumes."

Heath only smiled.

"It did give me a shock," Grayson continued, "you exposed that way, and I thought I had seen everything."

Heath dredged up a droll smile. "The world has seen more of me than *I* ever dreamed possible."

"She really is a naughty woman," Grayson murmured.

"Isn't she though?"

Grayson arched his brow. "Do you want some more advice?"

"By all means."

"Marry her as soon as possible," Grayson said. "A woman like that does not come along every day."

That same evening Grayson announced over dinner that he had invited a troop of traveling players to give a private performance at the end of the week. It was an annual tradition, a treat for the family and servants.

One troop or another had entertained in the old half-timbered barn on the edge of the estate ever since Heath could remember. Sometimes the players arrived in midsummer. Sometimes they did not come to Kent until Christmas. But never a year passed without a performance.

The Boscastle family enjoyed a good laugh and a good cry. Heath thought that Julia could use a distraction. He also liked the idea of involving her in a family ritual. Without a second thought, he had already begun to include her in his future. In fact, he could not imagine his life without her. For the first time in years he looked forward to the next day. He laughed more often. He wanted to make her happy.

He had been only half joking when he warned her that she could be carrying his child; she certainly had a good chance of conceiving before they left. He was astonished at how appealing he found the possibility of starting a family with her.

He would have to rush her to the altar. What he felt for her had become too overpowering to hide. He who had prided himself on his talent for secrecy suddenly could not be bothered with deception. In the past day or so, he had been caught standing too close to her more times than either of them could count. Everyone in the house, from Hermia to the housemaids, had to know that Heath Boscastle was smitten, desperately hungry for even a few stolen moments with the engaged widow who had sketched him in the nude.

His behavior went against everything he professed to believe. But he should have known that when he gave his heart, his would not be a gentle courtship, but a rather dark sensual dance that involved danger and risk. A Boscastle in love tended to be an unpredictable being. Perhaps because their breed did everything with passion.

His family understood, would not judge him, rather

would offer its support. He counted on that. He and his brothers might have half murdered one another while growing up. But God help the outsider who threatened one of them.

Explaining the situation to Russell would prove far more challenging. Unlike Julia, who confessed she dreaded the moment, Heath accepted it as an unavoidable task. He had no intention of denying his involvement with her. He wanted her, would announce his commitment to her to the world.

He could only hope that Russell would be able to put his personal feelings aside long enough so that together they could apprehend Auclair.

He glanced around the dinner table, taking in the laughter, the warm atmosphere of closeness, the zest for life. What a full house already, and the entire family was not even assembled. His sisters were not here; Emma was busy in London, with her fledgling students, and Chloe was safe and contented with her new husband, Dominic, after having helped him conquer his vicious enemy.

Drake and Devon should arrive any day, if a duel or pretty young woman had not waylaid the blackguards. He intended to enlist their talents locating Auclair.

Drake arrived the following day, which was a Thursday. Windblown, dark, and vital, he brought a dash of dangerous energy to the estate. His presence sent ripples of excitement and anticipation through the house. Several young ladies in the neighborhood appeared less than an hour later with their mamas to pay a social call, pretending to be surprised that Drake had just arrived.

The maidservants especially adored the two younger

Boscastle brothers, who were not above doling out outrageous compliments or cash tips to the loyal staff. Even the male domestics displayed a paternalistic pride toward their "brave young lords" and would not tolerate a disrespectful word in the village against them—although heaven knew, *everybody* knew, that those boys had committed sins aplenty to draw criticism.

The first thing Drake did, once he got Heath alone in the study, was to produce roughly one hundred of the pamphlets that displayed his nude caricature.

"There's a premium for these in London. I've got all my friends and the servants collecting them. Julia might have warned us you were going public, Apollo."

Heath shook his head in chagrin. "Damnation. I suppose that's the end of me in polite Society."

Drake laughed. "But what a dazzling debut in impolite Society. Audrey has offered a reward for the original."

"She would."

Drake's laughter died away. "It didn't sit well with Russell, I'm afraid."

Heath tossed the stack of pamphlets into the fire, turning slowly. "He's back? He must be on your heels."

"Not quite."

"Then he surely knows about me and Julia. That we are together."

"Oh, he knows, all right," Drake said quickly.

"And he did not come after us?" Heath's eyes darkened in disbelief. "That does not sound like the Russell I remember."

"Brace yourself." Drake took a poker to the pamphlets smoldering in the fireplace. "He'll be here soon enough."

"Why the delay?" Heath scowled. "Wrapped up in his mistress?"

"I wouldn't call it a delay," Drake said with a wicked grin. "More of a detour, actually. He came to me in a fury when he could not find you in London. I told him I suspected that you and Julia might have eloped."

"Eloped?"

"Well, I didn't use the actual word. I merely hinted that the family owned an ancestral pile in Roxbury. And every fool and his mother knows that Gretna Green is on the way."

Heath stared into the slow-burning flames, smiling in appreciation of his brother's devious mind.

"Aren't you even going to thank me?" Drake asked. "There's time to plan, or even to run off with Julia. Whatever pleases you."

"I don't think I'm the type to run away, but thank you."

"Always at your service." Drake lowered the poker to the hearth.

"I think you mean that."

Drake straightened. "Of course I mean it. Not to spoil the mood, but have you heard anything about Auclair?"

"No. I think it is dangerous to underestimate him," Heath said. "I wish I understood what he intends to do, and why."

"That seems perfectly obvious. Two spies on opposite sides. You got the better of him. He has not forgiven the insult."

"There's more," Heath said slowly. "I know there is, but I do not know why."

"Devon will be here soon," Drake said after a pause. He looked steadily at his brother. "You won't be alone this time, whatever you face."

Chapter 29

꩜

The traveling players performed the comedy *She Stoops to Conquer* in the barn on Friday evening. Following family tradition, the servants of the house were invited to attend and settled comfortably in the back, eager to be included in this annual event. Heath could not watch the play at all. The acting was awful, every other line flubbed and badly timed.

But everyone else was laughing, including Julia. It was a mindless entertainment, a release, and the very badness of the performance provided most if not all of the enjoyment.

Heath's enjoyment came entirely from sitting beside Julia, pressed shoulder to shoulder in the stuffy candlelit barn on bales of hay. It was dark enough where they sat that he could touch her, steal a kiss between acts. This was what he wanted their life to be.

His arm slid around her waist. His thumb flirted with the curve of her hip. "It's good to hear you laugh, Julia."

"How can I not laugh?" she whispered back. "The acting is appallingly bad. One of the players took sick at the last minute, and Mrs. Hardcastle is being played by a man. I think she—he—forgot to shave."

Heath glanced amusedly at the stage, but he was far more interested in the woman beside him. She looked lovely tonight in a light silver silk dress, her shawl sliding from her arms. He loved the supple line of her back, the way her sinuous muscles flared into her soft white bottom. He remembered the last time they made love, and his body reacted with a bolt of lust that could have sent the barn up in flames.

It was still early when the play ended. Hermia and Julia were strolling arm in arm toward the house, giggling as they discussed the performance. Jane and Odham were admiring the starlit garden, the wolfhounds trotting at their heels.

Heath followed behind Drake and Grayson. He could see the acting troop's wagons parked at the edge of the estate. Many of the players had remained in the barn, to disassemble the stage. This was the one place on earth where he should have felt comfortable lowering his guard.

"Hermia and I are going to take some refreshments down to the actors," Julia called over her shoulder at him.

"I'll watch you from the window," he said to her retreating figure.

Grayson pivoted to grin at him. "Do you really think she could meet mortal danger between here and the barn?"

He heard Drake's deep chortle of laughter. "You never know. A frog could jump out at her from the fountain."

"Or," Grayson added, "she could sink into a mud puddle and never be seen again."

"The rosebushes can be murder this time of year," Drake said.

"Rotten bastards," Heath said. But by the time he reached the house, he was laughing, too.

* * *

He lit a cigar and pulled a chair to the library window. He had promised Julia he would read the book she had given him on Egyptian hieroglyphics. He must have meant to at least a dozen times. Grayson and Drake had gone off with Hamm and Odham to the gaming room.

Heath had declined to join them.

He turned a page in the book and examined a drawing of undeciphered inscriptions, symbols believed to hold the mysteries of the ages. Scholars and linguists had struggled to decode these ancient passages. It was a study that fascinated Heath, but his mind wandered to another subject.

Keep her safe.

And keep her away from scandal.

He frowned, his dark head wreathed in a cloud of fragrant smoke. Ironic that he should remember Russell's parting words so clearly. Now that the two men were about to come face-to-face.

Well, he had kept Julia safe.

But free from scandal?

He shook his head. He could see her through the window. She was walking with Hermia across the lawn in the bright moonlight. Julia was a minor scandal unto herself.

He wouldn't have her any other way.

She and Hermia had reached the barn. He caught a last glimpse of Julia in her silver dress before she disappeared into the dark.

He opened the book again.

A folded scrap of paper fell out.

He read it three times before he came to his feet, his face draining of color.

*I had my first good look at her in the bookstore today.
She is lovely, about the same age as my sister would have
been had you not killed her.*

Will you mourn her, Boscastle?

*Or are you, like me, incapable of suffering that senti-
mental insanity called love?*

Armand

Heath stared down at the book, his face bleached white
with realization. The stranger who had picked the book up
when Julia dropped it outside the shop must have been Auclair. He had slipped the message inside before returning it
to her. They had all been standing together in the street.

Heath had missed him by mere seconds. Would he even
have recognized him from a drawing?

Julia's garden, the theater, a public street. Where next?
Auclair showed no fear. And what was this madness about
Heath killing his sister? He had never killed a woman . . .
dear God, had he? The month that had been erased from
his memory haunted him. He couldn't remember anything
substantial after being tortured.

What had he done?

What would Auclair do?

He felt the blood rush to his head as he backed away
from the window. Julia had given him the answer. If he had
paid more attention, he might have perceived the truth
himself.

*One of the actors took sick at the last minute, and Mrs.
Hardcastle is being played by a man. I think she—he—
forgot to shave.*

* * *

Hermia paused to rebalance over her arm the heavy basket of cold meats, cheeses, and bread that she carried. Her face was flushed, and she sounded a little winded.

Julia stopped to give her time to rest. "I knew we should have had Hamm help us. Or one of the other servants. Are you all right, Aunt Hermia?"

Hermia gave her an irate look. They were almost to the door of the half-timbered barn; although it was quiet inside, the lanterns were still lit, and the stage had not been completely dismantled.

"I am perfectly capable of carrying a basket, Julia." She resumed her stride.

Julia smiled. "Then why is your face red, pray tell? Why do you have trouble catching your breath?"

Hermia sighed, looking faintly embarrassed. "Odham, that's why. The fool kissed me as I was leaving the house. Oh, dear. The players aren't in the barn."

Julia glanced toward the small private woods. "They must have retired to their wagons."

"I wanted to meet the actor who played Squire Hardcastle," Hermia murmured, her gaze a little sad. "He reminded me of my late husband."

"Mrs. Hardcastle looked like my late husband," Julia said with a wistful laugh.

"Odham has asked me again to marry him." Hermia nibbled a piece of cheese from her basket. "This time I am seriously considering saying yes. I know it sounds silly, but when I watched the play tonight, I had the strangest feeling that my dear departed Gerald was telling me to be happy."

Julia turned her head. "Then take your basket to Squire Hardcastle and tell Odham you accept—oh, look. There's one of the actors in the barn now. I'll ask him to help us."

"I shall walk ahead."

"Don't be long, Aunt Hermia," Julia teased. "Odham will be missing you."

All but one lantern had been extinguished by the time Julia entered the barn. She approached the trestle table that had been used as a prop to set down her heavy basket of fruit tarts, a wheel of cheese, and two bottles of wine.

A lone actor remained on the crude wooden stage, practicing a swordfight with an imaginary adversary. Julia wondered if he were rehearsing for the next performance. Grayson had mentioned that *Romeo and Juliet* was part of the troop's repertoire.

He slashed a graceful arc in the air, his black cape billowing with a dramatic flair. Julia sensed that he knew she was there. He was showing off a little, not unusual for an actor. She stepped toward the stage.

"I enjoyed the performance."

He sketched a bow and jumped off the small platform. "My pleasure entirely."

She studied his face, rough-hewn, unshaven, attractive in an unrefined manner. His eyes were hard, glistening like black coals in the dim light. "You're Mrs. Hardcastle," she said in surprise. "I did not recognize you without your dress."

He bowed again, the sword drawn over his heart. "And you," he said in a soft, faintly accented voice, "are Julia Hepworth Whitby. The woman whom Boscastle and Althorne both desire. How nice of you to provide such a convenient revenge."

For an instant his words did not penetrate. It took her several moments to understand what he meant. But then she recognized him, the stranger in the street with the high beaver hat, and she realized with a jolt of terror that she was standing alone with the French officer who had tortured Heath so viciously in Sahagun that he bore the physical scars of it to this day. It did not seem possible. Not here, where she felt safe, protected. Not here, where he could inflict evil on so many innocent people.

"Auclair," she said, not moving, her heart pounding in her throat. The name defiled the air. This was the monster who enjoyed watching others suffer.

He tossed his saber to his other hand as if it weighed nothing. She saw the burn marks, the reddened scars on his knuckles. She cringed at the cold smile he gave her.

Where was Heath? How long had she been gone? Only minutes, surely. Not long enough for him to miss her. And Hermia—oh, pray God, let her aunt not become a part of this.

Auclair must have seen the desperate glance she darted to the door. He advanced on her until she was forced back against the stage. A sense of cold, of disbelief, gripped her. She wouldn't show him how afraid she was.

"He'll be here, I'm sure, the moment he realizes you are gone."

He closed the distance between them. She felt the sharp tip of his saber through her light dress. The barn had been unbearably warm earlier. Now the air chilled her like frost. Her mouth tasted like chalk, dry with fear. Auclair's dark eyes reflected no expression, beyond cruel . . . empty.

"Why are you doing this?" she asked, swallowing to counteract the sour taste in her mouth.

"He hasn't told you?"

"No."

"He killed my sister," Auclair said, frowning at her. "She was staying in a convent where Althorne and Boscastle took refuge after escaping me. They had demanded shelter, and the nuns gave it. Your lover shot her through the heart in broad daylight. She was dead when I found her."

Heath was running so hard that he almost knocked down Jane and her maid on the twisting path to the barn. "My goodness, Heath," she exclaimed as he gripped her shoulders to steady her. "Are you running after Julia or away from her?"

Her teasing grin fell the instant she saw his face. White, frightened, his eyes wild. "Auclair is one of the actors who performed here tonight," he said. "Find Grayson and Drake. For God's sake, hurry."

Julia heard her voice echo faintly in the rafters of the barn. From the loft above she could see the sliver of moonlight that angled across the unlit wing of the stage.

It was as if she were watching another performance. She felt detached, numb, barely conscious of what she said or did. She closed her fingers around the pistol concealed in the warm layers of her cloak. Her husband had given her the gun four months before he was killed. Heath's warning in the woods, and some instinct this evening, had prompted her to take it with her. Her late husband's words echoed in her mind. Was Adam trying to help her?

Do not carry it openly, Julia, but this is a savage world. I may not always be near to defend you.

She felt a rush of sorrow for him, a pain she had not acknowledged since leaving India. It was one of the few times she had allowed herself to grieve for Adam since she'd come home. She had been angry, bewildered at his death, uncertain what would become of her. Returning to England, to her dying father, had brought comfort but also a remembrance of deep regrets.

She believed she had lost Heath, the one man she had secretly loved. She had lost her young husband, and she had loved him, if not with the same frightening passion as she had Heath. She would reenter Society, which had never approved of her, with a wicked reputation and wealth.

She was Julia Hepworth Whitby, and she threw herself body and soul into whatever joy and tribulation she had to face. She would not die without fighting for her life.

"My sister was only nineteen," Auclair said, raising the saber in the air. "I left her in that convent to protect her. Your lover murdered her, and I—"

She lifted the gun. And braced herself to fire.

Chapter 30

She had closed her eyes reflexively as she prepared to pull the trigger. When she opened them, she saw Auclair crumbled on the straw in front of her. Blood soaked the wrinkled white ruffles of his linen shirt. Thankfully she could not see his face. His saber had fallen between her feet.

She shook out her dress to dislodge the blade. The echo of the gunshot seemed to deafen her for a few moments. She looked past Auclair's inert body to see Hermia frozen in the middle of the barn. She had no idea how long her aunt had been standing there. In fact, she did not even recall the instant she had fired the gun. She lowered it to the ground behind her.

Hermia's empty basket slipped from her hands. "Julia," she said in a faltering voice, her face gray, "I think . . . I think that I shall faint. You really have to curb this habit of shooting men."

Julia managed to move around Auclair as Hermia collapsed, her ample figure fortunately landing on a thick layer of straw. "Aunt Hermia," she cried, falling to her knees beside her. "Can you hear me?"

"Hear you what?" Hermia's eyes searched her face. "Did I faint?"

Julia rubbed her aunt's wrists between her palms. "I don't think so."

"Why not?" Hermia whispered.

"Well, your eyes were open the whole time, and you never stopped talking."

Hermia's frightened gaze drifted past Julia to the unmoving male figure only a few feet away. "Is he dead?"

Julia caught her lip between her teeth. She had started to shake, and she felt alternately hot and cold, as if she had suddenly taken ill. "I believe so."

"I wish I *could* faint," Hermia said, struggling to sit up.

"Yes, I do, too," Julia said. Her heartbeat felt erratic. "It's the first time I've actually killed a man."

"You didn't kill him."

She came unsteadily to her feet. She heard Heath's deep, reassuring voice from somewhere in the vicinity of the ladder to her left. It took her several seconds to perceive his familiar figure.

Her thoughts began to race.

He's still wearing his evening clothes. There's a pistol in each of his hands. That's the first time I've ever seen him slightly disheveled, and . . .

"You have straw on your trousers," she said, wondering if she were in shock. She had just killed a man—hadn't she? She worked up the courage to look more closely at Auclair. He lay unnaturally still.

Before she could even move, Heath was in front of her, grasping her in his arms as if he would never let her go again. She welcomed his warm strength and support, not certain how much longer she could keep her emotions in check. Her courage had never been tested before. Somehow she thought her father would have been proud of her. Only now could she admit how terrified she had been, grateful to whatever self-protective instinct had saved her.

"He is dead, isn't he?" she asked, gazing past his shoulder.

He turned her in the opposite direction so that she could not view the body. "Yes, he's dead, but *you* didn't kill him. I did."

She stared at him. The pistols he'd been carrying a few moments ago had disappeared. There was still straw on his evening clothes, and she wanted to cry. "How long have you been here?" she asked, her throat dry.

"I came shortly after you. As soon as I realized what was happening."

"You shot him from the loft?" she asked in wonder.

"I crawled up through the window. I thought for a moment that you heard me. You looked right at me at one point." His voice was uneven. "I was terrified of what might happen if I missed."

She felt his arms tighten as if to shield her. Still holding her, he looked past her and nodded tersely, his gaze on the loft. From the corner of her eye she saw Drake drop to the ground like a graceful cat. He moved swiftly toward Auclair's body, covering it with his own coat, his hard face dispassionate.

The door swung open. Voices echoed across the barn, the concerned voices of the Boscastle family and servants brought to help. Grayson and Odham were gently lifting Hermia to her feet, guiding her back into the fresh night air.

Drake and Hamm removed Auclair from view. And

Heath had not released her. Julia could hardly believe it had happened so fast, and that it was over. Heath had vanquished the man who had intended to destroy him. Her mind was in such a blur she could barely remember what Auclair had looked like. She wanted to forget.

"Did you hear what he said?" she asked softly. Heath was staring past her to the stage. His eyes seemed distant; she was afraid he was beyond her reach.

He glanced down at her. The hard angles of his face softened as their eyes met. "I heard everything, but I don't remember what happened at the convent the day I was rescued. I don't remember anything until I was being half dragged along an icy road by Hamm and Russell. We were dressed as peasants—they had disguised me to escape."

"There's no reason to believe him anyway," she said, aching for him.

He shook his head. "Why would he lie?" His eyes darkened with a bewilderment he did not bother to conceal. Had she ever thought him cool and detached? It seemed incredible that for years she had held an image of him as heartless and reserved.

The man who stood before her, who had killed to protect her, felt more deeply than anyone could ever guess. And she sensed he might have told her more had the doors behind him not opened quite so dramatically.

A breath of evening air scattered the straw littered on the ground. Grayson had returned to the barn. He strode up to where they stood like an outraged king who had almost lost his favorite prince and princess.

He picked up the pistol that Julia had dropped. His blue eyes glittered in hard approval. "Is she all right, Heath?"

"Yes. She will be."

"That was a damn good shot, Julia," Grayson said slowly, "although . . ." His voice trailed off. He was examining the pistol with a puzzled frown. "It's fortunate that your skill with firearms has improved since you shot my brother."

Heath sent him a meaningful look. "She didn't kill Auclair. *I* did."

"Ah." Grayson nodded in understanding and lowered the gun. "Well, that explains why her pistol has not been fired. What an ordeal."

"I'm taking her to her room," Heath said in a firm voice. Before Julia knew it, he had turned her toward the door. He broke away from his brother, who waited only a second before following them.

"Good idea," Grayson said. "Put her straight to bed."

Heath glanced at Julia sideways and smiled a little ruefully. "Isn't he an inspiration? Grayson, perhaps you should see to *your* wife. I gave Jane quite a scare on my way here. I do apologize if I upset her."

"Jane was more concerned about you and Julia," Grayson replied. He glanced back at the barn, shaking his head, his voice low with emotion. "On my own estate. Dear God, to think I invited that butcher into my home."

Julia slept in brief snatches throughout the night. She woke up twice, naked, in Heath's arms, and thought for an instant that she had dreamed Auclair's death. The scene in the barn had all happened too quickly, too unexpectedly, and Heath's lovemaking had seemed so passionate and spontaneous that the earlier events of the evening did not seem real. She wanted the scene with Auclair to fade away. She wanted to erase it from her mind.

Had Auclair held a saber to her hours ago?

"Was it all a nightmare?" she murmured as Heath's strong form moved over her.

She focused on the devilish smile that flitted across his face in the darkness. She tried to sit up. He eased her down effortlessly on the bed, his mouth capturing hers.

"It was very real." He kissed her deeply. "And it's over. My brave darling."

The low sensual tone of his voice sent a pleasant warning through her system. He sounded more dangerously sexual than ever. Could it be that in having conquered his enemy, he was able to unleash his deepest passions?

If so, Julia was in more trouble than she'd anticipated. Trouble of the most wicked type. Of course there was only one answer to her dilemma: submit, participate, and enjoy.

She wound her arms around his neck. "You are a formidable rival, Boscastle. I'm glad to count you as a friend."

"We're slightly more than friends," he said, spreading her thighs apart with his knee to punctuate his point.

He proved that statement several times over before the end of the night. Julia had never seen him so uninhibited, so highly erotic; she did not know whether she would survive this dark and decadently unrestrained side of the man she loved. She was more than willing to try. He brought out the passion inside her that she had suppressed.

He took her in one powerful thrust.

The tenderness in his eyes was as devastating as his wild sexuality. Heart and body, she gave herself to him. He took her greedily, demanding more, and she answered.

She raised herself to his lean, pumping hips. Met the untamed surge of his body with her own tantalizing movements.

He teased her. She teased him back.

More than once he withdrew, slowed the depth of his thrusts to torment her. More than once she squeezed her inner muscles around him to glove him in wet heat only to relax as he neared his peak. It was a game they played to bring each other maximum pleasure.

Heath was a master at it.

Julia was giving him hard competition.

They would both claim victory in the end, but the enjoyment came in playing, not in following the rules.

He was shuddering with enjoyment, the muscles of his taut body straining when she took her release. She could not fight it. He had hammered at her until she could not hold back another moment, his face dark with unadulterated desire.

At the moment of her climax, he claimed her mouth in a hot hungry kiss. Julia surrendered to him, yielded to her deepest impulses with abandon. She gripped his shoulders and felt herself shatter beneath him, fragment in unbearable pleasure. He groaned, sheathed inside her.

There was nothing left but to follow their instincts, no matter where they would take them. Julia savored the unrestrained power of him, the sensations that inundated her, the helpless spasms that swept through her. Only hours ago they had confronted a killer. Having survived, having watched Heath triumph over his enemy, made this moment all the sweeter. He craved raw sex. Perhaps he needed oblivion. She obliged him.

She caressed his tight buttocks with her fingertips and drew him tighter. He had stripped her of everything but pure sensation. She moaned softly against his mouth. She scored his back with her nails when he released a deep growl and exploded inside her. He held her so tightly she could feel his heart pound, the tension in his muscles slowly ebb away. She touched his face with her fingertips.

The fragrance of their lovemaking scented the bed-clothes and their damp, intertwined bodies. In another hour or so a new day would begin. Their intimacy would be interrupted, if not threatened. She knew that Russell would demand, and deserve, his explanation. She also knew that Heath would never be at peace with himself until he knew the truth about that day in the convent; Auclair's words had affected him profoundly. Had he killed Auclair's sister? Had he even been aware, in control of his actions? She would stand beside him no matter what he had done. He was a good man.

She thought of how the ton would look at them. The gossip that would erupt like a storm. Perhaps she would never return to London.

"We'll never be invited anywhere after this," she mused, not caring, wondering if he did.

He curled his arm around her waist. "One dead spy does not a scandal make. Besides, no one here tonight will talk."

She was quiet for a moment, her eyes closed. Men had a way of reducing everything to the most basic terms. Especially Boscastle men, who seemed to believe that whatever they decided would be law. Or that they were *above* laws. Particularly social ones.

"I think you've forgotten Russell," she said hesitantly. "The minor obstacle in the path of our illicit love. And when I speak of minor obstacles, I am referring to an obstacle the size of a small mountain."

He grunted. It was a rude sound, and it made her giggle. "I shall take care of Russell, as I told you before. I haven't forgotten him for one moment." He pulled her warm sated body against his. "I suggest that *you* forget him, though. In fact, as your future husband, I demand it. My family will support you, no matter what anyone else says or does. I really do not give a damn about the others."

"Perhaps I should have the first word with him," she said softly.

"I don't think that's a good idea."

"He isn't going to hurt me."

"I realize that."

She kissed his throat. "It's only fair, Heath."

True to Heath's prediction, the Boscastle family rallied around Julia the next day as if she were a royal relation about to be besieged by an army of peasants. Which, with their typical arrogance, the clan secretly believed everyone who did not support them to be.

The family met to have a civilized breakfast of tea, coffee, eggs, bacon, crumpets, and jam. Listening to the lot of them joke and make plans for the week, Julia found herself wondering if Heath *had* actually killed a man last night. And then she realized that their high spirits were a heartfelt celebration of overcoming. They shared in everything, the good and the bad.

Even Hermia and Odham were laughing and exchanging secret looks. But then they were in love, having conquered many obstacles to accept what they felt. Perhaps that made the difference. The Boscastle family loved life, and loved one another, sometimes with a clash of emotion and will that proved quite painful.

The Boscastles took extreme measures. The word *luke-*

warm did not exist in their world, and Julia found herself welcomed, embraced, a part of their passionate chaos.

The youngest devil of the brood, Devon Boscastle, appeared later in the morning, to the delight of everyone, then disappeared to take coffee and meet with his brothers. Julia did not know how Devon had learned of Auclair's death. But she could tell by the way he grinned at Heath that he had been told and wanted to be part of the celebration.

Heath's sisters Emma and Chloe, along with her husband, Dominic Breckland, Viscount Stratfield, had sent word that they were coming, too. The marquess would have a full house, or full house party, and his good spirits and enjoyment of entertaining were contagious.

Julia found herself seduced by the collective charm of the Boscastles, so swept up that she could have sworn the impossible had happened: she'd completely forgotten about the ugly complication she would have to confront.

Breaking her engagement to Russell.

He arrived at the house an hour after breakfast, as the family dispersed to change for a game of cricket on the lawn. Julia had lingered at the table over a last cup of tea, enjoying the sunny warmth that poured in the windows, a quiet moment to savor and reflect.

The sun seemed to disappear as a footman brought Russell to the room. She set down her cup and saucer, slowly rising from her chair. His face looked thinner, rather haggard, but he still cut a striking figure in his dark brown pantaloons and double-breasted riding jacket. His black eye patch, as always, gave him a dashing look. He was a familiar figure from her past, but her heart did not respond to him. They could never be happy together. She hoped he would accept that.

"Russell."

"How nice. You still recognize me."

It seemed that he wouldn't make this easy on either of them. She had not expected it, not deep inside, but all of a sudden she wished she'd taken Heath up on his promise to handle this. "I don't know what to say."

His voice lashed her. "I risked my life to save Heath years ago, and I would have done so to protect you. I left you with him because I trusted you both. How could you do this to me? Don't you care what people will say?"

She glanced out the window. Heath stood at the marble fountain in the courtyard, his broad shoulders and back toward her. His hair shone blue-black in the sunlight. Alone. He seemed so alone. She ached to join him, to lift the darkness from his expression.

What had he once confessed to her? That he thought he was destined to be alone? It wasn't true. She would walk through the flames of hell to be at his side.

She heard Russell move behind her, his voice imperious, urgent. He did not like to lose. He shoved a brass telescope out of his way. "Did you hear me, damnit?"

She hadn't really heard him. Heath had turned, distracting her. She studied his hawkish profile in the sunlight. Standing here with another man made her ache for her lover. What a wicked boy he'd been last night. She felt tender all over, a woman well seduced, indeed. She decided she might sneak back to Audrey for a few more lessons. Heath seemed to appreciate her knowledge. "Did you say something, Russell?"

"I know that the two of you have been lovers. Don't deny it."

He waved a paper in her face, blocking her view of the rogue she adored. Heavens above, it was the satirical cartoon of a naked Heath Boscastle mounted on a flaming chariot. That sketch refused to die.

"I would wager a guess," Russell said in an ugly voice, "that the pair of you had a good laugh at my expense over this. Can you explain it?"

She took the pamphlet out of his hand. "No. I can't."

"But it is *your* work?"

She stared down at the sketch, at Heath's magnificent body, all that sculpted muscle and sinew. "He's God's work," she said with an admiring sigh. "Magnificent, isn't he?"

"Magnificent?" A muscle jumped in Russell's jaw. "So you admit that you actually *drew* this disgusting thing?"

She smiled a little mysteriously but did not answer him. Her focus had returned to Heath. He had begun to walk toward the house with that lean-hipped, agile horseman's grace that made her breath catch. She knew exactly what he could do with those hips. She wanted him to do it to her now. She'd lost so many years of his love that she resented wasting even the time it took to properly end her engagement.

"Look at me, Julia," Russell commanded her in his terrifying soldier's tone.

She did. He was an attractive man, an ambitious man, not entirely bad. Or not bad enough. Julia certainly found herself drawn to devilish men. But Russell wasn't *her* devil. He never had been. Thank goodness she had been saved from marrying him.

He raised his brow, apparently satisfied that he had reached her. "That's better. Now I have your attention." He took her chin in his calloused hand. "The Boscastles are a seductive family. I know the rogue tempted you. I know how hard it is to resist the lot of them. Growing up I wished to be part of their world more than anything."

She swallowed, feeling sympathy for him against her will. Russell had been raised by an uncaring aunt, his parents dying while he was an infant. He had done well for himself, considering his circumstances. Ruthless ambition and hard work had carried him far. But he would never be satisfied with what he had gained. He would never amass enough wealth, enough acclaim, enough women to appease his restless nature. She had agreed to marry him for all the wrong reasons. Because she was alone, grateful for his support. She had not known, had not dreamed that Heath would wait for her.

"You were mine first," he said, a note of desperation in his voice.

"No." Heath walked into the room. There wasn't a trace of understanding or forgiveness on his face. "She was mine first." He leaned back against the door with his arms folded across his chest. "And you betrayed her. You have only yourself to blame. You asked me to protect her, and I have. From you."

Russell's gaze darted to her in disdain. "Is that how he lured you to his bed?"

"Do not be such an insulting idiot, Russell," she said indignantly. "You have a mistress. Judging by her condition, you've paid far more attention to her than you have to me."

He shrugged in bewilderment. "Every man in my position has a mistress. I suppose Boscastle ran back to tell you?"

"He did not," Julia said, "but I wish he had."

Russell placed his hands on her shoulders, apparently deciding he should try another tack. "*I* am the injured party. The wronged man."

Heath advanced on him, a muscle tightening in his jaw. "Take your hands off her, Russell."

Julia drew a relieved breath when Russell immediately complied. Watching Heath now, his face harsh and uncompromising, it was undoubtedly wise to obey.

"I cannot afford the scandal of a duel," Russell said coldly. "I am probably ruined as it is. Auclair has led me on a goose chase when it appears he was in London all along. My fiancée and friend have disgraced me—"

Heath glanced at Julia. "Leave us alone, please."

She looked at Russell. He refused to meet her gaze. Clearly he had not been told that Auclair was dead, that he had missed his golden chance for acclaim. Realizing Heath had stolen this, too, would not improve his temper. "I don't know what to say to you, Russell."

He laughed without humor. "I shall need time to think this over."

She drew a breath. She felt an overwhelming sense of relief. "It *is* over. I hope you can accept that as I have."

Heath closed the door as soon as she left the room. She and Russell had been given all the time they needed to end their engagement. He did not want her anywhere near the man again. He suspected that Russell would try to manipulate her, if not exert emotional blackmail to force her hand. More than anything his colossal pride had suffered a blow. He would recover. But not with Julia at his side. He did not deserve her. Heath would not allow Russell the chance to try to make amends.

"Auclair is dead," he said, without preamble. "By my hand."

Russell looked up in astonishment. "What?"

"He came here." Heath regarded him in thoughtful silence. "It seems that I was the one he wanted to punish the most."

"*You* killed him?" Russell's mouth tightened in an unpleasant sneer. "So even that was stolen from me? What a hero you are."

"Did you know that he wanted to kill me?"

"You escaped his guard, and he was mad. No one can find reason in the irrational. There was no logic in his insanity."

"Ah. Is it all that simple?"

Russell turned back to the window. "How the hell do I know what the bastard had in mind? He was a madman. Have you forgotten what he did to you?" He glanced around, his gaze challenging Heath. "I did not forget. You were half dead when I found you. You were practically mad yourself."

"Apparently I have forgotten even more than that." Heath shook his head. "Auclair claims I killed his sister."

Russell's shoulders tensed beneath his riding coat. He nodded without looking at Heath. "I saw no reason to remind you. It was an act of self-defense, and you had no idea what you were doing. She was French, after all, and she pretended to help you. She also had a gun. You killed her before she killed you. Or so it seemed."

Heath struggled to form an image in his mind of what

had happened. He could remember an arcade, washing his bloodied face in a frozen well. He remembered running, stumbling, his muscles weak. Hamm lifting him to his feet. The endless bumping on the wagon on an icy rutted road. Killing a young woman? He could not conceive of it.

"What difference does it make now anyway?" Russell asked dispassionately. "It was war. There is nothing to be done for it. The problem is how to fix the scandal that you and Julia have created."

"You had a chance to win her," Heath said, his gaze cynical. "You gambled and lost."

"So it would appear," Russell said sourly. "A woman can be replaced, but the damage to my career is irreparable. Auclair was meant to be mine. I have returned home empty-handed and a fool into the bargain."

"Perhaps not." Heath paused. "I have a suggestion, a gentleman's trade if you will. I do not want the credit for getting Auclair, but I do want Julia."

Russell stared at him, his mouth twisting in a bitter line. "Auclair for Julia? Are you proposing a barter?"

"No one outside this estate knows that he is dead yet. The authorities will be informed in an hour."

Russell did not respond, but Heath knew the decision had been made. It was a way for Russell to save face, to appear to have sacrificed his personal life for his country. Heath would protect Julia from scandal. The gossip of their love affair would begin to dissipate the day they were married. Society would accept them. They might not return the favor.

Russell bent to pick up the pamphlet that he had dropped on the carpet. "Have you seen this?"

Heath glanced down and suppressed a smile, his level gaze returning to Russell's face. "Yes."

Russell shook his head. "Don't tell me you *posed* for it."

"As a matter of fact, I did." Heath cleared his throat. "It was for charity."

Heath called for Drake to discuss with Russell the details of turning Auclair's body over to the authorities. He did not care to be involved. He would rather find Julia. They were both free now; he felt lifted from him a darkness that he had lived with for so long that it had become part of him. There was a time to be wise and a time to be wicked. A time for war and for love.

He ran up the stairs to cross the long private hallway to her room. He found Hamm standing at attention, guarding her room as he had been instructed. His gaunt, pock-marked face wore a somber expression.

"Is Lady Whitby waiting for me?" he asked.

"Yes, my lord, but . . . if I may have a word alone with you before you visit her?"

"Is something the matter?" Heath asked.

"I have a confession to make."

"If you dropped another dish, you needn't bother mentioning it."

"I had given my word that I would never tell. Sir Russell was my commanding officer, as well as yours. He swore me to secrecy."

Heath stared across the hall to Julia's door. "This sounds far more serious than a broken dish. Please continue, Hamm."

A look of distress darkened the man's rough face. "He left you standing there by the woman's body so that the other men would see you and assume you'd killed her. Forgive me. I did not mean to eavesdrop on you and your brothers last night."

"You knew about Auclair's sister?"

"I remember a young woman in the convent. I didn't know who she was at the time. I don't believe Sir Russell ever accused you openly of killing her. He simply did not disagree when it was assumed you'd done it. No one ever spoke of it until now."

Heath swallowed, another burden lifted from his soul. "Are you telling me that Russell killed her?"

"I did not see him do it. I can only suspect that he reacted in self-defense and was ashamed to admit it. You ran in to him when the shot was fired. My lord, you were in such a bad way I could have convinced you I was the king."

"It is done now, Hamm. You have given me more comfort than you know. Thank you."

"I was warned never to speak of it."

"It will never be discussed again."

Chapter 31

Julia met Heath at the end of the tower wing hallway the following morning. He looked so remarkably refreshed in his gray tailcoat and pantaloons that an innocent observer would never guess he had taken her in every position possible throughout the night.

In fact, they had parted company only an hour ago.

"You look exceptionally lovely today," he said and claimed her arm, as if he hadn't just seen her naked in her bath, then helped her hook her bodice.

She smoothed down the skirt of her cream wool morning gown. "I feel exceptionally ravished."

"I suggest we start to build your stamina. You have years of ravishment ahead."

They walked down the wide staircase arm in arm. "Once again it was not a complaint."

His lips quirked into a grin. "A compliment?"

She stared straight ahead, her voice lowering. "I'm ashamed to admit that it was."

"Passion is nothing to be ashamed of, Julia. Not between husband and wife."

"We're not married yet."

"We will be soon enough."

"Nothing will stop us this time, will it?" she asked, pausing on the bottom of the stairs.

"No. Why do you think I had Hamm guarding your room?" He drew her gently into his arms and kissed her, his love for her shining in his eyes.

Her breath rushed out in a contented sigh. "There are other people in the house."

"I don't see anyone."

"I can hear them."

He looked up.

There were voices drifting from the oval salon. Julia could not identify any of them to save her life. Heath's kisses were too distracting. She wound her hand around his strong neck and pulled him closer. She had always believed him to be brave and honorable, but last night she had seen into the soul of this man herself. His beauty was not superficial.

"We have to stop this," she whispered, laughing.

"Why?" He ran his hands down her sides. Her skin still felt warm from her bath. "Do you want to go back upstairs?"

"We just came down."

"No one saw us." He was already trying to pull her up to the next step.

"Julia! Heath!" a loud male voice boomed from the door at the end of the hall. "We thought the two of you were going to stay in bed the whole day."

Heath gave a sigh as Julia unwound her arm from his neck. "Good morning, Gray. And thank you for your subtlety."

"Morning? It's afternoon," Grayson retorted. "We were just about to sit down to luncheon. Are you joining us or do you have other plans?"

"Well," said Heath," we do have plans to make, actually. Wedding plans."

Grayson broke into laughter. "Say it isn't so."

"It is."

"I'm not at all surprised, but I am pleased. May I be the first to give my blessing?"

Heath wished to be married as soon as possible, within a fortnight, if the arrangements could be made. Julia agreed. They had waited years to be together. She wasn't about to take a chance on letting anything ruin their happiness this time. Her sister-in-law-to-be Jane was beside herself with delight and promised to help in whatever way she could.

Hermia expressed her concern that two weeks might not be enough time to make proper preparations. But as Heath's sister Emma, Viscountess Lyons, pointed out, "It is more than enough time for the two of them to cause another scandal. My students are still talking about that caricature."

Julia and Heath did agree, however, on a quiet country wedding. Well, as quiet as an affair could be when one had a mansion overflowing with Boscastles, brothers, sisters, in-laws, uncles, aunts, and an army of boisterous cousins, who proved that it was quite impossible to dilute the passion in their blood. And why would anyone want to try?

The wedding took place on a Saturday afternoon at the Marquess of Sedgecroft's country estate. Heath dressed and was shaved, then paused at the window of the upstairs gallery where his elder brother stood waiting for him. He took one look at the carriages lining the drive, and wryly asked if there was anyone in the whole of England whom Grayson had forgotten to invite.

"I thought you disliked weddings," he said as they lingered together at the window.

"I do. But it's not my wedding. You're the one who has to face the firing squad. I've done my duty, thank you. And lived to tell of it."

"Dear God," Heath exclaimed, recognizing a petite figure in a bright green satin dress waving up at them from an arriving carriage, "that's Audrey Watson. You invited a courtesan to my wedding."

"No, I didn't," Grayson said. "Julia did."

"And you allowed it?"

"Well, it's not my wedding."

"Still no sign of Drake?"

"Oh, yes. He sent word he'd be a little late. A duel detained him."

Heath smiled. "And Devon?"

"He took two young ladies for a stroll in the woods. I suspect they were headed for an infamous cave. You remember it?"

"In vivid detail."

Grayson laughed. "The legend still lives."

"I hesitate to ask—where is our dear, dictatorial sister Emma?"

Grayson lowered his voice. "Dispensing unsolicited advice to the socially ignorant. That's why I'm hiding up here."

"I can't hide," Heath said, removing his hands from his pockets. "I have a wedding to go to."

They descended the stairs. His sister Emma stood waiting for him, a small-boned woman with apricot-gold hair, blue eyes, and a warlord's heart.

"There you are," she said. "I do not blame you for hiding after having that pamphlet published for every man, woman, and child in the country to see."

"It's nice to see you, Emma," Heath said, adjusting his snowy white neckcloth.

"Well, it wasn't nice to see as much of you in print as I did," she whispered, then lifted her hands to readjust the neckcloth's folds. "Congratulations, rogue," she added with an indulgent smile. "I am happy for you and awfully proud."

The marquess had ordered the gardens as well as the interior of the house decorated for the wedding reception. The weather was mild but not overwarm, with the faintest hint of a breeze. Sedgecroft's private orchestra played from a hidden glade of ferns; servants in gold-braided livery and formal white wigs stood sentinel at every pathway to offer cake and champagne. The purebred horses in the immaculate stable were festooned with white silk rosettes and paraded around the estate.

The ceremony went off without a flaw. The bride wore an off-white silk wedding dress with a scalloped Brussels lace bodice over a pearl-white tissue slip. White kidskin gloves and white satin slippers completed her dress. Her bridal veil was secured by a wreath of deep pink rosebuds entwined with ivy leaves. She did not, as one newspaper later reported, carry a pistol.

The groom wore a double-breasted dark blue tailcoat over a white cambric shirt, embroidered waistcoat, and fitted black pantaloons. He cut such an achingly handsome figure that Julia had a hard time keeping her hands to herself.

Devon was sitting in the midst of a group of young ladies, who giggled at his every utterance. The Marquess of Sedgecroft served as the best man; his wife, Jane, watched the wedding with one of his aunts from the front row of the small family chapel in the west wing. Hermia and Odham sat beside them, not talking to each other. They had quarreled over breakfast, but agreed to appear together in public for Julia's sake.

Lord Drake Boscastle sauntered into the chapel a minute or so before the ceremony began with a voluptuous young woman no one recognized. Viscount Stratfield brought his beautiful raven-haired wife, Chloe, to serve as a bridesmaid while he watched the wedding, although his eyes never strayed from Chloe the whole time. Emma stood as matron-of-honor, gently insisting that Jane, expecting the family heir, was not an appropriate choice for the job.

Audrey Watson shook her head in wistful approval as Heath tenderly took his bride into his arms to kiss her. "Rogue," she murmured. "Another Boscastle has broken my heart." She glanced around the crowded chapel, her face brightening at the sight of his two younger brothers in dutiful attendance. "Oh, well. There's always hope, isn't there, Drake?"

"That depends on what you're talking about, Audrey, the altar, or an affair."

"What a rake you are, Drake Boscastle," the woman sitting beside him exclaimed. "Can't you behave even during a wedding ceremony?"

He glanced up at Heath and broke into a wicked grin. "It's not my wedding, thank God."

Voices rose around the chapel in congratulations as the minister pronounced the couple before him to be man and wife. Julia felt Heath's strong hand close around hers as the guests stood to cheer them. "There's no escaping me now," he said softly, brushing her veil back from her cheek.

She stared up at him. "That goes for you, too."

"You'll never be rid of me now. We did it, darling."

She caught her breath. She could not believe that he finally was hers. That she was Heath Boscastle's bride. Guests were bumping against them. He kept a tight grip on her hand, even as he dutifully kissed sisters, aunts, and cousins. His brothers naturally tried to outdo one another buzzing her on the cheek.

"Mine," he said politely, pulling her away. "Find your own."

"Are you ever going to let go of her hand?" his young cousin Charlotte Boscastle teased.

"No." He tugged Julia out of Devon's arms. "I'm not."

The wedding feast took place in the formal banqueting hall. Dancing went on until the evening in the domed-ceiling ballroom with a quartet playing in the balcony. Julia had never heard so much laughter in her entire life, and the music of it warmed her heart. Her own upbringing had been often lonely.

Heath looked down on the celebration, Julia's head resting on his shoulder. He'd spirited her away during a waltz. "How long do we have before they realize we're gone?" she asked.

"Days. Devon's toasted everyone but the gardener."

"We should have at least bid everyone good evening."

"Trust me. I'm a master at fading into the background. They'll never miss us."

True to his word, they were locked inside the east tower suite seven minutes later. A small fire had been lit. Two bottles of champagne sat on the table along with a tray of thinly sliced ham, crusty bread, and tiny French pastries.

Heath stripped down to his shirt and pantaloons while Julia sat on the bed sipping champagne. She watched him with growing desire, admiring the muscled lines of his body, that easy male elegance that never failed to stir her senses. Champagne and her husband. The combination went straight to her head.

"Nice wedding, wasn't it?" she asked, swallowing as he came toward her.

"I thought so."

"We were both on our best behavior."

"Until now."

He knelt before her to remove her slippers and pink stockings, spreading her legs apart as he did. Julia stared down into his dark sardonic face, her breath quickening with unabashed need. "Are we going to revert to our former ways?"

"Naturally." He rose up onto the bed to untie the back of her boned French corset. "You look very desirable tonight, Lady Boscastle."

"Look who's talking."

He peeled the corset from her breasts and leaned over her soft curvaceous body. "I've heard some titillating rumors about you."

She closed her eyes. His hand slid up her hip to squeeze her breast. "They're all true, unfortunately. I can't deny them."

"Deny them?" He rolled over and covered her mouth with his. "I was hoping you would *prove* them."

She brought her hands to his chest, tracing the deep indentations of muscle. "Is this what you had in mind?" she whispered against his lips.

"That will do nicely for a start. But, please, allow me."

"Allow you—"

She felt her wrists imprisoned in his hand, an enslavement of the most erotic order. She strained, testing him. He tightened his hold on her. He eased his other hand down her hip, into the warm hollow of her thighs. It was a fleeting brush of his fingers, a teasing promise. She felt herself opening to him, her body throbbing for more, begging in silence for him to do his worst.

"Please," she whispered.

"My beloved wife, our wedding night has just begun. I do not intend to rush it."

"Our wedding night," she murmured. "It seems so long ago that I dreamed of this."

"Did you, Julia?" he asked softly. "Then I think that we shared the same dream."

She laughed in delight. "What would people think if they heard Heath Boscastle, the consummate master of self-control, confessing that he dreamed about marrying the woman who had shot him?"

"I confess that I do not care what anyone outside this house thinks."

She studied him with a tender smile. "And you don't care that Russell has claimed your glory?"

"Glory." He gave a deep sigh. "There's no glory in killing, only peace, perhaps, in knowing that Auclair cannot threaten us again. Let Russell be a hero for as long as it lasts. God knows that I do not want the acclaim."

"Russell was never my hero," she said, smiling up at him.

"No?"

"It was always you. Perhaps I should have told him how I felt about you."

He shook his head. "You should have told me."

"May I tell you what I feel now?"

He gave her a roguish smile. "I know exactly what you feel."

"Then . . . "

"Our wedding night," he reminded her, "is an experience that I fully intend for both of us to enjoy."

He kept his word.

He stroked, brought pleasure to all the secret places of her body. He aroused her to the point where she was shaking, out of her mind with need. She gave herself to him, accepted each touch until she thought she would shatter if he did not allow her release. He caressed her everywhere but where she needed him the most. He refused to hurry. She was achingly damp deep inside.

"Sweet," he whispered, and drew the peak of her breast between his teeth. "Naughty," he added, lifting her legs over his powerful shoulders. "Delicious Julia. Thank you for agreeing to be my wife."

He gripped her bottom and thrust inside her to the hilt. For a moment she did not move. It was enough to simply feel. Then her body welcomed him with a passion more than equal to his. He flexed his spine as he sank into her passage. She lifted her hips to his and moaned in pleasure.

Heath released her hands and felt his heart tighten as she reached up to touch him. She traced the scars on his chest, sculpted the hard muscles of his back and buttocks with her fingertips, urging him closer, deeper. He studied her face, lost himself in the warmth and love he could see in her eyes. He had never looked at anyone, loved another human being as he did her. She had set his heart free so that he could give it to her as he had once meant to.

He caught her hands again, interlacing their fingers. He wanted to be joined to her in every way. He threw back his head and surged into her. She answered with sensual abandon, her muscles gripping his shaft. He felt his control slipping as the heat in his blood came to a scalding boil. He was still holding her hands when she came, and his heart thundered so hard he could hardly draw a breath.

"My God, you're beautiful," he said, squeezing his eyes shut to take his own release. "My wife." His voice was hoarse. "My love."

She lay tangled in the sheets beneath him when he was spent, her face pressed to his shoulder. For several minutes they held each other, warm, sated, and reluctant to break the mood. She felt cherished and protected, overwhelmed with appreciation that they had found each other again. When he spoke, it was almost as if he had read her thoughts.

"I did not believe I could ever feel as happy as I am now." He kissed the top of her head, threading his fingers through the heavy red hair that fell down her back.

"Nor I."

He lifted his head slightly. "Listen. Do you hear that?"

She opened her eyes and laughed. "It's your brother's orchestra—he's got them playing outside the tower."

Heath grinned. "I ought to strangle him."

"Not on our wedding night, please."

"Good point. I shall do it in the morning."

A few hours later that same brother sent up a servant with another tray of food and drink to be set discreetly outside the tower door. Heath did not stir. He had thrown on a dressing robe and was at the fire, sketching his naked wife in passionate absorption.

Julia glanced at the door. "Shouldn't we at least say thank you to all our guests?"

"That can also wait until the morning. Grayson will invite them to stay. Lift your right leg up onto the bed, darling. Bend forward a little. Hold up your hair."

"You are an incorrigible rogue, Heath Boscastle. This is a shameful position."

"Not from where I'm standing."

"May I ask *why* you are doing this?"

"To return the favor, my love. Is it wrong for a man to sketch his own bride?"

She let her hair fall down her back, gasping. "You aren't going to publish it?"

"Don't be insulting. It's a wedding gift."

She frowned at him over her shoulder. "I don't particularly want a sketch of my backside. Pearls, yes. Diamonds, possibly. But a drawing . . . of me undressed."

He circled the sketching easel, his eyes narrowed in contemplation. "Very nice—what did you say? Ah, the gift. It is for my enjoyment only. A gift to myself if you will."

"I won't," Julia retorted, straightening her back. "I mean, I won't pose."

He came up behind her, wrapping his arms around her waist. "I posed for you."

She turned in his arms but made no effort to disengage herself. "And look at the trouble *that* caused."

"I wish," he said quietly, "that we may cause each other trouble for the rest of our lives."

"I think you can count on that," she whispered.